THE ROAD TO DEADWOOD

A face wrapped in a red kerchief appeared just below the stagecoach window where I was sitting. When he jerked the door open, the Mexican beside me shot him through the kerchief. The Mexican dove out one side of the coach, I dove out the other.

There were three men still sitting their horses. I came up firing my Remington. I saw two of my shots kick up dust from the coat of one man. He threw up his hands, fell backward over his mount's rump, and landed in a heap.

The explosion of the stagecoach guard's shotgun roared overhead and I saw another rider flung to the dust.

The remaining bandit fired off several wild shots before he wheeled his horse around and raked its flanks with his heels. The Mexican fired his carbine. The wounded rider managed to hold his seat and escape.

The ride to Deadwood was proving to be full of surprises. I had started out thinking I was only going to be shaken to death by the coach over the next couple of hundred miles. Instinct and experience should have warned me that nothing is ever as simple as it first seems.

Going to find a killer was no exception.

WILLIAM W. JOHNSTONE
THE PREACHER SERIES

DEADWOOD

BILL BROOKS

Pinnacle Books
Kensington Publishing Corp.
http://www.pinnaclebooks.com

PINNACLE BOOKS are published by

Kensington Publishing Corp.
850 Third Avenue
New York, NY 10022

Pinnacle and the P logo Reg. U.S. Pat. & TM Off.

First Printing: January, 1997

Printed in the United States of America
10 9 8 7 6 5 4 3 2 1

*For Kelly and Wade, who accepted me before
the words were ever written
and helped heal me with their love.
Now the words are for them.*

1

Two things happened the day I rode into Cheyenne with Charley Weed draped across the back of a stolen roan horse: it rained so hard it crushed men's hats, and Nate Pliers, the only other detective besides myself working for Ben Beadle's Detective Agency, was shot and killed while taking a bubble bath with a married woman.

Ben was waiting for me in front of Dick's Diner, a false-fronted restaurant squeezed between the White Elephant Saloon and Jacob's Hardware Store. It was a clapboard, unpainted establishment with a plate glass window and red-and-white-checkered curtains.

The food at Dick's was bad, the coffee worse, but Ben Beadle always took his meals there routinely.

Little Dick Johnson was a busted-down cowboy who couldn't cook an egg with the directions written on it. But Little Dick had once pulled Ben's carcass out of the Canadian River while on a trail drive and had kept him from drowning. The truth was, Ben couldn't swim any better than Little Dick could cook. But Ben figured the least he owed Little Dick was his patronage. Ben was a man who believed in loyalty and friendship.

I reined in. Water spilled off me and Charley like we were ducks. Ben looked at Charley and said, "I see you got your man."

"What is left of him, anyway," I said, feeling the water sluice down the back of my neck. I stepped in under the overhang of the diner. My boots sloshed when I did; the slicker I was wearing seemed alive with yellow light.

"I was hoping you could have brought him in alive," Ben said. Ben Beadle was as tough a man as I'd ever met. He had killed his share of bloodletters in twenty years of pursuing the law but possessed the disposition of a Quaker when it came to violence.

"Well, I was hoping I could've too," I told him.

"You had to plug him?"

"No sir. He plugged himself," I said. I swept my hat off and slapped it against my leg, trying to knock out as much of the weather as I could. I noticed some faces peering out of the diner window at what I had brought back to their town.

Ben's shaggy brows wormed together and he sucked something out of a tooth, no doubt a piece of Dick's wang leather bacon, and laid his disappointed gaze on me. His eyes were the color of seawater, a warm wet green that the light seemed to float in.

"He plugged himself?" It was a reasonable question.

Ben shifted his attention to Charley, who was draped like a rug over the blaze-faced roan. It seemed somehow proper that Charley was still on the same roan he had stolen from Jake Goodlove before he left town. The roan had Jake's initials welted on its shoulder. Its hide was dark and slick from the rain.

"Why's he wearing that dress?" Ben asked. "I thought when I first seen you, you'd killed a woman and brought her back here for me to see."

"Well, that is what he was wearing when I caught up

with him," I told Ben. I could understand his curiosity about Charley's unusual appearance.

"You want to tell me about it?"

Ben's mouth was still working at whatever had stuck in his tooth. He was a clean-shaven man except for long sandy moustaches. His cheeks and neck were the red rawness of a man who had spent his life facing into the sun and wind. Tiny spokes creased outward from the corners of his eyes. Such a look was common of men who spent a lifetime squinting into the ceaseless sun and the great distances, scouting for danger.

Certain things—like a Cheyenne war party, or a tornado, or a fire sweeping across the prairie—were things a man hoped he wouldn't see but all too often did.

"I caught up with him in Julesburg," I said, watching the rainwater drip from my slicker and collect into puddles around my boots.

"He was staying with a woman named Belle Blue. You know Charley couldn't go ten feet without finding himself a consort. The first place I looked was in the sporting houses. It didn't take long to learn that Charley was in town. Not many men are as handsome as Charley was. I guess it was the one time that being so handsome did not have its rewards."

Ben stood staring at what remained of the notorious "Gentleman Bandit"—a sobriquet given Charley by the dime novelist Ned Buntline. Charley didn't look like much of a gentleman, or a bandit, dressed in a gingham dress with a sprinkle of lace tatted across the bodice and around the cuffs.

I doubted that even ol' Ned Buntline could stomach such a sight.

Ben noticed the round puckered spot just in front of Charley's right ear crusted to the color of rust. I could tell he was waiting to hear the rest of it.

The rain percolated in the muddy street and slanted off the edges of the overhangs and danced atop the tin roofs.

It sounded like shucked corn hitting the bottom of a wash-basin.

"I guess one way or the other, Charley was bound for a bad end," I said. "After all, I wasn't the only one looking for him. I heard that there was a Pinkerton man from Denver on his trail, also one or two bounty hunters. I heard that King Fisher and Ed Siringo were on his trail, too."

I saw Ben's eyes narrow at the mention of the Pinkerton man. Ben had once worked for that agency, now they were competition. He wiped a finger across his sandy moustaches and said: "I am not surprised about Siringo or Fisher. They would've made good detectives if it wasn't they enjoyed the violent aspects of the work so much." Both men had reputations as mankillers of the first order. King Fisher I could understand. But Ed was hard to figure; his daddy was a Baptist preacher.

"Anyway, I found Belle Blue plying her trade with a broken-nosed miner in a crib on Stillborn Alley. You know how Charley appreciated a woman that could and would work to support him. Women just fell all over themselves to please Charley. Belle was no exception. She was tall and round-shouldered and not an entirely bad-looking woman in the right light. She had a mole near her left eye the size of a dime. Charley preferred the unusual in a woman.

"The miner wasn't happy about my unexpected appearance, and neither was Belle; the miner was still wearing all his clothes because of how cold it gets up there in that high country. But it did not keep him from his business with Belle."

Ben Beadle pulled his makings out of his shirt pocket with the weariness of a man who had done it a thousand times before and rolled a cigarette and then offered the makings over to me.

"So Belle gave up Charley just like that?" he said through a cloud of blue smoke.

"Not exactly," I said.

Ben squinted at me.

I was about to tell him the rest of the story when three hard shots shattered the peace. I saw Ben stiffen with the instinct of a man that had heard the sound of gunfire plenty of times in his past.

"It sounds like they came from the Inter-Ocean," he said, turning in that direction. I hurried alongside him as doors popped open in spite of the hard weather and the idle and curious fell in behind us.

I saw city marshal Dave Beltrain come out of the Blue Star saloon across the street, where he spent the bulk of his time dealing faro. He wore a plug hat, a brocade vest over a freshly boiled shirt without the paper collar, and a fancy little Policeman's Model Colt stuck inside his waistband.

Beltrain acted reluctant to cross to our side of the street. He was no doubt contemplating whether to muddy his shoes and the cuffs of his checkered trousers. Dave Beltrain was a fastidious man, like most of his breed—gamblers hired on as the local law. They wouldn't ride out on a posse until they made sure their hair was combed and neatly parted and smelled of rosewater.

"What is it? What's happening over there?" Beltrain bellowed.

"Shots!" someone hooted.

Then one of his cronies came up and handed Beltrain an umbrella. He popped it open, then crossed the street carrying it high over his head, tipytoeing like a debutante going to a quadrille. I heard Ben grumble under his breath at the appearance of the lawman. They had kept up a running dislike for each other ever since Ben established his detective agency in Dave Beltrain's *town*.

"Don't need more law around here," Beltrain had openly complained as he watched the words "BEADLE'S DETECTIVE AGENCY" being painted in gold leaf on the small plate glass window of Ben's office the day Ben went into business.

Ben had ignored Beltrain's derision, just as he would any man he lacked respect for.

"Fancy name for an old broken-down drover—*Detective,*" the lawman derided in the presence of several cronies.

Then with the casual air of a man who had seen too much and done too much, Ben Beadle said, "I knew you when Harry Longbaugh put a pistol in your ear in a Denver whorehouse and told you to fight or run and you wilted like a rose in winter. Don't trouble me with your nonsense, Beltrain—you ain't up to a real fight."

It had been bad air between them ever since.

Now Beltrain tried crowding in the same front door of the Inter-Ocean along with the rest of us. He smelled like bay rum and sweat.

Jeeter Forbes, the desk man, was cowering at the foot of the stairs.

"Joe Roars . . . went upstairs . . . with a gun in each hand . . . and I guess he has shot Nate Pliers and . . . maybe Missus Roars as well!" Jeeter stammered. A woman was screaming. Several men had come from the bar and stood holding their drinks and long cigars. One man had a napkin tucked down inside his shirt and a drumstick in his right hand.

I saw Ben's jaw knot and he took the stairs two at a time with me on his heels and Dave Beltrain somewhere in the rear. A gauze of blue smoke hung in the hallway outside an open door.

Dave Beltrain said, "This is my jurisdiction," but Ben ignored him and stepped into the room with me alongside.

Nate Pliers was resting in a copper tub of warm water that was turning pale crimson from the ribbons of blood leaking from three dark holes in his chest. His head lay slumped forward, his chin resting on his chest. A cigar floated in the water. A whiskey bottle lay next to the tub, its contents staining the carpet.

Joe Roars was a wealthy cattleman who owned practically everything a mile out in any direction of Cheyenne. He was considered important, a man to be reckoned with. Now he sat on a red velvet settee, insignificant, a smoking pistol in each hand. The smell of nitrate and sulphur filled the room.

Roars was a man of bulk; he had a head the size of a bull, and close-set eyes. The pistols seemed small in his large hands. He didn't look half so important sitting there like that.

Roars's wife, whose first name was Anita, was too hysterical to even cover herself. She was as naked as any woman I ever saw (and I've seen a few). Some of her beauty seemed faded standing there like that, hysterical and exposed. She was a tall, slender woman with milk-white skin and bunches of autumn red hair that hung loose and unpinned down past her soft white shoulders.

She had high cheekbones and a long curved neck and dimples. And I reckon she had pretty eyes as well, even though they were smudged by her tears.

It was common knowledge that Joe Roars had met Anita at a local bagnio called Madam Drake's, and had taken to her like a horse to oats. Anita had what few of her sisters of the working class had: stunning good looks and the keen ability to make any man feel special. She also had a plan to marry the first rich man that came her way. That had been Joe Roars, a successful man, it seemed, with everything but women.

The wedding was written up in the *Wyoming Weekly Leader* and was the biggest event to take place in the territory that year. I didn't go, but I'd heard later that Joe had ordered in several hundred pounds of fresh oysters and fifty cases of champagne, among other delicacies. It was said that if Joe hadn't been so eager to get started on his honeymoon, the party might still be going on.

Ben pulled a spread off the bed and wrapped it around Mrs. Roars and set her in a chair by the doorway with her back toward the tub full of bloody water and Nate.

"What happened here?" he asked her. His voice was a

gentleman's drawl of smooth calmness but one that commanded attention. She dabbed at her eyes, her perfectly curved lips quivering as she tried to regain herself.

Dave Beltrain busied himself by wiping the mud off his shoes with one of the hotel's towels.

"We was just . . ." Then she looked over toward her husband and broke into sobs. Joe Roars looked as stunned as if he had been kicked by a horse. A spot just below his left eye twitched.

"Me and Nate . . ." she began again. "We was just . . ."

"I reckon it's plain what you and Nate were doing," Ben said, without the slightest hint of accusation; it would have served no purpose. Ben turned again to look at Nate's corpse and I could tell he was disappointed in equal measures at Nate's poor judgment and the fact he was dead.

"Well, Beltrain. I guess this is your business now," Ben said. "All that can be done has been done." Then he looked at Joe Roars, whose nearly crossed eyes were looking at something that none of the rest of us could see.

"I am sorry that Nate was involved in this, Roars. But I've never known a good reason to shoot an unarmed man. The least you should have done was let him get to his gun."

Roars bobbed his head.

"Of course, Nate would've killed you in a fair fight— he was one hell of a gun artist. I guess you didn't know what to do, huh?"

When Joe Roars didn't answer him, Ben concluded by telling Joe he ought to keep his wife at home or put her on the next stage to Denver, whichever was easier.

I followed Ben out of the room and down the carpeted stairway. As we reached the bottom of the stairs, I saw a row of porcelain cuspidors lined along the ornate oak bar. Behind the bar there was a long mirror etched with frosted cherubs. The waiters all wore white shirts and the bartenders cravats.

"This is some *bon ton* place," I said.

"I reckon if Nate could tell us," said Ben. "He'd have wanted to end it in a place like this. He always was a man who liked to live beyond his means. Now he has died beyond them as well."

We walked back down the street to Ben's office. The rain had slackened to drizzle and the wind had shifted east to west and carried with it a sharp chill. I was still wet from my ride and was eager to get into some dry clothing.

By the time we reached the front of the diner again, a group of callow youths stood in a circle around Charley Weed and the stolen roan. Their eyes were big, and some of them were laughing. Ben paid one of them—a tall, lanky boy with splayed teeth—fifty cents to take Charley over to Klingbill's Funeral Parlor and the horse over to the livery. We watched as they marched off in a parade, Charley draped over the back of the roan, his skirts blowing in the wind.

We stepped into Ben's office, a small, spare space containing a scarred desk; a swivel chair which, every time Ben sat in it, screeched like cats being kicked; a rack of shotguns and rifles on the wall; the mounted head of a mule deer Ben had shot on an expedition he had helped guide for Bill Cody and the Grand Duke of Prussia; a washbasin on a commode; and a blue china water pitcher with two glasses. The only other item in the room was a Shaker chair hanging on a peg. I took it down and sat my haunches in it. Ben sat in his swivel chair.

"Need to oil that thing someday," he said. He said it every time he sat in it.

2

A letter lay spread out upon his desk. He motioned to it.

"What is it?" I asked.

"The rest of the bad news," he said. "I got it just before the shooting at the Inter-Ocean. It's from a woman I once knew. Go ahead, read it."

"Looks personal," I said, before reaching for it.

"No, it's just more trouble," he said.

I looked at the name on the return address on the envelope before reading the letter. It was from a woman named Alexandra Dupage, although at the bottom of the letter she'd signed it "Alex."

> *Dear Ben,*
> *I can't explain to you how wonderful it was to hear of you residing in Cheyenne. And to receive the news at such a fortuitous time! Dodge seems so long ago.*
> *I hope this letter finds you well & in good spirits. Now for the tragic news I bear you in this letter.*
> *You see, this past summer, I and a few young women*

*who work for me, arrived in Deadwood. A business venture,
but not entirely what you may think. I won't go into details
so much at this time. But if you decide to accept my invitation, offer really, to come to my aid, then I will tell you
everything.*

*I will take the chance that we meant something special
to each other once. Enough so that you will hear me out,
read this to its conclusion before making up your mind as
to whether you are willing to risk your life for me. I won't
blame you if you refuse.*

*I won't belabor this longer. Three of my young women
have been murdered since our arrival. At first, it was believed
the deaths of two of the girls was accidental. But when the
third girl (her name was Flora) was found last week—it
was unmistakably murder. Without a great deal of proof at
my disposal, I am now of the belief that the other two girls
were also murdered and made to look like accidents.*

*I know that it must seem insensitive of me to come to you
with my problems after all this time of separation. But when
I found you again, I had to take the chance you would hear
me out.*

*However, I've taken the precaution to advertise for some-
one of experience in this line with the Territorial newspapers
on the chance that you might not be able to help me.*

*I hope this letter finds you well and I hope that I hear
from you, even if you choose not to come. I understand.
Take care, dear Ben. You will always have a place in my
heart.*

Yrs. affectionately,
Alex Dupage.
No. 24 Front St.
Deadwood, D.T.

I placed the letter back on the desk.

"Who is she, Ben?"

"The only woman I ever loved, other than Nettie," he
said. I saw in his stare the pain a man can have in remem-

bering a woman he's loved and lost. I saw it because I've
had the same pain come and go ever since Mary Lee.

"She was young, Irish, beautiful," he said as though I'd
asked him to describe her. The pain melted into wist-
fulness.

"It was in Dodge City, the last herd I took up there,"
he continued. I listened as he let the words flow out carrying his thoughts, his memories of her.

He looked up, his blue gray eyes watery, hurtful.

"You know I lost Nettie in "sixty-eight, then three years
later, I lost Arlo—you remember Arlo don't you?"

I did. Arlo was a handsome boy, good-natured, russet
hair like his mother, sea green eyes like hers. He was killed
in Wichita, Kansas, on a hot summer afternoon by a deputy
city marshal who said the boy was drunk and firing his
pistol off in a dangerous fashion. A coroner's inquest was
held and the shooting was termed justifiable. The deputy
quit and left town right after and just before Ben arrived.

Ben picked up the tintype that was sitting on the corner
of his desk and stared at it for a time; the pewter frame
shone dully in the low light.

I had seen the picture before; it'd been taken in a Denver
photographer's gallery: Arlo sitting against a painted back-
ground, wearing a pair of angora chaps and a wide-brim
hat. A cigar in one hand, a Colt Peacemaker in the other—
photographer's props. A sly grin on the boy's face revealed
just how innocent he was.

He was a sweet and gentle boy whom the prairie came
to claim long before it had a right to him.

"Anyway, I went a little crazy after that," Ben said. "After
Arlo's killing, I turned to whiskey, and I went looking for
the lawman that killed him, only I couldn't find the man.
So I found other men instead and took it out on them.
Didn't matter who. I just needed to take it out on some-
body."

Yeah, I knew how that went, but I didn't say anything,
just listened.

"I took one last herd up to Dodge, that's when I met Alex. She was working out of one of the houses, you know the ones I'm talking about. I had my pay and my saddle and a bottle, and it was all I figured I needed. Then I met her."

He set the tintype back down carefully from where he'd taken it. His eyes still held onto it long after his fingers set it free.

"She was different, Alex was. For one thing, she was smarter than most. She had dreams and ambition. Dreams was something I'd long forgotten about. But she had something else, too. She had a special way about her, a tenderness I couldn't touch with my anger. And that broke me down," he said, finally looking away from Arlo's image and down to his own hands.

"You know what it's like, a woman that can do that to you? That can be all the things you need, that can see into places so dark in your soul you're afraid to look at them yourself?"

There was one, my late wife, Mary Lee. She was like that for me.

"Yeah," I told him. "I know what it's like to be with a woman like that."

"Then you know why I fell so damn in love with her?"

I nodded, pulled the makings from my shirt, rolled a shuck, and smoked it there in the dimness of his office, the quiet sucking at our bones for a little while.

"I asked her to marry me," Ben said, his lips curving slightly.

"You know what she said?"

"No."

"She said she wouldn't marry a cowboy if a cowboy was the last living man on earth. I asked her why not and she laughed till she cried. She said she loved me. She said I was the first man to come along that took her heart, but she wouldn't marry me. I asked her why not, and she said, 'Don't ask me that if you don't already know.' Well, I already did know. I mean hell, what'd I have to show for my life? What'd any cowboy have to show?"

He was staring at something in the room only he could see.

"The truth was, Quint, she had brains and ambition and wasn't about to settle for anything less in life than what she wanted, and I couldn't hold that against her. How can you fault a person for knowing what they want?"

I didn't know of any way.

"She changed me," he said. "Changed me in ways I didn't expect. And by the time we parted, I had lost my hate and taste for getting drunk and mean. I did it because I couldn't touch a person like her with all my force and will, and I knew then and there that there was no point for me trying to go on like I had been. It was time to get up and get moving. Do something worth a damn in my life. It's when I decided to become something, make something of myself, just like she wanted to do for herself. I couldn't fight that. Hell, I admired her."

Then he reached in a drawer and took out a bottle, wiped the dust off with his hand, and handed it to me.

I took it and looked at him.

"I quit drinking for the wrong reasons," he said. "This one's for her."

We each took a pull and then he corked it and placed it back in the drawer.

"You still love her?" I asked.

He looked at me for a long, full moment, thinking about what I'd just said.

Then he smiled and said, "I'd be lying if I said I didn't, but I can't say I love her in the same way. Too many years have passed."

"Are you going to go and help her with her problem?" I said.

"I want to, but the thing is, I've got several commitments I need to attend to right here. I've given my word to men, and my word is my bond. I've agreed to handle certain matters for them. I can't just drop everything and go to Deadwood, not just yet."

I could feel it coming.

"You want me to go?"

His look said it all.

I thought about the last part of her letter, the part that talked about if she didn't hear from Ben in a reasonable time she would advertise in the papers. Then I thought about the type of men an advertisement like that would attract.

I looked at the postmark on the envelope.

"This was mailed nearly a month ago," I said.

Ben nodded gravely. "I know."

"I was thinking about men like Fisher and Ed Siringo," I said.

"Just to name a few," Ben said. "If Alex has advertised in the territories, that's the sort of men that will show up. That's another reason why I'd like you to get up there as soon as you can."

"I was thinking mostly of Fisher," I said. "He swore he'd kill me the next time we clashed."

"Then I guess if you run into him, you better shoot him first," Ben said.

"I was hoping I'd left that sort of business behind me in Del Rio," I said.

Ben smiled politely and said, "You don't ever leave it behind you, Quint. Not entirely."

He was right, of course. A man does what he needs to do, and along the way he makes enemies. King Fisher was one I'd made in Caldwell, Kansas, several years back when he was the law and I was a cowboy. Our first run in. Then, a year later in Tascosa, I was the law and he was the cowboy, and this time I returned the favor by busting him over the skull with my self-cocker for being drunk and disorderly. He didn't swear it to me directly, but spread it around later that the next time we met, he'd finish me.

The last I heard, he was doing stock detective work up

in the Montana Territory, shooting rustlers in the back with a long-range rifle. It was the sort of work that fit him, shooting men in the back.

"Maybe if you could just go and buy me some time," Ben said. "Until I can break free here and come up myself."

I knew Ben Beadle wasn't a man to ask favors lightly.

"I suppose you want me leaving on the next stage out?" I said, half jokingly.

He smiled.

"The ticket will be waiting for you."

His handshake was enough to let me know he appreciated my decision. Something told me we might not see each other again.

3

"The Cheyenne and Black Hills stage leaves in the morning, I'd like you to be on it," he said as I turned to leave.

The thought of two-hundred and forty-six miles riding in a Concord had all the appeal of being bludgeoned with a Walker Colt. I knew he wouldn't have asked me if he'd seen any way around it.

"I'll send a wire when I get there," I said.

"Keep a low profile, Quint. Anyone that would murder women is a man lacking charity. I can't afford to lose another detective. I'm down to my last one."

It was a weak effort at humor, dark as it was.

"I'll have to leave for Laramie and tell Kipper we brought Charley back," Ben said glumly. "I don't think it's exactly what he was hoping for, buying a dead man."

Ned Kipper had hired us to find Charley Weed and return him to Laramie—it had to do with Ned's daughter, Minnie, who Charley'd left with an unwanted gift. Minnie wasn't the best-looking woman in the territory, or the youngest. Ned figured the least Charley was going to do was to marry Minnie and make an honest woman of her and be a father to the child she was carrying.

The way I'd gotten the story was that after Minnie gave Charley the bad news about her condition, he stole Jake Goodlove's roan quarter horse to make his escape. He also robbed the First Bank & Trust but only got seventy-five dollars for his effort. But robbing a bank was enough to have a reward posted for him throughout the territories. And the reward was what attracted men like King Fisher and Ed Siringo.

I opened the door to step outside, then Ben said, "You'll have to tell me the rest of that story about Charley when you get back."

It had stopped raining. The miners, gamblers, prospectors and teamsters that earlier had been driven indoors by the weather, were now drifting back outside again and the town was beginning to get its rhythm back . . . a rhythm like a defective heartbeat.

I made my way to the room I kept at Kung Chow's. Kung ran a laundry and let out a back room. It was more private than the boardinghouses, and quieter than the hotels. I walked my gelding over to the livery on the way and had him put up. I saw Jake Goodlove examining the blaze-faced roan that Charley Weed had stolen from him—the one I'd brought Charley back from Julesburg on.

Jake was a barrel-chested man with a thick head of carrot red hair and freckled hands.

"Thanks for returning my horse," he had said. "I'm glad you killed that son of a bitch. He deserved shooting for stealing my horse." Then he added, "I heard he was wearing a dress?"

I didn't bother explaining that I hadn't killed Charley, or the reason for the dress. I was too weary and my bones felt like they still had rainwater in them. The barn had the sweet smell of hay and horse and held a warmth that made my weariness even deeper.

Kung Chow was eating watery soup with a spoon when

I came in. His dark beaded eyes glistened within the folds of his narrow lids. His long, sallow fingers held the spoon in the way a child would. He was wearing a red silk jacket and cotton pants. He was a man of indeterminate age. The only clue to him was the iron strands that streaked their way through his hair and wispy chin whiskers. I calculated him to be several years older than Ben Beadle. That would have put him somewhere in his sixties. But he might as easily have been a hundred.

"Ah, Mistah Quint—you back, eh? You catch your man?"

"Yeah," I answered, not wanting to go into it. To explain how it was that Charley Weed was wearing a dress to a man with Kung Chow's orderly mind was more than I had in me at the moment.

"Your room ready, like always," he said; a smile like that of an emaciated jack-o'-lantern creased his face. "You want some rice soup?"

"No thanks, Kung. I had something more substantial in mind—something that started out with horns and hooves."

Kung Chow's laughter was a series of short, hard cackles like the laughter of a man who didn't understand something but was happy to laugh anyway.

"Ah, Mistah Quint, you a funny fellow!" The soup sputtered from his lips. It would be hard not to like a man like Kung; He was kind, decent, and hard-working. And, he laughed at just about anything I said. I counted him among my friends.

I left Kung to his soup and went to the back of the laundry, where I kept a room. It was small, but clean and well maintained by the old Chinese, and it had a window that looked out on the back alley—not much of a view, but a window nonetheless. I heard the tinkle bell ring out front over the door, heard Kung talking to someone about their laundry, heard the bell ring again and the door close, then I heard Kung sit back down, heard the rattle of his spoon against the bowl.

I propped my Creedmore rifle in the corner, dropped my saddlebags on a chair, and made sure not to lay my hat on the bed; a woman in Ardmore once told me it brought bad luck, laying a hat on the bed. Not that I believed in superstition.

Then, I removed my Remington self-cocking revolver that I wore in a crossover holster and the Colt Thunderer I used as a backup. I felt ten pounds lighter and probably was. It was a lot of hardware to carry, the Creedmore and the two pistols, but not when you needed them.

The next order of business was a hot bath and dry clothes.

The barbershop and bathhouse were just two doors down. I took a set of dry clothes along with me and asked Kung if he'd dry out my boots by his stove.

"Oh yes, Mistah Quint—certainly. Ha, ha, ha."

Chester Stutts was a man who could talk milk out of a bull, but he knew how to cut hair and his baths were hot and if you got there early enough, the water was still fairly clean. A dollar would get you both a bath and a haircut. I preferred to do my own shaving.

Chester plied me for the details on Charley Weed while he and his man, an old curved-back fellow known as Persimmon Bill—who claimed (every time he was sober or drunk enough to tell it) that he had fought the Blackfeet up in the great Stony Mountains and trapped enough beaver to make all the hats east of the Mississippi River—

"I'm fond of fruit wine, you know," he rasped in a breath that would cause a mule to faint. Chester warned him not to disturb the clientele. I gave Bill four bits and thanked him for hauling the water.

"You ought not pay that old man a tip," Chester said. "It's like feeding a stray cat—he'll keep coming back for more."

"Maybe he really did fight the Blackfeet," I said.

"The only Indians Bill ever fought were wearing doeskin dresses—speaking of which, I seen you brought Charley Weed in. What was *he* doing in a dress and dead as last week's fish?"

"It's a long story. Remind me to tell it to you sometime. Right now, I'd just like a little privacy and to soak the ache out."

Chester was still fighting the temptation to persist upon me when a gambler came in seeking a haircut and shave. It was someone I hadn't seen before, but then, that wasn't unusual with the way Cheyenne was filling with new faces. It was on the road to the goldfields up in the Black Hills, and about everything with two legs, a deck of cards, a goldpan, and dreams of growing rich was pouring through.

I sank into the water to my chin, then closed my eyes against the steam and let it drag all the weariness out through my pores. It felt like a thousand tiny pinpricks against my skin. But it was one of the best damn feelings in the world. A man deserves anything in this life, it's a hot bath.

I tried not to think about it—the long ride to Deadwood.

I tried not to think about someone who would kill young women, no matter what the reason. I wondered if maybe the killings had something to do with their profession. Though she hadn't said exactly what her business was in the letter, I had a good idea judging from what Ben had said of her past. I thought of all the names working girls were called by the men who used them: Brides of the Multitudes, Soiled Doves, Cyprians, and Whores. I thought of another name I'd heard them called, too: Fallen Angels.

Nobody should have to fall that far, I thought—not even angels.

Maybe it was the hot bathwater soaking into my tired muscles, or maybe it was the whiskey, but memory took me back to the day I'd received Ben's letter asking me to come to Cheyenne and work for him.

I had been in Del Rio at the time, wearing a badge for

the past nine months for a man named Hector Ortiz, who headed up Del Rio's Peace Commission, such as it was. Actually, the Del Rio Peace Commission was just Hector and another man named Junebug Brown. The town was scarce on politicians. A week after they hired me as city marshal, Junebug Brown got drunk and fell from a wagon and died of a broken neck, leaving the commission a little smaller.

I'd drifted to Del Rio to escape the winters farther north; December and January in the Texas Panhandle can ruin a man on winters.

For a time, being the law in Del Rio was a nice change of pace from what'd I'd been doing—drifting. The weather was warm, the tequila good, and the señoritas plentiful. One in particular held my attention. She was a working girl, tall and beautiful, with long black hair and deep brown eyes. Her name was Juanita Delgado, and she was all a man could imagine himself wanting or needing. As it turned out, I wasn't the only man that wanted or needed her. Nor was I the only man she had eyes for.

I guess that was when the beginning of the end came: the day she introduced me to Pancho Vega, a border bandit who plied his trade up and down both sides of the Rio Grande, but never in my town.

Either I was too blind, or too trusting of Juanita when she said Pancho was a cousin she hadn't seen in a long time. We spent lots of nights, the three of us, laughing and drinking and going to the local dances.

I remember asking Pancho one night why he'd never pulled a crime in Del Rio. He said the reason was because of the old man, Hector Ortiz—the one that hired me. Pancho said he respected Hector and he would never do anything to dishonor him, such as committing a crime while the old man was head of the town's peace commission. He said Hector used to come to the village when he was a boy and give him and the other children candy, and that Hector and Pancho's mother had once spoken of marriage after Pancho's father had been murdered by the *ruales* in a gunfight.

"Well, that's good to hear," I remembered telling Pancho. "I thought at first it was because you might be afraid of me." It had been a joke between us at the time. But I remembered the slightest twisting of his lips as he replied, "No, my friend, I am not afraid of you." The exchange was lost in a blare of music, as Pancho swept Juanita to her feet and onto the cobblestones of the square where the *bailes,* the local dances, were held.

"He is just my cousin, Quint," I remembered her saying. "We've not seen each other in a very long time." I lifted my glass and saluted them as they spun to the music. I was in love with her; what did it matter if she missed her cousin?

A week later, Pancho would lie dead on the cobblestones of that same square, and I would be nursing a bullet wound to my right leg from his gun.

It was one of those things that happen when you are least expecting it, the sudden violence.

Pancho and Juanita were already dancing when I arrived late from making my rounds. They had been drinking mescal, laughing, lost in each other's gaze. I guess that's when I realized that Juanita and Pancho were more than just cousins.

How exactly it flared up between us is still hazy. First there was a little joking about this closeness of cousins, then a few more words that weren't jokes. Then Pancho did something he shouldn't have: he spoke the truth about him and Juanita. I'd just enough tequila in me so that it hurt, Pancho's truth.

He did something—pushed me, maybe. I called him a name. He reached for his *pistola,* I reached for mine. It was over in an instant.

Juanita cursed me, cried as she knelt over him, her tears falling onto his face.

Some of Pancho's relatives came across the *Río* and took charge of his body and carried him home to his village in the back of a wagon. Then I began to hear the rumor, that some of his people were vowing to avenge his death.

That was the same week I received Ben's letter asking me to come to Cheyenne and work as a detective for him. The timing seemed right. I couldn't find any reason to stay in Del Rio.

I remembered limping down to Hector Ortiz's saddle shop the same morning I'd gotten the letter and read it several times. I wanted to inform him personally that I was going to resign my position.

He didn't act surprised.

"It's just as well," he said. "Trouble finds you like thirsty men find liquor."

I thanked him anyway for having hired me and for his kindness.

"Where will you go, *señor?*" he asked.

"Cheyenne," I told him.

"How is the weather up that way?"

"I hear the winters are cold," I said.

He nodded his head as if that was all he needed to know about Cheyenne.

A part of me had hoped he would try and talk me out of leaving, that he would make a promise that he and the others who lived in the dusty little town would stand behind me if Pancho's relatives did come and try to avenge his death. Something like, No Señor McCannon, you don't have to leave because of those grieving people of Pancho's. We will protect you. We will fight for you.

But the only thing Hector said when I handed him my badge was, "I have a brother-in-law who needs a job. I guess now I can give him yours."

So I packed everything I owned into my saddlebags, threw my forty-dollar saddle on my twenty-dollar horse, and said *adiós* to Del Rio. But before I cleared the town's limits, I stopped by to see Juanita one last time.

She was back working at *The Conquistador Club* when I

rode up. It must have been a slow day because she wasn't with a customer at the time.

"I'm leaving Del Rio," I said.

"Do you expect me to cry, beg you to stay?" she asked sullenly.

"Why didn't you tell me the truth about you and Pancho to begin with?" I said. "It might've saved us all some grief."

"Because a woman has her beauty only so long," she said.

"What the hell does that have to do with anything?" I asked.

"I wanted you both, because you both found me desirable, and I know someday I won't be beautiful any longer and no man will want me when that day comes. Is there anything wrong in wanting what you want?" she asked.

It was a good question.

Three weeks later I arrived in Cheyenne.

Now, I was sitting in a tub with the water growing cold and the whiskey bottle showing empty. It was time to go nab a few hours rest before heading to Deadwood.

I figured Deadwood couldn't be any worse than a lot of other places I'd been.

I didn't know just how wrong I was.

4

Morning came with the shuddering force of someone opening a trap door and dropping me through it. I had slept the sleep of the dead and when Kung Chow shook me awake, I had fully forgotten where I was. My hands instinctively searched for something to defend myself with. The war had done that to me. The war did a lot of things to a man.

The war could make a man so tired he would gladly fall asleep in a trench of rainwater, caring not whether he drowned; for sleep became everything. It wasn't just the exhaustion of the limbs that made a man so tired; it was the exhaustion of the mind as well. And when a man did fall asleep, it wasn't really like sleep at all as much as it was a great falling into hell.

That kind of sleep, that temporary death, carries with it the shock of reawakening, of being jolted back into the temporal world. And often, such awakening was to the thunder of cannon and a thousand butternuts coming out of fog-enshrouded woods, their voices raised in a single yell that crawled down your spine and clawed at your groin.

And you knew they were coming to kill everything in their way, including young Union boys in blue tunics who had taken to sleeping in rainwater graves.

"Mistah Quint, you got to get up now. You told me to wake you up; it's me, Kung." My hands stopped searching and I swallowed against the thumping of my heart.

The old Chinese grinned hugely at me, then left and returned with a tin cup of coffee that was hot enough to boil shirts in. He smelled like incense and his silk jacket whispered against itself when he handed me the coffee.

"You leave this morning, Mistah Quint?"

"Deadwood," I said.

"Why that place?" Kung was curious as a two-headed cat.

"Business," I said.

"Ah," he said, as though that explained everything. Then he grinned again and said, "You don't look so good, Mistah Quint."

I got dressed, walked down to the livery, and got my saddle, then walked over to the stage office. The air was fresh and clean, the sky crisp and blue. Far to the east I could see the fringe of the cloud blanket that had passed over the day before. I could smell autumn coming down from the aspens high up in the Medicine Bow Mountains.

A round-trip ticket was waiting for me, just as Ben Beadle had promised. The office contained two benches, a regulator clock with a brass pendulum, a calendar with a rendering of a young woman holding a can of Arbuckle coffee, and a single spittoon that needed emptying. A small cast-iron stove with nickel plating and some of the isinglass busted out heated the room against the morning chill. The place was so dry you could smell the dust.

I looked over my fellow passengers.

A gambler stood by the window. He was wearing a claw-hammer coat and carried a leather kit under his arm that probably contained the tools of his trade. The weight of a small pistol bulked the inside breast pocket of his coat.

Sitting on a bench was a frail young man in buckskins whose fine-boned features were drawn tight as though he carried with him troubles or was expecting some. He wore a tan Boss-of-The-Plains Stetson that looked too much hat for him.

Across from him, sitting on the other bench, was a woman and what was obviously her daughter, judging by the way they each had the same corn-silk hair and china blue eyes. I guessed the woman to be in her late twenties, the girl, six or seven. The woman wore a small black velvet bonnet trimmed in scarlet, and so did the little girl. They both wore cloaks over their tieback dresses. It was hard to imagine why a woman and her daughter would be going to the Black Hills, unless she had a husband there—or was in search of one.

A dark-skinned man of solid, square build squatted on his heels in the corner. He looked to be part Mexican, with some other blood thrown into the mix. He carried a blanket roll and wore a wide-brimmed sombrero of dirty gray that shaded a good part of his features. He watched me from under that hat and I had the feeling that he was having some hard thoughts about my presence. He wore a corduroy jacket over a threadbare cotton shirt and faded Levis. His boots were scuffed and run down at the corners of the heels. He seemed not to breathe.

I walked back outside, set my Dunn Brothers saddle down, and rested the Creedmore rifle in the crook of my arm while waiting for the stage to come. I had taken the liberty to wear a linen duster as protection against the boil of dust the Concord would raise if the weather stayed dry. I was traveling light out of necessity. I carried only one extra shirt in my saddlebags along with spare ammunition, a Barlow knife, and clean socks. The duster would cut down on my need to change and still allow me a presentable appearance.

I checked the time on my Ingersol; it was ten minutes to seven. I saw the driver, a man named Shepherd, and his guard, a fellow named Billy Bean, leave the diner where they no doubt had eaten their breakfast. I watched as they shuffled across the street and down to the livery. Billy Bean carried a twin-barrel shotgun—the tool of his work.

In twenty minutes, they brought the Concord up pulled by a four-horse team—all bay horses except the right lead, a thick-chested dun.

In a half hour more, we were rolling out of Cheyenne on our way to the Black Hills and already we were being bounced senseless. The road was a line of ruts and rocks and other evil things.

I had picked a seat next to the door. The woman with the blue-eyed child sat next to me, her daughter alongside her. Directly across from me sat the gambler, his eyes full of disinterest. Next to him sat the slender young man wearing buckskins. To his right sat the Mexican. I had gotten a closer look when he'd climbed aboard the stage. He had light gray eyes but the cheekbones of an Apache; I had been right about his mixed blood.

The sun chased us all that day, and three times we stopped to change horses and twice to eat—except for the Mexican, who stayed to himself; whether too poor to afford the price of a meal or too disinclined, I could not be certain. I noticed he wore a thin silver bracelet around his wrist and always kept his blanket roll close by. I figured the blanket held a short-barreled gun. Maybe a carbine. Something small bulged in one pocket of his jacket—most likely a pistol near the same size as the one the gambler carried.

I figured he was trouble waiting to happen.

At the last stop of the day, the stationmaster, a big German named Faust, came out to greet us. A large-boned, apple-cheeked woman accompanied him. I took her to be his wife. She said her name was Greta, and then she showed us where to place our things inside the log hut that doubled as a hotel. Afterward, she showed us where we'd take our supper—at a long table outside fashioned out of lodgepole pine. There were the benches on either side of it. The shadows from the trees crossed the yard.

I noticed when we ate, the German kept staring over at the kid in buckskins while the wife talked nonstop about the privations of living so far away from civilization.

"Der savages are on da loose, ya know," she said. "Dey could come any time and kill us all in our beds!"

I saw the way that took effect on the woman with the little girl, saw the way the little girl's eyes filled with firelight and fear.

"Greta! Shut yer damn talk vid tellin' of der Indians, eh!" Faust ordered, his mouth full of half-chewed food that flew from his lips when he spoke.

Then, as though unaffected by her husband's angry chastisement, Greta fell to talking about the dresses the woman and girl were wearing and about how she only had but a few flour dresses to wear herself, being so far out on the frontier and away from any of the towns. The whole while the German kept his stare on the kid.

The rain came hard that night again, a storm out of nowhere. The white flashes of lightning danced through the sleeping quarters, a long room divided by blankets strung over rope to provide the women with a modicum of privacy. The crash of thunder exploded overhead like cannon shot.

I could hear the little girl crying because of the storm and I knew her fear from a long time ago . . . the same fear I had heard when the thunder of real cannon and the rain of shrapnel had torn through the trees at Cold Harbor and other killing places.

Fear comes to each of us in different ways. I wanted to draw back the blanket and tell the little girl that it was all right, that the storm wasn't going to harm her. Then I heard her mother say. "It's okay, Tessie—it's just rain. It won't hurt nothing. I won't let it." The little girl stopped sobbing and I wondered what fate awaited her in life, what other fearful things she might come to know.

I stepped outside and stood under the only overhang of the log structure and watched the silver wire of lightning dance through the sky. Like a photographer's flash against the landscape, the brilliance of the storm caused the rain to look like falling dimes.

I made myself a shuck and smoked it, felt the dampness crawl against my skin, and remembered a surgeon's tent where I had lain facedown on a table while pieces of Confederate lead were dug out of my back. A rain like the one that was falling now snapped against the tent's canvas and spilled under the edges, turning the ground into a soup of mud and blood that slathered the surgeon's boots. I remembered thinking that it was my baptism into this world, or maybe the next.

I finished the shuck and ground it out under my heel. That's when I saw the stationmaster climb out of the stage, buckling his belt. His features were frozen under a sudden flash of lightning, making his big frame ghostly. I watched him head back toward the front of the hotel as I leaned into the shadows.

Then the kid climbed out of the stage. He looked frail and thin, and he walked as if he was somehow wounded— his movements jerky, erratic in the popping light of the storm. Then the long darkness swallowed him and when the lightning flashed again, he was gone.

It was something I wished I had not seen. I waited for a time until I thought everyone was settled back inside again, then returned to my bunk and grabbed what sleep was left to me. I tried hard not to think about the kid and the stationmaster.

The next morning, I saw the Mexican squatting by the water tank when I came out. The sky had cleared to a flawless blue and the hint of a warm wind blew out of the south, taking with it the heavy, sweet smell of the corrals. He looked at me without moving his head, his eyes shifting with my movement. I washed my hands and face at a pump, ran fingers through my hair, and replaced my hat.

I saw the gambler stepping out of the privy; the woman and little girl went in next. The kid stood by the corrals, one foot hitched on the lower rail, watching the horses as though he did not want to show his face to the rest of us. The smell of fried bacon came from the main room of the station; its scent crawled down into my belly. I went to the kitchen and took a plate and filled it, then went back out and sat down at the long table. The kid stayed at the corral while the rest of us ate our breakfast. I saw the German looking in the direction of the corrals several times.

The German had close-cropped thick hair and a large forehead that rested atop a nose that was thick and flattened against his ruddy features. He had the sort of face you didn't enjoy looking at. His heavily muscled forearms rested atop the table as he ate. I saw fresh scratches on them. I thought of what I'd seen the night before. Then I looked at the German's wife. The secrets we keep, I thought.

In forty minutes, we were back to getting our bones rattled within the confinement of the Concord. The little girl whined, then slept with her head in her mother's lap. The gambler looked annoyed. Dust climbed through the open windows and we unrolled the canvas shades to keep it to a minimum. We went along another half hour like that, then it happened.

I heard the driver "whoa" the team and the stage lurched suddenly, then slammed to a stop so hard it threw the gambler and the kid halfway out of their seats. The Mexican had somehow braced himself. The little girl instinctively started to cry. My attention stayed on the Mexican. His face seemed to grow darker under that big hat and his eyes caught pinpoints of light enough to let me know he was watching me as well. I saw then that he had dropped the blanket off the carbine; he had it aimed at the center of my belt buckle.

The woman coughed against the dust and the gambler's

gaze was full of anticipation as he and the kid struggled to regain their seats. The kid kept his eyes lowered. The little girl said, "Mama?" and she hushed the child with a finger to her lips.

Someone outside the stage said, "Get the hell out here!" then a face appeared just below the window where I was sitting. The face had a red kerchief wrapped over it, and when he jerked the door open, the Mexican shot him through the kerchief.

I had no time to figure it out as I pushed the woman to the floor. She pulled the child down with her. The Mexican dove out one side of the coach, I dove out the other.

There were three men still sitting their horses as I tumbled out of the coach behind the bandit the Mexican had shot through the face.

Confusion helps the disadvantaged in such instances and I came up firing the Remington. I saw two of my shots kick up dust from the coat of a man sitting a paint horse. He threw up his hands and fell backward over his mount's rump and landed in a heap.

The explosion of the guard's shotgun roared overhead and I saw the effects of his Greener as it snatched one of the riders out of his saddle and flung him to the dust. He rolled over and tried to sit up. The front of his shirt was ripped by a dozen bloodspots the size of nickels. He said nothing; he just simply fell back and died.

The remaining bandit fired off several wild shots at the only thing he was sure to hit—the Concord. He was still firing wildly as he wheeled his horse around and raked its flanks with his heels. He was maybe fifty yards away when the Mexican stepped into the middle of the road, and as calmly as if he were aiming at a prairie chicken, fired his carbine. The rider slumped forward, nearly lost his seat, but somehow managed to hold on. Before the Mexican could reload another shell into the breech of the carbine, the wounded rider was too far out of range.

Then the woman inside the coach screamed.

The kid sat slumped on the floor of the coach. A ribbon of blood trailed down from under his hat and over his smooth face staining the front of his shirt. One of the bandit's shots had pierced the coach, and struck the kid somewhere in the head just above the hairline.

The gambler, who had not left his seat, said, "I think that boy is as dead as a rose in winter."

The Mexican came around and together we carried the kid out of the coach and laid him upon the ground. I had taken hold of the upper half of the kid, and when I did, I felt something that surprised me: the kid had small but very firm breasts. The scene of the previous night between the stationmaster and the kid coming out of the coach flashed through my mind.

The bullet had plowed a deep crease across her scalp but left the kid's brain's intact—bloody but not fatal. I wiped up her face with a linen hanky provided by the woman and wrapped the kid's head in a piece of the extra shirt I'd carried in my saddlebags.

"He'll live," I said. I figured it wasn't up to me to give away her secret. She obviously had her reasons for posing as a man. We put her back in the coach and then took tally of our work upon the bandits.

Two were dead. The one I had shot would be joining them soon, judging by the way the blood was frothing from his lips. I'd seen enough men shot through the lungs to know he wasn't going to make it.

The Mexican knelt by the dying man and said in good English, "What is your name and who are these others?"

The man looked into his face and uttered, "Why the hell should I tell a damn greaser anything?"

The Mexican reached over and took a Colt Army-Model revolver near the man's outstretched hand and stuck it in inside his waistband. I guess he figured the dying man wasn't going to need it anymore.

"Well, you are dying, *señor*. And two of your friends are already dead and the other one is carrying one of my bullets. It seems you have had an off day. Do you believe in God and Jesus Christ?"

The man's eyes filled with a mixture of contempt and confusion.

"Do you?" the Mexican repeated.

"Hell, no!"

"Then I feel sorry for you, *amigo*, for in a short time you will have to answer to *Him.* Maybe *He* will forgive you— I won't." Then the Mexican stood and walked back to the coach.

The woman asked if we would bury the dead men. The driver said he'd send someone back at the next stop.

She asked about the one who wasn't dead yet.

"We'll leave him a canteen of water," I said. "That is about all we can do for him. He won't live long enough to drink it all." I saw the way her eyes glistened with the tears forming in them. The terror had left her little girl mute and clinging to her skirts. Sudden violence has a way of blowing out the flames of innocence and leaving the soul a darker place.

Such violence on the frontier was a common event, like a wildfire or a killing snowstorm or a cyclone. There wasn't much you could do about it when it happened. The mother would have to somehow try to explain it to the little girl once she understood it herself.

We lifted the kid back inside the coach still unconscious. She didn't weigh more than a hundred pounds. With her hair cut short and her slender frame hidden under the buckskins, it was easy to see how she could pass for a boy. I wondered if when she awoke, she would regret her decision.

The gambler volunteered to ride on top of the coach so that the kid had more room to stretch out.

The Mexican started to climb in.

"Tell me something," I said.

He turned, looked at me with those dark expressionless eyes.

"Deputy United States Marshal Hector Torrez," he said. "I'm on my way to Deadwood on private business."

When he saw the next question form itself in my gaze, he said, "I thought maybe you were trouble from the way you were armed. This country's full of bloodletters. I thought maybe you could have been one of them. I'm a cautious man." Then he stepped into the coach.

The ride to Deadwood was proving to be full of surprises. I had started out thinking I was only going to be shaken to death over the next couple of hundred miles. Instinct and experience should have warned me that nothing is ever as simple as it first seems.

Going to find a killer was no exception.

5

For the next three days, the routine changed little, except the dust and the heat seemed to chase us all day and everyone in the coach was smelling gamy because of the lack of facilities. The jolt and jar of the trip were enough to fray the nerves of a *padre*.

The kid had regained her senses by late that same evening she'd been wounded, but she said her head felt like it had been split open by a maul.

"You are lucky," the gambler told her. "An inch lower and you'd have had a third eye to see out of." He wasn't much on sympathy or kindness, qualities unknown to his profession.

Deputy Marshal Torrez continued to remain to himself, forgoing conversation or the company of the rest of us. The woman, who said her name was May Smith and that her child's name was Tess, made several attempts to engage Deputy Torrez in conversation. He expressed little interest in her efforts. She was more than a little grateful to him for helping to save her and the child from, as she stated in a whisper, "Abuse of an unspeakable nature" at the hands of the men who'd held up the stage.

Several times she expressed her gratitude to me as well.

"What is your name, sir?" she'd asked, after several failed attempts with the deputy as the coach rocked along a smooth stretch of the Belle Fourche—the first decent piece of road we'd encountered since leaving Cheyenne.

"Quinten McCannon," I said.

She seemed to roll the name over in her mind, as though testing the sound of it. Her dress showed white salt stains of sweat, and strands of her dark hair had come loose from under the feathered hat she wore. Dust smudged her cheeks. I had to feel for her; she looked like a woman that was accustomed to regular bathing and toiletry—uncommon luxuries on the frontier. The trip must have been harder on her than anyone except for the child, who seemed each day to lose a little more of her energy and tolerance for the rough, hot ride.

Finally she said, "Quinten; that is a good strong name. Is it Irish?"

"No, ma'am. Mostly Scot—at least, my elders were."

She smiled softly.

"I apologize for the error."

"No need," I said. "If the truth were told, there's no doubt some Irish mixed in as well."

"Well, anyway, Mr. McCannon, I want you to know how terribly grateful I am that you and Mr. Torrez fought off those men. There is no telling what might have occurred had they been successful in their attempt to rob us." Her eyes lowered, diverting away from the obvious thoughts she was tendering about the bandits. I wanted to say that there was little chance that the holdup men would have taken advantage of her. I wanted to say that those poor bastards were just after the money. But I couldn't be sure that was all they were after.

The little girl, Tess, rested her head on her mother's lap, her eyes half-closed in that dreamy state of exhaustion and boredom that comes from a whole lot of doing nothing.

"It's none of my business," I said, "but Deadwood seems like a hard place to take a child."

Her hand stroked the little girl's head, her long fingers pale against the child's raven hair.

"My man is there," she said. She didn't say husband. She said man. I wasn't sure if the way she said it was intentional. I saw no wedding band on her finger. She seemed too fragile, like an expensive vase, to be going to a place like Deadwood, even if it was to meet a man. But I've known women to be fools when it came to love. Then again, love has made fools of us all. I thought briefly of Del Rio and Juanita Delgado.

I smiled at her and said, "Well, I'm sure he is anxious to see you both again." She didn't return my smile. I let the topic die there in the air between us.

The last night on the road, we stayed at a way station twenty miles outside Deadwood. The Black Hills surrounded us, their slopes dark with the ponderosa pine that grew forty and fifty feet high; the sun cast their long shadows over the road. And when the sun set, the hills claimed their name, their blackness growing deep and complete.

I took my usual leave from the confinement of the stationhouse and stepped out into a black night that was whitewashed end to end with stars. A cockeyed quarter moon rested just above the spiny tops of the trees. The air was cold enough to see my breath and it made my heart beat just a stroke faster.

I saw the Mexican lawman squatted at one corner of the log house, his blanket draped across his shoulders, the carbine resting across his knees. I walked over, knowing I was uninvited and held out my tobacco and cigarettes.

"Smoke?"

He took a short, sharp breath inward and let it out through his nose. "You don't look to me like a gambler," he said. "And you're sure not a miner." It was then that I could smell the whiskey coming off him. "I figure you for a *pistolero*—a hired hand of someone."

"I'm just offering you a smoke, Deputy," I said, wondering why I had bothered making the effort.

"You were cool under fire when those men tried to take the stage. You hit your man with both shots. I couldn't place more than two fingers between the mark. What's your game?"

"Nothing," I said, "Forgive me for disturbing your rest." I started to turn and go find a quiet spot to smoke my shuck.

"Sure, I'll share your makings," he said. "I've tried to give up the habit, but I can't seem to find a good enough reason."

I extended the tobacco pouch and papers again and this time he took them, rolled himself a cigarette in neat fashion, and handed me back the makings. He pulled a match out of his jacket pocket and struck it against the buckle of his belt. The flame danced white, then blue, in a flash of light, and when he snapped it out, my eyes had to readjust.

"I'm a cautious man, McCannon. I have to be in my business. It's caution or the boneyard for men like me. Don't take it personal that I'm trying to get a tag on you. I just need to know who I'm keeping company with." He had a drawl to his voice I had often heard down along the border. I wondered what he was doing this far north.

The tip of the cigarette glowed red against his dark features. He had a thin silky moustache, black, untrimmed. The moustache, along with those Apache cheekbones, added menace to his countenance. The smell of liquor on him just made him seem a bit more dangerous.

"I'm not any of those things you mentioned." I told him. "I'm just a fellow doing a favor for an old friend," Lawman or no, I felt it necessary to keep my business private.

He pulled something out from beneath the blanket, held it forth. I saw then, it was a bottle.

"Drink?" he said.

"What is it?"

He snorted.

"It's commonly referred to as Mexican Mustang Liniment; it's better than most doctors you could get in this country. They claim it cures everything including nightmares and carbuncles. It steadies the hand and steels the nerve, or so it is widely advertised."

It was cheap alcohol that burned the tongue and throat and sent a fire down into the belly. But it warded off the chill air and I handed it back to him.

He tipped the bottle to his mouth and took a long hard swallow, then wiped his lips with the back of his hand.

"Night is a fascinating time," he said.

"It can be."

"Night is when the thief comes. The Bible says that death will come to us like a thief in the night. There is more to night than just the darkness. There is the darkness of men's souls," he said, in a voice that was sinking in tone.

"The darkness of the night attracts the darkness in a man's soul; like attracts like. Night is the time of evil, is the time when the innocent sleep and the guilty do their dirty business. Predator and prey," he concluded.

"You don't talk like a border marshal," I said.

Again he snorted, drew on the cigarette, blew it out through his nose.

"I was educated back east at a school for Apache kids. I had four years of college and wearing shoes and neckties and white shirts and acting like a white man to prepare me for this," he said, waving the bottle in one hand, the moon's light reflecting off the brown glass.

"Only thing was, I wasn't a white man and I wasn't an Apache either, although I had a little of both running through my veins. Even got some German blood. Don't

ask me how or when all those folks got together with my
Mexican side, but they did.

"I learned to speak Latin in that school and can still
speak it some, although I find little need for it in my line
of work." He paused, drew in a breath of the smoke, put
the bottle to his mouth and took another swallow of the
busthead.

"I also have the failing of talking too much when I have
been drinking."

If he was drunk, he held his liquor well.

"I am the first Mexican Indian White man hired as a
United States Deputy Marshal as far as I know. I guess they
don't get many of my type applying for the job."

"I didn't mean to pry," I said.

He waved the hand holding the bottle, then offered it
to me. When I declined a second drink, he had at it some
more, his teeth flashing white in the dim light. He finished
its contents in one long swallow, then dropped it to the
ground where it clinked off a rock.

"I like what I do, McCannon. I'm good at it. I've got
more education than most white men I know, but it doesn't
mean spit. As far as most are concerned, I'm just a damn
mestizo—a man of color, less valuable than a mule. But
wearing this badge changes some of that." He pulled back
the lapel of his corduroy coat and touched a small nickel
badge pinned to his shirt.

"This," he said, "helps keep things even."

He stubbed out his cigarette and I finished mine and
the blackness closed in on us again.

The door of the hotel opened and closed again on a
pair of dry hinges; I turned my attention to the sound. It
was the girl in buckskins. She walked to the corrals where
the horses stood sleeping head-to-rump and rested her
forearms on the top rail. She looked small and shadowy
in the night light. Hector Torrez had fallen silent, his
breathing deep. The Mexican Mustang Liniment had done
its work.

I walked over to where the girl was. She heard my approach and turned, startled.

"You don't have to be afraid," I said. "I was just having myself a smoke. How's the head feeling?"

She seemed to shrink in my presence and I wondered if it was a mistake to have approached her in such a manner.

"You ain't going to hurt me, are you?"

"No. I just came out to have a smoke, like I said."

She touched the side of her face with her right hand as though it were hurting. I wasn't quite sure what to say to her.

"It's none of my business," I said, "but this country is a hard place at best. I can help you get back to Cheyenne or Denver or wherever it is you are from, if it's a matter of money."

She looked at me, the moon's light touching her face, her head slightly tilted, the dry stain of blood dark against her buckskin shirt.

"I need to get to Deadwood," she said.

"I can't imagine why," I said.

She had the nervousness of a deer about to run off.

"It's a personal matter," she said.

"It's not worth having to do what you've had to do to make it this far," I said. Her features grew stiff; I saw her swallow hard.

"What would you know about anything?" she said.

"I know you are not a boy," I said. "And I saw you and the stationmaster the other night. I didn't want to see it, but I did. You're too young to have to prostitute yourself. Let me buy you passage back to your home."

Her shoulders slumped noticeably, I thought she might fall down. I took a step toward her, and she took a step backward.

"Don't touch me!"

"I wasn't going to."

"I didn't prostitute myself," she said, her words fluttering out like wounded birds struggling for flight.

"It's none of my business," I said. "Life is hard enough for most of us as it is. I wasn't trying to judge you. I just wanted to help."

"I was out looking at the horses," she said. "He came out, took hold of me, told me not to fight him. I begged him . . ." The words caught in her throat, and she turned her face away from me.

"You don't have to explain," I said.

"No! I do. I have to explain to someone!"

"Okay."

"He forced me into the coach. He knew. Somehow, he knew that I was a female."

"Maybe. Maybe not," I said. "Men like that . . ."

"No. He said he knew I was pretending to be a boy, but that he could see right off that I wasn't. He said that his old woman couldn't pleasure him anymore, but that I could. He was too strong. He hurt me. He hurt me in ways I can't tell you . . ."

I reached out and put my arms around her. She trembled like the frightened child she was.

"You don't have to explain any more," I said. Her crying was something soft, muted, like the wind stirring in the tops of trees. Only the sound came from a deep and broken place, a place that might never be mended again.

"I can't go back," she said. "Not yet, anyway."

"Then you'll need to protect yourself," I said.

"I don't know how."

"I'll show you."

"You won't tell anyone about me?" she said.

"No. It's your secret. But remember, if Faust could see through your disguise, so will other men like him. Keep a caution always. Don't trust anyone."

She stepped away from me, looked at me with those innocent hurting eyes, and said, "Not even you?"

"I think you already know the answer to that," I said. "I don't think you'll have to worry about Deputy Torrez, either."

She reached out and touched the wrist of my left hand. The hoot of an owl drifted out of a tree; its sound was primitive and lonely and crawled under the skin.

"My name is Rose," she said.

6

Before we parted, I took the Colt' Thunderer backup with the two-and-a-half-inch barrel from my shoulder holster and gave it to Rose.

"It's got small grips," I said. "But it's enough power to stop a man, even one the size of Faust, should you need to use it."

She seemed reluctant to take it, her hands lying at her sides, not reaching for the nickel-plated pistol that looked like silver in the moonlight.

"You don't have to wear it openly," I said. "Wear it in the pocket of a jacket."

I bucked out the cylinder, showed her the empty chamber that I kept the hammer on and the five remaining shells. "It's a single action," I said. "You need to thumb back the hammer before you can fire it." I ejected the cartridges and showed her how.

"Just aim it like you would your finger, hold it steady while you squeeze the trigger." The hammer snapped down with a hard click. I took hold of one of her hands and placed the pistol in it.

"It's up to you, Rose."

She tried it, her thin frame silhouetted like a black paper cutout, her arm extended, pointing the pistol toward nothing more than darkness.

"Just squeeze it slowly, don't pull," I said. The hammer fell on the empty chamber. She didn't flinch, but the barrel of the pistol dropped noticeably. "Try it again," I said. The second time was better, the third was better still.

"How does it feel?" I asked.

"It's heavy for such a small gun," she said, lowering the revolver to her side.

"You'll get used to it."

"I don't know if I will," she said, looking at the pistol in her hand as though she couldn't comprehend its meaning.

"Remember what Faust did to you," I said. "There are other men who would do the same if given the chance. It's your decision. I won't force you to take it."

I saw her close her eyes against the memory, the pain that came with the memory. I waited for her to decide.

She held out her hand for the cartridges, I placed them in her palm and watched her slip them one by one into the chambers, snap shut the cylinder; it looked larger than it was in the smallness of her hand.

"Remember, keep the hammer on an empty chamber," I said. "And practice shooting it so that you get used to the feel of its kick—and so you can hit what you are aiming at."

She looked doubtful.

"It's not that difficult," I said. "The trick is not to be afraid. A pistol is a close-range weapon. Aim at the largest part of your target—the chest. Not many shootists can hit anything with a pistol at more than forty feet. Not under fire they can't."

She let out her breath all at once.

"The thing is," I said, "you may not have to use it at all. But if you do, at least you'll have it, and with some practice, you'll be able to hit what you're aiming at. Real important in a gunfight." I tried to put a touch of humor on it; I wasn't sure I did.

She looked at me then, the faintness of her eyes seeking my own. Her breathing was soft, like the muted purr of a cat.

"Why is it," she said, "that some men can be like Faust and others like you?"

"The world is made up of all sorts of men, Rose. Why we are who we are is just a matter of luck of the draw, I suspect. I don't know the true answer."

"You are very kind," she said.

"I'm not a saint, Rose. I just don't like to see people get hurt. It's real important you learn how to shoot that piece and protect yourself, especially in a place like Deadwood. Don't count on the kindness of others to protect you. It's a hard fact, but one you need to be aware of."

I saw the softness go out of her eyes.

"I suppose you are right, Mr. McCannon."

"You can call me Quint, I prefer it. Mr. McCannon makes me sound old, even if I seem that way to you."

Again, she touched the back of my wrist, the bones in her hand and fingers were as small and delicate as a bird's.

"I reckon we had better get some sleep," I said. "We still have twenty miles tomorrow in that Concord."

She hesitated before removing her hand.

"I will pay you for the pistol once I get to Deadwood and get settled," she said.

"No need," I told her, "it was a gift to me in the first place." I didn't tell her that it had once belonged to a Creek policeman over in the Nations whose wife had used it to murder him in a quarrel over an octoroon woman. The wife had sold it in order to pay for her husband's funeral. It had cost me twenty-five dollars, but I liked the way it balanced in my hand and didn't mind paying the extra for it. I had owned it for several years as my backup.

"It's generous of you," she said. "I don't know how to thank you."

"Just stay alive, Rose. Don't let anyone harm you. And when your business in Deadwood is finished, go back home. Go back to people who love you and will care for you. This country is no place for someone like you."

I stood there in the cold night air for a while after she had left and thought about another young woman I had once known who was in some ways much like Rose in her delicacy and her pain, and in my wanting to protect her. Only I hadn't been able to. It was a memory I tried hard to keep tucked away, like a tintype kept in a drawer under some shirts.

But Rose's vulnerability had dredged up the memory of Mary Lee McCannon and I saw my late wife's face behind the lids of my eyes as I closed them. And the softness of her voice whispered to me like the wind easing through the trees.

Quint, I don't want to leave you. I don't want to leave little Samuel. Please, make it so I don't have to leave you both. Quint . . . promise me that you will take care of our son and that you will never forget me and that you will tell him about me. Will you tell him about me? Will you remember me always as I was? Please, please, please.

They were her last words to me, and now they tumbled through my head like loose rock breaking down a mountainside, each word bruising my soul. She died that night and took some of me with her. Our infant son died two days later, taking most of the rest of what was left of me. They called it the Milk Sickness. I never understood it nor tried to beyond what it had cost me.

Someone once said, "That which does not kill you, makes you stronger." I am not so sure.

I could hear Torrez's breathing from across the way. It was deep and sonorous now, the rhythmic sound of the exhausted or the drunken. But I had the feeling that he was a man who would awaken instantly if approached. Men like Torrez never slept the sleep of the dead. Instead, they rested somewhere just below the surface of consciousness, their framework tuned to the slightest noises, their nerves frayed as the cuffs of their shirts. Men who could kill you while they were still sleeping.

The night was blue black and empty, the stars pinpoints of light, and the chill air held in it a warning of an early winter. I smoked another shuck and let all that day's weariness creep in, not wanting to go to bed, not wanting to think about girls like Rose or those who were being murdered in Deadwood or men like Faust and Torrez. I didn't want to think about Mary Lee, either, or a son I'd never get to see grow up. Maybe the dead were the lucky ones.

That night I dreamt about Rose.

She was pointing the silver pistol at me, thumbing back the hammer. I could see the slow turning of the cylinder, see the blunted dull gray heads of the bullets, hear the clicking of the mechanism, her hand steady, her face a mask of deliberate calm, and I knew within that moment that she would kill me and there was nothing I could do to stop her—and I wondered why.

The following morning produced a sky that was swollen with the gray bellies of clouds the size of Conestogas bunching together, crowding the canyon walls, obscuring the tops of trees that stood blue green in the cold dawn light.

We ate breakfast outside at a long table and the child, Tess, told her mother she was cold and everyone else ate their meal in the silence of people who are uncomfortable and not much given to conversation at that hour of the morning.

The driver and the guard went about their work of harnessing the team of horses without the benefit of exchanging words. Wood smoke rose from the stone chimney inside the log dugout where the cookstove was; everywhere there was the smell of burning pine, thick and tangy in the chill air.

Rose sat directly across from me and several times I looked up to see the gratitude in her eyes and I thought it was a good thing that other people can't know our fears.

The gambler ate with rapid deliberation. He wore a pinky ring that had a small diamond set in it and his hair was greasy from not having been washed. The pores of his skin were black from the road dust, and his growth of unshaven beard was a light rust that rolled with the movement of his jaw as he ate.

I saw Torrez hunkered by the corrals, watching the driver and guard hitch the team. He looked no differently than he ever did, the sweep of his sombrero's brim low over his dark eyes, his heels lifted off the ground so that they could support his haunches, his back bent to the wind that blew down from the northwest. He seemed not in the least disturbed by the cold weather or the effects of the Mexican Mustang Liniment from last night. I saw then that he was chewing what looked like a strip of jerky. I was still curious about his business in Deadwood.

Soon, we were once again inside the stage, including the gambler, now that Rose had recovered sufficiently enough to sit.

The road climbed farther up into the Black Hills, the sides of the canyon walls closing in so that not two wagons could pass one other at various places. One time the stage had to be stopped so that the driver and guard could climb down and remove a lodgepole pine that had fallen across the road.

By noon we arrived in Deadwood. The last twenty miles of the journey had seemed the longest. I had done some prizefighting at one time in my younger days, and after long bouts my ribs and arms and chest would be sore for days from the blows of other men's fists. It was nothing compared to the pounding the stage trip gave me, only the pain was in different places.

I climbed down and waited for my saddle and Creedmore to be handed down from the boot of the stage.

The woman, May Smith, approached me, her daughter clinging to her hand. I saw the listlessness in the child's eyes—small vacant pools of blue that were absent of light.

"I want to thank you again for what you and Marshal Torrez did to protect us," she said. "Perhaps later, after we've gotten settled, you will allow me the opportunity to show you my appreciation in a more tangible way—dinner, perhaps."

"Perhaps," I said. Her little girl looked up at me, the dark ringlets of her hair damp against her head, damp and uncombed and unclean, as was her dress and her shoes, which were spotted with dust. Then her gaze shifted impatiently to her mother.

"Have the driver tell you of a good hotel or boarding-house," I said to the woman. "Your child looks as though she could use some rest and decent food and a bath."

"Yes," she said. "I will." She looked into my eyes a moment longer as though searching for an answer to an unspoken question, then turned and went over to where the driver was standing at the rear of the coach, talking to a man whose belly hung over his belt buckle.

I watched the gambler pick up his valise, saw the glint of his pinky ring, then watched as he marched off down the walk and become quickly lost in the flowing mass of humanity that crowded the streets of the ramshackle town of Deadwood.

"It looks like hell on wheels," Hector Torrez said as he stepped past me, his carbine in one hand, his blanket tied over his shoulders. Then he paused, leveled his gaze on me, and said, "Last night . . . I talk too damn much when I drink. And I sometimes drink too damn much. Don't get the idea we're friends. I don't make friends. To me, you are just like everybody else—potential trouble." Then he turned and walked away.

Somehow, I understand what he meant about friendship and not trusting and knowing what you were about in this life. It was a good way to be if you wanted to stay alive very long in his business—or mine.

I hefted the Dunn Brothers saddle in one hand, the

Creedmore in the other and asked the driver where I might find a livery.

Before he could answer, Rose touched me on the shoulder.

"I'll keep your advice," she said. "I'll practice till I get it down. I just hope I don't ever have to use it." I started to say something but she cut me off. "If I do, I do," she said. "I ain't afraid."

I shook her hand, felt its smallness in my own, and said, "Good luck to you, Kid," and she smiled, the driver and the man with the big belly looking on.

"Thanks Mr. McCannon. Thanks for everything."

The driver told me where I could find a livery and I walked in that direction.

Deadwood was laid out on a long narrow street that was without a straight line to it. Trailing off at angles were one or two other streets. Every building in the town looked like it had been put up in a hurry. Everywhere stood the enterprise of a boom town: saloons, honky-tonks, gambling dens, whiskey tents, crib houses, a couple of hotels, hardware stores, jewelers, restaurants, opium dens, gunsmiths, butcher shops, and a shoe repair—all jammed cheek-to-jowl in raw lumber false-fronted buildings, canvas tents, and hodge-podge structures of lesser quality.

The street itself was clogged with teamsters, mules, horses, and oxen teams hauling more lumber and more mining equipment, all trying to pass and get around one another. The result was a lot of men cussing the air. The sharp report of hammers could be heard farther down the street. Still more permanent buildings going up. Men lounged about in bowler hats and claw-hammer coats—Attorneys-at-Law and real estate agents. Only they had another name for them in the South; they called them carpetbaggers.

Miners in their stiff dirty clothing, their eyes hollow and streaked like raccoons, leaned against the support poles of overhangs and squatted on the steps of several establishments watching the goings-on and each other.

Other men stood around in doorways: pimps, gun punks, pickpockets, judging by their eager, expectant eyes and their slouching postures. Frontier flotsam; every town had them, just like every town had mongrel dogs and tame Indians.

The foot traffic up and down the street was heavy with gamblers, faro dealers, vagrants, sloe-eyed women in colorful dresses cut high on the bottom and low on top. If there was a profession to be named, there was a face to match it somewhere in that crowd. Everyone wanted to strike it rich and take their share of the gold. Some took the yellow metal from the earth, others took it straight from the miners' pockets. That was life in the mining camps.

I found what I was seeking at the far end of town— Black Hills Livery & Rental.

An old gent whose features looked as though they'd been cut out of the very rock itself sat a three-legged stool; his grizzled, craggy face tilted toward the sun that now appeared between a split in the clouds.

"I might need to rent a horse while I'm here," I said.

His eyes opened with the slowness of a yawn. Tiny lines of dirt were creased in the folds of his skin. He was bundled up in a heavy buffalo-hide coat that looked several sizes too large for him. His unshaven face was a patch of gray briar. His mouth twisted downwards at the corners, the right side stained brown from a lifetime of chewing and spitting tobacco from that side.

"A horse?" he said, as though he had not heard that word before.

"That's what you do here," I said, glancing up to the sign painted over the double doors of his barn, "rent horses?"

"'Course I do, when I got 'em to rent. Trouble is, I ain't got one to rent right at the present." He looked irritated that I had disturbed his rest. His eyes trailed over me and he held up the palm of one hand to shade the sun's glare so that he could better see who it was that had come to trouble him.

"You're a long drink of water," he said, then spat off to the side from a cud he had stored in one cheek. "Ain't seen you before, have I? Folks coming in here a hundred a day to pan the gold. Cutters and shooters, there's a killing a night right out there on them streets. Had to carry two off just this mornin'. Somebody laid 'em out last night. Ain't nobody knows who done them boys. Ain't nobody even cares. Welcome to perdition, mister!" Then he spat another watery brown stream and wiped his mouth with the back of his hand.

"When do you reckon you will have a horse for rent?" I asked.

He looked at my saddle.

"That's a double rig," he said. "We called them rimfires, down on the Brazos. A Dunn Brothers, ain't it?"

"That's right," I told him. He smiled his approval.

"I should have a horse or two due in later on today, or tomorrow. Cost you a four dollars a day. And before you tell me how pricey that sounds, remember—I'm the only livery in Deadwood. You could always walk to wherever it is you need to go. You from down on the Brazos?"

"I've been in the neighborhood a time or two," I said. "Can I leave my saddle stored here?"

"You can. Set her down and I'll take her in soon's my siesta is up." I looked at his hands; they were rough, the fingers twisted and knotted at the joints.

"You cowboy for a time?" I asked.

Light came into his face, along with the first show of friendliness.

"Man. I must've drove ten thousand of them goddamn creatures. Five long, hard seasons. Drove them from the Rio to Kansas and Nebraska and later on up into Montana. Now there is some damn righteous country—Montana.

Purtiest place I ever seen. Would of stayed but I didn't,"
he said, and spat again.

"Come here instead. Tried mining gold and my hands
froze up in the creeks; the arthritis crippled up my fingers,
bummed my knees, crawled into my back. Then I took to
this. Horses is all that I know anymore, all that I care to
know. It ain't a bad business," he said.

He spat out the blanched cud into his hand this time,
looked at it, and threw it aside. "All gone," he said. "Dead
as Yankee soldiers on Pea Ridge. Har! Har! Har!" He had
a laugh like the bray of a mule.

"I'm looking for someone," I said. "A woman."

The angling light of sun caught in his gray-as-crawfish
eyes as he squinted up toward me, his hands jerked up
from his knees and his throat seemed to slide down inside
the loose skin of his grizzled neck.

"Hell, mister, I hope you ain't set yer sights too high
because there is only two kinds of women in Deadwood—
fat whores, and skinny ones. Take yer pick! Har! Har!
Har!"

"Her name is Alexandra Dupage," I said. A wagon filled
with freshly sawn boards of lumber rumbled past, the
boards slapped hard against one another as one of the
wheels hit a rock in the road. It sounded like pistol shots.

"To hell and Jesus!" shouted the driver, and he cracked
a bull whip over the head of a team of mules whose velvety
ears shone golden in the sun light.

Some of the joy went out of the old-timer's face at the
mention of Alexandra Dupage's name, his mouth stopped
moving, the soft, pliable skin under the rasp of dirty whiskers lay still.

"You talkin' of Alex Dupage?"

He brought a rough hand to his mouth, drew it down
across his stained lips, and shook his head in a slightly
agitated way.

"Goddamn, mister, I was you, I'd steer clear of Alex's

fer awhile. She's had some trouble lately. Fact, she's sorta suspended operations," he said.

"How so?" I asked, watching the movement of the old man's eyes. The eyes of a man can tell you a different story than his mouth. The eyes shifted past me; I could see black flecks floating in gray centers, jagged lines of bloody veins running through the white.

"They say some of her gals have been murdered," he said. The knot of his throat percolated, then settled back again just above the top button of his soiled shirt.

"Last one they found had a butcher knife stuck in her." He shuddered his shoulders. His lids closed against the light, pulling his bushy brows downward. Then he shook his head once more and opened his eyes again and looked at me.

"There's plenty of other places a man could take his pleasure," he said. "I'd avoid Alex's I was you."

"Why is that?" I asked.

"They say she's put out a reward for whoever it is killed them gals. Word has it King Fisher and some others like him has already hit town. You ever heard of King Fisher, mister?"

"Yeah, I have," I said, reluctant to acknowledge what I knew or didn't know.

The old man spat again, even though he had no tobacco in his mouth and rubbed the palms of his hands against the sides of his legs.

"King Fisher is a killing sonofabitch!" he said, some of the words catching in the phlegm of his throat. "If Fisher has come after that reward money, he's liable to shoot somebody just to say they was the one who killed them gals. Anyone doing their business down to Alex's is liable to wind up on ol' King's gunlist! You wanna get your ashes hauled, I'd do it at Crooked Nose Kate's, or Rabbit Alice's.

"Hell, I'd even take up with Calamity Jane first," he added, with a struggling chuckle. "She's less attractive than a chamberpot, even to an old coot like me."

His eyes glittered, he was obviously enjoying whatever it was traipsing through his mind.

"But at least with ol' Janey, you wouldn't run the risk of dying because of it, less it were from the clap, maybe." Then his laugh became lost in its wheeze.

The old man reached in his pocket and took out a fresh plug of tobacco and set about filling his cud with it.

I was still considering the presence of King Fisher in town. He had the instincts of a bird of prey when it came to knowing where the reward money was being offered. Alexandra Dupage had already advertised in the newspapers if Fisher had come.

The sun went back behind the clouds and just that quick, drops of rain the size of half dollars clanged off the tin roof of the livery.

"Well, so much fer a pleasant day," the old man said, then grabbed up my Dunn Brothers saddle and took it inside. He had the limp of a man who knew what it was to have horses fall on him.

I was left to my own fate standing there in the sudden downpour. Welcome to Deadwood, I thought.

7

The rain lasted less than five minutes, then the clouds parted once more and the sun broke through beautifully against a sky as clear as blue glass and a rainbow formed itself at the far end of the canyon. It was a touch of rare beauty set against a backdrop of such a scarred place. Several patrons of the Jerzey Lil Saloon had stepped outside to observe the rainbow.

The air smelled clean and new, and the sun mirrored itself in the puddles of rain lying in the rutted street.

Among the curious clientele of the Jerzey Lil that had been drawn by the spectacle of the rainbow was a slightly built man who wore blue-tinted spectacles.

I gauged him to be about five-six. He was well dressed in a frock coat, fresh white shirt, creased trousers, and polished boots. His features were sharp, bony, but the skin was sallow. He had a straight thin nose and heavy sandy moustaches. There were other things about him too: his hands. I noticed that his hands were well attended, as was the rest of his appearance. He had clean fingernails, for one thing. An unusual affectation on the frontier.

But it was the blue-tinted spectacles that first drew my attention. Not only did they hide his eyes, they also gave him an air of mystery.

And though he posed no outward sign of threat, I got the feeling he was dangerous. The feeling I got was that Doc was dangerous the way a diamondback is dangerous in the quiet way it coils under a bush.

Standing next to him was a woman of robust build; her left hand was hooked through the crook of arm. The woman was paying more attention to Doc than she was the rainbow.

They seemed an odd couple, the pair of them. He stood at least a head shorter than she and hardly matched her in size and bulk. She had thick, short-cut hair tinted a deep reddish color. She wore a black velvet dress that fitted tightly against her figure. The swell of her breasts were exposed by the low cut front of the dress. Her skin was slightly ruddy and healthy in appearance, unlike that of the man's.

She had a plain but not altogether unattractive face. A prominent nose and red full lips. She held a little yellow parasol in her right hand.

Even though his eyes were hidden behind the blue-tint glasses, I knew he had taken notice of me as I passed by.

I heard the woman say, "Come'n Doc, let's go back inside."

And then in a voice that was soft, almost feminine, he replied, "In a moment, Kate—I haven't seen a rainbow in years."

I knew then who the man and the woman were.

I saw a sign across the street that advertised the Deadwood Hotel & Billiard Parlor. I needed a room and a change of clothes, although I'd have to buy another shirt after having used my spare as bandages for Rose. I needed a decent meal and bed that didn't hold the company of graybacks. They were just a few of the things I *needed* before introducing myself and my reason for being in Deadwood to Alexandra Dupage. But the thing I *wanted* was a bath with enough hot water to burn through the soreness the Black Hills Stage Company had pounded into my carcass for the last two hundred and forty six miles.

The man at the hotel counter looked me over when I asked about renting a room.

"You're lucky," he said. "We got one vacancy on account a July Fitzimmons being killed last night in the Variety Club."

"Unlucky for him," I said, "lucky for me."

The clerk grinned.

"Miner stuck him with a stiletto over a card game. They say July's blood squirted high as the ceiling. July fancied himself a prizefighter, but I guess he didn't count on fighting no knife."

"I'll take the room," I said.

"Don't mind his stuff, I'll come and pick it up later," the clerk said, handing me the pen to sign the register with.

"How much for the room?" I said.

"Dollar fifty a day, clean sheets included. We got the best rooms in town. Ask anybody."

I laid five dollars on the desk. "I'll take the room for five days, and if it's as advertised, I might stay longer." He stared at the money knowing it was short of the asking price then handed me a key.

"And if I fall to the same fate as Mr. Fitzimmons," I said, "you can keep the change and rerent the room. How'll that be?"

That seemed to satisfy him, the macabre logic.

"Top of the stairs, down the hallway to your left. Last room on the end. There's a stairway just across the hall from you that leads down the back and out to the privy in the alleyway." It was a skeleton key that would have fit any one of the doors. I took it and slipped it into my pocket.

"Anything else you'll be needing, Mr.—" He glanced down at my signature on the register. "Mr. McCannon," then peered up at me through the dark circles that formed his eyes. "A woman, maybe?"

"No, thanks," I said, and climbed the stairs.

It was a common room, bare of all but the essentials: a cotton tick mattress upon a bed of iron springs, a single plain chair, a tin washbasin, and a china pitcher of fetid water resting on a roughly hewn commode. Lying next to the pitcher were a towel and a yellow bar of soap. A small framed mirror hung from a nail above the commode where a man could shave if he wanted and had his own razor. And of course, Mr. July Fitzimmons's belongings which I collected and piled in the hallway.

I laid my saddlebags on the bed, propped the Henry in a corner, and hung my hat on the chair before pouring water into the basin and washing my face and hands, then strung wet fingers through my hair before drying with the towel.

When I looked up, I saw my image in the mirror: the clear, almost colorless eyes of my father and his father, the square of face that needed the burnt red stubble scraped clean, the sweep of moustaches of the same deep rust color that draped along the sides of my mouth. I saw weariness and a man who needed a shave and a bath and his moustaches trimmed: the face of the McCannon clan.

I saw what Mary Lee saw the night she died, the same face that the man I killed out on the trail to Deadwood had seen just before he died. It was the same face that some Confederate boys coming out of a stand of hardwood trees saw as they swept down on our position at The Wilderness and a lot of other places where we set about killing one another.

It was a face less inclined to either sorrow or joy than it once was. What had happened to all the years? I wondered. How had it come to be that I was in this place at this time?

As I stood there staring at the image that seemed both mine and not mine, I remembered one young boy in particular in that bloody campaign. He could not have been more than thirteen or fourteen and carried the Rebel flag on a tree branch. He was leading a small company of Rebs up our right flank at Pickles Gap.

He had lost his cap as he charged out of the trees holding his flag, the wind tearing through his long wheat hair as he ran. His screams rippled through the meager gray ranks, and they, in turn, set their voices to the yell. It was not so much a yell as it was a howling curse. And in that small, spare, frozen moment, I could not bring myself to pull the trigger on him. He seemed only a boy playing a boy's foolish game, and I could not kill him.

All around me the crack and pop of rifle fire pierced the air and the smoke from our guns and their guns lifted over our line in a thick blue cloud that obscured our vision and scorched our throats.

The whine of minnie balls split the air, kicking up dirt and snapping leaves off the trees. It was a horizontal rain of lead killing and maiming everyone in its path, cutting men down like marionettes whose strings were suddenly broken.

And somehow, miraculously, through a break in the choking smoke, the young flag bearer emerged, the ragged bunch of butternuts behind him, and on they came directly into our guns.

And still I couldn't pull the trigger on him. He was just a boy.

But someone did shoot him, for his head suddenly jerked backward just as he was leaping over the dead body of a fallen Union man. A bloody spray of red flew from his golden head. The flag he carried fluttered to the ground like some great wounded bird. Dead or dying, his legs continued to carry him several more paces. Then he became entangled in his cherished flag, fell, and came to rest just inches from where I was kneeling.

And for a long, full moment, the war stopped. The flat pop of rifle shots faded, and a calmness descended upon that small square of ground there in front of me as I looked down into the open eyes of the dead Rebel flag bearer. A halo of bright red blood soaked the ground. His right hand lay stretched out before him, nearly touching the toe of my boot as if he were reaching for me, reaching for someone to take his hand and hold it in those final fateful seconds. Only death had come too quickly for such sentiments, and he, like a lot of other boys, had died alone.

As I stared into my own eyes there in the mirror, I remembered something that I had long tried to forget. Just before the boy was shot, our eyes had met for the briefest moment and he had stopped yelling as though in that moment he'd forgotten that we were at war and that our only reason for being in this place was to kill one another because of the color of our uniforms. And for a long, fateful second, he was just a boy in the wrong place at the wrong time; we both were.

The memory touched a spot in me that caused me to take in a deep breath and let it out slowly. It was a spot next to the one I kept for Mary Lee and my son, Samuel.

I was drawn back up out of the well of remembering by a knock at the door.

I slid the Remington out of its holster and held it behind my back before opening the door.

The man was tall, slump-shouldered, wearing a coat made out of dyed black sheepskin. He wore a pinch-brimmed fedora pulled down tight to his ears. He had brown eyes that were flecked with green and pocked skin around his jaw and neck. His ears were prominent and he had the flat nose of a boxer. His thick, meaty hands rested at his sides.

Before I could ask, he pulled back the lapel of his coat and showed me a small badge cut from a silver dollar.

"I'm Constable Johnny Slaughter," he said. His long dark moustaches lifted, then fell back into place when he spoke.

"I saw you get off the stage today." He continued when I did not reply to his introduction. "I watch and see who gets off the stage," he said. "It's part of my job—to see who's coming into town."

He fell silent, his eyes searching mine, waiting for me to tell him who I was and why I was here. When I didn't, he said, "Ever since she put it in the papers about the reward she was offering, they've been riding into my town. I figure you're one of them. Tell me if I'm wrong."

He didn't say who "she" was, but we both knew.

"You're wrong," I said.

"No. I don't believe I am."

"Believe what you want," I said.

His gaze slid to the hand I was holding behind my back with the self-cocker in it.

"If you was just another gambler or a gold panner," he said, "you wouldn't be coming to the door holding a pistol behind your back. I could arrest you, run you out of town."

"No. I don't believe you will do that," I told him.

"Why wouldn't I?" he said.

"Because if you were going to, you'd have already done it."

Something determined left his gaze, and the left side of his face twitched, stretching the muscles in his neck.

"I've got my hands full here," he said. "I don't need men like you to make my job harder than it is."

I took the opportunity to ask him the obvious question: "Seems you could have saved yourself all this trouble of worrying about the gun artists showing up in town if you had found whoever it was that killed Miss Dupage's girls in the first place."

I saw the knot form along his jawline, saw the color of anger rise in his face.

"If you know that much," he said. "Then I'm right about your reasons for being here. Your type always comes to gather over the carcass. And as far as those gals of Alex Dupage's, they're just fancy whores whose living or dying don't mean a whit in the long scheme of things. People get killed here all the time and for a variety of reasons. I don't have the time or inclination to spend all my energies looking for someone who has a bent against sporting gals."

"It would seem to me the reward alone would make you interested," I said.

He took a deep breath, then let it out, his irritation with me growing.

"I get paid regular mister, every week for pinning on this badge, and I get to run a faro game over at the Jerzey Saloon and I get to go home and sleep at nights when I'm done working. It's honest, steady work. I don't need no more than that."

It didn't figure, his answer. But I let it rest where it lay.

"I'll tell you this," he said. "I figure you for trouble. You and the others that already arrived and are bound to come. The way I see it, comes to trouble out there on those streets, I'll shoot you without warning, you give me reason."

I knew the type. Men who were brave enough to wear a badge and back up their authority with a gun, but not so brave they'd give an opponent an even chance. They were the kind of men who would walk up behind you and shoot you in the back of the head, then arrest you for whatever law it was they thought you had broken. I harbored no doubts that Constable Slaughter was probably very dangerous in that regard.

"I'll keep your warning in mind," I said. "Now, if you will excuse me, I'd like to see about the chances of a hot bath and a meal."

He looked at me with the dull, vacant look of a man who had already written me off his list of someone to share a drink and a cigar with. Then he touched the brim of his hat and turned and walked away. I could hear his heavy steps on the stairs as he descended them. Then I heard him say something to the desk clerk in a muted voice. I closed the door behind me.

I stretched out across the bed, suddenly weary from the

stage ride, the sleepless nights, old memories, and the thought of men like Constable Slaughter and Hector Torrez and King Fisher—any one of which might kill me if given half the chance.

8

Sometimes you sleep the sleep of the dead. And other times you visit with the ghosts. It's those other times when you force yourself to come awake and sit on the side of the bed and smoke a cigarette. The times when you can't seem to escape the gloaming images, all the dead faces, and whiskey rivers. And in that hour of deep lonely, you also remember the women, too. Women who've held you and loved you for a night at a time. Maybe you forget most of their names, but you never forget them completely. And remembering that much at least helps you get through the worst of it, the long nights.

In the nightmare I'd just awakened from, we fuzzy-faced boys of the thirty-second Michigan Volunteers had been crossing a low, swampy area, the fetid water up to our waists, the muck sucking at our boots, making every step an effort. Some of the boys were afraid cottonmouth snakes would slide through the coffee-stain water and bite their legs. We could hear the bullfrogs croak, then stop, then croak again. The mosquitos rose like clouds off the water, taking their toll on our arms and faces and working their

misery into our eyes and noses. Our clothes were damp
and rotting away, our flesh sloughing off our bones.

It was in the false dawn of morning, when the light tricks
you into believing that you are safe from the night and a
warm breeze plays among the Spanish moss that hangs
from the cypress trees like the molted hair of dead southern belles.

I wasn't sure why we were crossing that swamp or how
we had gotten there or what our purpose was for being
there. But I knew that we were surrounded by the floating
shadows of Confederates dressed in tattered uniforms as
gray as the very dawn itself. And through the swirling mist
I could see a gallery of faces, faces that were drawn with
hunger and hatred, their yellow eyes burning brightly,
their mouths set in ghostly grins of broken and missing
teeth.

It seemed like we had been in the water a long time.
No one talked. A great silence empaled us with fear, a fear
so heavy it lay against the chest and pinched the heart.
The water and the muck pulled at us, wearing us down so
that once we made the other side, we'd be easy prey for
the waiting rebels.

And then, suddenly, a large man in a slouch hat and a
butternut jacket torn at the shoulder hovered above me.
And I saw what he was holding: a Springfield musket with
a long, rusty bayonet attached to the muzzle. Before I could
move, he plunged the steel into my guts, pinning me to
the ground, his weight behind it. I thought that it would
hurt. Only I didn't feel any pain.

I knew that I was going to die. And in knowing that, I
knew something beyond pain, something indescribable.

I looked up into his face and saw there was no hint of
compassion, no expression of forgiveness in the glazed
eyes of the man forking me to the ground, for the war
had cost him what it had cost us all: everything.

We were not brothers or men of the same color or even
men of the same country. We were simply men who had

lost ourselves, who had come to understand only one thing: survival. And that need had brought us to this moment: one man killing the other so that one could live, for another day, another hour, another minute.

I closed my eyes and waited for the end.

I awoke against the pull of the dream, my mouth dry, the rest of me soaked in sweat. I sat up on the side of the bed, the room deep in darkness. I struck a match to the lamp on the little stand next to my bed. The flame guttered low, flared, and filled a corner of the room with dull buttery light. I adjusted the wick and closed the glass chimney down around it, my hands unsteady, my breath short, labored.

I reached into my pocket and took out the Ingersol, checked the time: it was nearly nine in the evening. Then I rolled myself a shuck and used the lamp to fire it. The smoke felt good and powerful against my lungs. I realized that I was grateful to be alive . . . grateful and ashamed at the same time.

I thought of those who were still lost and wandering aimlessly in the dreams of the living, those still seeking release from the world of my mind: Mary Lee, Samuel, the rebel boy who carried his flag, the men who'd died by my hand. Faces and memories. Hard to forget; hard to remember.

From the earth we are born, and to the earth we return. But what of our souls?

I dressed, took my hat from the back of the chair, and left down the rear stairway. The night air was cold and black, the sky filled with stars.

I walked out to the street, where a few heelers and loafers were hanging about; most everyone else was staying inside the dens of iniquity where they could indulge their desires and conduct their business, one seeking the other. Desirous men and wanton women; Johnny-Behind-The-Deuce, and bottom dealers; billiard boys and coon-eyed miners.

Pieces of the dream were still with me like broken bits

of glass shattered inside my skull, wounds that would never heal completely.

I stepped inside one of the saloons. Whiskey sounded good to me just then.

The room was long and narrow, a fancy oak bar running down one side with a back bar; a mirror reflected the bottles and the faces of the men staring at their reflections as they stood drinking their whiskeys, one foot resting on the brass rail.

Suspended from the ceiling were old wagon wheels that supported oil lamps and could be lowered or raised by ropes. Opposite the bar were the poker tables. Further down, a faro rig was set up and men were bucking the tiger. And in the back, a keno game was going on.

I noticed a chair hanging high up on the wall, suspended from a peg. On either side of the chair were the stuffed heads of a bison and a black bear. The black bear's yellowed ivory teeth were exposed in a frozen snarl; the glass eyes stared impassively.

One of three bartenders lifted his chin and said, "Name's Tommy O'Dule, what'll it be?"

"Whiskey," I said. "Mash whiskey, if you have it." His eyes were blue, creased in a broad face, and he was wearing a white apron.

"Sartainly," he said, and took a bottle from the bar behind him, poured a glass full of it, and shoved it across to me. "Will Jack Daniels do you, sar?"

"Tennessee whiskey," I said, "but it'll do me just fine."

I drank the first glass and had him pour a second.

"Come for the gold, did ya?" he asked, his face was as expectant as a child's, his accent cheerful, and full of Irish charm.

"No," I said. "I came for the whiskey."

His grin was huge, his cheeks florid. He had large arms and a thick chest beneath an apron that was tied around his neck and again around his waist.

"Yer smarter than most, then," he said, tippling the bottle for a third time when I failed to protest.

"Oh, some will get lucky, strike it rich. But most will end up with whatever gold they do manage to muck out of them blackened hills being taken by the professionals: the gamblers and the sporting garls. Them's the real miners."

"Tell me," I said, "why do you have that chair hanging up there on the wall?"

His gaze traveled upwards to the chair, and a pleasant expression settled into his face.

"Oh, that's ol' Bill Hickok's chair," he said. "The one he was sitting in when Jack McCall came up from behind him and relieved him of his salad days." His right hand contained a damp rag and he ran it in circles over the polished bar.

"He was quite a talent, you know," Tommy O'Dule said. "The boss says he's honoring Bill by keeping his chair up where nobody can ever sit in it again. Personally, I think he keeps it there for show, to draw a crowd, don't you know?

"A fellow from Denver came in last month and offered to buy it for a hundred dollars, but the boss said he wouldn't sell it for a thousand. Although I think he would if someone was to offer him that much for it. The man would be a fool not to, it's nothing more than an old chair."

"I heard they let McCall off on a verdict of self-defense," I said.

Tommy O'Dule nodded, his blue eyes crisp in the smudgy light.

"That they did, and it's a crying shame, for the man was as guilty as Judas. It wasn't no legal jury, of course, just some drunks and miners who thought Bill was too much a dandy to begin with," Tommy said, still looking up at the chair.

"Jack left town right after. There was talk that some of

Bill's friends would carry out their own justice. Parsonally, I never believed it. There are very few tried and true men that come to Deadwood—Bill included, I'm sorry to say. God rest his soul!"

He snapped out the rag and flipped it over his left shoulder.

"I'll tell you this," he said, leaning over the bar in order to speak low. "Talk has it that McCall was a hired man, an assassin for some of the hard element here in town that didn't want to see Bill become the law and take things over."

Just then, a commotion started up by the front door: several miners led by a rowdy teamster swept into the place. The teamster was short, wiry, dressed in a butter-soft fringed jacket and canvas trousers stuffed into the tops of long boots. He wore a billed cap and the butt of a pistol was exposed from his waistband.

"Oh, piss and feathers," said Tommy O'Dule at their appearance. "It's that damn Calamity Jane and her friends!"

I looked but still couldn't make the determination that the teamster was, in fact, a woman. She had a narrow, homely face that was bereft of any femininity. The hair was short and dark and chopped and sticking out from beneath her cap. There was nothing in her gait or manner to suggest womanly qualities. Unlike Rose, this woman appeared to be a mistake of nature.

"She'll cuss the air blue and try to pick a fight with any man that looks at her wrong," Tommy said. "And it don't take much for a man to look wrong at Calamity Jane."

"I've heard it said she and Bill were an item," I stated, turning my attention away from the arrivals who had taken up chairs along the back part of the bar.

"According to her version," Tommy said with a wink, "she and Bill were husband and wife. Longtime lovers. She saved his life, he saved hers." He hunched his large shoulders. "Depends on which night she's telling it, and to whom. Depends on how drunk she is or ain't and who she's trying to get to buy her drinks that night or bed down with. Me parsonally, I never seen the two of them together—would've been surprised if I had. Bill Hickok was sartainly no saint, but he wasn't no blind man, neither!''

My own interest was more in the hard element that Tommy had mentioned as possibly having a hand in killing Hickok. If there was a certain element trying to control the illicit trade in Deadwood, then maybe there was some connection to the killings of the women who had worked for Alexandra Dupage. How or who this element was, and what role they might have played in the killings, would only be an unfounded guess. But still the mention of such an element intrigued me. When I met Miss Dupage, I could ask her what she knew of such men.

"Tell me something, Tommy," I said. Tommy's features were muscle tight as he continued to stare toward the back room, where Jane and her crew were in the process of raising general hell.

"What's that, sar?" he said, twisting his head back around in my direction.

"This hard element you spoke of, concerning Wild Bill's killing—do you know any of the parties that might be a part of this group?''

I saw the last traces of Irish humor fade from his eyes. He blinked twice.

"No, sar, I would not. Nor would I care to find out. Men that would lay Bill Hickok low are not men I'd want to make the acquaintance of. Bill may have had his faults, but he wasn't afraid of anyone. It would take some real nerve on the party that'd want to assassinate him."

Then he leaned forward again and said, "If I were you, sar, I'd be watchful of who I asked about sartin matters, if you want to keep on breathing the air of our lovely little burg.''

"To tell the truth, Tommy," I said. "It seems strange

to me that you'd have heard such rumor and not have heard any names to go with it."

His gaze danced over the rest of the room beyond my shoulder and down along the bar before leaning toward my ear again.

"I only just arrived myself—a week or two before it happened. No one seemed to be all that stirred up over it. Except there was this one odd little fellow who claimed he was Bill's best friend, a man named Charley Utter. "Colorado Charley" they called him. He told me soon after it happened that he thought Cross-eyed Jack was put up to the whole thing by some of the local bosses—men who control most of the gambling and confidence games. Charley claimed they didn't want Bill to get elected as the law because of his reputation, and so paid McCall to put a bullet through his brain—which he did right smartly.

"Anyway, Charley didn't say any names, he was commonly drunk the day he told me and it was not even yet ten in the morning."

"Why'd he tell you if you were just new in town? Why not someone he knew and trusted?"

"Drunks talk to the men who pour them their whiskey," Tommy said. "It ain't unusual. I've had men tell me things I would be reluctant to tell a priest—things about their wives, for instance. Who can say what it is about liquor and loneliness that makes a man want to speak so freely?"

"Where could I find this Charley Utter?" I asked him.

A slight bit of relief returned to his eyes.

"Oh, that I couldn't tell you, sar—other'n to say he left town shortly after paying for Bill's funeral and seeing that he was properly buried up on Mount Moriah. Some say he left and went back to Colorado. Others have said he went back east, to Boston or New York, where he had come from originally. I haven't seen him around since that morning."

Just then, I heard Jane yell an insult to someone in the back room and a voice yelled back for her to "Shut the hell up!'' followed by a lot of laughter and more swearing and more laughter.

The mash whiskey had worked its wonder and I thanked Tommy for his time and laid a pair of silver dollars down on the bar that he picked up with fingers thick and reddened as sausages.

"Come back again anytime," he said, the Irish lilt of his voice ringing above the noise of the crowd.

I stepped back out into the night and felt the chill air through the linen duster, felt it crawl along the back of my neck. The whiskey helped warm me.

Yellow light spilled from the windows of the hurdy-gurdies and saloons all up and down both sides of the street. The town was cranking up for another night of revelry and hellraising. I could hear the drunken, boisterous chorus of the miners singing their sentimental songs of home and sweethearts left behind. The lovesick and homesick men were joined in song by their chippies—the closest those men were ever going to get to a sweetheart in such a far-flung camp as Deadwood.

But I knew the loneliness of such men, and I didn't blame them for wanting to raise a little hell and have the company of a woman, any woman, to share the long, cold nights with. I wanted to go and join them and forget about the reason I had come to the gulch. Ever since I'd arrived in town, I'd been getting a bad feeling about the place. I didn't reckon it to get any better the longer I stayed.

But my conversation with Tommy O'Dule had given me a hook to at least hang my hat on as far as the killings went, and I knew I needed to forget all about joining the rowdy miners and their painted ladies for at least this night.

It was time to pay a visit to Alexandra Dupage.

9

I found the address Alexandra Dupage had given in the letter: 24 Front Street.

It was a small white clapboard house at the north end of the gulch, sitting by itself next to an empty lot. It was freshly painted, and its small square windows revealed light seeping through the parts of maroon drapes. There was a white picket fence guarding the structure.

It could have been the house of a parson or a bank president.

I opened the gate and went in.

There was a set of three wooden steps leading up to the door. Just as I reached the first one, the door suddenly opened to a quadrant of saffron light. A man, one hand still holding the doorknob, stood there, silhouetted against the light. For a brief moment he did not move. Then he descended the steps and walked past me without greeting.

He wore a greatcoat, but I recognized him as he brushed past me. He wasn't wearing his blue glasses now, but it was the same man who earlier in the day had been standing in front of the Jerzey Saloon watching the rainbow: Doc Holliday.

Although I had never personally met Holliday, his reputation as gambler and gun artist was known to me. I also knew that he supposedly was a consumptive and a drunk who had a penchant for meanness. I had never heard or read anywhere that he had actually killed anyone in a gunfight, although I did read of a shooting scrape he had been run out of Dallas for.

The territory was full to overflowing with men like Doc Holliday, men of little known fact and a whole lot of rumor who did little to dissuade the public of their dangerousness.

A mulatto girl answered my knock. She was tall but finely put together. She had cinnamon skin and dark freckles dotted the bridge of her nose and her eyes were a soft gray. She wore a dark blue blouse and a long black skirt, and several silver bracelets encircled her forearms. Large gold loops dangled from her earlobes.

"Yas suh?" she said, her eyes fixed upon me.

"I've come to see Miss Dupage," I said.

"Miss Alex not be seein' any gentlemen callers tonight, suh." She had a voice that reminded me of bayous and tall cotton under a hot dry wind. It was a soft southern drawl I'd not heard since the war.

I glanced down the street, and saw Holliday pause in the light of a saloon window to tip a small silver flask to his mouth as he leaned against the wall of the building. His cough erupted in the air, then he wiped his lips and moved on into the waiting shadows.

"That man," I said. "The one that just left here. He was a gentleman caller?"

Her eyes shifted downward.

"No suh, he a friend of Miss Alex's."

"Well, you might go and tell her another friend is here to see her," I said.

"Who should I say be calling?" she asked, her gaze once more lifting to meet my own. Her lips were slightly separated and I could see the porcelain of her teeth, even and white against the dark ruby mouth.

"Tell her Ben Beadle," I said.

"Yas suh," she said. "You wait here." Then she closed the door gently, but all the way. I glanced back down the street toward the direction I had last seen Holliday. He was gone.

The door suddenly flew open. The interior light shone brightly.

"Ben!"

I saw then why Ben Beadle had said the first time he met her, he knew he was going to fall in love.

She was uncommonly beautiful. Her russet hair was combed straight back from her oval face, pinned by a pair of silver and abalone shell combs. Her eyes were the green of emeralds. Her skin smooth and white and flawless.

When she saw that I was not Ben, she looked sharply at the mulatto girl.

"Cherry Bee, I thought you said—"

I stopped her and said, "My name's McCannon, Miss Dupage. Ben Beadle received your letter and asked me to come in his place, at least until he could come himself."

She took her gaze off the girl and placed it back on me. Her eyes were the sort of eyes a man could easily fall into and drown.

"Ben never replied saying he was sending someone in his place," she said.

"He figured it was best to keep whatever business we might have as private as possible," I said.

"Why didn't he come himself?" she asked.

"He's unable to just at the time."

There was a instant of doubt, but then the eyes relented. And this time, as she looked at me, she really looked at me.

"Ben must trust you a great deal," she said.

"We go back some."

She took a breath and let it out again, then said, "Come

in, Mr. McCannon," and stepped back away from the door while the mulatto girl held it open for me. I followed her into a small, well-appointed parlor. A matching pair of green upholstered chairs sat facing each other. Across from them was a serpentine-back sofa with half-lyre–shaped armrests. A light brown brussels covered the floor. The walls were done in flocked wallpaper; a pair of Currier and Ives prints hung on the east wall. A small tea table stood in the center of the room. I'd seen one similar to it in a cathouse in Denver.

"Have a seat, Mr. McCannon," she said.

She was wearing a dark blue sateen dress that caused her skin to seem even more white and un-flawed. The dress was clasped at the throat by a cameo brooch and the sleeves were decorated in an arabesque of black beads from wrists to elbows. The light in the room shimmered against the material, seemed almost to swim in it.

"Cherry Bee, bring us some cognac," she said to the mulatto girl, who turned quickly and wisped out of the room.

The room was warm and comfortable and intimate and held the scent of crushed flowers. She sat across from me, her gaze never leaving my face.

"Tell me," she said. "How is dear Ben?"

"He's fine," I said.

"And married?"

"No."

She smiled, her teeth were even and white, her lips curved in a perfect bow around them.

"I thought by now . . ." she said. Her voice still held traces of an eastern accent running through its smokiness. Her hands rested in her lap, the long fingers bone white against the blue dress.

"I think maybe he's waiting for the right woman to come along again," I said.

She tilted her head just very slightly and everything softened in her face.

"He's a fine man," she said. "I would wish him the best of everything." There was a tenderness to her words, and I know she meant it.

"I read the letter," I said. "Do you care to tell me about what's going on?"

I saw the light fade from her eyes, the slight smile disappear. She swallowed, but before she could say anything, the mulatto girl brought in a cut-crystal decanter and glasses on a small silver tray and set it down on the table.

"That'll be all, Cherry. You can go on to bed."

Cherry Bee said, "Thank you, ma'am," twisted her eyes in my direction then slipped out of the room again as quietly as a whisper.

I waited while Miss Dupage poured us each a glass of the cognac; the amber liquid seemed alive in the soft light of the room. It had a smooth, unfamiliar taste to me, but I liked it. I watched her sip it as though it were something precious, something not to be disturbed in the drinking of it.

Without setting the glass back down on the table, choosing instead to hold it within both her hands, she said, "Someone is killing my girls."

"Yes, you stated that in your letter," I said.

"Three so far, Mr. McCannon, since my arrival here this summer. At first, with Dotty, I thought it was a suicide. A bottle of poison was found by her bedside. Then, a couple of months later, Eva was found with her neck broken—" Something caught in her throat, her gaze shifted to the right of me, a luster of wetness filled her deep green eyes.

"Still, I did not think of a connection between the two," she continued, touching the tip of a finger to the corner of one eye. She didn't seem to me a woman who would cry easily.

"But then about a month ago, another of my girls, Flora, was found stabbed to death. A butcher knife was . . ."

She brought the glass up to her mouth again and drank from it, only this time she drank without the same restraint she had earlier. This time she drank like someone who meant to have the liquor take hold of her and tear her loose from soberness. I remembered a time when I had done the same thing with good success and a lot cheaper brand of alcohol.

I watched as she refilled her glass and mine.

"I think it's a warning to me," she said.

"What sort of warning?"

"I think someone wants me to leave Deadwood, to close my business."

"Why would someone want you to do that, Miss Dupage?" I asked, feeling the warmth of the cognac course through my blood. "I'd think a town like this would welcome your services."

Her eyes came to focus on mine, I shifted slightly under their gaze. I knew it would be easy to cross over the line, to let the matters at hand become secondary in my thinking. There was something about her beauty, something vulnerable and insurmountable all at the same time. And everything about her seemed to lie just beneath the surface of those alluring eyes that made me want to go over to her and put my arms around her and kiss the smoothness of her jaw.

"Let me make something clear to you, Mr. McCannon."

The eyes that were drawing me down into them did not waver or blink as they stared into my own.

"I know what it's like to be a working girl. I've been one. But I was luckier than most—luckier or smarter, however you want to look at it. I saved my money and I didn't marry the first cowboy who came down the pike and asked me, and I raised myself up out of the *life*. But there aren't many ways for a woman to be independent on the frontier. And the life never lets you go, not completely it doesn't. I've seen first-hand what happens to most working girls." She paused, took another drink from the cognac.

She rested her dark fluid eyes on me again.

"Have you ever been to the bottom of the barrel, Mr.

McCannon? Can you possibly know what it is like to be twenty years old and have to sell your body to a dirty miner for fifty cents, or hope that a pimp likes you well enough not to beat you, or worse, scar your face?''

Her eyes smoldered with old angers and hurts. Then she added, "No, how could you possibly know such things."

"I know where the bottom of the barrel is, Miss Dupage. I've been there. Maybe not in the same way as you've described, but I've been there."

"I haven't," she said, her jaw jutting outward, her look one of self-possessed dignity. "I was lucky, and I was smart, and I was determined. And I never fell to the mercy of but one man, and just one time. But I've known lots of girls who weren't so lucky. By the time I left Dodge, I knew that I'd never again let a man control my life or my future.

"I came here to Deadwood with the express purpose of running an escort service. I brought with me five young women who wanted the same thing I wanted. I made them a promise that I would take care of them. I do not run crib girls or streetwalkers or women who will drug you and steal your money or have their pimps knock you over the head with a lead sap.

"A man knows that if he is with one of my girls he doesn't have to worry about such things. And my young women know it as well. That way, everyone is happy."

"In the end, though, it still boils down to the same thing, doesn't it?" I said. "The ladies still have to sell themselves to the miners, or anybody else who wants them."

"No, Mr. McCannon, it is not the same thing. The ladies who work for me have a choice in the matter, and that is the difference. The men who use my service know that they are to treat my girls with respect and charity, that they are not to abuse them. When it comes down to the more intimate details, it is by mutual agreement between the customer and the young woman.

"In return, the men pay handsomely for the privilege of a first-class escort for the evening."

"But it doesn't always work out that way, does it?" I said.

"It had, until the killings began. Now the other girls are afraid. They want to leave Deadwood. But I have convinced them to stay, even though I've temporarily suspended operations."

"Maybe it's better they leave than be murdered," I said.

"You don't seem very sympathetic to the situation, Mr. McCannon. Perhaps it is a mistake, your coming here instead of Ben."

"Don't misread me, Miss Dupage. I don't like to see people hurt. If three of your girls have been murdered, I don't blame the others for wanting to clear out. Whatever life they may return to has to be better than being murdered. Leaving might be something for you to consider as well."

"I won't run or be driven out of town," she said. "Whoever did this needs to be caught!"

"I agree, that's why I'm here. Tell me of your suspicions."

She sighed, sipped the cognac, fixed her gaze on me.

"As I said, I think someone wants me out of business. I've thought about why. The reasons are few, if any. But there may be one or two."

"Tell me."

"Well, first, the best girls in Deadwood come to me because they know my policy. The second thing is, once men have been escorted by one of my ladies, they are rarely willing to settle for less the next time out. My girls remind them of the sweethearts and wives they left back home. Money to a miner doesn't mean a thing if he can't spend it on his own pleasure. I think whoever is responsible doesn't like the fact that the miners are spending most of their money on my girls. Maybe it's a pimp, or a joy house owner—I don't really know."

"And maybe it's someone who is killing them for his own strange reasons," I suggested.

She bit her lower lip, her eyes tearing over again.

"Maybe it is," she said, her smoky voice barely audible.

"There is something I am curious about," I said. Again she swallowed.

"What would that be, Mr. McCannon?"

"How were you able to ensure that your girls were unmolested while escorting their customers?"

She drank the last of the cognac left in her glass and brushed at the corners of her eyes with her fingertips.

"I pay a man to watch out for the welfare of my ladies. He is quite notorious. Very much feared."

"Doc Holliday?" I said.

She looked surprised.

"How did you know?"

"I saw him leave just as I came up."

"I needed someone of well-known reputation," she said. "He was in town. I offered him the job. It pays well."

"Which leads me to another question then," I said.

"Which is?"

"Why didn't you simply have Doc find the man who is killing your ladies, since he's already on the tab?"

"Obviously you don't understand," she said. "I pay Doc for his deadly reputation. He is not a well man. His vice is liquor, his energies limited."

"There sounds like more to it than that," I said.

Her green eyes shifted away.

"Perhaps there is, Mr. McCannon."

"What might that be?" I asked.

"I suspect Doc has a personal interest in me . . . one I'd just as soon not encourage." Her voice trailed off, but I knew there was more.

"That sounds like only half the reason," I said. "What's the rest of it?"

She seemed reluctant to speak about it further. But when she saw I wasn't leaving, she said, "I am not entirely sure that Doc isn't somehow involved with the killings. After all, his job was to protect the girls and that he failed to do, or so it seems. To be honest with you, I don't know of anyone here in Deadwood I can trust. It is why I have sought help from the outside."

"But you did more than that, Miss Dupage."

I saw the uncertainty in those velvet eyes.

"You advertised in the territorial papers. And now, men like King Fisher and Ed Siringo will be coming and you'll have to deal with them."

The eyes snapped.

"You seem to know a lot about my business," she said.

"Have you ever dealt with a man like King Fisher?" I asked, and before she could answer, I added, "Do you know what sort of man King Fisher is? Do you know what the others who'll come for the reward are like?"

She looked at me as though I had thrown her an insult. But she needed to know she was playing a dangerous game if she was playing it with manhunters like King Fisher and the others that would swoop down on Deadwood like turkey buzzards on a dead possum once they read her advertisement.

She quickly regained her composure.

"I won't stand by and do nothing," she said. "I'll do whatever it takes to find the killer."

"Sometimes the cure is worse than the ailment," I told her.

"Maybe it is," she said. "But what choice have I?"

"None now."

"Are you certain you want to involve yourself in this, Mr. McCannon?"

"I guess I'm like you, Miss Dupage, I don't see any choice. I gave Ben my word."

I couldn't tell if those eyes were grateful or unhappy.

"I have one last question for you," I said.

"What is it?"

"Why, if someone wanted you out of business, wouldn't they just come after you? Why kill three of your ladies instead?"

She shrugged her shoulders, her lips pursed into a

momentary thought, and said, "I honestly don't know, Mr. McCannon. Maybe the angels are watching over me, the fallen angels of my girls."

"Yeah, maybe so," I said.

"What will you do now?" she asked, as I stood and placed my Stetson back on my head.

"First thing?" I said. "I'll go and find me a hot bath; I haven't had one in four days. Then, come tomorrow, I'll do what I get paid to do—I'll start investigating."

She stood and extended her hand. I took it in mine and shook it lightly. Her fingers felt warm and graceful as they closed on mine. I could smell the scent of her perfume and it did something to me, something that made me shift my weight and wish that I had found that hot bath earlier and scraped off the stubble from my chin.

"Then you'll remain in touch, Mr. McCannon?"

"You can count on it," I said. Keep it business, I told myself as I released her hand.

She saw me to the door, held it while I stepped out into the night, a raw wind had picked its way down through the canyon and blown trash along the street ahead of it. I turned then, looked at her standing there in the lighted doorway, and said, "Do you keep a pistol?"

She smiled and said, "Yes, as a matter of fact, I do. And I know how to use it."

"Somehow, I'm not surprised," I said, then bid her good evening.

"Goodnight, Mr. McCannon." Her words trailed me down the steps.

As I neared my hotel, a shot rang out of the darkness and clipped a chunk of wood from a post inches in front of my face. I had been thinking about Alexandra Dupage, about the way her perfume smelled and the way her hand felt in mine, when the bullet whistled through the air and slammed into the post. Instinct put me on the sidewalk, the self-cocker already in my hand.

I did not see the flash but knew by the sound that it was

a pistol shot and not a rifle. The abrupt bang was lost within the din of the night's revelry. No one bothered to come rushing out into the street to investigate. In towns like Deadwood, pistol shots were as common as hogs at a trough. And by the time I was cocked and ready to defend myself, whoever had taken the shot had disappeared into the cover of night.

I felt the pulse thicken in my wrists and throb against my temples as I slipped the Remington back into the cross-draw holster. A few inches closer and I would have been tomorrow's gossip, displayed out in front of the local funeral parlor. I remembered on my way to catch the stage in Cheyenne how the undertaker had trussed up Charley Weed with baling wire and propped an empty Winchester through the crooks of his arms so that folks could have their photographs taken with the body for a dime. Death always seemed to magnify a man's celebrity.

It wasn't the sort of attention I wanted.

10

Instead of going to directly back to my hotel room, I bought a bath and sank down into the tub of hot steamy water and paid the kid working the bathhouse two dollars to bring me a meal. I wanted something that had beef on the plate and something to wash it down with. I gave him two bits more to take my clothes down to a laundry and get them cleaned and wait for them.

The steak was two inches thick and covered the entire plate and I ate it down to the bone, then washed it down with beer and waited for the water to do its magic and the kid to return with my clothes. I thought of Nate Pliers reposed in the crimson water of his bloody bath, his expensive cigar floating on top.

One minute you're alive and the next you're dead.

I could still hear the gunshot ringing in my ears.

I turned my thoughts elsewhere, to something more pleasant. Alex Dupage's image filled my brain. I could still smell her perfume. She had stirred something in me that had long lay cold and untouched, something that went beyond the usual desire a man can get for a woman.

And yet there had been that air about her that suggested she was a closed door. A door behind which no man was allowed. What really troubled me was, I wanted to be the one to go through that door.

I thought of the women who had come along in my life after Mary Lee died: the widows and the whores and the ones in between. Seemed I'd drifted between one and the other not knowing which I preferred. Part of me wanted what I once had: a good stable woman and a home where I could hang my hat after a long day. The other part of me wanted just the opposite: a woman as wild as the West Texas wind and just as hard to hold. Warm nights and tempting smiles and plenty of mescal.

I wondered if Juanita Delgado had found herself a new man yet.

Alexandra Dupage was another matter altogether, though. She was neither saint or sinner, as far as I could judge. She wasn't needing or wanting. And now she was floating around in my mind in a way that good whiskey will, making me feel slightly off kilter and more pleasant than I had a right to.

I settled into the thoughts of her and allowed myself the pleasure.

The door opened with a slight click of the latch. I brought the Remington around from where I had it resting on a chair next to the tub; its action was smoothly mechanical, all its vital functions ready and set as I thumbed back the hammer.

He stood there staring at me, the light soft in those nearly colorless eyes, eyes that were stern and without humor, the hollow cheeks puffing in and out below the prominent bones of his face. His mouth, partway open under the heavy sand-colored moustaches, showed a set of good teeth. His breathing was raspy and faint.

The eyes shifted enough to see the self-cocker in my hand, then drifted back, collecting my gaze.

"What'll it be, Doc?" I asked him; I had the front sight of my pistol aimed at a spot just above his breastbone.

"It's not what you think," he said. "I didn't come to shoot it out with you."

"That's good," I said. "Because if you had, I'd have to pull the trigger and I don't think you could stand the grief."

He coughed into a crimson-stained handkerchief, wiped it back and forth across his lips twice, and then balled it in his fist.

"What's your business with Alex Dupage?" he asked.

"That's just it, Doc—my business."

"That's not good enough."

"It has to be."

"You know of me?" he said. "You know the type of man I am?"

"Yeah, I've heard the talk."

"Dying doesn't mean a damn thing to me," he said. "Does it to you?"

"Did you come to discuss philosophy, Doc, or was there another reason for this unexpected visit?"

His gaze grew to fixed points within his skull, his hands flexed and unflexed by his sides. His cheeks worked hard, like a bellows against a fire, trying to work the air in and out of his weakened lungs.

"I will ask you again," he said. His voice was raspy, full of phlegm, rough, the way a hard drinker's will get after a time. Still, it was a voice stubborn with a southern accent—the voice of a Confederate gentleman who had maybe lost some of its gentility.

"What is your business with Miss Dupage?" he asked again.

"Like I said, it's personal."

"Then you and I, sir, have a problem."

"Only if you believe so," I said.

He stood there, unmoving except for the labored breathing. He didn't look like a killer; he looked like a man who had lost hope that he was going to live a long time.

"Someone took a shot at me tonight," I said. "Maybe it was you."

Something moved just under his left eye, a small twitch like a tiny worm working just below the skin.

"Had I been the one," he said, "you would have now been wrapped in the arms of death."

Coming from him, the expression did not seem florid.

"Well, Doc, I guess I was lucky, then, that it wasn't you."

"Miss Dupage is a special friend of mine," he said. "We enjoy a business relationship as well. It is incumbent upon me to see that she and her employees are not to be troubled. Do you understand my position, sir?"

"I know, she told me," I said.

The spot below his eye twitched again. He swallowed, the paper collar around his neck moved, the string tie moved with it. His shadow hovered against one wall. I was fully prepared for him to produce a pistol. Hell, I was half expecting it. And I knew if he did, one or both of us would be killed somewhere in that space of uneven time.

"She told you," he said. It was not quite a question, not quite an assertion. Then, impossibly, the eyes became more cold, more void of any emotion and he said, "Then you understand?"

"I understand that your business with Miss Dupage is your own, Doc. I expect the same consideration."

"Then you understand?" he repeated.

"Let me ask you something, Doc."

He did nothing to invite the question, but I asked it anyway.

"If your job was to protect the girls working for Alex, then why didn't you?"

The slightest blush of color rose in his neck, the side of his jaw moved almost imperceptibly. They were the little things you needed to be aware of when challenging a man of Doc's reputation. The hands will kill you, but the look in a man's eye will tell you whether or not he's thinking about it.

On the frontier, there were two types of men who would kill you: there were those like Doc, who might just pull their piece and have at it; and there was the other type, the ones that would lay for you in an alley, or shoot you in your sleep—fill your brains full of lead or shoot you in the kidneys and walk away.

With Doc, I sort of got the sense he could do it either way.

"You are intruding where you are not welcome," he said.

"You know about the reward she's put out for those responsible for killing the girls?" I said.

"You are here for that?" he said.

"It's what I do, Doc."

Then the hard stare eased a bit and one corner of his mouth lifted into what could only be described as mild amusement.

"I hope that your journey to this place was not a long one," he said. "For you have come here for nothing."

"I'm not the only who has come, or will be coming," I said. "One of them might already be in town. King Fisher. You ever heard of King Fisher, Doc?"

The small amusement fell from his mouth.

"He is a low-heeled assassin," Doc said. He said it like a southern senator denouncing an opponent. A cough rattled high up in his chest and bent him forward at the waist. The hand with the balled-up hankie jerked upwards to his mouth and the veins of his neck distended into small purple ropes as the paroxysms rattled through him. He gripped the jamb of the door with his free hand in order to steady himself. Finally, after several seconds, the cough abated and he wiped his mouth and swallowed several times.

He looked weak and frail, a man ready to step through death's door.

"Do you mind not dropping the hammer on that piece?" he said, his gaze falling to the revolver in my hand. "I need a drink of my whiskey. I have it here, inside my coat."

I motioned for him to do so. His hand, a tremble of bones, reached inside the greatcoat and brought out a small silver flask which he held aloft and said, "I would offer to share it with you, but not many men will drink from the same container as a lunger, so I won't bother to extend the invitation." Then he tipped it to his mouth and I watched the sharp edge of his Adam's apple jerk in his throat as he swallowed.

His breathing was labored, but he replaced the flask inside his coat, then swiped a finger across his moustaches, sweeping away the dew clinging to them.

"Your involvement with Alexandra," he said, his voice a tinge weaker now, "will come to nothing. There are things that you do not understand."

"My water's getting cold, Doc," I said. There was nothing I was going to learn from him that I did not already know, except that he saw me as a rival, a threat to whatever it was he thought he had going with Alex Dupage.

He blinked. Just once. Drew in a deep breath through his nostrils and let it out again.

"Perhaps the next time we meet, sir, the odds will be more even between us," he said, again his gaze falling to the self-cocker in my hand.

"Maybe so, Doc. You just never know."

He adjusted the greatcoat over his shoulders, pulling it tighter about him, then he turned and closed the door behind him, the scent of his bay rum still lingering in the air.

Doc Holliday, King Fisher, Johnny Slaughter. The number of gun shooters I'd have to keep an eye out for was beginning to add up.

11

The next morning I walked down to Johnny Slaughter's office. The sky was leaden, lying low over the canyon, and the streets were muddy from a late night rain. An icy wind blew down through the canyon and the pedestrians, what few there were that time of morning, were huddled against the cold, their hands bunched inside their pockets, their collars turned up. One man's hat was racing down the muddy street; its owner running behind it.

Constable Slaughter looked up when I entered; he had been drinking coffee from a tin cup, an unlighted cigar clamped between his teeth. The wind blew in behind me and stirred some papers on his desk.

"You mind?" he said.

I closed the door as he restraightened everything.

His coat was off, and through the tight fit of his shirt I could see the bulk of his shoulders and chest and arms. He was a man who could do a lot of damage with just his fists. I had been in the ring with men like him back when I did some prizefighting. I knew what it was like to hit a man like him and what it was like to be hit.

"I see you ain't left town yet," he said, blowing steam off the coffee as he brought it to his mouth.

"I came to get some information from you," I said. He didn't bother to invite me to sit down or have some of his coffee.

"You've wasted a trip down here, then," he said. "I ain't in the information business."

"What do you know about a ring here in Deadwood?" I waited for a sign of recognition: a muscle twitch along the jaw, a shifting of the eyes, the unsteadiness of the hand holding the cup of coffee.

Either he was a good poker player or he didn't know what I was talking about, because I didn't see anything in him that gave away whatever secrets he might be carrying.

"McCannon, right?" he said. "If I read your name right, the one you signed on the hotel register, it's McCannon?"

I waited for him to say what was on his mind.

"I got no time for gun artists and bounty hunters, just like I got no time for drunks and troublemakers."

"Does that include murdered prostitutes?" I asked.

He set the cup down. Some of the coffee spilled onto his desk staining the edges of some Wanted posters. His lips compressed and his jawbone worked into a small knot under his left ear.

"You've been warned!" he said. "You go on back to the hotel and get your things and climb on the next stage out."

"I'm afraid not," I said. "My business isn't finished here yet."

He moved good for a big man, but I was ready for him.

I ducked the first blow from his huge right fist. The left one followed, angled downward, and grazed the side of my face. I drove a right to a spot just below his ribs, the only place you might hurt a man his size with a body blow. I heard him grunt, but at the same time he swung a looping left hand that missed but caught me with the elbow to the

side of my head as it came around. It was like being struck
with an anvil.

As I stumbled sideways, stunned, the inside of my head
ringing like mission bells, my old prizefighter's instincts
took over. I lashed a left to his cheek, felt it drive hard
against the leathery skin, strike bone. I followed with a
right and another left, then two more rights in rapid succes-
sion—each blow driving him backwards.

His face was cut high on the cheek from where I had
hit him with the last right and a knot bulged over his left
eye and blood leaked from his nostrils.

But he was big and he was a gamer, and he hit me with
a series of pounding blows that drove me off him and into
the chair of his desk, my feet tangling in the rungs.

I slammed hard against the floor, the palms of my hands
stinging from trying to break the fall. Then he hit me with
something that shattered my senses and dropped me into
a long dark well of nothingness.

I awoke to a drunken chorus of "I'll Take You Home
Again, Kathleen." The voice was scratchy, raking like cat
claws against my skin. I tried moving, tried sitting up. And
when I tried, my head felt like shattered glass. I reached
up, probed the sources of the pain; there were many. The
worst, however, was at the back of my skull, where the
constable had hit me with something I hadn't seen. My
hair was sticky from where my scalp had been split, and
when I touched that place, it took my breath away.

The voice stopped singing long enough to say, "Looks
like ol' Johnny Slaughter gave you the bum's rush and a
whole lot more there, mister." Then, without further
pause, it broke back into song.

I adjusted my vision enough to see I had been locked
up in a small cell with none other than Calamity Jane
Canary. She was horribly drunk and reeked of anquitum,
a common concoction used by miners to keep down the

body lice population. She squatted in her bunk, howling the same chorus of the song over and over again.

The room was small, maybe six feet by eight feet, with one window that had a set of bars which let in a small amount of light. Through the gloom I could see a heavy iron door that I didn't have to try to know was locked.

Against my own better judgment, I managed to sit upright.

When she saw me do this, she stopped singing again.

"Wah there, yer a damn sight more alive than I would've guessed!" she said. "You don't have no whiskey hidden on ya, do ya?"

Carrying on a conversation with her was not something I had in me just at the moment. And when she saw that I wasn't a talker, she took over.

"I'd a nursed ya if I had some bandages and bear grease," she said. "Hell, I've nursed a lot worse than ya! I've even nursed folks through the pox and measles! Goddamn if I couldn't stand a drink—'scuse my French, in case yer a Christian—which I am most of the time myself, except when I'm drunk and feelin' blue. Which I am at the present!"

My only hope was that she would pass out, but she didn't.

"Hell, ya like singin', mister? I should've been a singer like one of them opry gals, travel the world over, see everything, do everything!" Then her face shrank into a frown as she examined something on the front of her shirt.

"Trouble is, my bosoms ain't big enough to be one of them opry gal singers! Ya ever notice how big a bosoms them gals have?"

Then she tittered.

"But I ain't missed much in life besides having big bosoms. I've seen and done things most folks couldn't even dream about."

She laughed and slapped the top of her leg.

"Whoo boy! I mean I have *done* some things, believe

you me!" Her fringed jacket was stained dark in places and her canvas pants were muddy at the knees.

"Ya ever hear of Wild Bill?" she said. "Hell, of course ya have! Everybody's heard of Wild Bill!" She had small, blunted teeth, evenly set but yellowed. Her eyes shone fierce, alive with a restless energy.

"Me and Bill was married!" she said. "Oh gawd!" Her face twisted suddenly and she began to bawl aloud and flung herself across her cot in a highly dramatic way. I'd seen worse performances.

"Me and Bill have us a child—a baby girl, back east! And now Billy's dead and will never get to see her, and she won't get to see him, either! Oh Gawd!"

Her grief was exaggerated, just as her singing had been. She may have not made an opera singer, but she would have made a pretty fair actress.

Her loud sobbing went on for several more minutes as I sat there trying to overcome my own grief—the grief of my injuries.

"Ya sure ya don't have a drink on ya, mister?" she said, suddenly changing moods again, wiping at eyes that were absent of tears.

When I nodded my head, she took on a forlorn look.

"If I was wearing some bloomers," she said, "I'd a taken them off and made ya a bandage and wrapped that poor head a yars. Did I tell ya I used to nurse folks?"

"Look, I appreciate the offer, Miss Canary," I said. "But the truth is, I'm not up to conversation just now."

"Ya know my name!" she shouted. "Hell's bells! Then I guess ya have heard of me?"

She seemed as delighted as a child that I knew who she was.

"What's yar name, mister?" she asked, completely ignoring my request for some peace and quiet. I gave up on the hope that she would settle down, at least for the present.

"McCannon," I said. "Quint McCannon."

Her gaze studied me for several seconds.

"Nope! Ain't never heard of ya," she announced. "I thought fer a minute I might've known ya. I've known plenty a good lookers in my time, shame to admit! Har, har, har." Her laughter was dry, shrill, something that seemed to crack against my skull.

"Ya ever consort with Texas Jack or White-Eye Johnson?" she asked. "Maybe that's where I might've known ya."

"Don't know either," I said.

She twisted the ends of her short, choppy hair; it was greasy and lank, what there was of it.

"Whiskey gives me the blues," she said. "Having too much of it, or not having enough." She waited to see my reaction to her self-made joke and when I offered none, she slapped her knee and laughed. "Har, har, har.

"Johnny busted ya good, didn't he? Drug ya in here and tossed ya on the floor. I said to him, Johnny, what'd ya hit this feller with? And he said, 'I busted him with the butt of my double-barrel whanger, and I'll do the same to you, you don't shut yer yap!' Then I looked him in the eye and said, "There ain't a day in heaven or hell that'll ever pass by when ya'd ever bust me like that, Johnny Slaughter." Then he slammed the door and skulked off!"

For a long moment she stared at me as though seeing me for the first time.

"It's a wonder he didn't bash out all yar brains!"

"Yeah, a wonder."

"It was me that lifted ya up on yar cot and put that blanket over ya so's ya wouldn't catch yar death!"

"Thanks," I said, and meant it.

"Pshaw! Don't need to thank me. I nursed plenty like ya—or have I told ya that already? Anyway, you wasn't the only one that paid the devil's price. Johnny wasn't lookin' so tip-top hisself. I seen how his face was all cut and his eyes all big and swellin' up. I'd a paid to see that go round!"

She fell silent for a minute and the break from hearing her talk was a welcome gift, but it only lasted for a minute before she was back at it.

"They killed my Bill, ya know?"

"Who did?" I asked, slightly more interested in what she had to say.

"Some right here in town. They paid that old ugly skunk McCall to kill him. Paid him fifty dollars and gave him a stolen pistol and sent him off to do it and he did, by Gawd!"

"Who paid him, Jane?"

But I could tell, looking into her startled eyes, that she was lost somewhere in her own fogged thinking, unaware of half of what she was saying.

"He wan't cross-eyed, neither, like they said he was. He could see good as you and me. He was just a plain damn ugly sumabitch, excuse my French!"

"Jane, who was it that paid McCall to kill Bill?"

"Poor Billy, laid low like that! We was goin' to make a big score and go get little Janey and start a home, maybe in Nebraska along the Platte. Bill said how he always like the Platte. Me, I never could see it, livin' up in that lonesome Nebraska. But I'd a gone anywhere with ol' Bill." Her features grew genuinely sorrowful.

"But that's all dried up dreams now, thanks to *Mr.* Jack McCall . . ."

She wound down at last, sat silently, her head tilted over to one side, her mouth open, the blunted teeth showing behind her pale, thin lips. A string of drool leaked from one corner of her mouth and then she slumped over, her eyes closing as she did so. In a few seconds she was snoring.

She may have been drunk and she may have been half crazy, but she was the second person to tell me that someone had paid McCall to assassinate Hickok. And if that were true, then maybe the same party had a hand in the killings of Alex's girls. It was a stretch, but it was all I had to go on so far.

The heavy door rattled open; two people stood in the frame of light. One was Johnny Slaughter, the other was Alex Dupage.

She waited for me to stand. The pain raced through me like a wildfire through dry grass.

"I've paid your fine," she said.

I looked at Slaughter. The damage I'd done to his face couldn't have hurt half as much as my head did.

"Are you able to walk?" she asked.

"Enough to get to my room," I said.

"Come, let's go."

I thought it strange that Johnny Slaughter would accept a fine and let me go, considering the circumstances. But he said nothing.

As we stepped outside, I could see that the jail was little more than a log structure set in an alleyway back of Johnny Slaughter's office. I wasn't sure of the time, but the sun was already setting beyond the surrounding hills and the sky had begun to turn brassy.

"How'd you know where to find me?" I asked.

"Word spreads fast," she said.

I looked at her.

"Johnny's face," she said. "He couldn't hide it. The woman he sees when he's not seeing his wife told me about it. I guess after the fight, he needed some special comfort."

"Tell me," I said, "how was it you got him to let me go without a fuss?"

"It's a simple matter of economics," she said. "Johnny has a wife and a mistress to support. He needs money more than he needs his pride. Besides, he knows that I know all about him and Lulu Divan, the other woman. He wouldn't want to risk my having a chat with his wife about the matter. I simply suggested that the whole affair of the fight between you two could be resolved in a peaceful manner and allowed him to suggest an appropriate fine for your indiscretion."

"Yeah. Well, thanks," I said.

"Come back to my place. I'll have Cherry Bee stitch your scalp and we'll get you cleaned up and feeling better."

The thought of turning down her offer never even crossed my mind.

Cherry Bee washed the blood out of my hair and with a needle and some black silk thread sewed the gash on the back of my scalp together while I nursed the pain with plenty of Alex's imported cognac.

"What dat ol' fool hit you wid?" Cherry Bee asked, as she stitched the wound.

"I was told the butt of a shotgun," I said. "It feels more like it might have been the roof."

"Lawdy, you lucky he didn't knock you silly!"

"I'll let you know if he did in the morning."

She giggled.

Afterward, I sat and let the cognac work its magic. Alex sat across from me. She had changed from the gray jacket and overskirt she'd worn to the jail into a soft long-sleeved white blouse that veed down the front and was tied loosely with a loop of string. Her skirt was long and flowing and of a soft black material.

She held a glass of cognac, her long, slender fingers encircling it, the glass and the fingers equally delicate.

"Feel better?" she asked me.

My head was filling with a light blue smoke that was both warm and gentle. The sharp edges of pain were slowly receding to another place.

"Yes," I said. "This cognac does wonders."

"I'm having Cherry Bee fix us some dinner," she said. "I hope you like roast duck."

I sipped more of the cognac, and lost any thought about my fight with Johnny Slaughter as I looked into her green eyes that under the low light, seemed more jade than emerald. I told myself through the warm fuzziness of the liquor that I was making a mistake. I told myself that a smart man wouldn't allow himself to mix his business with his pleasure. Then I thought of Nate Pliers sitting in that tub of bloody water. Lots of men had made that mistake.

I told myself another thing: she was once the woman

Ben Beadle was in love with, and maybe still was. I had no right to violate our friendship.

But right at that very moment, I wasn't able to take my eyes from her.

We ate, the two of us sitting directly across from each other, Cherry Bee serving us the meal at a modest table that was lighted by candles. I thought I'd seen Alex's beauty already, but there, in the light of candles, in that very instant, she looked glowing. I ate the meal without tasting it. The conversation was kept to a minimum.

Then we reclined to the parlor where we had first talked.

"More cognac, or would you prefer something stronger—whiskey, maybe?" she asked.

"My preference would be for something else altogether," I said. I felt like I was standing on the edge of a cliff and had decided to jump off just to see what it would feel like to fall a long way.

"I think the cognac has affected you," she said. Her presence seemed to fill the entire room. I could smell the perfume in her hair, I could feel its silkiness touch the side of my face. I could taste her mouth on mine. Even though she sat there across from me and offered no indication that she was being anything more than polite and compassionate toward me.

"I think you are right," I said. "I had better go before I say or try something really stupid."

She sipped from her glass, her gaze fixed on mine.

"I'm aware of what is going on here between us, Mr. McCannon. But that doesn't mean I want it to happen."

"You're right," I said. "It shouldn't happen."

"You need to understand . . ." she said. The cognac was really beginning to bury me beneath a warm, heavy blanket of sweet comfort.

"No," I said. "The reasons don't matter. I came here as a favor to an old friend, I can't betray his trust."

Her face seemed to soften under the shadows and light of the candles.

"What was between Ben and me is in the past," she said. "It's not Ben standing in your way, is it?" Her voice was smoky and I couldn't think clearly and the room seemed to shift.

"Let's just leave it at that," I said. "There's no point in discussing what I want to happen and what you don't want to happen."

"I confess that I find you an attractive man," she said, lowering her glass of cognac. "But there are two reasons why I can't allow myself to become involved with you. I want you to know what they are."

Either I'd had drunk too much, or I hadn't drunk enough. I waited for Alex Dupage to explain without wanting to hear what she had to tell me.

"The first thing you need to understand," she began, "is that I vowed a long time ago not to let myself get emotionally involved with anyone. Ben was the exception. I was young, he was tender with me. He needed me in a way no man had before. It was love and it was something more than that, but I wouldn't marry him because I wanted more from life than being somebody's wife. I wanted independence. Most men wouldn't understand that. And if they did, they wouldn't appreciate it."

She paused, turned the glass of amber liquid between her fingers, and never once stopped looking into my eyes.

"The other reason I have for not wanting anything to happen between us," she continued, "is that I already have a male friend. A man whom I see. It would not be fair to him."

"I thought you just said . . ."

"I didn't say I was in love with this man. He is a companion. Someone who doesn't question me or force his life on me. We share certain things. It's convenient and without too much demand. I like it that way."

"I see," I said. It must have showed my disappointment.

"Do you really?" she said.

"Yeah. I really do." It was a lie, but I didn't have it in me to argue the point.

"I better get going," I said, and stood, nearly forgetting that I had a head full of misery.

She rose from her side of the table, came around, and touched her hand to my wrist.

"No, I don't think you fully understand what I've just told you," she said. Her face was inches from mine, her eyes searching mine, and when I breathed, her scent flowed into my senses and mixed with the cognac and left me unsteady.

"You're right," I said. "I don't understand,"

"Maybe in time you will," she said, and released her fingers from the back of my wrist. "Goodnight, Mr. McCannon."

Then she was gone. I was still standing there holding onto the back of the chair when Cherry Bee brought me my curled Stetson.

"You goin' to be able to put that thang on your head?"

"I wouldn't go out without it," I said. She looked at me with the sweet curiosity of a child.

"The trick is going to be taking it off later."

She giggled.

"Thanks, Cherry Bee. Thanks for the supper and sewing my head back together." She smiled a smile of bright teeth and her beauty was a comfort against my pain and weariness.

I was halfway to my hotel room when I ran into Hector Torrez.

"McCannon," he said, his gaze assessing the damage Johnny Slaughter had done me.

"Marshal," I said.

He shifted his gaze.

"I'd just as soon you kept my position to yourself."

"Yeah, I forgot; you said you were on personal business."

"I'm looking for someone," he said. "I'd just as soon they not know that."

"You don't have to worry about me, Torrez. I've got enough problems of my own."

"I can see that." There was no sympathy or compassion in his manner. He was a man of unchanging characteristics.

"There's some bad business going on in this place," he said without bothering to elaborate.

I started to ask him what he meant when someone shouted, "Hey ya!"

I turned to see Calamity Jane weaving down the street. She was in the company of a miner. They were both drunk. It was a day that seemed to have no end to it.

She crossed the street, nearly got run over by a wagon carrying nail kegs. Ignoring the curses of the driver, she came to stand just inches from me, her breath as sour as kraut.

"Ya ain't got a dollar for me and my pal Ted, over there, do ya?" And when I hesitated, she winked and said, "Maybe I could rid myself of ol' Theodore and me and ya could go up to yar crib and have us a sweet time, eh?"

I gave her the loose change in my pocket and would have given her more if she had persisted. She shook my hand like it was a pump handle and she was dying of thirst, then rejoined her friend on the far side of the street. I saw them kiss. When I turned back, Hector Torrez had vanished.

Suddenly, I was alone and glad of it.

12

The dreams came hard that night. I tumbled down into them and everyone was waiting for me. Mary Lee held the shattered head of the dead Confederate boy, his rebel flag wrapped about him like a bloody shroud. She kissed him delicately on the cheek, just below where the minnie ball had entered. His eyes fluttered and his breath came in gasps. Nearby, a cradle carved of cherrywood rocked in the wind. In it I saw my infant son, Samuel.

I could hear gunfire in the forests that surrounded the glade where Mary knelt holding the dead boy. The woods were full of Confederate soldiers. I could hear the Rebels howling; their shrieks causing the tops of the trees to explode blackbirds.

Some strange, powerful jealousy rose in my chest at the sight of Mary holding the boy, at the way she kissed him as though she were his lover. The boy turned his head and looked at me, his gaze a mixture of sadness and pain.

Alex Dupage was there, too—reclined on a quilt of soft yellow flowers. She called to me, held out her arms. Mary Lee smiled, content to hold the broken child that changed from the dying boy to our son, Samuel. Without willing it, a force drew me toward Alex and away from Mary and my son; I knew that I was betraying them, but I could not stop myself from going to Alexandra.

Alex was warm and sensuous and I lay down atop her, her arms reaching round, holding me tightly to her. She kissed my mouth over and over again and my passion was on fire for her. But then I turned just enough to see Mary. She was crying, the hurt pouring down her cheeks. She was asking me why I was doing this to her. *Why was I being unfaithful to her?* And shame overcame me, but I could not bring myself to leave Alex.

Doc Holliday stepped from the trees dressed in Rebel gray, the sunlight shattering off the brass buttons of his tunic. His right hand was perched inside the gray coat. I could see the outline of a pistol against the fabric. His smile was craven as his hand slid from inside the jacket bring a pistol with it.

Alex, now naked in my arms, whispered things to me I could not understand. She clawed at me and thrust her hips against mine, oblivious to Doc and the pistol he had pointed at us. I could not move, could not escape her or him or the Rebels who suddenly came pouring out of the woods from every direction, their heads bandaged and bleeding, their faces contorted in hatred and pain.

Mary Lee's long, slow wail of anguish rose from an open grave. I struggled to go to her, to set myself free from Alex. As I struggled, Alex became Rose, the girl on the stage, and she was frail against me and she was crying and asking me why I was doing this to her. *Why was I hurting her in this way?*

Then Doc pulled the trigger and the sound shattered the dream.

I surfaced from the dream like a drowning man struggling against the smothering grip of some dark, bottomless river. My lungs ached for wanting air and my heart pounded. I lay there for a long time, waiting for the effects of the dream to subside.

When the world righted itself in my mind again, I made it to the washbasin and pulled water over my face with both hands. My head ached from the wound. I was soaked in sweat; my skin felt hot, feverish. I wanted to crawl out of it.

The room was dark, full of stillness, except for my breathing. I didn't know what time it was. It felt like I was in a tomb.

Someone knocked at the door.

I didn't move.

There was another knock.

I withdrew the self-cocker from the holster, then opened the door. I eased the hammer down on the pistol when I saw who it was.

"Miss Dupage." At least, I think I said her name. She looked at me.

"Can I come in?" she asked.

I stepped back. She saw the Remington in my hand. I replaced it in the gunbelt and lighted the lamp. She stood there looking about the room.

"What time is it?" I asked.

"Well past midnight," she said.

"What's wrong?"

"I couldn't sleep," she said.

The flame guttered in the lamp, its yellow tongue of light dancing back and forth as if it were alive, trying to escape its glass cage. The lamp was nearly empty of oil.

She was dressed in the same clothes she had been wearing earlier, the cotton blouse and black skirt, only she was wearing a dark blue velvet jacket that was stitched with black beads across the front. Her hair was loose, cascading past her shoulders. Just to look at her took my breath away.

"I don't have anything to offer you," I said, looking around the room. "I don't even have a bottle of whiskey or a glass to pour it in. You'll have to excuse my accommodations.''

"I didn't come for a drink," she said, slipping into the room. She was close enough to me that I could smell her perfume. Then her hands were touching my bare forearms.

I hesitated, then kissed her. Her mouth was as warm and sweet as I had imagined it to be. My fingers wove themselves into the smooth silkiness of her thick hair. My left arm encircled her waist and she slid her hands to my sides.

Her kisses were passionate, full, and I felt my own passion rising out of places I had long forgotten existed.

It felt awkward, eager, but somehow we managed, without letting go of one another, to make it to the bed. My mind raced with questions as to what had changed her resolve from a few hours earlier until now. But they were questions I didn't want to take time to ask. They didn't seem important.

I unbuttoned the jacket and removed it from her. Then I lifted the cotton blouse over her head and the warmth of her breasts pressed down against my chest. Her hair fell down into my face, a silken shroud, as she leaned over me.

"I don't know why I'm doing this," she said, her voice as thick as smoke.

"Let's not talk," I said.

Her face closed on mine again, her lips brushed the side of my cheek, she kissed the bruise there and ran the tips of her fingers over my lips, then down across my chest, and down further still. I shuddered from a deep, deep place.

My hands caressed the smooth curve of her back, touched the swell of her hips. Then she stood, removed the skirt and the underskirt, and stood naked before me in the dying, dancing light. She seemed more than my eyes could take.

She knelt before me, took one of my hands into her

own, brought it to the side of her face, held it there. Then she looked into my eyes and said, "Is this what you want?"

"Yes."

I pretended not to see the small flicker of pain behind her eyes when I said yes. She held my gaze for a moment longer, then rose to the bed alongside me and kissed me again, a long, slow kiss that seemed to last forever.

She moved over top of me with animal grace and at the same time reached down for me, touching me in a way that caused me to swallow the rush of pleasure it gave me. My hands floated upward, encircling her breasts. The pain from my injuries was numbed by her presence, by the sweet anguish of my passion for her.

Her sweetness flowed over me and through me and I finally knew what it was like to stand at the edge of a cliff and jump off and fall freely through the waiting space.

Later, she lay silent in my arms, her breathing even, warm against my chest. Somewhere in the time since she had arrived, the lamp had burned itself out; the only light came from ghostliness of a full moon that crept through the window.

"Tell me about your friend," I said.

She took a long time before she spoke.

"Why does it matter to you?" she asked.

"I don't know why it matters," I said. "I'd just like to know what sort of man you find interesting enough to share your time with." She knew what I meant.

She looked at me, withdrew her face several inches, and stared.

"What sort of man are you?" she said.

"I'm not sure I understand the question."

"You asked me what sort of man interests me. What sort of man are you?"

"I meant other than me."

"If it is a problem for you—" she began to say, but I stopped her by kissing her gently.

"It's not a problem for me," I said. "I'm just curious."

She waited for a long moment.

"His name?" she said. "Is it his name you want to know, or do you just want to know what he is like?"

"Both," I said.

She sighed, her hand rested on my chest.

"His name is Edwin John-Davies. He's English," she added.

"And probably very handsome," I said.

"Yes, I suppose you could say that."

"Rich, no doubt?"

"His family is well off, but if you think that is why—"

"No, I was thinking it is just my luck."

"What is?"

"That'd you be interested in a rich English gentleman."

"You're talking foolishness," she said. Only she said it half seriously.

"Deadwood is a long way from England," I said.

"Edwin has come here to invest in mining," she said. "He seeks to be his own person."

"Easy enough to do when you have money behind you," I said.

"You're being unfair to the man. You don't even know him."

I started to defend myself; I didn't think I was being unfair to *Edwin;* I thought I was just calling a spade a spade. But she stopped me by placing her fingertips against my lips.

"Do we really have to discuss this?" she asked.

"Of course not," I said. But I wanted to.

She leaned her face closer to mine.

"Remember, you wanted to know," she said.

"Yeah. I had to ask, didn't I?"

"Yes, you did," she said.

"He's probably gracious and has good manners, too."

Her lips brushed the side of my jaw.

"All that, yes."

"Damn, last time it was a Mexican bandit, this time a charming Englishman."

Her fingers crept across my chest.

"What are you talking about, Quint?"

"Nothing."

Her body pressed against mine, warm and soft, the way a woman's body ought to be, and the passion reawakened in me.

"Let's talk about something else," she said.

"No," I said. "I'm tired of talking." I pulled her closer.

She floated above me, her hair dangling against my face. I could smell the scent of her, the womanly scent that can drive a man to madness. Her lips brushed my cheek, floated to my chin, then sought my mouth.

"Yes, no more talk," she said.

13

Somewhere beyond the passion, I sank into a deep, undisturbed sleep. There were no dreams this time, no ghosts, no pain. There was just the sweet nothingness.

When I opened my eyes again, Alex was gone. The scent of her lingered there in the bed with me, lavender and female. When I tried sitting up, something sharp and painful pierced itself behind my eyes; I'd temporarily forgotten my encounter with Johnny Slaughter. I felt around on my scalp, touched the stitches. They were stiff. My head still hurt like hell, but the rest of me felt just fine.

I gritted my teeth and sat up, then stood. I felt slightly off kilter, but the pain and dizziness passed in a few seconds and I made my way to the washbasin. I drew water over my face and examined my image in the mirror. I looked like a scruffy hound, but at least a contented one.

I collected my straight razor out of my saddlebags and shaved, then carefully drew a comb through my hair. I strapped on the self-cocker, pulled the duster over it, and settled the Stetson on my head as best I could. By all appearances, I looked almost normal.

I left the hotel. The weather over the gulch had cleared and the sky was a flawless blue. The sun sparkled in the puddles of rain, reflected against the windows. The labor in Deadwood had slowed. And for the first time since my arrival, the boomtown had taken on a casual air. Deadwood didn't seem like such a hell town just at that moment.

It was Sunday morning.

I realized then that I was hungry—hungry in a way I hadn't been in a long time.

I entered the first restaurant I came to—a place called Lou's Cafe.

Even at that hour, it was doing a good business. The all-night crowd of red-eyed gamblers, weary prostitutes, and men who'd had their pockets cleaned and their souls tarnished were steeling themselves for another twenty-four hours on earth, if they could just make it through this one more morning.

They sat, leaning over plates of yolky eggs and greasy hash and crisp strips of bacon. The steam from their coffee cups rose in tiny clouds and broke against their fatigued faces.

I took a table near the window—an old habit lawmen get. Outlaws, too.

A young Irish girl who was plump and apple-cheeked and wearing an apron came and asked me for my order. I took the special.

I made a shuck and smoked it and watched the street outside, but my thoughts were on Alex and last night. A part of me didn't want to believe what had happened; it didn't seem real. I wasn't so sure it was.

I wanted to believe that whatever had taken place between Alex and me was something special; that it wasn't just another case of two lonely people burning up the night. I tried to think through it over the plate of fried eggs and slab of ham the Irish girl brought me.

I was still thinking about Alex when a voice I hadn't heard in a long time called me out of the pleasantness.

"McCannon."

I looked up and saw a face that didn't offer me any comfort: King Fisher.

I laid my fork down with my right hand, and at the same time slid the cocker out of its holster under the table with my left. The red-checked tablecloth hid the action. The only damn problem was, I never was able to hit anything using my left hand.

The dark blunt features of King Fisher were peppered with a wiry beard. Black, pitiless eyes half hidden by hooded lids fixed themselves on me.

King Fisher was a tall man for one thing, real tall. He wore a greatcoat, dusty and heavy and down past his knees, which made him appear even taller than he was. I could see the bulge of his pistols underneath the coat—how many was hard to tell.

His gaze drifted over me, over my food, like I was something he'd never seen before.

He drew air through his nose.

"Why ain't I surprised you're in Deadwood?" he said with a voice graveled by too many cigars and snakehead whiskey.

"You're standing in my light," I said.

He shifted his weight. They say it's the hands that'll kill you, not the eyes, so I made sure to watch his hands.

"You come for the reward money?" he said.

"I like to keep my business my own, King. You can understand that, can't you? A businessman, like yourself?"

"It's why *I'm* here," he said, "the money." Then added, "I don't much care if you know that."

"Well, thanks for sharing the information, King."

Fourth button from the top of his coat: that's where I'd shoot him if I had to. I hoped it wouldn't go that far.

"Recall the time you screwed me out of that reward money on Shanghai Doolittle over in Ardmore," he said. "Twenty-two hundred dollars."

"You got a good memory," I said. "That was five years ago."

"Told myself then I'd never let you screw me outta no more reward money."

"I've got a sore skull," I told him. "It makes me edgy, the headache I've got from it. I came in here for some coffee, a little breakfast, a little something to take the edge off. Now you show up, stand in my light, talk about the past like I care to hear it. I'm in no mood. What do you want?"

I wasn't half as upset as I made it sound, but I was growing weary of the conversation.

"I ought to just go ahead and plug you here and now, McCannon. You know, pull my pistols and air you out like a bachelor's bedsheet."

"It'd be a mistake, King."

"Mistake?" He grinned the stupid grin of a bully suddenly unsure of himself.

"I've got my self-cocker under the table here, and it's pointed at your buttons. I couldn't miss if I tried. Hell, if I was just to fall off the chair by accident, I'd probably kill you. It wouldn't even be a contest. You wouldn't want that, would you?"

Then some of his features sagged, the hoods lifted over the eyes like shades going up. His gaze fell to the table.

"You do, huh?" He cocked his head just a little, as though trying to see under the table but afraid to move too much.

"Yeah. Primed and ready."

Was I lying or wasn't I? That was the question dancing behind King's eyes. And if I wasn't lying, then he had a problem and we both knew what it was: all that hardware he was carrying under his coat wasn't worth a tinker's damn. Even a fast man isn't that fast.

I saw the truth of it settle in his gaze, the hard reality he was beaten this time around.

He gritted his teeth, trying to see under the table but

not able to, and not sure if or when I might pull the trigger on him. Finally, he quit trying to see.

"There'll be another time," he said.

"My eggs are getting cold," I said.

His nostrils flared, then he let go of it: the temptation to see if he could jerk the pistols before I killed him.

Men like King Fisher don't wish for death so much as they sometimes invite it. I knew one thing, sooner or later, I'd have to kill him, or he'd have to kill me. It was just a question of when.

Slowly, his hands relaxed at his sides; I still held the self-cocker aimed at his coat buttons.

His mouth twitched.

"Next time, no talk," he said, then turned and left.

I let out my breath as I saw him pass by the window and walk out of view. I don't know if I could have hit anything or not, holding the pistol in my left hand. It would have been some trick on my part. I was glad I didn't have to find out.

I slid the piece back into the holster and resumed eating. The eggs had lost their taste and the slab of ham was cold—so was the coffee. It was a bad end to what had started out to be a good morning.

I reached for the money to pay my bill when something suddenly blocked the sunlight coming through the window.

Without taking the time to look, I threw myself sideways just as King fired his pistols. The window exploded into a shower of glass. Falling, taking the table with me, I saw a gambler grab his neck and slump facedown into his plate of food; a ribbon of blood spurted through his fingers.

The table I threw up as a shield took two of King's bullets before I could clear my own gun.

Over the clatter of plates and tableware and scrambling patrons, I could hear King Fisher say, "It's time to finish it, McCannon. I've come back to kill you! Just like I said I would."

He said it as calmly as if he were announcing the playbill at the local opera house.

A shard of glass had buried itself into my left wrist; a single drop of blood bright and red as a ruby percolated from the wound.

Time seemed to stop, and for a long, frozen moment, I could hear my own breathing.

A bullet shattered the air, slammed into the table, splintered past my face and bore a hole through the floor.

I knew when I raised up from behind the table I'd have one chance and only one chance to kill him. Once I raised up, all he had to do was hit the mark. It wasn't a thought I had much time to dwell on.

He fired twice more just as I came up over the table. How he missed both shots, I don't know. My shot took him dead center.

It was like some invisible hand had snatched him off the sidewalk and flung him into the street.

He landed on his back, flopped in the mud, dead as he was ever going to be.

Someone shouted to get a doctor, but it wasn't for King; it was for the gambler who'd taken one of King's stray bullets in the neck.

I stepped outside onto the walk and stared down at the body, the boots pointing skyward, the lifeless eyes no longer menacing, the hands no longer quick. I didn't feel good about it. I didn't feel bad.

Johnny Slaughter came charging up the street, his gun drawn. Maybe it was going to be a day of killing. I turned on him, held the self-cocker straight out, the front sight in a direct line aimed at the center of his body.

"Hold it there," I ordered.

He stopped short.

"It was self-defense," I said. "You can ask these others."

He looked uncertain. Several confirmed my side of it; he slipped his own gun into his pocket. I lowered mine.

He leaned over, looked at the face, straightened, and

said, "King Fisher," like it was a cussword that had slipped out of his mouth in church. It sent a buzz through the crowd. Lots of folks had heard of the gunfighter.

"Goddamn it!" Slaughter swore. "I don't need this aggravation."

"Nor do I," I told him.

"He won't be the last to show up," Slaughter said, his face patchy with dark bruises.

"I want you out of town."

"Then you better make it happen here and now."

It doesn't happen often, but when a man tries to kill me, like King Fisher had just tried to do, my blood gets hot in a way that burns up all my reason. I was at that point now, ready to fulfill the destiny of any man who was looking for it, including Johnny Slaughter.

"You threatening me?" he growled.

"Take it how you will."

I watched his right hand, the one hanging near the pocket he'd put his gun in.

"I didn't come here to raise hell, but I'll take all of it you want to hand out, Constable. You want to finish it, finish it!"

We were both at that point, ready to die in order to stand our ground. I couldn't speak for Johnny, but I no longer cared.

Then a voice spoke from the crowd of onlookers.

"You ought to let it go, Constable. I saw the whole thing. This man was just eating his breakfast, just having some runny yellow eggs, when that fellow tried to shoot him through the window. I don't think you want to die over some piece of dogshit like King Fisher. 'Course, maybe I'm wrong. Maybe you do."

I didn't have to look to recognize the voice: Hector Torrez.

Slaughter turned his attention to the Mexican-Apache-White lawman, saw the simple way he was dressed, the cold stare, the carbine cradled in the crook of one arm.

"Who the hell are you?"

"That doesn't matter, does it?" Torrez said. "A fact is a fact, and the plain fact here is, Fisher brought on his own trouble."

Torrez glanced in my direction. Nothing in his look told me he was being anything other than a truthful witness. He was hard to figure out.

Finally, Johnny Slaughter let go of it reluctantly, like a dog giving up a bone already chewed clean of its meat. He asked some of the more able-bodied to help him carry the tall, lank corpse of King Fisher over to the undertaker's parlor.

"I ain't known you but less than a week," Torrez said, stepping a step closer to me. "And already I've seen you kill two men cold as ice beer. I know why I'm here, you want to tell me why you're here?"

14

"Why the sudden interest?" I asked Torrez, as we walked down the street.

"I could stand a whiskey, how about you?" he said.

"It's early for that," I said.

"This looks like a good place," he said.

It was Nutall and Mann's Number Ten, the place that had Wild Bill's bloodstain on the floor and his chair hanging on the wall.

"Sure, why not?" I said.

I noticed Tommy O'Dule was not yet on duty. Instead, there was another man rubbing down glasses behind the bar. He looked tired and miserable.

"A bottle," Torrez said. The man looked at him briefly, just long enough to see the hard, frank stare. Just long enough to see this wasn't a man he should ask a lot of questions of. Questions like why a man would want to drink hard liquor that time of the morning.

Torrez took the bottle, dropped a dollar on the counter without asking the price, and poked his fingers in two empty glasses the barman had just rubbed down and set on the bar.

"Let's sit over there," he said, pointing with his nose to a table in the far corner. A man with his trousers rolled up past his knees was sleeping on the pool table.

I waited while Torrez filled each of the glasses with Red-Eyed Jim. He tossed his down, looked at me, then at my untouched glass.

"Like I said, it's a little early for me."

He refilled his own glass, turned it between dark, blunt fingers.

"So what's the story on you, McCannon? You sure in the hell didn't come up here to muck for gold."

"You answer my question first," I said. "Why the sudden interest in me?"

I thought I saw something that could've passed for a smile play at his lips, but it would be a stretch of the imagination.

"I'm looking for someone," he said. It's what I'm good at, looking for people."

"What's that got to do with me?"

"Tell me first why you're here."

I took a breath, thought about the whiskey, about whether or not I needed a drink this early in the day, decided I didn't.

"There's been some killings," I said. "Prostitutes. I came up here to check into it for a friend."

Torrez didn't take his eyes off me.

"The dead girls worked for a woman named Alexandra Dupage. She's the one who wrote my friend, asking for help. I came in his place. He's in the detective business."

He still had that somewhat-near-a-smile look and his fingers continued to twist the glass of whiskey around between them without spilling any of it.

"That must be good drinking liquor, the way you're fondling it," I said.

"Detective, huh?" he said. "That what you are, too? A detective?"

"I guess you don't think much of the title or the profession," I said.

"First goddamn detective I ever met," he said. "Would you believe it? All these years, and you're the first one. Your friend, he's a Pinkerton man?"

"No. He's in business for himself. His operation is a lot smaller than Pinkerton's."

"Who's your friend? Maybe I've heard of him."

I told him Ben's name. He shook his head, said no, he hadn't heard of any Ben Beadle.

"Beadle Detective Agency, out of Cheyenne," he repeated after I'd told him. He half rolled his eyes, trying to remember if he'd ever heard of it. "No. I ain't never heard of it."

"It doesn't matter," I said.

"Well what the hell does a job like detective work pay, anyhow?" Torrez said.

"Depends on the assignment," I said.

"What, maybe a hundred a month, something like that?"

"It's not regular pay," I said. "It all depends on the job."

Torrez lifted the glass of Red-Eyed Jim, sipped it, held it out, looked at it, sipped it some more.

"How's a man get in that line of work, detective?" he said.

"It isn't hard to get into," I said.

"No, I bet it isn't."

"Why the interest?" I asked again.

"Just curious, about the detective work," he said.

"What about the other?"

"You mean, your reason for being here?"

I nodded.

"Yeah. Like I said, I'm looking for somebody. You could be him."

"How so? I rode up here on the stage with you. You'd know if I was the man you're looking for."

"No, not necessarily. It could be anybody."

"Why're you looking for somebody in the first place?"

He set the empty glass down gently, like it was an egg he didn't want to break.

"I had a brother come up here nine, ten months back," he began. "Come up here to muck gold. Him and another man, a man named Leotis January. The way my brother described this Leotis January, he was a gold panner. Bob was a fool, I told him that first off when he talked about it. But you'd have to know Bob to understand why he wouldn't listen to me. Bob's young, full of piss and vinegar. A dreamer, that's what Bob Torrez is."

Hector Torrez didn't seem to be talking to me as much as he was to himself. I listened while he told the rest of it.

"Bob and this fellow January, they came here saying how rich they were going to get. I heard from Bob once. Said they'd found something, but he wouldn't say what or how much exactly. Then, a month ago, someone sent home his things. They were wrapped in butcher paper and sent home to the old woman. His shirt and extra pants and a dollar watch he owned. No money, of course. I went to the house and the old woman showed me Bob's things wrapped up in that butcher paper. She said to me, 'Hector, Bob's been killed, I know it. Go see if you can find your brother and learn what happened to him.' She cried a little. It's mostly because of her that I came here. For me, too."

I watched him pour another inch of the whiskey in his glass and take his time drinking it.

"I ain't sentimental, like some," he said. "But goddamn it, Bob was my brother, the old woman's youngest boy. You can see how a thing like that would affect her, can't you?"

"Yeah."

He blinked, dropped his chin a little.

"See, Bob was always chasing after something that wasn't there. He was an unsteady boy, but damn if you couldn't help but like him the first time you met him. He was that way. Everybody liked Bob the minute they met him."

Then, Hector Torrez stiffened in his chair and his eyes grew fixed.

"They shouldn't have sent his goddamn clothes home in butcher paper," he muttered. "Not even a goddamn note to say what happened to him!"

"Somebody must have cared enough about him to do that much," I said. "A woman, maybe. Sounds like what a woman might do if she cared about him—send his things home."

"Butcher paper . . ." He said it like they were the only words he remembered from a forgotten prayer.

Then, he drank the whiskey, drank it like there was a fire in his gut he was trying to put out with it. And for a long time, there was nothing but the sound of flies droning the air.

"The writing on the butcher paper," he said after a while. "It could've been a woman's. I didn't think of that till just now, you mentioning it." The thought stirred behind his eyes, bringing some new hope.

"Bob liked women, and they sure in hell liked him." He lifted his gaze toward me as he poured some more of the whiskey into his glass a little less carefully than before. Some of the liquor spilled over onto his blunt fingers.

"But if it's like you say, McCannon, how come she didn't take the time to write a note with it, to say what happened to Bob? How come a woman would take the time to send his things and not bother to tell his own family what happened to him?"

"Maybe she thought she'd done her share," I said. "Or maybe she was afraid of getting more involved if it was something bad that happened to your brother."

"Maybe that was it, she was afraid," he said.

"Maybe so."

This time he drank the whiskey like he was just plain thirsty for it.

"It's a damn weakness," he said.

"What is?"

"Drinking."

"To some, maybe it is," I said.

"To me," he said. "It'll get me killed some day. I know that as sure as I know anything."

"Then why do you do it?"

This time his lips edged into a genuine smile.

"Two reasons," he said.

I waited for him to tell me.

"I can't stop. And it don't matter."

"Dying ought to count for something," I said. "The same way living ought to count for something."

"Not to me, it don't."

"No sweetheart waiting back in Texas?" I asked.

He grunted.

"Do I look the type?"

"It was just a question," I said.

"Yeah, I guess it was."

He poured out another glass, only this time, he filled it all the way to the top.

"I guess we both came here because of the killing going on in this town," Hector Torrez said, before draining his glass.

"Maybe you should begin asking about the women Bob might have been friendly with," I suggested. I wasn't sure he'd heard me, for his head had dropped slightly, like a weary old bull's.

I stood and the chair scraping over the floor brought him around.

"Detective . . ." he said, staring up at me.

"Good luck, Mr. Torrez, I hope you find your brother."

Something pinched the muscle below his left eye; disdain, maybe.

"What's something like that pay? That detective work?"

I left him sitting there, his hand gripping the half empty bottle. The company of Hector Torrez had suddenly lost its appeal.

I walked up the street to the stable where the old man was sitting, his face tilted to the sun.

"You get a horse in yet I can rent?"

He opened his eyes.

"You ain't dead yet," he said.

"Was I supposed to be?"

He coughed a laugh, then spat, then wiped his mouth and nose with the back of his hand. His eyes searched around in my face like a prospector looking for quartz in a field of stone.

"I heard the shots," he said.

"About that horse . . ."

"Saw them carry a man over to Principal's funeral parlor. I thought maybe it was you."

"Well, you can see it wasn't," I said. "Do you have a horse to rent, or not?"

He scratched the loose skin of his neck.

"Got a buckskin. He ain't fer beginners, ya know what I mean?"

"Bring him out."

The old man stood like it was the greatest effort in the world to do so, wiped his hands along the legs of his trousers and disappeared inside the stable. In a few minutes he led out the buckskin; he put my Dunn Brother saddle on the gelding and I appreciated the fact he had.

"Four dollars," the old man said, holding out his hand. "Up front, ya don't mind."

I paid him and climbed abroad. I barely got both feet in the stirrups and the buckskin was off. I gave him his head; it's the best thing to do with a horse that wants to run. Just let him. Hell, I wanted to run, too.

I let the buckskin run for a long time, then slowed him to a walk. I followed a trail off the main road that led back in among the tall dark pines. We climbed a ridge, worked our way along a ridge and kept going until we came to a blue mountain lake that lay glittering in the sun.

The buckskin was balky about the descent, but this time I was in charge, and together we went down—all the way down to the edge of the lake, then in up to the buckskin's belly.

I let him drink, then rode him out and back up on the shoreline. I dropped his saddle and let him crop grass while I pulled off my boots and everything else I was wearing.

The water was cold, damn near like knives cold. But I went in anyway and it sucked the breath out of me and tempered the pain shrinking my skull. And after a while, everything quit hurting and feeling bad and I could breathe again.

I soaked in the icy lake until I couldn't feel my legs and arms, then worked my way out and lay in the grass, letting the sun warm me. I refused to listen to the voices of the ghosts. Instead, I listened to the gentle cropping of the horse and the way the wind floated over the meadow grass and the way the water kissed against the rocks there at the shoreline. It was enough, just enough. All I needed. And I remembered an old Baptist preacher telling me once that it wasn't what a man wanted in life so much that counted, as it was what he needed. And if a man just got that much out of life, he was damn well blessed.

Lying there on the sweet grass with the sun warming my skin and Deadwood a long way off, I had just exactly what I needed.

I closed my eyes and was nearly asleep when I heard the drumbeat of riders approaching.

15

I raised up in time to see four riders pressed against the horizon, their horses throwing up clods of dirt. I could feel the pounding hooves rumbling up through the ground like a thumping heart.

I pulled on my trousers and shirt and shoved the Remington into my waistband.

Three of the riders were wearing red shirts and the brims of their hats were flattened back against the crowns. They had the same squinting eyes and long, wild moustaches and vandyke beards. Quirts swung from their gauntlets, and their chaps flared and flattened as they lifted and fell in rhythm with their lathered ponies. But it wasn't the red shirts I was watching as much as the man who rode out front.

He was riding a large blooded stud with four white stockings. A horse like that would cost three, four hundred dollars. I noticed then the saddle. It sure wasn't anything the Dunn Brothers would've made. It had iron stirrups and a small flap of leather for the seat. It was the kind of saddle a man would want if his horse gave out on him in middle of the plains and he had to carry it a long distance. It didn't look like it weighed anything at all.

My attention went from the horse and saddle to the man.

He was tall and well built, wearing a tailored gray suit and a tweed cap. He would be hard to mistake for a frontiersman. And the way he rode told me he wasn't a westerner.

The riders drew up ten feet away, sliding their horses to hard stops, except for the dude riding the thoroughbred. He circled around me, then came to a halt.

The other three were fanned out in a semi-circle behind him. The three red shirts could have been brothers, for all their similarities. They looked on with curiosity while the dandy riding the big stud tipped his cap before addressing me.

"I say, my dear man, is it your habit to take your leisure on private land?"

Hell, I didn't have to guess to know who it was by the accent: Edwin John-Davies, Alex's English gentleman—for lack of a better term.

He had soft brown eyes and a nose that had never been broken and a narrow square chin and overall soft features. He wore a cravat, a bright blue one, and tall, polished boots with small silver spurs. I noticed the checkered stock of a sporting gun protruding from a hand-tooled scabbard just behind his right leg.

The stud pawed the ground and snorted and tried tossing its head, but the Englishman held him in check with total command. He might not have been your typical bucko, but he knew how to handle a horse.

He wore gloves—nice soft kid gloves, expensive, like the horse and the rest of his outfit. He was the kind of gent you might see at some cattleman's club, sipping port from a crystal glass, or relaxing in a private rail car, smoking dollar cigars while out shooting up a herd of antelope on one of Pawnee Bill's hunting expeditions.

I was trying hard not to make a judgment about him, but it was damn difficult not to, considering how it'd gone between Alex and me the night before.

He waited for me to answer his question. The other three sort of sat there, resting their forearms on the horns of their saddles, curious, like monkeys.

"Didn't know you could own this land," I said.

He smiled at that.

"What makes you think not, sir?"

"Well, the last I knew, the Sioux owned it. I believe that is why they killed that poor crazy bastard Custer—because they were under the impression that the Black Hills was still theirs."

"Ah, I see," he said, almost politely. "The Sioux, that would be the redmen in this part of the territory, is that it?"

"Yeah, that'd be them," I said.

I could see the red shirts were enjoying the conversation.

"Full of it, ain't he?" one of them said to the other two. They all grinned like can-eating goats.

Edwin John-Davies looked at his hands as though he were admiring them, or the kid gloves he was wearing. He looked at them a moment, then back at me.

"You see, my dear man, this *is* private land—I've purchased it."

"To hell you say," I said with mock surprise. "How'd you manage that?"

One of the red shirts edged his horse closer to get between me and the Englishman.

"Hold on now, Mr. Coffey," Edwin John-Davies said. The mention of the name rang a few old bells. I looked at the kid and he looked back.

Charley Coffey had grown some since the last time I'd seen him. He'd grown a moustache, for one thing. It made him look foolish. The last time I'd laid eyes on him was when he'd been locked up in a Kansas jail for stealing a man's union suit off a clothesline. Charley was just a kid then; fourteen, fifteen, maybe. No one thought he'd amount to much. But Charley'd proved them wrong. He made himself into a gun artist of sorts. He killed a few old outlaws on his path to glory: a petty thief in Fort Riley; two army deserters in Hays.

Off and on over the years, I'd heard rumors about Charley Coffey. Kid Charley, some called him. Then I'd heard last winter he'd killed Jim Ketchum in Telluride. Some claimed it had been a fair fight. If it was, that would make Charley the genuine article; Jim Ketchum was no slouch with a gun.

"No sense in letting this man backtalk you, Mr. Davies," Charley said, feeling brave, I guess, with the others to back him up.

"No, Charles, I don't think that is what the gentleman was doing. I simply think he is misinformed about matters. Wouldn't you say that was the case, sir?" It hadn't taken me long to dislike him, the manner in which he spoke.

"You're Edwin John-Davies," I said.

He offered me a look of mild surprise.

"I am, sir, and might I ask who *you* are?"

"Name's McCannon," I said. "Quint McCannon."

Charley Coffey lost that slouched surly, look he'd had when he heard me tell Edwin who I was.

"I know this sumabitch!" Charley declared.

"Watch your mouth, boy," I warned. "Only my friends call me sumabitch."

He wasn't quite sure how to take that—as a joke or not.

His holster was half turned around from the hard riding he'd just done; his pistol was resting just about the middle of his spine. I could see he was trying to figure out a way to reach it without me shooting him first: there was no way. He knew it and I knew it.

"Hold up Charles," Edwin John-Davies ordered.

"Take his advice," I told Charley, "even you're not that fast, and I'm not that slow."

The other two were waiting for the play to begin. Most

men won't enter a fight that's not their own—not for thirty a month and board, they won't. One spat, the other scratched his jaw. I guess both were a little more than disappointed that Charley hadn't shot me or I hadn't shot him, or somebody hadn't shot somebody. They'd probably been having a slow week until I'd come along.

"Have we met, sir," Edwin said, "you and I? Have we met somewhere along the way?"

"No, I don't believe we have. But I met a friend of yours and she mentioned your name."

A quizzical look troubled his brow.

"It's the accent," I said. "It stands out in this country."

He smiled, showed me his teeth. He had a lot of teeth, I thought.

"Jolly well," he said.

"Well, now what?" I said.

"Well, I hate to seem an old fussbudget about it all, Mr. McCannon, but if I allow you to stray onto my property, then I invite everyone, don't I? And then you can see how that would become a problem, can't you?"

"Is it the grass?" I said.

"Pardon?"

"Are you worried that someone will steal your grass?"

Again that furrowing of the brows. He didn't quite get it.

"I mean, is that what you're worried about, a man comes and takes a swim in your little lake here, rests himself, then when he's ready, he'll steal your grass? Because to tell you the truth, I don't see anything else a man would want with this country other than to look at it. So I guess I don't understand your concern about trespassing."

"Let me handle this, Mr. Davies," Charley said.

For a long moment, Edwin John-Davies didn't say whether or not he *would* let Charley try and handle me.

Then he laughed hard and loud.

"Grass! Steal my grass, indeed!"

I saw the other two red shirts grinning. They weren't

quite sure what the joke was, but if Mr. Davies found it funny, then they reckoned it had to be funny. Like I said, it must have been a slow week around Deadwood before I came along to cheer everyone up.

"Can't you see, Charles, that Mr. McCannon is implying that the reason I don't want trespassers on my land is that I'm worried they might steal the grass?" This was followed by some more of the deep laughter.

Charley said, "No I *can't* see, Mr. Davies. It don't sound like no goddamn joke to me!"

"Oh, but it is, dear Charles," Davies said. Then his laughter drifted away like a hot wind that dies out at sunset, and his gaze narrowed sharply.

"You see, Charles, Mr. McCannon here obviously cannot see the point of why I don't allow trespassers and he has made some sort of a joke about it. A rather sly joke, I must admit. But a joke nonetheless."

Then the nostrils of that unbroken nose of his flared and I knew Davies no longer appreciated either my humor or my presence.

"Tell Mr. McCannon what the usual penalty is for men who trespass on my property, Charles."

This time it was Charley Coffey's turn to look happy.

"Well, Mr. Davies, usually you have me and Fork and Tolbert whup a man with our quirts. Whup him all the way back to the boundary line where your property begins."

"Indeed I do, Charles. Indeed I do. What do you think of that, Mr. McCannon? Charley. Charley and Mr. Fork and Mr. Tolbert punishing trespassers in the way just described to you."

"I think a man who would allow himself to be whipped by these sisters of yours isn't much of a man," I said.

Edwin Davies straightened slightly in his saddle.

"I see," he said. "You're portending that you won't allow my men to mete out the usual punishment on you, is that it?"

"If you mean to order them to whip me, that's it exactly."

He swallowed. He was close to the edge, I could see that veiled anger just behind the glass of his eyes. Anger just waiting to be set loose from under all the breeding and fine rich upbringing he'd had. I figured a man like Davies enjoyed it more than most, seeing a man whipped, broken down. All his refinement didn't stop him from liking the taste of a little blood now and then. He probably saw it as some form of high sport.

"Well then," he said, adjusting his jaw. "It would appear we are faced with a dilemma, then."

"Call it what you will."

"What say you, gentlemen?" he called to the other two red shirts, Tolbert and Fork. They offered him looks of uncertainty. Then one of them said, "Whatever you say, Mr. Davies; we work for you."

He looked pleased to hear the right answer. He was a man used to hearing the right answers to his questions.

"There, you see?" he said, turning his attention back to me. "My men agree with me."

"Then let them begin," I said. "But first, I'll shoot Charley there, then you. Him first, because I figure he's the fastest. Then you. I'll take my chances those other two won't have the stomach for it. How'll that be, Davies?"

I saw the effect of that, how it settled in those eyes that had been enjoying everything so much up until now.

"That sound all right with you boys?" I said, without turning my attention completely to Tolbert and Fork.

I could hear the way the leather of their saddles creaked when they shifted some of their weight. The sudden prospect of a gunfight was something they hadn't counted on.

Charley was another matter, however. He wasn't a real smart boy, judging by the looks of him; most gun punks lacked good sense but made up for it with pure meanness. But the fact was, Charley was still sitting there with his Peacemaker halfway up his butt, so it wasn't doing him much good just at the moment. Still, the odds were long in their favor if they did decide to fight.

"Is it worth it?" I said, pushing the point home, because a situation where men are being tested can turn south real quick.

"I seemed to have misjudged you, sir," Davies said, after a long, unsteady moment. "I don't enjoy this business with trespassers, but then, a man must protect what is his, wouldn't you agree?"

"Depends on the price he has to pay," I said.

"Quite true. And in this particular case, the price would most certainly be much too high. I will, however, insist that you vacate my property immediately."

"I've never been one to stay where I'm not welcome," I said.

"You won't mind if I have Mr. Fork and Mr. Tolbert and Charley here escort you to the boundary line?"

"Not Charley," I said. "You want those other two to ride along, that's fine with me, but not Charley. I don't care for the man's company."

I could see Charley would have given up his mother's virtue just for the opportunity to reach that .45 slid round to his tailbone. But his mama could rest easy; she wasn't going to have her reputation stained this day.

I cleaned camp, mounted the rented horse, and turned back in the direction I'd come, with the two red shirts in tow. One was smoking a shuck and the other rode with his right leg wrapped round the horn of his saddle. Bored men doing a boring job.

We reached the boundary of Davies's property just above the treeline, high up the ridge I'd descended earlier.

"This is it, McCannon," the one smoking the shuck said. "Don't come back here, okay?"

"What's a job like this pay?" I asked.

The other one dropped his head and said: "Thirty-five a month, and board."

"Somehow, it don't seem worth it," I said, "you want my opinion."

The first one said, "It's steady work, though, working

for the Englishman. There ain't many good jobs to be had. Not around here there ain't."

"You mean as long as you don't mind whipping a fellow with quirts for stretching out on some grass, maybe watering his horse?"

Neither of them took any offense, but they were plainly uncomfortable with my end of the conversation.

"We do what we're told," the one smoking the shuck said. "There's plenty of hands'd be willing to take our places we don't take orders. You can understand that, can't you?"

"No, I can't," I said.

They looked off, back toward the lake.

"Tell me something," one said. "Were you really going to shoot John-Davies and Charley and me and Fork here? Were you going to go up against all four of us?"

I looked them in the eyes.

"What do you think?" I asked.

They looked sheepish.

"A man'd have to be crazy going against four," the one smoking the shuck said. "You don't act like somebody that's crazy."

"Well, that's the thing," I said. "You just don't know about a man, do you?"

I could tell by their stares they weren't certain.

"We better be heading back," the one called Fork said. "You ain't intending on coming back this way, are you?"

"If I do, I'll let you know."

"Most likely you do, Mr. John-Davies'll have us whip you. That's if Charley don't shoot you in the head first, or the spine."

"I'll take my chances with Charley Coffey," I said. "I knew him when he was stealing other men's underdrawers from a widow's clothesline."

That raised a couple of smiles.

"He'd be the type," Tolbert said.

We shook hands.

"There's work down in Texas," I offered, as I turned my horse around toward the direction of Deadwood. "A top hand might do well for himself a little farther south." They didn't reply.

And as I rode back toward Deadwood, I knew that those two boys had one thing and only one thing on their minds: counting the number of days left till payday. That and maybe some plain-faced gal waiting for them down in the low country somewhere.

I didn't hold anything against them, though. They were just a couple of good men doing a bad job.

16

By the time I rode back into Deadwood, the sky was bunched with heavy gray clouds and the wind drew sharp and cold down through the gulch.

The old man was still sitting out front of his livery when I arrived. It was like he hadn't moved since I'd left that morning.

He eyed the horse.

"You come back," he said, like it was a surprise to him.

I dismounted and handed him the reins.

He ran his hands over the haunches.

"You looking for dents?" I asked.

He grinned, showing me his missing teeth.

"Just an old habit I picked up in my droving days," he said, "running my hands over 'em, checking their legs and such."

Then he jerked the saddle free, set it up on a barrel, and led the horse inside.

I was hungry, but I wanted to swing by and see Alex first. I didn't have to give myself a reason; I already knew the reason.

Cherry Bee opened the door a minute after I knocked.

"Mistuh Quint," she said. Her smile was pleasing; she was an attractive girl.

"Is Alex home?" I asked.

"Miss Alexandra be with somebody," Cherry Bee said.

"Oh."

"Some young man," she said. "Wanted to talk to Miss Alex."

Dust blew up from the street. The gusts of wind pinned some pages of yellow newspaper against the white picket fence.

"You want to come inside?" Cherry Bee asked. "Look like a storm fixin' to come."

"I'd like that."

She stepped back, led me into the front parlor.

"I can take your hat for you," she said.

"That's all right," I said. "I take it off, I'll just have to go through the grief of having to put it back on."

When she smiled, so did her eyes.

"Would you like me to bring you something to drink, Mistuh Quint?"

"A little of that cognac would do the trick," I said.

When she returned, she was carrying the crystal decanter of cognac and two glasses on a silver serving tray. She set the tray down on a small black walnut table in front of me.

"There you go," Cherry Bee said.

"You want some of this?" I asked, pouring out a couple of inches of cognac.

Cherry Bee's hand flew to her mouth and her eyes grew wide.

"Oh, no, suh. Miss Alex'd whup my bottom she was to catch me drinking that devil water."

This time it was my turn to grin.

"I could dust off your coat while you was waitin'," Cherry Bee offered.

I was about to decline the offer when a door across the

hall opened. I stood thinking it was Alex coming out of the room.

But I was a little more than surprised to see the Kid, Rose, coming out of the room. Alex appeared just behind her, supporting her by the elbow.

I stood to meet them.

Rose saw me, stopped, looked uncertain.

"Mr. McCannon, what are you doing here?" she asked. Her cheeks were strained with tears, her eyes red, and full of hurt.

"I was going to ask you the same thing," I said.

Rose looked like she was about to come apart. She looked at Alex, then back at me.

"Oh, Mr. McCannon . . ." she cried, then threw herself at me, and suddenly I was holding that frail body again, uncertain about the cause of her pain and grief.

My gaze lifted past Rose's shaking shoulders and were met by Alex's questioning stare.

"What is it, Rose? What's the matter?" I whispered to her.

"Maybe we should all go in there," Alex said, pointing to the parlor.

I led Rose into the room, helped her to the settee. She didn't want to turn loose of me.

I looked at Alex again, looked for answers.

"Cherry Bee, bring some water," Alex ordered. Cherry Bee brought a glass of water, offered it to Rose. She wiped her eyes with the back of her wrist and sipped some of the water. She looked up at me, then at Alex.

"It's my mama," she said.

"What is?" I asked.

"She's been killed . . . murdered," she sniffed.

I glanced across the room at Alex; she nodded.

"Do you remember the matter we discussed," Alex said, "the reason you've come?"

"The killings?" I said.

"Yes. Rose's mother was one of them."

"Her name was Flora," Rose said. "Mama's name was Flora."

"She worked for you, Alex?"

"Yes. She was the last one to . . ."

I remembered what Alex had said: how they'd found the last woman murdered by a butcher knife. I knew Alex wouldn't have gone into detail with Rose about it. At that moment, I felt as sorry for Rose as I had ever felt for anyone. She was frail in lots of ways.

Rose's hands trembled as they tried clinging to me.

"That's why I came, Mr. McCannon. I came looking for Mama . . ."

"I'm sorry, Rose."

She had the look of the lost now; the look that comes when the hard cold reality of a loved one's death sets in.

"I didn't know Flora had a daughter," Alex said hesitantly. "She never told me . . ."

"Mama left me when I was little," Rose uttered. "But I was old enough to know she was my mama; she promised she'd come back. Left me and Daddy 'cause Daddy went a little crazy with drinking and quoting the Bible all the time and swinging his fists at her. I guess Mama couldn't take no more of Daddy hurting her. But I remember her saying she was coming back. I remember her saying that to me . . ."

Alex's hand closed over her mouth, the fingers pressing her lips.

"Maybe you ought to lay down for a little while, Rose?" I suggested. "Just rest a little. Alex, how would it be if you poured a little glass of that cognac for Rose?"

Rose was still staring into that netherworld, talking the whole time about her mama leaving her and about her daddy and how he went crazy afterward. I put the glass to her mouth and encouraged her to drink it. She made a face, but drank it anyway. Alex had Cherry Bee pull the covers down on one of the beds.

"Don't leave me, Mr. McCannon. Don't leave me here

in this room alone," Rose pleaded. I helped her to the room, and Cherry Bee undressed her and helped her into the bed.

The light outside had grown dark from the coming storm and the room had a gloomy cast because of it. I pulled a chair up next to the bed.

"Let yourself rest, Rose."

She looked up at me with those sad, bittersweet eyes of a woman who was not quite a woman yet and not quite a girl any longer. I didn't know the words to say to her, at least the ones that would make it better, make the ache go away.

So instead, she held onto my hand, and I to hers. And we stayed like that until the room grew dark and the silence and the cognac soothed her and her fingers grew limp in mine. She fell asleep like that, with me holding her hand.

"How is she?" Alex asked, when I rejoined her in the parlor.

"Resting," I said.

"How do you know her?" Alex asked.

"We rode here on the stage together."

"Just that?"

"There was a problem out on the road. I offered my help," I said. "That's all."

Alex handed me a glass of cognac. I didn't bother to sip it.

"She showed up at my door an hour ago," Alex said. "She said she was looking for her mama, Flora Cash. It was totally unexpected. At first I thought she was a boy, in those clothes she's wearing. But then I could see it when she took off that big hat; it was Flora all over again, only younger. Only her name wasn't Flora Cash when I knew her, it was Flora Reed."

"How'd she learn of it?" I asked.

Alex shrugged her shoulders.

"She had a small tintype, showed it around to some of

the locals. Flora was a pretty girl, the kind men wouldn't forget seeing."

"How much did you tell her?" I asked.

"The truth, but not all. She didn't need to know it all," Alex said.

"I met your friend today," I said, pouring myself a second glass of the liquor, feeling a need to change the subject.

"Oh," she said, her eyes widening slightly.

"A real son of a bitch," I said.

I saw how that took effect. Her face flushed red, those lovely green eyes turning more jade.

"You don't have the right—" she started to say, but I cut her off.

"Why'd you leave before I woke this morning?" I asked.

"I thought it was better I did."

"Better for you? For me? Better for who?"

"For everyone concerned."

"I don't understand you," I said, feeling an anger toward her that I didn't want to feel.

"Would you be happier if everyone knew that I'd spent the night with you? Is that what you want, for everyone to know?"

I wasn't good at this sort of business, of dealing with feelings I knew I shouldn't be having. I didn't want to get into a fight with her over something that wasn't her fault, or mine. It'd been a bad day all around, and I was carrying a lot of anger from a lot of different sources, and this day didn't seem to be getting any better.

I drank half the cognac. I didn't know if I wanted to walk out the door or pull her to the floor. I wanted to do both, but found I couldn't bring myself to do either.

"I've had a long day," I said.

"I heard about the shooting this morning," she said. "Why didn't you come to see me?"

"I needed time to think about things, to get away."

"Everything's becoming entangled, isn't it?" she said. "Us, the killings, now Rose?"

"It's my fault," I told her. "I shouldn't have allowed things to get out of hand—I mean, between you and me."

"Could you've stopped it?"

I looked at her, looked into those ever-darkening green eyes that I'd never seen on any other woman, and knew the answer.

"No, I couldn't have stopped it," I said.

"No one could have."

I wanted to kiss her mouth, kiss it and never come up for air.

"It's going to get me killed," I said, "the way I'm feeling about you."

"No, don't let it."

"I didn't tell you the other night, the first time I met you, that on my way home someone took a shot at me. I was thinking about you when it happened."

Her hand reached up and touched the side of my face, her fingers cool and graceful, light against my jaw.

"Then you must leave Deadwood," she said. "I can't ask you to stay any longer. There will be others to help me, but not you."

"Others?"

She nodded.

"A man named Ed Siringo stopped by at noon. He said he was answering the ad I'd placed in the *Rocky Mountain News*."

"Jesus, Alex, another gunhand."

"He said he was a detective, a Pinkerton man."

"Christ!"

"Just go, Quint. Leave Deadwood. Tell Ben there was nothing you could do for me. Tell him I decided to leave and the matter resolved itself."

"Have you?"

"No. I won't be forced out. I won't start my life over

again, go on to the next mining camp and the next, until I turn myself into a crib whore just to survive!"

"Christ, Alex, you're going to wind up dead if I can't find out who it is killed those women!"

"No, you don't owe me that," she said. "You've risked your life enough."

"That's it?"

"That's it. I want you to leave Deadwood as soon as possible."

"Makes no damn sense. I thought there was something more between us."

"Does it matter?" she asked.

"It matters to me."

"But if you or I die because of it, what have we gained?"

"How can I protect you, Alex?"

She shrugged, studied me, shook her head.

"I don't know," she said, her hands cradling my face, her eyes brimming with tears.

I thought about Edwin John-Davies and that tailored suit and four-hundred-dollar horse and all that grass he owned, and all the rest of it. I thought about the two of them together, riding, picnicking, in bed. It made me feel brutal and angry and helpless. Alex was right, everything had become entangled.

I'd come here to help an old friend and instead had betrayed him with the woman he had once loved and maybe still did. And worst of all, I was *still* no closer to resolving the murders than the day I'd stepped off the stage.

And my mind was full of this woman.

"Do me a favor, Alex. Take care of that kid in there. See she gets a stage ticket back to Cheyenne."

She looked at me, and for a minute I thought she was going to kiss me, to tell me not to go. But she didn't.

I stepped out into the cold wind that was sweeping down through the gulch. One day rainbows, the next storms.

That was the way life seemed here in Deadwood, no matter how I looked at it—rainbows and storms.

I wasn't even sure where to begin. Then I saw what might be an answer, standing in the opening of an alley cussing two cowboys a blue streak.

17

The cowboys were half drunk, and Calamity was completely so. They had pinioned her up against the wall of a harness shop just inside an alley. It was the supper hour and there was hardly anyone on the street except for Jane Canary and those two cowpokes.

"Goddamn ya to hell, mister!" Jane was saying, as they held her there.

"Look here, gal," one of the cowboys was saying back, as he struggled to hold her wrist and keep from getting kicked in the sweetbreads.

"Look here yarself!" Calamity screeched.

"We paid you five damn dollars for what you're wearing under them buckskins. Five dollars and a whole lot of good liquor, now it's time you paid up."

Jane was stomping at their feet with her heels and thrusting her legs out in kicks, and every time she cursed them, spittle flew from her lips and sprayed their faces. Even I could tell they weren't enjoying it much.

"What kinda gal ya think I am?" Jane cried.

"Hell, darling, we already know what kinda gal you are,"

one of them said, trying to hold her and wipe some of Jane's spit from his eyes. "It's just a case of proving it, that's all."

"Let her go," I said.

Their heads jerked around like I'd roped them.

"Who the hell—"

"A friend," I said. "I'm a friend of this woman's, and I hate to see her being abused."

Jane smiled hugely in that sloppy way a drunk will when she recognized me.

"McCannon!" she shouted. "Get these apes off me, will ya?"

They were just boys. Bare-cheeked, freshly shorn boys just off the range, with their new haircuts and big bandannas hanging from their necks. The haircuts made their ears stick out from under the brims of their Stetsons.

Tricked by Jane, their big ears were red with anger.

One was buck toothed, and I would've been willing to bet, neither of them had ever had a woman before. Now, they'd picked the wrong one to marry for an hour.

"She's got five dollars of ours, mister," the buck-toothed one said. "Said she take us both on for five dollars cash."

"Yeah, and we bought her drinks all afternoon, too," the other one said.

"You gentlemen new in town?" I asked.

"Got here today," Buck-tooth said.

"Kansas, somewhere like that?" I asked.

They traded glances.

"How'd you know we was from Kansas?" Buck-tooth's friend said.

"Just a guess."

"Well, that don't change anything," Buck-tooth said, "just 'cause we're from Kansas."

"Just that you've been bamboozled by the best," I said.

They blinked hard, like startled owls.

"You gents know who you're holding there?"

"Damn flim-flam artist," Buck-tooth said.

"That, gents, is Calamity Jane Canary. She can outdrink, outfight, outshoot, and probably outlove any man in the territory. You are both lucky you didn't get what you paid for," I said. "And equally lucky all she got from you was five dollars."

They seemed uncertain.

Jane was grinning like a weasel.

"Jane, give these boys back their earnings," I said, "and maybe they'll turn you loose."

"Ain't got but three damn dollars left, Mac!" she shrieked.

"I'll make up the difference, if that's all right with you gents."

"Well, what about all the whiskey we bought and poured in her?" Buck-tooth's friend asked.

"What about it? You want her to puke it up?"

Still, they seemed reluctant to let it go at something that simple.

"Take your money and go over to the Number Ten," I said. "Ask for Tommy O'Dule. Tell him to line you up with one of the regular girls, one that won't cheat you or have her pimp knock you over the head. Tell him McCannon sent you. You'll both feel better for it come tomorrow morning."

"Wadda you say, Elbert?" Buck-tooth asked his friend.

"Sounds good to me." Then, looking at Jane, "Probably beat this homely sot any day."

"Say! Watch yar goddamn mouths!" Jane swore.

"Go ahead, turn her loose," I said. "Jane, give them the money." She looked at me like I'd just announced her sister had died, but dug down into her greasy buckskins and produced three silver dollars. I gave the cowboys two more and watched them head off for Nutall & Mann's.

"Well, hell, Mac," Jane blubbered. "I'da whipped them boys' butts, ya hadn't come along and stopped me."

"Yeah, I know, Jane. That's why I did it. I just couldn't stand by and watch those two youngsters take a whipping."

She laughed, slapped her leg with her miner's cap and said, "Hot damn, let's go have ourselves a drink. Whadda ya say?"

"I need to ask you some questions," I said.

"Honey Mac, ya can ask me any damn thing ya wanner, just buy me a round first. Wrasslin' them boys has made me as dry as a dead man's pecker. They was damn lucky ya showed when ya did, or I'da whupped 'em like puppies."

The Zenobia Saloon was just across the street.

"How about over there?" I suggested.

"Sure, sure," she said, "any ol' damn place at's got a fresh bottle of ol' John Barleycorn will do." She tried hooking her arm in mine, but I sidestepped her effort. She didn't seem to notice.

It was a big open room, the Zenobia. Full of blue smoke and noise. The usual kind of noise you hear in a saloon: glasses clinking, rough talk, laughter, the sound of a piano being played by a professor.

Jane slapped a few of the gents standing along the bar as we made our way to an empty table toward the rear. Some of the ones she slapped on the back turned and greeted her and tried to grab her, others tossed her angry looks.

I ordered a bottle and one of the bartenders brought it over to our table along with two glasses that were still wet from the last washing.

I didn't think she needed anything more to drink, but it was plain she talked best when her tongue was being oiled.

She eyed the operation while I poured us each a jigger's worth of mash, then her hand snaked out and snatched up one of the glasses. She downed it like she was desperate then set the glass back down all in one swift, sure motion.

"'Nother," she said.

"I need to talk to you, Jane."

"Sure, Mac, like I said, 'nther if ya damn please."

"Can't talk if you're passed out on me, Jane."

She licked her lips and spread her fingers atop the green felt of the table. The nails were dirty, the ends blunted.

"Ya married, Mac?" she asked. Her voice went from high pitched to nearly hoarse when she spoke slowly, which was seldom.

"Let's discuss other things," I said, taking a sip of my drink.

She took the bottle from my hand and poured herself a good portion of it into her glass.

"Handsome racehorse like ya," she said, "I wouldn't be 'tall surprised ya was married to two 'er three women. Har! Har!" Her laughter was harsh, unpleasant to the ear.

"I'm not one of those fresh-faced cowboys," I said.

"Whadda ya mean, Mac?"

"I mean, I'm not going to sit here all night buying you drinks and not get anything for it."

She grinned lasciviously.

"What is it ya want there, Mac?"

"You know what I'm referring to."

She offered me a sly, hesitant look.

"Go ahead, ask me anything ya want, Mac."

I watched the knot of her throat slide up and down as she guzzled another glass of the liquor. It gave me time to take her in more carefully. She was larger than she first appeared. And when her hand reached out for the glass, I could see her forearm was knotted with muscle. But she was thin, too. Sickly.

"Back in the jail, when we were locked up," I said, "you mentioned something about how Jack McCall was put up to killing Wild Bill . . ."

She looked at me over the rim of her glass without removing it from her mouth, her eyes wide, staring.

"I said that?" she said, lowering the glass an inch or two.

"Yeah, that's what you said, Jane. You were hung over at the time, a little drunk, maybe, but that's what you said."

"It's true, goddamn it!" she blurted suddenly, then looked around, then jerked her eyes back in my direction.

"Tell me," I said.

She looked around again, squinted as though trying to see through the haze of the miners' cigars.

"Gotta be careful what ya say around this place," she said, lowering her voice.

"Why?"

She looked at me dumbly. "'Cause, ya get heard by the wrong people, ya wind up dead like my darlin' Billy."

She leaned forward across the table, nearly spilling the bottle.

"Oh, Judas!" she said through a short, hard sob. "They killed him! And they'll kill me, too, I don't clear out soon!"

"Who are *they*, Jane?"

She blinked several times.

"See, that's the damn worst of it, Mac, ain't nobody knows who *they* are."

"But somebody suspects something, don't they, Jane?"

She looked around again.

"Names," she said. "Lots of names get said around."

"Like which ones?"

Her hands shook, she poured another glass, downed it, wiped some of the dribble from her chin with the heel of her hand.

"All kinds of names," she said.

"Come on, Jane."

"Why ya want to know for?" she said, suddenly sounding wary of me.

"Just interested, that's all."

She scoffed at that.

"Not ya, Mac. Ya don't seem like no kinda man that'd ask questions just to be askin' 'em."

"I'm looking into it for a friend of mine," I said. "He's the one that's curious."

I could see I was losing her to the whiskey again. Her

gaze had grown suddenly unsteady and her lids drooped and her jaw became slack.

"Jane!"

Her eyelids snapped open. She looked at me.

"What?"

"Names," I said. "Tell me what names you've heard."

"Goddam, Mac, I loved ol' Bill. I surely did. He had his ways, goddamn if he dint. Fussy about his appearance, fussy about his hands being clean, fussy about his guns. Fussiest man I ever knew. But goddamn if I dint love him much as I ever loved any man."

"Then why not help me out here and give me the names you've heard?"

"McCall," she said. "He was in on it."

"Not McCall," I said. "Everyone knows he shot Bill. Give me some other names."

Her eye lids were drooping again and her head lolled to the side.

"Loop," she muttered.

"Loop? Who is Loop?" I asked her, shaking her by the arm.

Her eyes came open partway, began to close.

"I heard maybe Leo had some hand in it . . ."

Her hands slid off the table, dangled by her sides. I wasn't going to get anything more from her.

"Come on, Jane," I said, lifting her under the arms. It didn't take much effort, as thin as she was.

I hustled her out the door and down the street to the Custer Hotel, a one-story flophouse catering mostly to miners.

The desk clerk looked up when he saw me enter and laid his copy of *DeWitt's Ten Cent Romances* face up on the counter. The cover featured a story about Wild Bill: *"Wild Bill The Indian Slayer."*

He looked at me and he looked at Jane.

"It's not what you think," I said.

He grinned sheepishly.

"She'll need a room for the night."

"Two dollars if you bunk up together," he said.

"It's just for her," I told him flatly.

"Dollar," he said. I paid him, took the key, and dropped Jane on the bed in the room, then covered her with a blanket.

"See she gets some breakfast in the morning," ʼ told the clerk on my way out.

"You ain't staying?" he said.

"Does it look like I am?"

Maybe it was the long day or my own weariness, but when I stepped back outside again, the wind seemed damn cold and my duster too little protection against it. If I was going to stay in Deadwood, I'd need a better coat. I made a cigarette and smoked it on my way back to my own hotel room.

The name Jane had given me rolled around in my mind. Leo Loop. Who the hell was Leo Loop?

18

A hard cold rain began to fall; the kind of rain that stings the flesh and seeps into the bone.

I ducked in under a butcher shop. Inside, a man was dressing out an antelope. I watched the loafers and the heelers duck doorways, trying to avoid the same cold rain. Then the rain changed to sleet and I could hear it pelting the windows up and down the walk. A man rode his horse at full gallop down the middle of the street trying to get home.

I rolled myself another shuck, hoping the rain would let up before I started for Alex's place. Anyone would know who Leo Loop was, I figured Alex would.

The smoke tasted good and the whiskey I'd had with Jane earlier had warmed my blood just enough against the chill dampness.

Then something drew my attention to the front of the Number Ten. I saw two men standing there in the low light of the doorway, talking. Normally, I wouldn't have paid them much attention. But then I saw who they were: Johnny Slaughter was one of them. He was wearing a yellow rubber slicker against the cold rain, saying something to the other man, his head tilting from side to side as he talked. I was too far away to catch any of their conversation. But Tommy was standing there listening, his hands plunged into his pockets, no doubt because he was cold. He was standing there in just his shirtsleeves, and it made me wonder if Johnny had called him outside, out from behind the bar, for the express purpose of talking to him in private.

Then Tommy started gesturing with his hands, as though he was explaining something difficult to the lawman.

Then, stepping from the shadows, a third man joined them: Doc Holliday.

Rain spilled off Johnny's hat brim every time he tilted his head. He towered over Doc, but somehow Doc still seemed the more imposing.

Slaughter immediately turned his attention to Doc. Doc stood there listening, then said something to the lawman. Johnny cranked his head around, looked over his shoulder, turned back to Doc. And for a minute more, they stood there, Johnny still talking. Then all three went inside the Number Ten.

The rain slackened and I flipped the shuck into a puddle and headed for Alex's. I got almost as far as the front gate, then stopped short. Tied up outside was Edwin John-Davies's blooded stud horse. The feeling I got left me colder than the rain had.

I could see a light on in the front parlor, between the split of the drapes. I saw another light on toward the back, where Cherry Bee's room was, the one we'd taken Rose to earlier.

Alex knew how I felt about the man. That she'd chosen to entertain him after what I'd told her left me angry. Truth was, I felt betrayed. I was tempted to confront them.

I waited for a time, thinking John-Davies would emerge, but when he didn't after several minutes, I gave it up and headed back to my hotel room.

The rain started up again and I did my best to stick to the sidewalks and whatever cover I could find, ducking in a doorway here, another there.

Between my anger and trying to stay dry, I failed to notice the shadows that moved on me.

There was the sound of shuffling boots on the boards and as I reached for the self-cocker, I was hit from behind and sent off balance. I was quickly shoved into an alleyway into the darkness of cover. I guessed there were at least three of them, maybe four.

The blows were delivered with short, hard grunts and each one seemed to find a new spot against my ribs and kidneys. Two or three times a boot found its way into my shoulders and back as I rolled around in the mud, got to my hands and knees, and was knocked back down again. A kick to my chest knocked the wind out of me and I stopped trying to get up.

The rain boiled up in the mud, next to my face. I could feel the blood leaking from my nose and lips. It was hard as hell to breathe, and I clawed at the mud trying.

Then I heard the double click of a revolver being cocked just above me and I knew I was going to be shot in the head. I closed my eyes and waited for the journey to begin. I didn't know if I was ready to die, but a great peacefulness came over me knowing that the time had finally come.

Like a dream, only this time it wasn't a dream. This time, I pressed my palms into the mud trying to raise myself up, to see the man who would do it, but a foot pushed down hard in the middle of my back, pinning me. I waited for the explosion of the pistol, wondering if I'd even hear it.

Bang!

It didn't hurt.

Then something slammed to the muddy ground next to me. I opened my eyes and saw the shadowy details of a man's bloody face under the pallor of yellow light coming from a second-story window of one of the buildings lining the alley. The dead man's features were distorted, the eyes frozen in a surprised stare. I could hear the sound of boots splashing through the mud, followed by the distinct metal click of a shell being ejected and another being jacked into the breech.

I lay there trying to breathe, staring into the face, what was left of it.

Then I heard the unhurried approach of footsteps, the sucking sound of mud. I waited. Maybe it wasn't over. I saw the muzzle of a carbine dangle in front of my eyes for a brief moment, then watched it swing over and poke at the dead man.

"You still alive?" the voice of Hector Torrez said.

"I think so," I managed to whisper through the shortness of breath that'd come with being kicked in the chest.

"I could only get the one," he said. "The others scrammed into the dark. I guess if I'd been carrying a repeater, I might've gotten more. But this old single-shot . . ."

"That's okay," I said. "One seems enough."

"You know that man?" he asked, poking with the muzzle.

"No. But then, there's not a whole lot left to identify."

"Yeah," he said. "Those big grain bullets create a lot of damage. Can you get up?"

I nodded. Felt him lift me under my arms until I could sit up. He leaned me against the wall of a building, squatted down, took stock of me.

"I seen worse," he said. "You were lucky."

"How so?" I asked.

"That one there, the one I shot, he was about to cap you." He stood, went over to the dead man, bent down, and picked up the pistol still clutched in his hand. Hector held it aloft where the light was better under the upper window.

"Forty-four, forty. Merwin & Hulbert model. Don't see

many around. Mean little bastard of a handgun," he said, then shoved it into his pocket.

"You think you could help me up the rest of the way?" I asked.

Again he squatted in front of me, looked into my eyes.

"Somebody wants you dead, why?"

"I don't know."

"Because you came here looking into the killings," he said. "That why they want you dead?"

"It would be my guess, if I had to make one."

He looked back at the dead man briefly.

"Whip you, then kill you," he said. "They wanted you to make you suffer a little before they capped you with that forty-four, forty. I'd say you've made some real enemies."

In spite of the beating, I didn't feel there was anything broken—no ribs, no bones.

"I think if I can stand, I'll make it back to my hotel room allright."

"I'd think you'd want to wait right here until the next stage left tomorrow," he said, "then crawl on it. You look like a man who's running out of chances. Maybe the next time I don't come along, then what?"

The rain splattered off the brim of his hat, danced in my eyes, along my skin, feeling good and cool and welcome.

I pushed against the wall, worked myself upwards. He watched as I did.

"It's a hard rain," he said, "cold."

"Yeah."

I looked around for my self-cocker, saw it lying in the mud a few feet away. It took some doing, but I managed to bend and pick it up and straighten back up again without falling down.

"You better clean the mud outta that before you try firing it," he said. "Blow up in your hand."

It was hard to breathe through my nose. Maybe I was wrong about nothing being broken. I pinched off the blood between my thumb and forefinger.

"You just happen to come along?" I said.

"I was over there," he said, nodding toward a bagnio across the street. I could hear the laughter of women, the bark of eager men.

"Drinking?"

"Yeah—that, and keeping an eye on things," he said, looking in that direction. "I heard there was a girl that maybe knew Bob works in there."

"The same girl who sent your brother's clothes?"

"Maybe."

"She admit to it?" I asked.

He hunched his shoulders. "I didn't ask her anything yet," he said.

"Then you just happened to be over there watching and seen this?" I said.

"Something like that."

"Lucky for me," I said.

"That's what I said."

"I owe you."

He didn't say anything, whether or not he thought I owed him.

"Like flies and shit," he said.

"What is?"

"Trouble and you."

"Maybe I'm just having a bad week," I said.

"Man," he shook his head, "nobody has that bad a week."

"Like you said, I'm lucky."

"Yeah, you are."

"What about him?" I asked.

Hector looked at the dead man.

"I guess it's too late for him. I guess he had a worse week than you."

"No, I mean, you just going to leave him there?"

"Well, I guess his friends will figure it out, come back for him soon as they think it's safe. I guess it'll be up to them to see he gets buried. I don't see where that concerns me."

"What about that girl?" I asked.

He looked over at the house across the street, the laughter from the women louder, pitched, like someone was tickling them, the men barking like dogs.

"I'll probably go back over, hang around a little, see what I can see."

"Remember, she probably had some feelings for your brother," I said. "Why else would she have done what she did? Go easy, if you find her."

He cocked his head, the rain slanting off his brim to the side, sluicing down over the shoulder of his coat.

"You think just because I was never married to one, I don't know how to handle a woman when I have to?" he said.

"No, I just meant that you need to remember that whoever sent Bob's clothes back to you probably didn't have anything to do with his disappearance."

"That's what being a detective teaches you? To think that way?" he said.

"You're a smart man, Hector. You want to find out about your brother, do it the right way."

He looked at me with those fearless dark eyes that were hidden in the shadows of his face. I could hear his breathing.

I started to turn to the street, everything feeling loose, unattached.

"Another thing," I said. "You need my help, let me know."

He didn't say anything. I didn't expect he would.

19

I asked Graves, the hotel clerk, to have a boy get me a bottle and bring it to my room.

"Look like you fell down in the mud," he said.

"Make it mash whiskey," I said.

I climbed the stairs; they might as well been the Rockies. I fumbled with the key to my door, found it already unlocked.

The lamp didn't need to be on for me to know there was someone in the room. I could smell her fragrance.

"What do you want?" I asked, without bothering to reach for the lamp. I struggled with my duster, wet and heavy with rain and mud, as were all my clothes.

"Mr. McCannon," she said. From the sound of her voice, she was sitting on the bed.

"Who are you?" I asked, pulling out the tails of my shirt, working the buttons with my muddy, cold fingers.

I heard the glass chimney being raised. Then a match flared and the flame touched the wick; the room slowly filled with soft, warm light. It illuminated her face. It was a face I hadn't expected to see again: May Smith's.

She looked different than on the stage, less prim and proper, less plain. Her hair was loose and down around her shoulders, for one thing. She wore a waistcoat over her blouse and a long heavy skirt.

"What're you doing here, Miss Smith?" I asked, still struggling to get out of the wet shirt. No matter how I moved, it hurt.

"I know this seems odd, my being here in your room like this, the light out," she said.

"No," I said. "The way things are going, there's not much I find odd. But it still doesn't answer the question of *why* you're here."

"I don't know . . . where else to be," she said.

Then I saw, on the bed beside her, bundled under the blankets, the small, still form of her daughter, the toss of dark ringlets upon the pillow.

May Smith saw my gaze, and said, "She's exhausted. I'm sorry . . ."

"Don't be."

"I had no intention to impose myself on you . . . I barely know you. But you see, Mr. McCannon, I have no one else to impose myself upon."

"If you don't mind," I said, "I need to get out of these wet clothes." I waited for her to avert her eyes, but she didn't. The room was small, not built for privacy.

I pulled off the shirt, then the boots, and then my pants. I was still in my underdrawers, but they'd need to come off as well. I reached for a towel, turned my back to her, and with as much dignity as I could manage, traded the drawers for the towel.

When I turned back, she was still staring at me.

I scrounged a shirt out of my saddlebags, the one purchased to replace the one I had torn into bandages for Rose. I put it on, keeping the towel tied round my waist.

"You mind I smoke?" I asked.

She shook her head.

"Normally I wouldn't in the presence of a lady," I said.

"No, go right ahead, Mr. McCannon. It is your room, after all."

Mud was clinging to my hair. I ran my fingers through it.

There was a knock at the door. She started, her right hand coming to her throat, just above a cameo brooch she'd pinned there.

"I think it's the bottle I ordered," I said. I reached into my pants and pulled out the money.

The kid had corkscrew red hair and he tried hard to look past me into the room. I saw him grin when he spotted her, the freckles spreading out across his nose. A kid that age.

"Anything else you be needing, you just let me know, sir. Name's Deke. Just ask Mr. Graves downstairs to have Deke get whatever it is you be wantin'. I'll do it."

I closed the door with him still trying to get a better look at May Smith.

I pulled the cork on the bottle, found the water glass, wiped it out with my fingers, and poured enough of the mash to get my blood circulating again. Then I remembered what manners I still had.

"You?" I said, holding the glass forth.

She nodded just a little. I handed her the glass, watched her sip the mash, saw the flinch in her eyes as she swallowed it. She steeled herself, drank the rest, and handed me back the glass. I poured another, this one for me.

"So what's this all about, Miss Smith?" I said, feeling the liquor rip through me.

She lowered her eyes at last. Her hands fidgeted, one against the other, the gray gloves she was wearing thin, and tightly formed over her long, slender fingers. I imagined those gloves holding a parasol as she strolled along a tree-lined lane, a beau at her side, eager to please; a gentleman. And she, as delicate in her manner as spring rain upon pretty flowers.

"You see . . ." she began, then drew a sharp breath. "I

have no one to turn to, no place to go with my child, no one to take me in. And worst of all, Mr. McCannon, I have no money left.''

Her voice stumbled and she gripped the bedpost with one hand, the knuckles showing through the cotton glove.

Then she lifted her gaze with as much pride as she had left.

"It's not much," she said, "but you're the only one I could think of.''

"You mind?" I said, indicating the foot of the bed.

"No, please, sit down." Then, as I moved closer, she said, "Your nose, it's bleeding.''

I touched the back of my hand to it, pulled it away, saw a smear of blood.

"I fell down," I said. "It was an accident.''

She looked at me a minute longer, knew I was lying about falling down, then swallowed, willing to let go the rest of the questions she had about what had happened to me.

"I thought you said on the trip up you were coming to meet someone, a man." I said. "What happened you didn't find him?''

"I found him," she said.

"And he disappointed you?''

She blinked several times, trying to hold back the tears that were building just behind her pale blue eyes.

"You see," she said, her spine suddenly becoming a rod of stiffness, her chin jutting forward in an effort to compose whatever dignity she had left to her. "John has already married someone else. He said he sent a letter explaining it to me. But, I never received it. At least, he claims to have sent a letter.''

"The little girl?" I said.

She turned her attention to the sleeping bundle of child beneath the blankets.

"She's his daughter," she said. "John's and mine.''

"That didn't seem to bother him?" I asked. "That you came all this way, brought her with you?"

"She was three when he left us to, as he put it, find a better life for us. That was nearly two years ago," she added. "I couldn't wait any longer in Denver. We were nearly out of money then."

"So you thought you'd just come and find him, and everything would be all right after two years," I said.

She turned her face away.

"I thought that it would . . . yes."

"But you were mistaken about this John?"

She took a deep breath and let it out, her eyes wet, still wanting to be fiercely loyal, it seemed, to a man who'd abandoned her and their daughter.

"He promised me . . ."

It was like an unanswered prayer, the way she said it.

"Look, I'm sorry, Miss Smith. You and your daughter can stay here the night. In the morning, I'll see what I can do to get you tickets back to Denver. You have people back in Denver, folks that could help you and the little girl out?"

She shook her head. "No one."

She was doing her best to maintain, and I was doing my best to keep from closing my eyes and falling into the exhaustion that was pulling at me.

"Well, try and get some sleep, we'll discuss it over breakfast in the morning, what you and the little girl are going to do."

"I'm a proud woman, Mr. McCannon," she said. "At least, I always was until now. If it weren't for Tessie . . ."

"Don't think about that right now, Miss Smith. I'll go out in the hallway and finish my smoke while you get yourself ready for bed."

It's the worst kind of way to be, beholden to strangers. I didn't want to make it any harder on her than it already was. Besides, I had the bottle of mash and my makings, and for me, right then, that was just about all I needed.

I stepped out in the hallway and smoked the cigarette slow and deep, taking turns with the mash, trying not to think about anything beyond the moment. Trying not to think about Alex and her visitor and Rose or the men who'd nearly killed me out in a dark alley, or even why they'd tried to kill me.

My exhaustion was deep; events seemed to be turning faster than I knew how to keep up with them.

It'd been a damn long day, that's all I knew. That, and the shuck and the whiskey tasted good.

I waited for what I thought was long enough for May Smith to get undressed and into bed. I knocked lightly before stepping back inside. The flame of the lamp guttered low and I could barely see her face. I unrolled my soogins, stretched out on the floor, propped my back against the wall, still holding onto the bottle. I closed my eyes, listened to the buzz inside my head, medicated myself with the liquor, shifted my weight now and again whenever one spot got to bothering me. I let the whiskey begin its journey through my flesh and soul, let it carry me on a long, slow ride down a peaceful river.

I didn't mind resting that way; hell, I'd done it a hundred times before in my life. Sleeping in places a man wasn't meant to sleep: the hard ground, trenches filled with rainwater, and saddles. Sleeping on the floor wasn't hardly even an inconvenience. I heard the little girl cough in her sleep, it pulled me up a little, then the whiskey river carried me back down again.

I was nearly asleep, not quite, but just at the edge of it when I heard May Smith say something.

". . . You want, it's okay."

I thought she was saying something to the girl. My mind was adrift, thick, heavy with exhaustion, the numbing effect of the whiskey.

I thought maybe I'd been dreaming that she'd said something. Then she said it again.

"It's okay if you want to lie here in the bed next to me,

Mr. McCannon. I don't mind. You don't need to sleep there on the floor."

It was soft, her voice. Soft like a butterfly landing on the petal of a flower. Soft and gentle and sweet. It drifted through my weariness. I thought about her in the bed. I thought about accepting the offer.

When I didn't move or say anything, I heard her say, "I wouldn't mind if you were to come and lay here next to me, Mr. McCannon. I wouldn't mind having you here."

Only this time when she said it, it wasn't so much as though granting me permission as it was a request. And for a long couple of minutes more, I thought about it. I thought real hard about it.

"Miss Smith . . ."

"You don't have to say anything," she whispered. "Words aren't necessary. Not tonight they're not."

I remembered how she looked with the shadows of the light from the lamp edging over her face. She'd proved to be an attractive woman with her hair loose and free like she'd had it. At first, I told myself it was the whiskey, or maybe the exhaustion, or even the damn whipping I took in the alley, that made me consider her offer. I was hurting and halfway to being drunk and maybe that was all part of it, my wanting her just then.

Now, she was making it easy for me. Too easy.

"It's been a long day, Miss Smith. Thanks, but no."

For a long moment, she didn't speak. Then she said, "May I ask you why not?"

"The truth?" I said.

"Yes. I'd like the truth, Mr. McCannon."

"The truth is, Miss Smith, I can't give you an answer. I can't think of one single good reason, to turn you down. But I've got my hands full right now and I think if I were to come to bed with you, it'd just be one more thing I'd have to deal with. And I don't know I can deal with one more thing right now."

"I must sound needy to you, desperate," she said.

"No, Miss Smith. You don't sound that way at all to me. I understand what it is to want to be held."

"I'm sorry," she whispered.

"Don't be. Another time, another place, who knows how I'd feel about it. You're an attractive woman, Miss Smith. Don't be sorry for feeling what you feel."

For a long time more she didn't say anything. I could hear the soft breathing of the child next to her, sleeping the sleep of the innocent, and I thought that must be the way an angel sleeps, soft and still and undisturbed like that.

"Mr. McCannon . . ."

"Call me, Quint, Miss Smith. I guess we've gotten to know enough of each other in this short time you can call me by my first name."

"I just wanted you to know, I'm not needy. Not like that."

"I know, May."

"It sounds good," she said.

"What does?"

"Hearing you say my name."

I closed my eyes. Even though the flame had burned out and the room had become dark, I still closed my eyes.

Something about her had touched me. Her and the little girl. They were like angels that had fallen from the sky, their wings broken, unable to fly any farther. Brought down by the false promises of a dishonest man and the unshakable weight of disappointment. Their wings, broken by hopelessness and despair.

Two angels fallen to the ground, left there untouched by kindness.

How many other women had shattered through the clouds of love and dreams and hope only to fall to this mortal earth?

Fallen Angels.

"May," I said.

"Yes."

"What's your man's last name?"

"I thought I told you," she said.

"No, you just said, 'John'."

"Oh," she whispered. "It's Johnny Slaughter."

20

I left the room early, dawn was just breaking over the Black Hills. The pine trees along their slopes stood shrouded in a languid mist. That hour of morning, the air was cold and sharp as a knife blade.

May and her daughter remained asleep as I gathered up my things and quietly dressed. Every piece of clothing but the clean shirt I'd put on the previous night was stiff with dried mud. I was a hell of a sight to anyone that might've taken notice of me.

I saw a few miners heading off into the hills, their mules loaded down with gear: pick axes, shovels, tin pans, their beans and bacon and dreams. But with the exception of those few eager men, the town itself was as quiet as the little cemetery up on Mount Moriah, where Bill Hickok's bones were resting the eternal rest.

I walked to Nutall & Mann's Number Ten.

The place was all but empty, the heelers and loafers having long since fled to their tents and shanties. The smell of stale smoke still clung to the air. Stale smoke and stale beer—it was a smell I'd long been familiar with, and first thing in the morning, not a smell you appreciated.

Tommy O'Dule was the lying on the bar asleep, stretched out fully on his back, his arms folded across his chest, his shoes lined up neatly by his head, the laces left untied.

I bounced a silver dollar off the oak. He opened one eye, screwed it around until he saw me standing there.

"Mr. McCannon," he uttered, half sitting up, wiping drool from the corner of his mouth with his shirt cuff.

"Are we open yet?" he asked with uncertainty.

"I'll have coffee," I said.

He looked around the empty club.

"I'd say we're either ain't open yet, or we've lost all our business."

"No jokes this early, Tommy. Make the coffee, if you don't mind."

He eased his bulk off the bar.

"Damn poor bed," he grumbled, "oak is."

I waited while he got the Arbuckle going, then watched as he combed fingers through his thick red hair, saw the muscled forearm as he did, the arm itself thick as a piano leg.

He seemed less inclined toward chatter this time. Maybe I had awakened him from his dreams.

He excused himself to go out back to "make his water," he said. When he returned, he poured me a cup of the pitch black coffee. It looked and smelled like something other than coffee.

"I never claimed to be any sorta cook," he said as he poured. He pushed the coffee and the silver dollar my way.

"On the house," he said. "How could I charge anyone for that poison?"

He wasn't far from the truth, about the coffee being close to poison.

"Tell me something, Tommy," I said, blowing off the steam. "You a friend of Doc Holliday's?"

That opened his eyes a little wider.

"I know of the man, yes sar."

"That's it, you just know *of* him?"

"I've seen him around, spoken to him once or twice, that'd be about it, sar."

"So you're not a friend of his then?"

He shook his head.

"No, I don't think anyone would classify me and Doc as chums."

Then he seemed to think it was his turn to ask the questions.

"You look like you've had yarself a bit o'trouble, sar."

He was staring at my mud-stiff clothes, the nick above my eye, the nose that was maybe broken from the fight last night—if it could be called a fight—the bruises that were beginning to turn plum color just below my skin.

Something told me he already knew about the trouble I'd had.

"How about Johnny Slaughter?" I said. "You friends of Johnny Slaughter's?"

Trouble filled his eyes.

"Why you so interested in who my friends are, Mr. McCannon?" he said.

"Just that I'm trying to get a handle on things around here, Tommy. Trying to figure out who's who, who it is I've got to watch out for, who I don't."

"Well, sar," he said, picking up a rag from under the counter and wiping the bar top with it. "I ain't but fairly new in town myself, like I told you already; I don't know very many folks I'd call friends of mine."

"So you're not a friend of Johnny Slaughter's, either?" I said.

It wasn't setting well with him, the questions I was asking; I could see it by the way he stiffened, the way he pushed the rag over the bar, the coldness that crept into his gaze, the way a man will look when you start to push him too far in a direction he doesn't want to go.

"I know Officer Slaughter," he said, "if that's what you mean."

"Know him well enough to have private conversations with him? How about, Doc? You know Doc that well, too?"

I guess he thought the bar was clean enough, because he stopped wiping it with the rag. He placed both hands on the oak, his thick arms showing through his shirt.

"Finish yar coffee, sar, and leave, we ain't opened yet."

It was what I'd been wanting, a place to start. Tommy had just given it to me with his denials, such as they were. There had to be a reason he didn't want to admit Doc and Johnny Slaughter as men he knew more than just casually.

"They in on it?" I said, setting the coffee cup back down along with the dollar.

"What would that be, sar?"

"The killings."

His head twitched, just a little.

"You're trying my patience," he said. "I don't know nothing about the killings of those prostitutes. That's what yar talkin' about, ain't it? Those girls being murdered?"

"Yeah, Tommy, that's what I'm talking about."

He could do it one or two ways if he wanted to: he could just come over the top of the bar and brawl, or he could reach below the bar there by his knee and snatch the hickory wood billy and bring that with him. I was prepared for him to do it either way. I was surprised when he didn't.

"Looks like you've already had your share of misery and hard times, sar," he said. "I was the boxing champ of my county—Cork—back home. You wouldn't want to test me. Not in a fistfight you wouldn't."

I figured I had three choices. I could shoot him, fight him, or leave. I decided I'd gotten enough of what I'd come for, that to try for more would only lead to unnecessary violence. An old Texas Ranger I once knew cautioned me on the virtue of not becoming greedy by saying in a simple drawl, *"Hogs get et."*

"Your coffeemaking," I said, turning to leave, "it needs practice."

I stepped outside, rolled a shuck, and watched as the sun lifted over the Black Hills, its light shattering against the tops of the spiny pines and splaying out in long golden shafts. And I thought to myself, I'd survived another night in Deadwood, thanks to Hector Torrez. The real question was, how many more nights would I be able to survive?

I wanted to go see Alex, ask her about last evening, about the visit of Edwin John-Davies. But then I thought, to hell with it. If she wanted, she could find me and tell me about Edwin John-Davies and his visit.

I started down the street, back toward the hotel. Maybe May and the little girl Tess would be up by now, maybe they'd have had enough time to get dressed.

Hector Torrez stepped out of the front door of the bagnio he'd been standing in front of last night when he saw whoever it was push me into the alley.

This time, he was still putting on his coat.

"Torrez," I greeted him, as soon as he saw me.

I could see his uneasiness at running into me. He finished buttoning his coat, acting like it was a common occurrence, a man like him coming out of a cathouse.

"What're you doing out this time of morning?" he said. "You didn't manage to get yourself shanghaied or killed after I left you last night?"

"I didn't know you were given to humor, Deputy," I said.

"I ain't."

"How'd you do last night," I asked, "with the girl? You find her?"

He shifted his glance.

"I might've found her."

"You're not sure?"

"I said maybe I did."

He shifted his gaze to up the street, refusing to acknowledge much of whatever he'd discovered in the fleshpot, though it was obvious he'd spent the night inside.

"You find something in there beside information?" I said.

"Hell, McCannon, you're just full of damn curiosity, ain't you?"

"There's nothing wrong with a man needing the company of a woman."

He looked at me hard then.

"Jesus Christ, McCannon! You must've gotten your brains scrambled in one of those fights you're always losing."

"Look, Hector, it doesn't matter to me what you do—in there, or anywhere else. I was just asking if you'd found out anymore about your brother, that's all. You want to take it a different way, go ahead. There's no shame in bedding a whore."

"Well, thank you very goddamn much for the lecture," he said.

"You know, Torrez," I said, trying to keep a lid on it, "you are about the touchiest man I ever met."

He shook his head, like a man in disbelief.

"I'm starting to hear things about you, McCannon," he said.

"What sort of things?"

"*All* sorts of things. Your name's become a cussword in this town. There's talk you're dangerous, spoiling for any fight you can get into. Especially since you doused King Fisher's lights the other day. That lawman Slaughter, he's been throwing your name around to his friends. You wouldn't exactly get elected mayor if you were to run," he said.

"That means I'm stirring the pot."

"What pot?"

"The one where I find out who killed those women."

"Yeah, well, if you're not careful, you're going to wind up in that pot with them."

"Not as long as I've got you around watching after me, Hector."

"I wouldn't count on it, McCannon, my being around next time."

"I'll see you later, Hector. Good luck with finding Bob, huh?"

He looked back at the bagnio, the one he'd just come out of, and tilted his head up toward a second story window, one that had lace curtains hanging in it. I saw one of the curtains draw back just a little. A face appeared. Young, pretty, dark.

May and Tess were up, sitting there dressed, waiting, by the time I reached my hotel room.

"How about some breakfast?" I offered.

Tess looked at me, looked at her mother. "Mama?"

"For her," May said. "Maybe a little something to eat for her."

"For both of you," I said.

"No, just for her," May insisted.

"Come on," I said, opening the door for them.

"What about our things?" she asked, pointing to the two small trunks in the corner of the room.

"Leave them, we'll pick them up later."

We found the cafe, the one I'd been sitting in the day King Fisher had tried to kill me through the plate glass. There was a new window already installed, the putty still fresh along the casing.

Tess ordered flapjacks and maple syrup and a glass of goat's milk. May ate little of her eggs, nibbled at her toast, sipped her coffee. She was prettier sitting there in the light of day. I remembered our conversation of the night before, wondered if maybe I'd made a mistake turning her down. It was funny how much my opinion of her had changed since the stage ride up from Cheyenne.

I enjoyed watching the child eat, hungry, full of energy,

the way a person should eat a meal. I watched her pour too much syrup on her flapjacks. It ran off the sides before she cut into them with her fork. She grinned with each mouthful.

"I'll find a way to repay you," May said.

"No, you don't have to concern yourself with that," I told her.

She tried to persist.

"Look, May, it's really not a problem for me to help you and Tessie out. Why turn it into one?"

I saw the way her soft blue eyes searched for an answer to my question.

"I had a son once," I said. Why I said it, I don't know; but I said it as I watched Tess eat her flapjacks. Maybe that was it, watching a beautiful child enjoying herself, thinking how it would've been if I'd gotten a chance to watch my own son doing the same thing, pouring too much syrup over his flapjacks.

"I'd like to think if it were my wife and child needing it, someone would be willing to help out," I said.

"You said 'once'," she said. "What do you mean, 'once'."

"He died of the Milk Sickness just after he was born. Him and my wife both died of the same thing."

She didn't say anything; she didn't say the usual about how sorry she was to hear of my loss. She didn't make words just to make them. She just sat there looking at me with those soft sea blue eyes that let me know she understood in ways that words could not.

"What I mean to say is, May," I continued, trying to assure her, "it is not a bother to me to help you and Tess. Don't let it be a bother to you, okay?"

She nodded.

"I accept your kindness," she said.

"Good. Soon's we're done eating, we'll go over to the stage line and see about a pair of tickets to Denver."

May reached across the table and touched the knuckles of my hand with her fingertips.

"Mr. McCannon."

I didn't move my hand away.

"About last night . . ."

"I know," I said.

"I didn't mean it to sound—"

"I don't know much," I said. "But I know what you were feeling last night. I was feeling the same way. But it didn't seem right. Not for either of us, not just now."

Her lower lip quivered slightly, the eyes misted over.

"I just meant to say that I didn't want to sound needy to you—not in that way."

"To tell the truth," I said, "it felt to me more like needing and not being needy," I said. "There's a difference."

"You're an unusual man, Mr. McCannon."

"No, not so different than anyone else," I said.

Tessie asked if she could have a second glass of goat's milk. I ordered it for her.

"I can't go to Denver," May said.

"Why not?"

"What would I do once I got there? I've no money, no family, no one there waiting for us."

"I'll give you enough to rent a place, tide you along until you can find something," I said.

"No. Why squander the money it would take to travel to Denver when I can stay right here, find work here."

"You've seen Deadwood, May. Is this a place you want to raise your daughter in?"

"It will have to do until I can get myself square again."

"May, I don't even think they have a school here for Tess."

"Then I'll tutor her myself."

"What sort of work do you think a town like this would have to offer a woman?" I asked bluntly. "You've seen the female population here. What do you think those women do for a living?"

"There are other things a woman can do besides what you're referring to, Mr. McCannon."

"Look, after last night, May, I think you can drop calling me 'mister'. 'Quint' will do."

She gave a weak smile. It felt awkward, me lecturing her on the vices of Deadwood. Maybe if it hadn't been for Tess, I would have kept my opinions to myself.

"Besides the obvious, what sorts of other things would there be for a woman to do here?" I asked.

"I can take in laundry and sewing," she said. "I'm a very capable seamstress. With all these bachelors here, I would think there would be plenty need of my services."

"And Johnny Slaughter," I said. "What about him? He's still the law in Deadwood, in case he didn't tell you."

"What about him?" she said, stiffening her lower lip.

"You don't think that'd make him uncomfortable, to have you and Tessie living here in Deadwood, under his gaze?"

"I hope it *does* make him uncomfortable, Mr. Mc— Quint. Besides, what's that to me? I have my daughter to look out for; that's my main concern."

"I don't think its a good idea, May. That's all."

Now her fingers did more than just glide over my knuckles; they encircled my wrist.

"Your wife," she said. "Did you always give her your opinion on matters you felt strongly about? Did she ever disagree with you?"

"Yes. Matter of fact I did, and she did."

"And how did you take that, when she disagreed with you?"

I remembered exactly how I took it.

"I respected her for having strong beliefs," I said, unashamed.

"You see, Quint, that's the way good women are. They

stick to their beliefs, no matter what anyone else tells them.''

"You can have my room at the hotel," I said, not seeing any reason to continue trying to talk her out of leaving Deadwood.

"I've already paid a week's rent. It'll give you time to get settled, maybe find something better, a small house, maybe." "No, I won't see you out on the streets because of me," she stated firmly.

"Just till we find you something better," I said. "You and Tess."

I started to rise, pay the bill for breakfast. Her fingers closed around my wrist, stopped me from getting up.

"I want you to know something," she said, her eyes searching mine. "What I offered last night, I haven't changed my mind about it. If you change yours . . ."

"A man doesn't often get asked," I said. "At least, not asked by a woman like you. It'd be hard for me to tell you exactly how that makes me feel."

"Promise you'll at least think about it," she said, before taking her hand away from mine.

"Yes," I said. "I'll think about it."

21

I told the clerk at the hotel the situation, and gave him another five dollars to extend the room stay, in case May needed more time to find her own place.

"She your missus?" the clerk asked, looking at May and Tess waiting in the lobby. "That your little girl?"

"Mind your own business, friend," I warned. He shifted his gaze back to the money.

"Sure, sure. It's your room, I reckon you can have who you want in it. You can keep an ape in it, you want. It wouldn't make no difference to me."

"See that she gets fresh towels, sheets," I said. "Soap for her and the little girl. Have your boy, Deke, take their clothes down and have them laundered. Have him bring some fresh fruit up to the room." I laid another ten dollars down. "Meals as well, in case Miss Smith chooses not to go out."

He looked at me. I could see it running through his mind, the name, the questions that came after it.

"You make sure Deke takes care of it, okay?"

"Sure, Mr. McCannon, anything you want for Miss Smith, I'll see it gets done."

I told May I'd check on her later. Tess held her hand, looked up at me.

"Thank you for the flapjacks, mister," she said, then smiled, showing a missing front tooth.

I went outside, pulled my makings, rolled a shuck.

What the hell was I getting into here?

I decided it was time to wire Ben, asking him when he might be coming to Deadwood. There were some things I wanted to tell him about—the situation with me and Alex, for one. I also could use the help, after what'd happened last night in the alley. I needed someone to watch my back. I'd been lucky so far, thanks to Hector Torrez. But how much longer could I stay lucky was another question.

I started to cross the street when I heard my name called.

"McCannon!"

I turned to see Johnny Slaughter coming down the street; a skinny deputy hurried alongside him. By the way he was walking, in that stiff-legged manner of a man going somewhere, it was plain to see that Johnny wasn't just out for his morning rounds.

"I need to talk to you, McCannon!"

I turned in his direction. My duster was unbuttoned, he could see the butt of the self cocker; I didn't mind that he could.

"What is it?"

"In private." he said. "I wanna talk to you in private."

I looked at the other man.

"Around here," Slaughter said, thumbing toward the alley.

"The alley? You got to be kidding!"

"What the hell's wrong with a little private conversation in the alley?" he said. The blood had gathered just under his skin, along the jaw and cheeks and neck, the way a man's will when he's angry and heavily built like Johnny was.

"You first," I said and waited until he and the other man stepped into the ally. I followed but kept a distance between us.

"Okay, we're here, private, like you wanted, Slaughter," I said, after he and the other man had gone in a short way and turned around.

"Tell him, Skinny!" Johnny said to the man.

"Saw you and that woman over to the cafe," the skinny deputy said. "The little girl, too. Eating."

I looked at Slaughter.

"There a crime in having breakfast in this town?" I asked, already knowing what it was that'd made the blood crawl up into Johnny's face and turn it plum.

"You know what this is about!" he said.

"Don't tell me," I said. "You're the jealous type."

"I don't need a reason to kill you, McCannon."

"Get in line, Constable."

Watch the hands, that's what was going through my mind. *His hand's move, shoot him! The other one, too.*

"Stay away from May!" he said. "I won't tell you twice!"

"What is it with men like you, Slaughter? You won't keep to a woman, you won't let her go." I didn't mind airing Johnny's dirty laundry if he didn't.

"Get lost, Skinny," he ordered the deputy.

"You sure, boss? You sure you ain't gonna need me in on this?"

"Get lost!"

Skinny retreated like a dog that's been kicked by its master, a little at a time.

"What do you want, McCannon? You want to kill me, blow a hole through me with that big Remington? That what you come here for?"

"You know why I came," I said.

"No. I know why you *said* you came. But ever since you've arrived, you've done everything you could to test me. Now it's May you're testing me with. I whipped you once. Maybe I should've killed you. But I didn't. I gave you a chance. And look what it's brought me. You see how that is, me giving you a break, not killing you when I could have? Now May shows up out of nowhere, and you and her are all of a sudden cozy, sitting down having breakfast together. Skinny seen you coming out of the hotel with her. That's how you repay me for not killing you, squiring around my woman?"

"You left her in Denver. You forget that?"

"Stay out of it, McCannon, it's between her and me."

"No, not anymore, it isn't," I said.

"Since when?"

"Since she asked me."

He walked around in a tight little circle, hands on his hips, bent forward at the waist. Then he stopped walking in the tight little circle.

"You don't know," he said. "You just don't know a damn thing about anything! You leave May alone!"

I'd grown tired of Johnny Slaughter's threats and bullying.

"It's too late for that," I told him.

He cocked his head to one side, his face flushed with anger.

"You want to end it here and now," I said. "Go ahead, pull your piece. This conversation is getting old."

And for a long, drawn-out moment, I thought he might just pull his pistol. He was breathing hard and the sweat was beading on his forehead. Then the air seemed to go out of him.

"Why don't you just climb on the next stage and go back where you came from? Why do you have to try and bring more trouble to this place than what's already here?"

Something had changed in him, the voice, the stance, the eyes. Whatever it was, it had changed him from just two minutes before. He looked suddenly like an old bull all worn out, ready to lie down.

"I lost track," he said. "I lost track of who I was. Lost track of May and Tess . . . everything. I came here, found it to my liking, married a woman. I figured May—a good-looking woman like her—wouldn't have trouble finding another man. Me, I didn't consider myself that much of a find. You can understand that, can't you, McCannon? How a man can get like that, start thinking like that?"

He looked at me, the eyes set close together in that brutal face.

"I'd almost forgotten about her. Now she shows up outta the blue. Her and Tess. What'm I supposed to do? Leave the woman I married? Leave Deadwood, my job? Give everything up for a woman I ain't seen in three years? Someone I'd written off?"

"May will take care of herself," I said, "as long as you let her alone."

"First you, then her . . ." he said. "Things was going good for me. Now all this has to happen."

"It could get worse," I said.

"How?" he muttered. His brooding face was full of anguish.

"I could find out you were involved in the killings of those women."

"Alex Dupage's girls? You accusing me of being part of that? Who're you to accuse *me* of being part of *that*?"

The right hand shifted slightly.

"Don't!" I warned.

"You come into my goddamn town and accuse me of murdering whores!"

"I'm not accusing anybody, Constable. Not yet I'm not. But it doesn't matter to me whether or not you wear that badge if I find out you were involved. I'll take you to the nearest court and see you hanged."

"You're not just some damn bounty hunter, are you?"

"I didn't come for the reward, if that's what you're asking."

"You're a federal man?"

"No."

"Who sent you, then?"

"It doesn't matter."

"I didn't kill those damn whores."

"If you didn't, I'm willing to bet you know who did."

A muscle in his cheek twitched; his hand held steady. He was thinking, wondering if he could pull his piece and fire it into me before I could pull mine and do the same to him. But you can only think about something like that for just so long. You wait too long, more than a second or two, it's too late. Anybody that's ever been there knows that much.

I could see it in his eyes, he knew it was too late to threaten me any more.

"If I knew who killed them," he said, "I'd have arrested them."

"I'm not convinced," I said.

"What, that I didn't do it, or that I'd have arrested them?"

"Either one."

"Believe what you want," he said. "But proving it is another matter. You won't be able to prove anything in this gulch. Hell, there's not even any law here, other than me. Or did you forget that?"

"That law is whoever is willing to enforce it," I said. "I don't think that's you. You want to tell me anything, now's the time."

"You're way off, McCannon. *Way* off."

"Mac! Goddam, honey, what ya and ol' Johnny doin' back here, the dosey-do?"

Calamity Jane came down the alley, swinging her arms in that exaggerated way she had, a half-used whiskey bottle in one hand.

"We finished here?" Slaughter said.

Jane had been drinking. It was plain the way she strutted, the way her face was flushed pink. She had a Navy revolver stuck inside her belt.

"Mornin', Johnny," she hooted, and did a little dance around him.

"Go to hell, Jane!"

"Well, ain't ya just the most gracious thing?" She grinned as he stepped past her. "How's Lulu Divan? And how's the wife?"

Johnny threw her a hard look. I could guess what he might have done to her if I hadn't been there.

"That Johnny's lost his sense of humor," Jane said, twisting slowly around in a circle, her arms spread wide, like wings.

Seeing her again called up the name she'd given me the night before—Leo Loop.

"Good ta see ya, Mac! Ya ready for a real woman yet?"

"Tell me about Leo," I said.

She didn't stop twirling, lost in her own revelry.

"Leo? Where'd ya hear that name, Mac?"

"You," I said. "Leo Loop. You remember, Jane?"

She stopped twirling and pulled the cork out of the bottle she held in her hand. Fumbling, the bottle slipped from her hand and the contents leaked out. She fell to her knees, trying to save some of it, the whiskey dribbling through her fingers.

"Jeezus, Mac!"

I pulled her to her feet still clutching the bottle and what was left in it.

"Who's Leo Loop, Jane?"

She looked at me with eyes like those of a terrified bird. She felt puny, all bones, her body wasted away from the drink and the life.

"I need a drink . . . Mac!" she said, those wild bird eyes peering down to the bottle in her hands.

"No, you don't need a drink, Jane. You've had a drink, you don't need another, not right now."

Her mouth drew down. She squeezed her eyes shut like I was about to hit her. I eased up on my grip. She shoved the bottle to her lips and drained what she'd saved from spilling into the dirt.

"Tell me about Leo Loop," I said.

"Jeezus Mac," she uttered, her mouth opening and closing like a fish out of water. "Leo's 'bout the majorest player in the whole damn gulch, that's all!"

"Go on."

She reeled away, now that I let her.

"Billy knew Leo. Leo wanted Billy to front fer him. Wanted Billy in his vest pocket 'cause of who Billy was, 'cause of Billy's rep. But Billy told Leo to kiss his white shiny behind—that he wasn't no shill fer nobody. Leo told Billy, he dint go along with things, Billy wan't goin to be around long in Deadwood." She paused, put the bottle to her lips, but it was empty. She held it out in front of her, looked at it, then flung it aside. "Damn and hell!"

"You know for certain this conversation took place between Bill and Leo?" I asked.

She looked at me the same way she looked at the empty bottle, with a lot of disappointment, like we were both something to be pitied.

"Know? Dint I tell ya me and Bill was married? Dint I tell ya that? Don't married folks tell one another things at night when they're laying in bed together? Billy told me all about Leo Loop and his offers to have Bill shill fer him. Bill said it'd be a cold day in hell fer he'd shill fer a pimp like Leo!"

How much was the truth? From what I knew, Jane and Bill were never married. And there was little evidence to prove that they were anything more than casual acquaintances. How much was the truth, and how much had Jane made up in her own besotted mind?

"Where can I find this Leo Loop, Jane?"

She stumbled toward me and got close enough for me to have to turn my head to keep from breathing her breath.

"Ya don't want to find him," she whispered, in a voice that was near a growl.

"Why is that?"

"'Cause he'll kill ya, just like he killed my darlin' Bill." She let out a groan, caught the brim of her hat in both hands, and danced around in a circle. "'Cause he'll kill ya just like he did Bill! . . . Just like Bill!" Her voice turned sing-song.

"You've never met him, have you, Jane, Leo Loop?"

She stopped circling long enough to glare at me, squinting her eyes, unsquinting them.

"Ya sayin' I'm a damn liar, Mac?"

"Did you ever meet this man?"

"Ain't no one calls Jane Canary a damn ol' liar!" She tried jerking the Navy from her belt. I grabbed her hand, twisted the piece free, looked at it. It was rusty, pitted, the hammer missing. She couldn't have shot me with it if I had pulled the trigger for her.

"Jane, you're not only drunk, you're crazy pulling a busted pistol on a man!"

She sat right down on the ground and began to bawl. Whether the performance was real or not, I couldn't tell. Whether or not what she'd told me about Leo Loop and his threats toward Bill Hickok was something else I couldn't be sure of.

I waited for a few minutes to see if Jane would come around again, talk a little sense to me, stop the playacting, if that is what it was. But when she didn't, I offered her a hand up.

"Don't need no dang help," she bawled.

She was wretched and sad, and who knew exactly what secrets she kept within that frail and fragile heart?

I pulled her to her feet in spite of her protest.

"I'm sorry you spilled your bottle," I said, reaching into my pocket. "Here, buy one on me, for the one you dropped."

She blinked, and brushed back the tears that had been forced from her eyes.

"I ain't no charity case, if that's what yar thinkin'."

"Did I say that?"

She narrowed her eyes.

"I ain't no liar, neither."

"No one said you were, Jane."

She looked at the money I was holding out to her.

"I dint mean to pull my Navy on ya, Mac. Ya know I'd never shoot a friend."

"I know."

"Ya believe me, don't ya?"

"I believe you wouldn't shoot me, Jane."

"No, I mean about that other, about what Billy told me about Leo."

"I'll follow it up."

A crooked smile eased itself across her mouth and suddenly she was childlike again. That was the best way to describe her at times, childlike.

She scratched at her hip.

"I could use a loan," she said. "But it'd be just a loan, ya unnerstand?"

"Sure. Pay me back when you get it," I said.

"Yeah, Mac. Jane don't welch on her loans, ya can ask anybody."

She took the money carefully from my hand, like it was a fresh bottle of whiskey and she didn't want to spill any of it. She patted my hand.

"Yar all right, Mac."

I watched her strut down the alley toward the street.

"Jane?"

She half turned around, nearly fell.

"Maybe you could use some of that money to buy yourself a meal. It might not hurt you to eat a little something," I suggested.

She nodded her head.

"Ah, Mac, I'll consider it. Ya know, I ain't ever had much of an appertite."

I made myself a cigarette and smoked it as I headed for the telegraph office.

It was time to send that wire to Ben.

22

I sent the wire to Ben, told him what I'd learned so far, and urged his presence as soon as he could free himself of his obligations in Cheyenne. I needed to explain some things to him, the part about Alex and me. Only I didn't mention any of that in the telegram.

My next move was to try and locate Leo Loop.

I began asking around. It didn't take me long to learn Leo owned a place called the Lucky Strike Saloon, up the street from Nutall & Mann's Number Ten. At least I'd learned that Leo Loop actually existed.

I had to admit—entering the Lucky Strike—it was a lot more elegant than you'd expect in a town like Deadwood.

Shafts of light filtered in through the front windows and angled across the floorboards coated with sawdust, tobacco plugs, and brass spittoons. Hanging on over the back bar was a large painting of reclining nudes, their eyes cast heavenward.

The place was quiet at that time of day, except for a back table of four men wearing plug hats conversing with one another.

A swamper was going around carrying out the spittoons. He limped; another busted-down cowboy doing the only work left to a man whose only education was horses and cows.

Two burly bartenders were carrying in barrels from a beer wagon parked out front.

I waited until one of the bardogs took a break, wiped his brow with a kerchief, and said, "Wadda'll it be?"

"Coffee, if you've got any," I said.

He looked perturbed.

"Nickel," he said. "That's how much a cup of coffee is." When I tossed a nickel on the bar, he said, "Refills are free."

His shirt was soaked with sweat from carrying the barrels.

"Anything else?" he asked, as he took the nickel off the bar and looked at it like it wasn't worth his time.

"Leo Loop," I said. "You know of a man named Leo Loop?"

He cocked his head, looked at me with tired eyes.

"You gotta be joking," he said.

"Why's that?"

"Everyone in Deadwood knows Leo Loop."

"I'm new," I said.

He grunted. "You and a hunnerd others that pour in every day. That's Leo in the corner—he owns the place."

"Which one?" I said.

"This one," he said.

"No, I mean, which one is he?"

"Oh, the fat one with the fancy vest and the cookie-duster."

"Thanks," I said.

"Don't mind, I'll be gettin' back to work now. Red get's peeved if he thinks I'm slacking."

"A couple of more questions, you don't mind?" I said.

He offered me a look of impatience.

"Mister," he said. "Red won't like me standing around yakking. It's delivery day, or didn't you notice?"

I laid a pair of silver dollars on the bar.

"That's for you if you'll answer a couple of my questions," I said.

He picked them up and slipped them into his pocket, making sure the other guy hauling the beer barrels didn't see him do it.

"Say, Harve, what's up, ya helpin' out here or not?" the other barman said.

"Can't you see I got a customer, Red?"

The guy grunted, settled the barrel behind the bar and went back outside muttering something to himself.

"Hurry up, ask your questions," Harve said.

"I hear Leo is the boss dog around Deadwood," I said. "If you want to do any business in this town, you need to get Leo's blessing first."

"Depends on what you mean," Harve said.

"Don't be coy," I warned. "That's good money in your pocket."

"Yeah, maybe you heard it right," Harve said, leaning over the bar and speaking softly. "Leo's sorta the man in town, you want to put it that way."

"He runs things?"

"You could say that."

"I'm asking."

"Yeah, I'd say he pretty much run things."

"Gambling, whores, things like that?"

Harve nodded.

"Somebody want to set up a game, maybe run a few of his own girls, they'd have to see Leo first? "Suppose a man skipped seeing Leo and just set up his operation? What then?"

"Look," he said, keeping his voice low, "I could lose more than just my job here for being out of line about things—you understand?"

He swallowed, looked over to Leo Loop and the other men with him.

"Maybe you ought to go talk to him," Harve said, nodding in the direction of the fat man at the rear table.

Then the other guy, Red, brought in another barrel of beer, set it down, and wiped his face with the sleeve of his shirt.

"This going to take all day?" he asked Harve. "You serving this fellow a cup of coffee or planning an evening out at the opera?"

"I gotta get back to work here," Harve said.

I took my cup and walked over to the table of the men wearing the plug hats.

"Mr. Loop," I said.

Four unhappy faces looked up at me, Leo's one of them.

They were all well dressed: clean white shirts, cravats, claw-hammer coats. Their hands were soft, the nails neatly trimmed. They were hands that didn't know work, other than the work it takes to count money or cut into an expensive steak.

The fat man with the cookie-duster mustache said, "We're having a business meeting here, sir."

"Your bartender makes a good cup of coffee," I said.

He didn't try to hide his displeasure with the interruption. His soft gray eyes shifted toward the two men carrying in the barrels.

"Yes, well, I'll bring that to his attention the next opportunity I get," Loop said sarcastically.

"I'm new in town," I said, before he could turn his attention to the three others with him.

The soft gray eyes shifted, grew agitated.

"That's all very interesting," he said. "I applaud your enterprise!" Then he returned his attention to the others, grinning, like he'd made some sort of joke. They chuckled, two of them. The third man looked like he'd never know a moment's worth of pleasure in his whole life. He was a lean, cadaverous man with drooping bloodhound eyes and a sagging face, long and folded in lines. Probably on a full moon, he bayed.

"I'm thinking of going into business," I said.

That got Leo's interest just a little.

"What sort of business would that be?" Leo asked, without bothering to look up.

"A gambling operation, maybe some joy girls. I heard I ought to see you first. So now I've seen you, now you know."

He turned his head, the thick flesh under his chin bulging over his tight paper collar. His skin was an ash gray, smooth yet from a morning shave, no doubt from the local barber, not his own hand. He smelled of bay rum and sweat.

"Who told you you needed to see me?" he asked, his manner nonchalant, but still curious.

"Let's just say that's the word on the street, that if I want to do business in Deadwood, I should see you first."

"Gentlemen, if you'll excuse me," he said, scraping his chair back away from the table. "It seems this gentleman and I have a matter that needs discussing."

They all muttered their assent like the fine businessmen they were.

"My office is back there," Leo said as he stood up, his bulk pressing against the wool jacket he wore.

I followed him back to a small but well-appointed room. A large desk took up most of it. He took up residence in a brass-tack leather chair and indicated for me to sit in the one across from him. The chair was made of elk horns, the seat covered in hide.

"I didn't catch your name, sir," he said.

"Quint McCannon," I said. There was no point in lying to him about it, he'd find out if he wanted to.

He rubbed a place behind his left ear with his forefinger.

"So you've come here to Deadwood to get rich, have you?"

"Something like that."

"And you aim to do it by setting up your own operation—gambling, prostitution, that it?"

He had a smooth voice, oiled, like a man that sells cura-tives off the back of a wagon; elixirs that he mixes up out of coal oil and alcohol and snake heads, promising the customer that it will cure lumbago, dropsy, and waning sexual desire. A man like Leo with that smooth voice could sell a lot of snake oil, I figured.

"Something like that," I said in answer to his question.

"And you were told you needed to check with me first?"

"That's why I'm here, to let you know."

"Because I sort of control things, is that what you heard?"

"Yeah, that's what I heard."

"Indeed." He smiled, the fatness of his face becoming a gray moon.

"So, if it's not true," I said, "then why the private meeting?"

He removed a cigar from a hand-carved box atop his desk. He bit off the end of the stogie and held a match an inch under the tip until it caught fire, then he drew in a long, deep lungful of smoke before slowly blowing it out in a blue stream.

He held the cigar between his fingers and rolled it back and forth as he took stock of me. Finally he gave a smug smile.

"I have to plead innocent," he said, his gray eyes expres-sive. "What can I tell you? The things you've heard about me are false. I have only this modest club, a small, simple operation out of which I do a meager business. I am, like everyone else who has come here to Deadwood, merely a man looking for the golden promise."

"So, then, I guess it doesn't matter to you that I start up my own operation, go into competition with you?"

His left hand slowly came up, the fingers touching the ends of the cookie-duster as though testing to see if the barber had waxed them well enough this morning.

"I have no concerns about your wanting to become a

businessman in our booming little town, Mr. McCannon.
What you do is strictly your business."

"Then I was misinformed," I said, not buying it for a
minute. "Sorry to disturb your meeting."

I stood, ready to leave.

"Ah, there is just one little matter, however," he said,
clearing a throat that didn't need to be cleared.

"Go on," I said, waiting to hear the rest of it.

"You see, I am the head of the business council here in
Deadwood, elected by the Deadwood Business Commission, some of whom you met out there at the table. And
as such, I am responsible for making sure that any new
business that goes up here in town has a proper business
license. And of course there is the matter of monthly associ-
ation fees that must be paid as a member of the council.
It helps to regulate the town's growth, and also to police
our own, you see."

"How much?"

He beamed.

"A man who gets right down to it—I like that," he
said, clearly pleased that I had not challenged the obvious
shakedown.

"How much?" I repeated.

"The license will cost you a thousand dollars. The
monthly fee will be twenty-five percent of your gross take,
as audited by me personally. It's what I do best," he said.
"Count money."

"And if I fail to buy a license and pay the monthly dues?"

"Then, sir," he said with feigned disappointment, "you
shan't be doing your business here in Deadwood, or anywhere else in the Gulch, for that matter."

"How long do I have to think about it?"

"Take all the time you want, Mr. McCannon. Only don't
attempt to open up your operation until you've paid your
fees."

"I'll let you know," I said.

"Yes, do that. And best of luck to you, sir."

Harve and Red were going at it outside near the beer wagon. A smashed barrel lay in a pool of foam near the back of the wagon. Both men had their fists raised like prizefighters, dancing around each other in a small circle, cussing each other, and making lots of hard threats.

I sidestepped them and headed for Alex's, now that I had something solid to go on; I needed to put the next piece of the puzzle into place. At least, that's the reason I gave myself for going to see her.

23

Cherry Bee opened the door to my knock.

"Mistah Mac," she said; her smile told me she was happy to see me.

"Miss Alex home?" I asked.

"She's taking her bath."

"I can come back," I said.

"Oh no, suh. She say that if you come, to send you to see her."

"You sure?"

She grinned.

"Yas suh, I'm sure."

Cherry Bee took my hat. My head was nearly back to normal, so I didn't mind taking the hat off.

"My, your clothes sho could use a cleaning," Cherry Bee said. "Looks like you been rolling around in the mud, or somethin'. An' look at that face! Mistah Mac, you've been in trouble again, ain't ya?"

"Accident this time," I said, choosing not to go into it again. I took off the duster and handed it to her. She held it out away from her and wrinkled her nose.

"Well, at least you wearing a nice clean shirt," she said. "That's the gentleman in you. A gentleman always makes sure he's got on a clean shirt, if nothin' else."

"I'll have to take your word for it," I told her. "I've never thought of myself in quite that way, as a gentleman."

She giggled.

"Miss Alex is back there, just knock on the door."

"Maybe I should wait," I suggested.

"No, suh, I don't think so. She say that if you come, to send you back."

I knocked lightly.

"Come in."

She was reclined in tub of water and soap bubbles that reached the notch just below her throat and hid her beauty. A bare knee protruded from the water, wet and shiny. Her hair was pinned up, drawn away from her oval face, the milk white skin. Her arms rested along the top of the tub, the hands dangling over the sides.

"I wondered when you'd be coming," she said.

"I don't like having to stand in line."

Those beautiful green eyes narrowed at the remark, darkened just a shade.

"What's that supposed to mean?" she said.

"Last evening," I said. "I came by last evening, but you already had company."

She didn't say anything. One of the hands reached over and took a glass of red wine that had been sitting on a small marbletop stand next to the tub. She brought the glass to her mouth, the wine deep red against the light in the room. She touched the glass to her mouth, to the curved lips that I remembered so well for their sweetness and delicacy.

She held the glass of wine there to her lips, her eyes watching me. I waited for her to say whatever it was she wanted to say. But instead she just stared, the lips pursed to drink, the long, slender fingers wrapped around the glass's stem.

"Edwin came to visit," she said.

"Yeah, I know."

Her gaze refused to look away, almost as if it were challenging me.

"That bothers you," she said, "that Edwin was here?"

"Hell yes, it bothers me."

"It shouldn't, Quint."

"I'm sorry I can't be as casual about it as you."

This time she flinched—just a little.

"You make it difficult between us," she said softly.

"What am I supposed to feel?" I asked.

"I don't know, Quint. I've never lied to you about who I am. You're free to believe whatever you chose. But I thought I made it clear the other night how I felt about you."

"I won't apologize for how I feel about you seeing him," I said.

"No, I didn't think you would. But you're making something of this that doesn't need to be."

I was tired of talking about Edwin John-Davies. Instead, I wanted to talk about what she knew of Leo Loop.

"Tell me what you know about Leo Loop," I said.

She shrugged, her bare wet shoulders lifting slightly out of the bathwater.

"I don't know that much about him," she said. "Leo and I are somewhat in competition, I suppose you could say. But not really. As I explained in our first conversation, I'm not a madam and my girls aren't what Leo's girls are. There's a big difference between us."

"How come you didn't mention his name the first time we talked?"

One long fingertip trailed itself around the rim of the wineglass, a light, delicate movement.

"There was no reason to mention his name," she said. "He does what he does, and I do what I do."

"He does more than just that," I said. "The way I hear it, he controls the pleasure trade in Deadwood."

"Yes, I've heard that, too. But it has nothing to do with me."

"It seems to me it has everything to do with you, Alex. If it's true, then you would've had to pay him off in order to run *your* business. That seems to me like an important piece of information you left out of our conversation that first night."

Her gaze settled on the glass again, watching the tip of her finger rub the lip. I remembered just how delicate those fingers felt, the way they traveled over my bare skin, pressed into my back.

I remembered at one point kissing her hands.

"Mr. Loop paid me a visit when I first arrived in Deadwood," she said, the tip of her finger touching her upper lip to remove a bead of wine.

"He stated that his position was as head of Deadwood's Business Commission, I believe he called it. He said that I would need to pay a licensing fee to him and his group. He also said that in addition, I would be obligated to pay a percent of my gross income as a monthly fee. I told him I wouldn't be much of a businesswoman if I were to pay such exorbitant fees."

"And?"

"I declined his . . . offer."

"Just like that? He didn't do anything about it when you started your escort service?"

She set the empty wineglass down, the fingers reluctant to let go, always reluctant to let go of whatever they might be in contact with. I could feel my skin tingle.

"Oh, he came a time or two after that and restated his position on the matter. Each time, he was a little more insistent that I buy a license. But I simply refused."

"Wait a minute," I said. "You mean he let you operate your escorts without a problem?"

Her eyes widened just a bit.

"I'm not as naive as you may think, Quint," she said. "I hired Doc to protect my interests and my business. I'm sure without someone like Doc to represent me, Leo Loop might have been less amicable about my doing business in his town."

"So he left you alone because Doc was working for you?" I said.

"Yes."

"No, he didn't," I said. "Three of your young women have been murdered. Doc didn't stop that."

I saw the wounded look invade her eyes.

"You think Leo killed them?" she said. "Dottie and Eva and Flora?"

"You said it yourself the first time we talked, that it could've been a joy house operator, someone warning you to take your business elsewhere. Leo seems the logical choice, don't you think?"

"But as you stated," she intoned, "why not just kill me if that was the purpose—to put me out of business, why the others? They were just working for me."

"I don't know. But I'd say Leo Loop is the man who's behind it. Now, it's just a matter of proving it. And in this town, that's going to be a little difficult. Everyone seems to be in everyone else's pocket, and there is no law here except for Johnny Slaughter. And unless I'm wrong about him, he's in Leo's pocket as well."

Suddenly she stood up, the soap and water sliding off her except for the dark triangular patch of her womanhood. She stood there unashamedly allowing me to look at her, wanting me to look at her, it seemed.

"Would you hand me the towel, Quint?"

I handed it to her. She waited to see if I would do anything else as she hesitated in taking it.

And when I didn't do anything else, she took the towel and wrapped it around herself, strands of her russet hair clinging to her neck and in places around her face where it'd come loose from the combs.

Still she stood there looking at me, small puddles of water collecting around her feet.

"How *will* you prove that Leo Loop was responsible for the murders?" she asked.

I pulled my makings and started putting together a shuck, something to occupy my hands, my mind, my thoughts from what I really wanted to be doing.

I put the smoke together, spilling just a little of the tobacco, and fired it with a match, snapping out the flame, then taking in a deep breath of the blue smoke before answering her question.

"The way I see it," I told her, "Leo's not the type to do his own killing; he hires it done."

She moved the towel, using a loose end to touch the damp strands of her hair along her neck. I wanted to take it from her and drop it to the floor.

"So, you'll find whoever it was that Leo hired and get him to tell you the truth," she said. The way she looked at me, I was willing to bet she knew exactly what I was thinking about the towel.

"And then, when you do," she said, stepping closer to me, "you'll have enough evidence to see that he's arrested."

"I'd like to think that's how it will go," I said.

"Yes," she murmured. "That is how it will go."

She dropped the towel.

She was still wet in places. Places that soaked through my shirt when she kissed me.

"Is this a good idea?" I asked.

"Do you think it is?" she whispered.

"Probably not . . ." My face was buried in the softness of her hair as she reached up and unpinned the combs and let her hair fall free.

"We agreed, didn't we . . . ?" she said softly.

"Yeah."

Her mouth was wet, her skin dewy, soft, warm from the bath. I could taste the wine on her lips, her tongue as it searched my mouth.

"I'm glad you're here," she whispered.

Those fingers, the ones that were holding the glass a minute ago, circling the rim so delicately, were tracing over my chest now, down along my ribs as she reached her hands inside my shirt, undoing the buttons. My skin prickled from her touch.

"You like being here, don't you?" she said, the throaty whisper of her voice intoxicating me.

"Yes, I like it."

Her teeth bit into my lip, then she kissed me again, only this time the kiss was more wet, more full, more wanting. And so was I.

The bathwater was still warm when I slipped into it.

Alex insisted I enjoy the luxury while she had Cherry Bee take my clothes and clean them.

Alex sat by the tub and washed my hair, back, and chest.

She paused several times, kissed my jaw, my chin, my mouth in little light ways, while her hands slipped below the water to tantalize me.

It seemed I couldn't get enough of her.

"I wired Ben," I said, feeling the need to be completely honest with her, and maybe myself.

The caressing paused for a brief moment, then continued.

"I asked him to finish up his business in Cheyenne and come here. That was before I found out more about Leo Loop."

"So now you won't need him to come," she said.

"Maybe not. If I can get this cleared up before he leaves Cheyenne."

"You will—I'm sure of it, Quint."

"I need to be honest with Ben," I said. "If he comes to Deadwood, he might be expecting to renew old feelings with you, Alex."

Again the hands stopped, but just briefly.

"I doubt that he would still have an interest in me after all this time," she said.

"Either way, Alex, I need to tell him."

"Do whatever you want, Quint. Tell him whatever you must."

Her lips brushed my throat as I leaned my head back to look up at her. I reached up and brought her mouth around and kissed it.

She seemed perfect in every way. And that's why I couldn't understand that one little part of me that was holding back, a feeling I couldn't quite pin down. I wondered if maybe it was because I'd been too long without the right woman in my life, or spent too many nights with the wrong women.

I even wondered if it had something to do with my late wife, my reason for not completely letting myself be swept up in Alex.

Whatever it was, it was something disturbing, subtle, like a knock at the door in the middle of the night. It was something I wished I hadn't felt.

We finished up the bath, and Cherry Bee delivered my clothes, fresh and clean, smelling like they were full of wind and sun.

We ate a nice lunch of oysters and cheese and drank glasses of red wine and spoke without speaking; talking with our eyes.

The sun outside was giving way to more stormclouds. Cherry Bee brought us coffee to go with a cobbler she'd baked.

"They say the snow comes early to the Black Hills," Alex said, as we watched the clouds gather over the gulch.

"I ever mention I don't care for winters?"

She smiled.

It was small innocuous talk, the sort of talk lovers engage in after they've made love, but not the sort of talk that people who are *in love* have. Maybe it was just me, my jaded history since Mary Lee died. Lots of women, lots of failed attempts at happiness, had left me lacking in the conversation department.

I wasn't sure that Alex was any more comfortable than I was with the small talk.

We were sitting there like that, watching the storm, sipping our coffee, when Cherry Bee knocked at the door, then opened it and said, "Look who's up and about."

Cherry Bee had Rose with her. Rose looked wan but rested. Her eyes were still rimmed red, but she offered me a smile when she saw me.

"I guess I slept like crazy," she said.

"Won't you have some lunch?" Alex offered.

Rose looked first at me, then Alex, then back at me. Unless I was wrong, I thought I could see the fleeting disappointment in her eyes as she sat down between us.

I wasn't certain, but I thought I knew why.

24

I hoped I was wrong about Rose, about her feelings toward me. I had one woman too many in my life right then. Between Alex, and May, back at the hotel, I didn't want to be juggling another woman's feelings. I figured with Rose, it was something other than love. But I didn't know well enough to guess if that was it for certain, and I had no time to try and figure it out.

The skies over Deadwood had turned almost black, the clouds bunching up like they were trapped. Then it began to snow.

I excused myself from the company of Alex and Rose; Cherry Bee brought me my duster, most of the mud brushed out, and I put it on before going outside. I'd need a heavier coat, now that the weather had turned bad.

The wind kicked up and the snow swirled down in large flakes and some of the town's citizens came out on the street to watch. Kate Elder and Doc Holliday were among the spectators.

Kate was dressed in a long ash gray coat with black fur collar and black fur trim around the cuffs. She wore a small gray matching hat. She had an arm through Doc's, looming over him. He seemed frail by comparison.

"Oh, look, Doc! It's snowing!" she said jubilantly, as I came within earshot.

"I can see that, Kate," he said, his voice barely audible. He coughed and she supported him against the spasms.

The way she looked at him during that moment was the way a woman looks at a man she has love for. The same wistful look of love a woman has for a child. She looked at Doc like he was her manchild.

Doc's face was ashen, with a bluish tinge to it, and his hands shook as he fought the coughing spell and Kate kept saying, "At's all right, Doc, 'at's all right, baby."

I don't know if he saw me or not; I didn't much care. I felt sorry for him, but we weren't friends, and we were never going to be friends.

As I started across the street, I saw another old face from the past; it was like someone had called a convention in Deadwood for every gunhand, pistoleer, and shootist in the territory. It was a credit to the damnable advertisements Alex had put in the territorial newspapers.

Ed Siringo rode a tall piebald mare. He drew back on the reins when he saw me.

"McCannon," he said, sitting there high up on that sixteen-hand horse.

"Ed."

"You come too, huh?"

"Not for the same reason," I told him.

"Not the money?" he said. "Then why?"

"As a personal favor for a friend. You know him, Ben Beadle," I said.

"Yeah, I know Ben. How's he play into this?"

"It's a long story, Ed, and it's snowing, and I'd just soon get down the street to the mercantile and see if I can find me a warmer coat."

"I talked to that lady yesterday," he said. "That Alex Dupage. She's a looker, damn if she ain't."

"Yeah. Well, Ed, like I said, I'd like to see about that coat, you don't mind."

He walked the tall piebald alongside me as I continued down the street. It was already beginning to turn muddy, that's how heavy and fast the snow was falling.

"Heard you killed King Fisher," he said.

"News travels fast," I said, without any interest in discussing the matter with a man that was cut from the same cloth as King Fisher.

"Well, I don't suppose the world's going to mourn his loss," Siringo said, in a joking manner.

"I wouldn't know," I said, trying my best to keep the conversation between me and Ed at a minimum.

"I guess it couldn't be helped," Siringo said.

"He brought it on himself."

"That's what I heard. Tried to shoot you through a winda glass." Ed's laugh broke through the crust of his beard. "Sumabitch never did have much sense. Shoot you through a winda glass!"

I arrived at the mercantile only to find a sign hanging in the window: *Having a Tooth Pulled, Come Back Tomorrow,* it read. Just my luck, I thought: to run into Ed Siringo the same day the only man I could buy a coat from was having his tooth pulled.

Damn!

"Looks like you're outta luck on that new coat," Ed offered. "Cold as a sucker, ain't it?"

"Let me ask you something," I said.

"What's that?"

"What would it take to get you to leave town?"

He stood in his stirrups, stretching his legs, scratching at his backside.

"Carbuncles," he said. "I get carbuncles rubbed on my ass from these long rides."

I waited for him to answer my question.

Finally, after he'd stretched his legs enough, he said, "It'd take me getting that reward money that woman's offerin'. I come all the way from Ogalla. You know how far a ride that is, Ogalla? Especially for a man that's got carbuncles?''

"How much would it take, Ed?"

"Two thousand, that's what she said."

"How about five hundred and you don't have to do a thing but leave town? How would that be?"

He sat back down again, the snow collecting on the shoulders of his capote, in his beard.

"Well, now that's a tempting offer," he said. "But it still ain't no two thousand, is it? It's a dang long ways from two thousand."

"So is a bullet in the back of your skull," I said.

His eyes grew larger under his heavy lids.

"You ain't trying to scare me, are you?"

"You know this business," I said. "You're not the only gun in town wanting to collect that money."

His mouth curled up through the hair of his face.

"I'll take my chances, same as you,"

"I'm here for a different reason, Ed, like I told you. I'm not here for the reward money."

"Yeah, and I don't piss yellow, McCannon. Same as you."

"Suit yourself," I told him. "Five hundred for leaving Deadwood isn't the worst offer I ever heard of."

"See you around, McCannon," he said, and turned the piebald's head back toward the direction of the saloons and whorehouses.

It was just one more complication, the way I saw it, Ed's presence in Deadwood. But what else was new?

I continued on to the livery. The old man was standing out front, staring at the storm. He had an old wood burner pulled out front, its door busted off, the flames cooking a pine log he'd been feeding it.

"Hey, sonny," he said. "Look at that damn snow, would ya?"

"How much for that coat?" I asked him.

He looked at me, the watery eyes pulled back within the bony brow of his skull.

"How much fer the coat?"

"Yeah, the one you're wearing."

He looked at it, back at me.

"Hell, I wouldn't take a hunner dollars fer it—can't you see it's snowing? It'll be colder than a well digger's nuts around here, now that the snow's come."

"Tell you what," I offered. "I'll give you twenty-five for the coat, and when I leave here in a few days," I'll sell it back to you for five. How'll that be?"

He twisted his lips thinking about it.

"That for sure?" he said. "You leaving in a few days?"

"For sure," I said, and meant it.

"Done!" he said.

It was a lot of coat, heavy as hell, but it was warm. The main trouble was, it'd take some doing to reach the self-cocker under all that curly hair. So, I took the pistol out and slipped it into the pocket of the coat.

I left the old man counting his new money. He didn't seem to mind that it was snowing and he was only in his shirtsleeves.

I decided to go pay Tommy O'Dule another visit. I needed to find out who was doing Leo Loop's killing for him.

"Tommy ain't here," the man behind the bar said, when I asked for him.

"When will he be here?" I asked.

The man was of slight built, nervous with a bad tic just below his right eye. His hair was long and straight and plastered down with rosewater. I could smell it, the cheap scent of the rosewater coming off him.

"About never," the man said. "That's when Tommy'll be back. He left town this morning on the stage for Cheyenne."

The bartender's manner was like that of a small unpleasant dog.

"He say anything?" I made one final attempt. "Tommy, why he was leaving?"

"Yeah, he said, 'See you around, sucker.' That's what he said."

"Just like that," I said. "Tommy ups and leaves his job?"

"You think pouring drinks for miners and whores is some sort of a plum job?" he said, his arms crossed over his chest, "standing on your feet ten hours a day, cleaning up men's puke 'cause they don't know when to give it a rest? You think that's a job a man would hate to leave?"

I'd grown a little tired of the man's attitude; he was one of those men you didn't like the instant you met him.

The doors suddenly blew open to a gust of cold wind and swirling snow trailed by a lone figure who stood for a moment in the quadrant of pewter light.

He paused long enough to let his eyes adjust, the carbine he carried rested in the crook of his arm. Then, when he saw me standing there at the bar, he crossed the room. He ordered a whiskey and drank it, then ordered a second before turning his attention to me.

"That little gal on the stage, the one dressed in buckskins pretending to be a fellow," Hector Torrez said. "She just blew out Johnny Slaughter's lights. Thought you might want to know."

25

By the time we arrived on the scene, a sizable crowd had gathered around the stricken form of Johnny Slaughter. He was lying there in the mud, stretched out on his back, his arms flung wide, the snow gathering in his dark moustaches, glazing his eyelashes. His mouth was partly open, his eyes wide and staring at a sky he could no longer see. A neat dark hole trickled a ribbon of blood across his brow. His head was slightly tilted to the side, like he'd tried to duck away from the bullet.

"How'd this happen?" I asked Torrez, pulling him aside.

"I was over there," he said, indicating the front of the bagnio he'd been hanging around since the other night. "I was keeping an eye on things. I saw your man here coming down the street. I guess he was making his morning rounds. It was quiet, me and him were the only ones out here."

The part about Rose hadn't made any sense to me from the instant Torrez said it was she that'd killed Slaughter.

"Then what?" I asked.

"He got to this point here," Torrez indicated with a

thrust of his jaw. "She come around the side of that building, just there. She said something to him, he said something back; I didn't hear what they were saying, but ol' John there seemed to get upset with her, raising his hands. That's when she shot him. Once, in the head, like you see."

"Anyone else see what happened?" I asked.

He nodded his head. "Like I said, the streets were clean, except for the three of us."

"Then what," I said, "after she shot him?"

"She went that way." He indicated the direction with a nod. I knew where she'd gone.

"I saw you talking to her alone that night out on the trail. I saw how she looked at you the rest of the trip. I figured maybe you'd want to know about this first."

"Look, Torrez," I said. "I know you're a federal lawman, but I'm asking you to steer clear of this. At least give me a chance to talk with her, find out *her* side of the story."

He looked at me, those lawmen's eyes questioning what was legal, what was duty.

"You want me to let it go," he said, "pretend like I didn't see anything, that it?"

"For her," I said. "Do it for her, not me."

He glanced at the crowed gathered around Slaughter's body. Some of them were talking about revenge, about hanging whoever'd done it.

"I've got no interest in this damn hellhole," Torrez said without changing his expression. "Other than to find what happened to Bob, I don't give a coon's ass about what goes on here."

"Thanks," I said. I turned to go. Torrez said, "Here." I looked. He had the Colt pistol in his hand. "She dropped this afterwards," he said. I took the gun and slipped it inside the pocket of the curly coat. Torrez turned his attention to the crowd, walking over and pushing them aside.

"Well, you men going to stand around gawking?" I could hear Torrez chiding them as I headed toward Alex's. "Or is someone going to carry this poor son of a bitch over to the undertaker's?"

He was a strange and unpredictable man, Deputy U.S. Marshal Hector Torrez was. And I could still hear him berating the gawkers as I made my way down the street: "He's not a goddamn circus to be looked at! Pick up his arms and feet!"

The same question kept running through my mind every step of the way: why had Rose shot Johnny Slaughter? As far as I knew, she didn't even know the man. And even if she had, it made no sense; not Rose, not that shy, troubled creature.

I knocked on the door. This time it was Alex who answered, instead of Cherry Bee.

"Thank God it's you, Quint. She's in my room!"

I went in and instinctively took my hat off when I saw her sitting there on the side of the bed, her head down, her body shaking. Cherry Bee was sitting next to her, trying hard to comfort her, her arm around Rose's shoulders, saying, "Now girl, now girl, just calm yourself down."

"Rose," I said.

She lifted her face to look at me.

"Mr. McCannon . . ." Her lips trembled, her hands shook.

"What happened out there, Rose?"

Her eyes were full of fear, tearing as she looked at me.

"He hurt . . . Mama," she stammered.

I looked at Alex for an explanation.

"She found a diary Flora kept among her things. It was in a trunk of Fora's effects. I had it stored since her death. I gave it to Rose."

"Rose," I said, sitting next to her on the bed. "Is that what the diary said, that Johnny hurt your mama?"

She nodded and bit her lower lip until it turned white.

"Where is it?" I asked Alex.

She pointed to a pile of things exposed in a small open

trunk sitting in the corner. A brown leather book lay atop the clothes; its pages were marked by a thin red ribbon.

I took the book and opened it to the place where the ribbon lay between the pages. The handwriting was delicate, small, a little difficult to read because of the misspellings. But there it was, the part about Johnny's abuse of Flora: how he'd beaten her on several occasions; how he'd always apologize for the beatings; how much she was in love with him; how he'd promised to leave his wife for her.

It was a tale of a woman left longing, clinging to unkept promises, to unrequited love, to pain and shame.

". . . I hate him and love him," the first line of the last paragraph began in that tender, unschooled hand. "I wisht he wouldn't hurt me so bad. I wisht he'd love me more and marry me like he said. I don't know if I can stand much more of this life! Oh, Dere Johnny, please, please don't hurt me no more!"

I flipped a few pages more, to the last entry. It was dated July 4th, 1876.

"I asked Johnny last night when he was going to leave—! I told him if he didn't leave her, I wood make things hard on him (tho I didn't really mean any of it). Johnny knows I know all his dirty secrets. Secrets about this town, not just about him. He got real mad when I mentioned it, about his dirty secrets. We had quite a row because of it. He slapped me and threatened me, said he would kill me if I said anything! I was sorry to have upset him so. I cried, but it did no good. He called me a b—! & cussed me in terrible ways! I'm worried that now I've gone and done it. Johnny can be a terror. Still, I love him . . ."

I closed it and handed it to Alex.

"You didn't know?"

She shook her head. "It was among her things. I didn't bother to go through them, considering the circumstances. I'm not even sure why I saved them."

"I need a word with you," I said.

We stepped outside in the hall.

"I thought you told me you never allowed your girls to be abused."

"I didn't. This was something different, something I didn't know anything about. I knew Flora was seeing someone privately, but a girl's private life is her own; I never get involved with that. Johnny was not a customer as far as I knew. They could have met anywhere—Johnny likes women. Flora was the type to be taken in by a man like Johnny. She always had these romantic notions that someday the right man would come along and he would be the answer to all her problems."

I could see that Alex was shaken by the sudden turn of events. No one who saw the anguish of the young woman sitting on the side of the bed could help but be drawn into her suffering.

"Where'd she get the gun, Quint?"

"I gave it to her," I admitted.

"Why? Why would you do a thing like that?"

"I told you, there'd been some trouble on the trail. I wanted her to be able to protect herself."

"Well, she's done more than that now. She's killed a lawman! They'll probably want to hang her for it."

"That won't happen," I told her.

"What makes you think it won't?" she said, her words sharp, angry. "Johnny has lots of friends in this town!"

"I'll need your help on this, Alex."

She cast a fretful glance toward Rose's room.

"God, Quint, this whole thing has become such a mess."

"I know, but we've got to finish it, not let it finish us."

"What is it you want me to do?" she asked.

"I want to keep her here, out of sight. Don't let her out of the house and don't let anyone in. I need time to tie Johnny to Flora's murder," I said.

Alex looked confused.

"I thought you said it was Leo you suspected."

"I think Leo was behind it, but he's not the sort that does his own dirty work. He hires it done. I think he had

Johnny on the payroll. I think Flora was getting too much under Johnny's skin and when she threatened him with the secrets he'd told her, he went to Leo with it and Leo ordered it done."

"Flora I can understand, maybe," she said. "But why would Leo and Johnny have the other girls killed? Why wouldn't they just kill me if all it came down to was wanting me out of business?"

"That's something I'll have to ask Leo," I said. "Johnny's in no shape to tell me."

There were other possibilities running through my mind—Doc Holliday, for one. The other night I'd seen him and Tommy O'Dule and Johnny having a private conversation out front of the saloon. Now Tommy'd left town suddenly and Johnny was dead. But that still left Doc, the man Alex had hired to protect her girls, but hadn't. Doc was still on my list of suspects along with Leo. Somebody knew something.

Alex's eyes were full of concern.

"Maybe I . . . we," she said, "maybe we should just get out of here."

"You know you don't want to do that, Alex."

She placed her hand on my arm, stepped close.

"I might," she said. "I've been thinking a lot about us."

"What about your friend Edwin?" I said.

"Quint—"

"It's gone too far, Alex, we've gotten too close to them."

"I'm afraid," she said. "For the first time, I'm really afraid."

"Maybe it's not so bad a thing, being afraid," I said. "Maybe it will help keep us alive."

She pressed herself against me until my arms reached up and held her. I could feel her heartbeat, her warm breath against my neck.

"I'm afraid for you," she whispered.

"Don't be. Just keep a watch on things here, Alex. Buy me some more time."

She kissed my jaw.

The feeling came over me again: what was it between us that wouldn't allow me to be completely free with her? It was a question I still didn't have an answer to. And just at the moment, I knew I couldn't afford the time to figure it all out.

There were other things to worry about; like keeping a vigilante mob of Johnny's friends from finding it was Rose that'd killed Johnny. Then I needed to tie Johnny to Flora's murder, and maybe tie Johnny to Leo Loop. Doc Holliday was still a candidate to be a part of the killings. Plus, someone had been doing their best to kill me ever since my first night in Deadwood. And even with all that to think about, there was still the matter of May Smith. How did I really feel about her? And what about her standing offer?

As I headed to the Lucky Strike, I passed the place on the street where Johnny had been shot and killed; there was a pink stain in the snow with new snow falling to cover up even that small trace of a man's death. It reminded me of just how quickly the land devours the evidence of our existence once we're gone.

When I arrived at the Lucky Strike, Leo wasn't there. The bartender, Harve, stood glumly at his post, a white apron tied around his bulging waist. His eyes were puffed, his lip cut, the dark bruises starting to form under his flesh from where Red had punched him a goodly number of times. I guess it'd turned into a real fight after all. At least looking at Harve it had.

I asked Harve where Leo was; he shook his head.

"Don't know."

I placed some silver on the bar.

"Would that help you to remember where Leo went?" I asked.

He touched fingers to his split lip.

"That Red, he hits like a son of a bitch," he said.

"Leo," I said. "Where'd he go?"

He swept up the coins, held them in his hand; his knuckles were scraped.

"Left about an hour ago," Harve said, checking the looseness of a tooth. "Climbed in his hack and took the north road. Ain't seen him since."

"Tell me something," I said. "You get in any punches?"

Harve winced. I headed for the stables.

The old man was perched outside on a three-legged stool rubbing his hands over the stove he'd been feeding the pine log to. He was wearing a blanket around his shoulders.

"Come to sell me back my coat?" he asked, his rheumy eyes, expectant.

"Not yet," I said. "But I'll rent that buckskin off you again."

"Awful damn weather to be going fer a ride, ain't it?" he said.

"You want to rent him, or not?"

"Sure, sure. If I don't, he'll just stand around and eat hay and drop horse apples I'll have to clean up."

He went inside, saddled the lineback with my Dunn Brothers and brought him out.

"Four dollars," he said. "Or did you forget?"

I paid him.

"I'd be back before dark, I was you," he said. "Storm like this could get a hell've lot worse before it's done."

"What's up that north road?" I asked.

He looked at me, gave that toothless grin.

"Hell, nothing but them hills. But if you foller it fer enough, you'll be crossing onto Mr. Davies's land. You know Mr. Davies?" he said.

"Yeah. I know him."

"Private son a buck!" the old man said. *"English.* Don't 'low nobody to trespass. Say he's had men whipped fer trespassin'. Got gold mine claims all over up there. I'd stay away, I was you."

I didn't wait around for more advice.

The snow continued to fall in large swirling flakes, just like everyone had said it would. The snow was piling up fast, and by the time I'd gone as far as what I figured was Edwin John- Davies's property line, it was nearly a foot deep.

The snow lay in white bundles on the boughs of the pines and was draped over the rock outcroppings. And where I crossed a stream, the water looked black against the whiteness of the banks.

It was deceptively beautiful, snow in the Black Hills. I could see why the Sioux were reluctant to give up this land. I could see why the white man wanted it. But the white man didn't want it for the same reason the Sioux did.

But any man with eyes could see how such beauty could seduce as well as any woman, any sin. All you had to do was take a deep breath and let your gaze travel over those black, black hills.

I didn't hear it, the bullet that struck me. It was a blow to my upper body, hard and sudden, and it carried me out of the saddle and flipped me over and over, tumbling me down the side of the ridge I'd just ascended and into a snowbank that swallowed me whole.

I lay stunned for a second, waiting to die, trying to suck air into my numbed lungs.

It was a silent world, there under the snowbank, silent and peaceful, and for a few long moments, I was willing to let it take me to that place where Mary Lee and Samuel and the Rebel flag bearer were waiting for me.

It seemed I was at peace. I tried not fighting it, the dying.

But then my lungs caught fire and instinctively I clawed through the smothering tomb of snow and gasped in a lung full of cold air.

I dug the snow out of my nostrils and rubbed it free of my eyes and sucked air until I didn't need to any longer. I could see farther up the hill that the buckskin had run a short distance, then stopped. The snow was too deep for him to want to run far. He stood there as though waiting for me to come get him.

I unbuttoned the woolly coat and looked for the bullet wound. Damndest thing was, I couldn't find one. I checked the coat and saw a small, flat matted spot where the bullet had struck but must have bounced off. Either the bullet had been of a low caliber, or it had been fired from too long a distance to go through the heavy coat. Either way, the buffalo coat had saved my life, and I was damn glad it had. I was sorry now that I'd promised the old man I'd sell it back to him.

I scrambled to a nearby rock outcropping and crawled under it just as a second shot kicked up a spray of snow inches from face. The sound of the shot echoed down the mountain and I saw a shower of snow break from a pine bough about two hundred yards from up above where I was. The buckskin was startled by the gunfire and crow-hopped through the deep snow a few paces before stopping again.

There was no point in returning fire with my self-cocker at that distance. In my haste to find Leo, I'd forgotten to bring the Creedmore with me. I might as well have tried throwing rocks as to try and hit anything so far away with just my pistol.

I hunkered down and waited. If they wanted me bad enough, they'd have to come down the mountain and get me; that's the way I saw it.

I waited a long time, listened, and kept an eye on the buckskin, who was eventually working his way back down the slope, pawing through the snow looking for grass.

I figured it was Charley Coffey up top. Maybe Fork and Tolbert, too. But at least Charley; it was his way: shooting a man from cover. Fork and Tolbert, I could only guess. But if they worked for Davies, and Charley was riding ram-rod over them, maybe they weren't above bushwhacking, either.

I checked the loads in my self-cocker, made sure they

were dry by putting in fresh ones. Checked the Colt Thunderer Torrez had retrieved and given back to me. I kicked
out the spent shell, the one Rose had popped Johnny
Slaughter with, and put in a fresh one.

I waited some more.

Finally they came. The sound of boots crunching in the
snow. Little trailing balls of snow rolled down the slope
ahead of whoever it was that was coming. Little by little
they were coming. I got ready.

From where I was squatting under the rock outcrop, I
saw Charley Coffey run out from the trees and snag the
reins of the buckskin and lead him back toward the shelter-
ing pines.

I thought about swinging around and firing off a shot,
but it was too far off, and I figured the others, Fork and
Tolbert, were perched up above, waiting for me just waiting
for such a chance to put some of their own rounds into
me.

Not today, boys.

After another several minutes, they got close enough I
could hear them whispering back and forth, asking one
another had they seen anything yet, any blood, me laid
out stiff. Naw, naw, they said; ain't seen nothing. Sumabitch
had to be down there somewhere, they assured themselves.
I was.

Tolbert stepped onto the rock outcropping I was under.
I knew it was Tolbert when I raised up from below and
shot him in the only place I could: through the groin. I
didn't aim, didn't try to pick the right spot; I just swung
up and shot him and he toppled headlong out into space
and landed with a thud ten feet away, clutching himself,
squirming in the snow, his blood turning the snow crimson
between his legs.

A shot rang off the rocks and I could feel the sting of
shattered stone against my cheek.

I ducked away again, heard Fork shout back up the ridge

that I'd just killed Tolbert. That wasn't quite true; Tolbert was dying, maybe, but I hadn't killed him yet.

Then I heard Charley Coffey call back down for Fork to close in, finish me off, and I thought, Yeah, Charley, why ain't you doing it?

It was a little bit of a risk because he was lying ten feet away and exposed in the open, but Tolbert's Winchester was lying there at his feet and if I could grab it, I increased my odds by a good bit.

I gave it a count of three, then went for it. Two, three shots cracked the air. One of the rounds slammed into Tolbert's back and he stiffened, sucked in a lungful of air, and died.

Nice going, Fork.

I grabbed the Winchester and missed getting killed by luck or poor marksmanship. Maybe both; I don't question things like that, not anymore I don't.

Charley was up there calling to Fork, asking whether or not he'd nailed me, and Fork was yelling back as to how he wasn't sure if he'd gotten me or not. Clamoring like a pair of gossips at a church social. I gauged where Fork was from his mouth.

The next time Charley called down to him about what was going on and Fork yelled back, "Nothing," I raised up and shot him with the Winchester.

He clutched his side and dropped over. He didn't say anything, didn't scream or call out for help. He just fell over into the snow. Either stone dead, I figured, or tired of answering Charley's dumb-ass questions while staying hidden up in the safety of those pines.

For a long time, there was just the silence of the snow falling.

Then Charley called out, "You get him, Fork, or what?"

I called back, "It's just you and me now, Charley. You want to come down here and settle it?"

Charley must have run out of ideas because he didn't answer. A few seconds later, I heard crashing up in the trees and saw Charley spanking the rump of his pony with the barrel of his rifle as he charged over the top of the ridge and out of sight.

I found the buckskin still tied to the bough of the pines where there was a lot of cigarette butts stubbed out in the snow.

The sun had suddenly appeared between a break in the clouds over the western horizon. It made me feel good to know that I was still alive and could still take notice of something like that, the sun breaking through the clouds. It would be dark by the time I got back to Deadwood.

By the time I rode up to the livery, the old man was properly drunk. He had a fat squaw sitting with him, warming her hands in front of the woodburner. She looked properly drunk as well.

"See what some of that coat money bought?" the old man said, holding the bottle out toward the squaw.

"She's Crow Indian. Fat, ain't she?" he said happily.

I handed him the reins.

"I like 'em fat," he said, his lips spreading across his dark gums. "More to hold onto." His laughter was phlegmy.

She said something to him in her language.

He looked at me and said, "I don't unnerstand a damn word of Crow, do you?"

My feet and hands were cold, stiff. They'd gotten wet from the snow, from falling in it and lying in it and waiting in it.

"Have a drink," he said, holding forth the bottle.

I didn't object. The whiskey put some of the fire back in my blood.

"Ya want," he said, "you can have her after I'm done."

I walked back toward the hotel.

I'd been thinking about how close I'd come again to being killed. And I'd been thinking about May Smith and all the rest of what was waiting for me in Deadwood.

26

The child was asleep, the room quiet, peaceful.

May sat in a chair, her gaze fixed on the window, staring out into the night, the sky red now from the storm, the snow collected against the sills; the glass had patterns of frost on it.

I removed the heavy coat, thankful once more that it had saved my life, and dropped on the floor over my bedroll. In spite of the cold air outside, my shirt was soaked from sweat. May watched me in silence.

I waited for her to say something.

I sat down, cross-legged on the floor and pulled off first one boot, then the other. Still she watched me. My chest was bruised from the slug that never made it through the curly coat. I winced when I touched the spot.

"Are you all right?" she said at last, as I rested my back against the wall.

"I've been better," I told her. I searched for my makings, but for some reason wasn't able to do much because of the cold stiffness of my fingers.

She moved from the bed, knelt beside me, looked into

my face. The light in the room was soft yellow. The shadows played against her face as she took the tobacco and paper from my hands and began to roll the cigarette for me.

"How bad are you hurt?" she asked.

"Not very," I said.

She wound the tobacco in the paper, licked the edges, sealing it, then twisted off the ends and handed it to me. I struck a match off the floor and the flame from it danced in front of our eyes. She moved behind me, placed her hands on my shoulders, and began to knead the flesh there where my muscles were tight and aching. Her hands were cool, the fingers strong, knowing just where to squeeze. I closed my eyes and leaned into the pleasure of it.

"I worried about you today," she said, as her hands continued working at the knots in my shoulders and neck.

"May, there's something I need to tell you," I said.

"Hush, don't talk, just let me do this, let me take away your pain."

The cigarette tasted good to me.

I reached up with my right hand and placed it atop one of hers, stopping it for a moment

"Am I hurting you?" she said.

"May, Johnny's dead."

Something audible caught in her throat, but she didn't say anything. Her other hand ceased its movement, its cool strength resting just at the back of my neck.

"He was killed earlier today," I said.

She lay her head on my shoulder near the hand I was holding.

"Why?" she said. "Why was he killed?"

"It's complicated," I said. "Maybe we can talk about why in the morning. Right now, I just need to rest."

For a long time she left her head there on my shoulder, her breath warm and soft and sweet against the side of my face. A single teardrop fell onto the back of my hand. It was warm, like rain in summer.

"I'm sorry I had to be the one to tell you, May."

She swallowed. "I didn't love him anymore," she murmured. "But I feel badly for him, and I feel sorry for myself for feeling that way."

I moved around, took her face in my hands.

"Don't be," I said. "Don't be sorry because you feel bad for him, May."

"I'm sorry for Tessie," she said. "She will never know her father now."

"Only what you choose to tell her about him," I said. "Maybe she just needs to know the good parts, May."

And for a long moment, she didn't speak except with her eyes and she moved her face closer to mine and I closed my eyes until our mouths touched.

It was a tender kiss, not at all like the way Alex had kissed me, not at all hungrily, full of heat and passion. My fingers wove themselves through her hair and she kissed me again, full and sweet and just as gentle as the first time.

"Why do I feel so alone?" she whispered.

"You're not alone," I said. "At least, not tonight."

This time, *I* kissed her.

The tips of her fingers stroked my jaw as I kissed her mouth. She made murmuring sounds and I felt her body tremble against mine and I wanted to hold her forever. Her hands lifted my shirt, pulling it over my head. Her mouth traced kisses down my neck, over my chest, as I parted the buttons of her blouse.

She whispered my name over and over as she kissed my chest and neck, and I felt the smoothness of her bare flesh under the blouse as I undid the buttons and ties.

She arched her back and I buried my face against her breasts and she moaned when I did. And I wanted her as much as I'd ever wanted anyone. But then my gaze came to rest on the sleeping child, Tess, there on the bed, and the sight of her jarred me back to reality.

"I can't do this with you, May," I said, pulling back.

She looked at me, her eyes questioning.

"I just can't feel right about it, damn if I can."

"Why, Quint?"

How could I tell her all the reasons? My affair with Alex, the murders that plagued me, my growing sense of how I'd been caught up in a situation I was never going to walk away from? How could I explain to her my own confusion about what I really wanted? And how could I explain to her that I didn't have any room in my life for her right now?

Rejection is a hell of a thing, especially when it comes from some drifter on a cold stormy night in a room full of loneliness. She didn't deserve to wake up the next morning feeling worse than she'd been feeling since she'd found out the truth about Johnny. I didn't want to be the next man in her life to cause her pain.

She withdrew.

"Twice I've asked you to my bed," she said. "Twice you've turned me down. I guess I must seem a foolish, lonely woman to you."

"No," I said. "You don't seem anything like that." She turned her head to the side, refusing to look at me. Ashamed, maybe, but without reason to be.

My hand touched the side of her face, brought it round so I could look into her eyes, so that she would know I wasn't lying to her.

"Look at me, May. Tell me what you see."

At first she avoided my gaze, but when I held her that way, she finally looked.

"I see someone who I've asked to my bed," she said. "I don't make it a habit of asking men to my bed. That should tell you something about what I see."

"What you see, May," I urged, "is a man who has spent most his life drifting. What you see is a man who lost the only woman he ever learned to love and who has never quite drifted far enough or long enough to get over it." I could see the denial in her eyes, but I couldn't allow her to deny in me what was the truth.

"You had one man who hurt you, May, you don't need another. You deserve better."

"You don't know what I deserve," she said, her voice breaking, her tears spilling onto my hands.

"I know me, May. That's what I know."

She wiped at her eyes.

"Tell me something," she said, straightening, holding back her pain. "Are you afraid that you might meet a woman that's worth falling in love with again? Or is it that you're afraid if you ever stop drifting, you'll learn the truth about yourself, that you deserve to be happy, like we all deserve it?"

"Maybe both, May. Maybe both."

She leaned and kissed me lightly on the mouth.

"Our loneliness comes from the same place, Quint McCannon," she said. "Believe it or not."

I lay awake a long time that night, thinking about what May had said, about our loneliness coming from the same place. I thought of Alex, of the passion between us, and wondered what it would be like, Alex and me, once the passion burned itself out. Alex was like prairie fire burning across my soul, burning up my logic and reason, burning up all the will I had to resist her. But when the fire finally burned out, would there be anything left, I wondered.

Was that where my loneliness had led me, in the path of a wildfire?

And what of May? What was I supposed to do about her? I didn't desire her in the same way I had Alex. But where Alex was more passionate, May was more tender. And where Alex always held secret the key to herself, May was an open book. I suspected that Alex would forever remain a mystery to any man she was with. And even though she was fully capable and willing to share herself, her body, and her bed, a part of her would remain untouched, unoffered, and that was the part that I most wanted from her—that part I knew I could never have.

And yet, here was this woman, May, who would give herself to me completely, and I refused to take it.

Lying there in the dark on the floor of a Deadwood hotel, I thought of how cruel life seems to treat us sometimes, by giving us what we need, but seldom what we want.

I don't know why, but my thoughts turned to another town and another woman. A woman I had killed a man over without meaning or intending to. A woman who in the end, saw me as just another sorrow for her to have to learn to live with—at least, until the next man in her life came along.

Juanita Delgado, that was it.

27

I awoke to find May packing clothes into the carpet-sided satchels. Tess sat on the side of the bed, watching her.

"I'll accept your offer of a pair of tickets to Denver," she said, seeing that I was awake.

"You've given up on the idea of staying here in Deadwood, then?" I said, not sure that I wanted her to go now.

"I've decided to take your advice and leave this unholy place," she said as she cast an eye toward Tess, who was holding a bisque doll dressed in a white linen dress.

"Just like that?"

She paused for a moment, the child's bonnet in her hands.

"I realized after last night that there really would be no point of my staying on . . ."

I didn't know whether to try and talk her into staying or not. My head was still unclear about what I wanted, and my dreams had been crowded with the same old ghosts. It seemed sudden, May wanting to leave.

"We'll get some breakfast and then I'll get you the tickets," I said.

"Fine," she said, but I could tell she was as unenthusiastic about it as I was.

The meal was somber, May speaking mostly to Tess, urging her to eat her flapjacks and not dawdle. I'd gone over and checked on the stage's departure, it was in less than an hour.

I handed May the tickets, along with what money I'd gotten in an advance from Ben when I'd left Cheyenne. She was reluctant to take the money.

"We've already had this conversation," I said. "Let's not have it again."

Her lips were compressed. I knew she wanted me to say something more, to ask her not to leave. But I couldn't bring myself to ask that much of her.

We finished the meal and I carried their satchels over to the stage office and waited until the Concord was brought around. The weather had cleared, but the air was cold, and snow still covered the roofs of every building. And wisps of black smoke curled from every stovepipe. It was a dreary day in more ways than one.

I held the door open for May and Tess, Tess climbing in first and taking a seat next to a man whose bulk took up the space of two.

Then May climbed in and sat next to the door. The canvas curtain was drawn up to allow light; later, on the road, it would be rolled down to help against the cold.

May reached out and touched my wrist.

"The offer holds, Quint. If you ever change your mind or figure out what it is you want, you come look for me in Denver."

"I'll remember, May."

But somehow, I believe we both knew that that was the last we would ever see of each other. I said goodbye to Tess, and she smiled and thanked me again for the flapjacks. She was a sweet little girl. I didn't know how Johnny Slaughter could have denied her.

The other passengers boarded, then the driver and the guard climbed up top. Then I heard the driver "haw" the team and snap the reins, and the Concord jolted, breaking free of the sucking mud, and I watched as it rocked down the street, the wheels shattering plates of ice where the ruts and puddles were.

Then they were gone, the stage and May and the little girl, Tess.

"You and that woman," he said. "Something up between you?"

It was Torrez, his usual stalking self, out of nowhere, suddenly there, silent as a cat.

"No, not today," I said. "Not tomorrow."

"How's the other one," he said, "the little gal that sent Johnny Slaughter to the happy hunting grounds?"

"I've got someone taking care of her, keeping her out of sight."

"That's good," he said, "because the way I hear it, some of that constable's friends are talking about revenge."

"They know who it was that killed him?" I asked. "They know it was Rose?"

"They think they know," he snorted.

"Let them think what they want," I said.

"You might not want that if you knew who it was they're saying killed him." Torrez was a damn mysterious soul, and sometimes his ways could be irritating.

"You want to tell me who?"

"You," he said. "They think *you* killed, Slaughter."

That was something I didn't need to hear.

"They think maybe you had a reason to kill him because of the way he opened your head with the butt of his shotgun. Not only that, but lots of folks saw business between the two of you out on the street the other day when you shot King Fisher. They say you were ready to kill him then.

They're pretty sure it was you who killed him," Torrez concluded.

"I guess you didn't bother to tell anyone it wasn't me," I said.

Torrez was doing his usual: scouting the street with his eyes as we talked.

"You mean tell I should have told 'em it was the girl that did it, not you?"

"No, that's not what I meant."

"What, then?"

"Nothing," I said.

"The other thing," he said, "they brought in two bodies this morning."

"Who did?"

"Fancy-talking Englishman—him and his ramrod, boy named Charley Coffey. You ever hear of Charley Coffey?" he said.

"Yeah."

"Charley's made a name for himself," Torrez said, a wry smile playing his lips. "If they had a contest for low-heeled assassins—men that'd shoot you in the spine—I imagine Charley would win hands down."

"I killed them," I said. "The two men they brought in."

Torrez didn't act surprised.

"You have any more tobacco?" he asked.

I watched as he rolled himself a cigarette with the tobacco and papers I gave him; then he handed them back to me before striking a match with his thumbnail.

"That's four," he said.

"What is?"

"The number of men you've killed since Cheyenne."

"I wasn't keeping count," I said.

"Maybe you should," he said, blowing out a stream of blue smoke.

"It's a violent world," I said. "What can I tell you?"

"More so in your case than in others," he said. "Why'd you kill them?"

I told him why, about my suspicions of Leo Loop and of having followed him into the ambush. He nodded and smoked and kept his gaze scouting the street.

"So, you think it's this fellow, Loop, is it? You think he's behind the killings of these prostitutes you come up here to investigate?"

"I'd be damned surprised if he wasn't."

"How'd you come to figure it out?"

I told him the part about my visit with Leo Loop, about passing myself off as a new dealer in town, about asking Loop's permission to set up shop. I told him how Leo wanted to shake me down.

"That it?" he said. "You have a conversation with this man and you figure from that he's been killing whores? Why, because they're not paying for permits to operate?"

I knew he was challenging my investigative skills, what few they were. He was testing me to see how I matched up to himself—a professional lawman.

"I think maybe the Englishman's in on it, too," I added.

He looked at me through the haze of blue smoke lifting upward from the cigarette that clung to his lips, his right eye squinting.

"What makes you think so, that this Englishman's in on it, too?"

"My guts tell me."

"Guts," he said, then ground the spent shuck under his heel. Torrez was a man you could easily dislike, but a man you had to respect. It was out of respect that I didn't tell him to go to hell.

"There's another consideration," he said.

"What's that?"

"Something that calls themselves the town peace commission held an emergency meeting right after the Englishman and his gunner brought in those two corpses. They hired Charley Coffey as the new town constable. Your man, Loop, is he a big man, belly out to here?" Torrez asked, holding his hands out in front of him.

I nodded.

"He's the one that suggested it, that they hire Charley. The Englishman backed him. Everyone else went along with it."

"Charley was the one that set up the ambush," I said. "Then when it came to the real fight, he damn near beat his horse to death trying to get away."

"I'm not surprised," Torrez said. "You want, you can go over to Nutall & Mann's and finish your business with him. He's over there now having drinks bought for him by a grateful community of his peers."

"You got to be kidding," I said. Torrez only offered that little smile that let me know he was enjoying the turn of events.

"You think I am, go over and see," he said.

"What are they claiming, the Englishman and Coffey, about the two men I shot?"

"Said you ambushed them. Charley said you were a professional assassin. Then the fat man said they should get a warrant for your arrest. But before they could do that, they needed someone to serve it on you. That's when the fat man nominated Charley, and Charley jumped to his feet like a schoolboy asking permission to go piss. They gave him Slaughter's badge and shook his hand and said go ahead, arrest you. But Charley said he needed deputies, case you had friends about. You got any friends about, McCannon?"

"Counting you, Hector, or do you mean others?"

He gave me that look that said, "We'll see how tough you are."

"Charley and his would-be deputies are over there getting themselves oiled to come looking for you. Because of Johnny Slaughter, and now those two dead cowboys. Thought maybe you'd want to know what they have in store for you."

"How far does your jurisdiction reach, Deputy?" I asked.

He looked at me.

"However far I want it to reach," he said. "I'm an employee of the United States. The rest is my discretion."

"Does that include investigating the murder of innocent women?" I asked.

He shook his head.

"Far as I'm concerned, McCannon, there's been no requests to the federal government to investigate the murders of whores."

"That's what you need," I asked, "an official request?"

He gave me a hard stare.

"Don't push your luck with me, McCannon. I've got other things on my mind. This damn gulch still belongs to the Indians as far as I know. I haven't heard differently."

"Here's what I know," I said, and told him my suspicions that Johnny Slaughter had killed Flora, and maybe even the other two prostitutes. I told him about Flora's diary. I told him about why I didn't think that Leo Loop was a man to dirty his own hands. I told him about Jane and what she'd told me and that maybe there might even be a connection to Bill Hickok's murder. He wasn't impressed.

"You forget," he said. "I'm here looking for my brother and Leotis January, or someone that knows where they're at. I didn't come here for any other reason. And until I find out about my brother, I'm not much interested in sticking my nose in business that has nothing to do with me."

"Let's go," I said.

"Where?"

"To see a friend of mine. Maybe she's heard of Bob, or this January fellow."

He looked skeptical, but then, most lawmen do when it's not something they thought of themselves.

Cherry Bee let us in, then, at my request, brought Alex to the parlor where Torrez and I stood waiting.

I made some quick, unadorned introductions between Hector and Alex.

"Mr. Torrez is here looking for his brother," I said. "Maybe you've heard of him, Bob is his name."

I could see Alex running the name Bob Torrez through her mind. Finally she shrugged.

"Sorry, I haven't."

"How about a man named Leotis January?" Hector interjected.

She thought again for a few moments, testing the name, then a light of recognition flared in her dark eyes.

"The name's unusual enough," she said, "that I do remember it. He used the services of one of my girls at least once, maybe even twice."

Hector shifted his gaze from Alex to me, then back to Alex.

"I'd appreciate it if you could tell me which girl it was," he said.

"It would be Alice," she said. "Alice, I think, is the one who accompanied him on a picnic, I believe it was."

"Where might I find this Alice?" Bob was eager, his hands opening and closing in anticipation that he'd finally gotten a break on his search.

"She and the others—the girls I had working for me until the killings—are all staying at Alvina Pea's boarding-house."

"Where does this Alvina Pea live?" Torrez wanted to know.

She told him it was at the other end of the gulch, between Harris's Tent Manufacturer and the Black Hills Brewery.

"I can take you there, introduce you to her," Alex volunteered.

"Not necessary," Hector said, in his usual loner fashion. "I can find her, this Alice—"

"Fournier," Alex said. "Her name is Alice Fournier." He nodded.

"Thanks," he said. Then, twisting the door handle, he turned halfway back to me. "Another thing, McCannon. Charley may be a back-shooter, but he's got plenty of drunken miners arming themselves, ready to get a little revenge. They're all bored and drunk, and that's the worst sort to deal with. You want my opinion, I don't think you're any match for that crowd."

"Thanks, Hector."

"For what?"

"The vote of confidence."

He didn't smile, he just closed the door behind him.

Alex asked me what was going on and I told her about the ambush the day before, about how it was Edwin's men I'd shot. I told her about what Hector Torrez had told me about the town council appointing Charley Coffey constable.

"I think you should leave," she said. "Ride out and don't come back. They're going to kill you, Quint."

I told her the rest of what Hector had told me, the rumor about a hanging party for Johnny's killer. She swallowed hard.

"They wouldn't hang Rose," she said.

"It's not Rose they think did it," I said. "They're saying it was me. But if they get wind that it was Rose, who knows what they might do, especially if they're drunk and need to taste a little blood."

She struggled with that.

"You and Cherry Bee and Rose," I said, "you need to leave here tonight, find someplace safe to stay for a few days until I can straighten this out."

"How will you do that?" she asked.

"Hell Alex, I don't know how."

"The old man," she said. "We can go to the old man's cabin."

"What old man?" I asked.

"Toole, he runs the livery stable."

I was skeptical. "He's a boozer," I said. "A gossip, to boot."

"No. He owes me," she insisted.

"Owes you?"

"I put him on the tab once when he was broke," she said. "With one of my girls. He wept like a child. He came here and wept, he was so grateful. I can trust him. He has a cabin up in the Hills."

I had her draw me a map of the cabin's location and stayed with her the rest of that day until the sun went down. Then I walked her down the back way to the old man's livery.

The Indian squaw was gone, the fire in the woodstove now a smolder of embers. We found him inside, in one of the stalls sleeping on his back. The barn was warm and sweet with the scent of horse and hay.

I shook him awake. He came up swinging feebly, cussing, trying to grab me, trying to shake out of whatever nightmare he'd been having.

"Whoa," I said. "Slow down, dad."

Alex held a bull's-eye lantern so the old man could see us.

"What you want?" he rasped.

Alex bent closer until he recognized her.

"Toole, I need a favor."

He looked at her and some of the tightness went out of his leathery face.

"Alex . . ."

"Take it easy," she said.

Then he looked up at me again, then back to her.

"What kinda favor?" he said.

"Two," she said. "Actually, I need two favors."

He shuffled in the straw.

"First, I need to use your cabin up in the Hills," she said. "Is it still there, Toole?" He nodded. "The other thing is, I need you to keep this a secret, that I want to use the cabin. Can you do that, Toole? Can you keep it just between us?"

"Wah, I guess I could," he corked.

"No guess," I told him. "Either you can or can't."

He looked disappointed that I was there.

"Yeah, sure I can," he said finally.

"Good," Alex said.

"Goddamn . . ." the old man muttered, and lay back. "What day is it, anyhow?"

"It's Tuesday," Alex said. "Only it's night, not day."

"Oh!" he gasped. "I've lost some more of my life somewheres. Oh!"

In seconds he was snoring again.

I saddled three of the old man's horses and put Alex on one, me on another and led the third back to her place. It was cold and snowing again, and no one was out on the streets that time of night because of the weather.

Cherry Bee said she didn't know much about riding horses. Rose said she did and that she would help Cherry Bee by taking hold of her reins for her and leading the pinto mare. Rose told Cherry Bee that all she had to do was hold on to the saddlehorn.

"Stay up at the cabin until I come for you," I told Alex.

"And if you don't?" she said.

"If I don't," I told her, "you're smart enough to know what to do. Just don't come back to Deadwood. Keep on going."

"Maybe when this is over . . ." she started to say, but I cut her off from the thought.

"We'll talk about it when I get up to the cabin," I said, and slapped her horse on the rump, and waited there on the street until they disappeared into the blackness and the swirling snow.

I thought of my odds, standing there alone on a cold, dark night in a town full of men that wanted to see me dead: hanged, shot, or otherwise. I thought of the odds and how I might change them. There were damn few options, but there was one.

The only man I knew in town who might have an interest in whether or not Leo Loop and Edwin John-Davies were involved in the murders of Alex's girls was the man who'd come for the reward money Alex had offered in the territorial newspapers—Ed Siringo.

Like the old man, Toole, had told me that first day I talked with him, Ed Siringo was a killing son of a bitch! And right now, that's what I could use on my side—a killing son of a bitch.

28

I kept to the shadows of Deadwood that night in my search for Ed Siringo. Several times I passed the open doors of saloons where the talk was running high about the killings of Johnny Slaughter and the two cowboys Tolbert and Fork.

If I knew anything at all about Ed Siringo, I knew he was in either a saloon, a whorehouse, or an opium den. There were enough of all three in Deadwood. It was just a matter of finding out what his pleasure was that night: whiskey, women, or dope.

The first place I checked was the Number Ten. The crowd there was small, the place as somber as a wake. I slipped in the back door, stayed along the wall, out of the glare of light, scanned the room, saw Ed wasn't among the patrons, and slipped back out again. Then, I did the same thing at the Black Hills Brewery and the Jerzey LiL and the General Custer. Ed wasn't in any of those places. I thought, How hard can it be to find someone in a town three blocks long?

Finally I came to the Gold Strike, Leo Loop's pleasure

palace. I checked the loads in both my pistols before going
in the back door.

The place was crowded, mostly along the bar, where
Charley Coffey was still holding court. They were drunk
and they were loud, with Charley doing most of the talking.
Charley was decked out in a long cowhide coat and that
Montana Peak hat he wore with the four creases in it, his
jug ears holding it up. Only now, the peak hat was tilted
back on his head and his face was flushed from drinking
all day and he was barking threats and bragging how he
was going to kill me personally. I thought, Yeah, Charley,
here I am. All you got to do is look over to the back wall,
if you want me that bad.

I scouted the rest of the place to see if Ed Siringo was
among those being mesmerized by Charley's tough talk.
He wasn't.

I gave the crowd around Charley one last glance before
departing the same way I'd come in. They were brave
enough with the red liquor burning in their blood and
carrying those long-barreled pistols down inside the waist-
bands of their pants. I thought if I stepped out of the
shadows and yelled real loud, half of them would shoot
their peckers off.

Sitting at a table listening to Charley boast were Leo
Loop and Edwin John-Davies. They were sharing a bottle
of expensive brandy, the stuff they keep for heroes and
rich men, the stuff they keep hidden behind the bar. I saw
Charley wasn't drinking any of it, the expensive brandy.

Leo had a cigar clamped between his pudgy fingers and
Edwin John-Davies wore a gray wool suit that wasn't made
anywhere closer than St. Louis. They exchanged conversation now and then, their eyes darting toward Charley and
his lynching party.

Then Leo would say something and Davies would smile
and nod his head. And Charley would shout something
and the men would hoot and slap him on the back and
wave their hats in the air. I thought the only thing that

would make the picture complete would be my head in a brine jar atop the bar. I'd seen enough to convince me that my decision to find Ed Siringo was the right one in spite of the misgivings I had.

I had seen enough and slipped out the back again. The air was cold as hell and chilled the sweat that had collected inside my collar and along my ribs.

I started knocking on the doors of the bagnios and crib joints. I interrupted a lot of four-bit romancing but still didn't find Ed Siringo. That left only one place for him to be: the underground opium dens.

I made my way to that strange little section of Deadwood by taking to the back streets and alleyways. At first glance, the Chinese section was a small collection of shacks and tents. Most of the businesses were restaurants and laundries. But there was another business that went on in China Town, too. Opium.

I asked around, got a lot of inscrutable stares for my troubles. But finally I found one old fellow whose skin was the color of candlewax. I told him what I was looking for.

At first, he said he didn't understand, asked me if I wanted to smoke some opium, or wanted to buy some opium pills. I explained it to him again, until he understood, that I was looking for a white man and described Ed as best I could.

The old man led me to an opening that led underground. I followed him down a flight of wooden steps that descended into what appeared to be a mine shaft. At the bottom of the stairs, there were several small rooms cut out of the rock and earth. The rooms went off in several different directions and there were lanterns lighting the way.

"Maybe the man you look for in there," the old Chinese said. "You want, you can go looksee." I gave the old man a silver coin for his trouble, took one of the lamps, and started going from room to room.

The air in the underground apartments was cool, damp,

but not unpleasant, unless you counted the sweet, heavy sent of the opium that was being smoked.

Each of the earthen rooms had two or three cots, and on each cot a figure reclined, hidden mostly by the shadows, but visible enough to see.

I approached each cot and held the lantern close in order to see the face of the person. Two or three were white women, prostitutes, I imagined, their eyes half-closed, their jaws slack, mouths open enough to show their teeth. Like the dead, only not dead. Most were Chinese men and women, each one in a dreamy world that only he or she could know. The army surgeon who took the Rebel lead out of my back gave me laudanum so I wouldn't scream and fight the pain. I knew, looking into the eyes of these people, what they were feeling. I'd felt the same thing, and I knew how easy it was, once you were there, not to want to come back again.

When I found Ed, he had that peaceful smile on his face most of them had: like a man who'd seen something too beautiful to describe, like the face of God. His eyes were glazed, and when I brought the lantern in close, they shrank, then jerked away from the light. They tried to hide themselves under his hooded eyelids, like night creatures scampering from the sun.

"Siringo," I said in a harsh whisper. I touched his shoulder.

The eyes crept out, like the way a turtle's head will come out of its shell after being scared—slowly, ready to hide again at the first challenging shadow.

I spoke his name again in the same harsh whisper. He lifted his head.

"Whaa—" he muttered, his voice floating from somewhere down in the cavern of his being, the eyes edging more toward the center of their sockets. I grabbed him by the lapels of his coat and pulled him up.

That startled him, and he squeezed his eyes closed and his hands fluttered like wild birds trying to knock me away.

"Come on," I said, pulling him to his feet.

"No, no!" he hissed.

"Come on, goddamnit!" I was loosing patience fast.

I pulled him outside, out into the cold. He stumbled, his limbs loose, unwilling or unable to stand. I half dragged, half carried him to a water trough. I stomped through the sheet of ice that had skimmed over the top. The ice shattered like cheap glass, much the same way the window at the cafe had shattered when King Fisher fired his pistols through it.

I pushed Ed's head through the jagged hole, held it under for half a minute, jerked it out again in a rooster spray of icy water. He coughed and sputtered and cussed. I'd made sure I had reached inside his coat and taken out the piece he was carrying as I held him under the water. It was a .36-caliber Whitney Navy revolver, long and crooked as the hind leg of a dog.

His hands struggled for it. I shook him hard.

"Listen, Ed!"

"What? What the hell do you want?" he coughed, the wet hair hanging in his eyes.

"I want to make you a wealthy man," I said. "Two thousand dollars wealthy. That's why you came here, isn't it, to become wealthy, collect that reward money?"

He shivered against the cold, his fingers pushing the hair out of his eyes, trying to get me to release my grip on him. But the opium had sucked all the strength out of him, had swallowed him whole.

"What the hell you talkin' about?" he cried in full anguish. I let him shake free of my grip. He rubbed his face with both hands, trying to rub away the freezing pain.

"Je . . . Jesus!" he stammered at how cold the water felt, how it shocked him to have his head plunged into a trough like that. "You nuts or somethin'?"

I checked the street to make sure no one had been roused by the ruckus of me pulling Ed out of the opium den and putting his head into the water.

It was quiet—so far.

I pulled him to his feet. He didn't like that, but I did it anyway.

"Take your damn hands off me!" he moaned. He didn't have any fight in him, much as he wanted to; the dope had cut his strings.

"We need to talk, and this isn't the place I want to do it!" I said, pulling him along by his coat collar.

He slapped at my hands, but I pulled him anyway—into the nearest alley.

I held him against the wall with one hand.

"What? What?" his cry more a squeal than a howl, shrill.

"Shut up!" I said.

He moaned, trapped by the dope and me, trapped in a place he didn't want to be. He offered a feeble struggle, then he finally settled down.

"If you can make out what I'm saying, Ed, just shake your head, okay?"

He looked at me, the eyes struggling to focus, his mind fighting the effects of the dope and the heart-stopping cold of the icy water. It was the look of something worse than fear, like he'd been caught in a nightmare he couldn't wake up from. I'd been there myself.

"I've got a problem, Ed. And I need you, and this," I said, holding up his Whitney.

The eyes narrowed a little; I knew he understood.

"You back me, I'll see you get the reward money Alex Dupage was offering. How'll that be?"

He rubbed his cheek with the back of his hand.

"I don't understand," he mumbled.

"You don't need to. You still now how to use this, don't you, when you're sober?"

He looked at the Navy. "That looks like the one I own," he said.

I shoved it in his pocket.

"You want me to kill somebody, that it?" His eyes crawled

over my face looking for an answer, a solution to the nightmare he was having.

"I want you sober," I said.

He tilted his head; his tongue lolled out of his mouth, he gave a deep sigh and moaned.

"Don't get melancholy on me, Ed."

He blinked several times, not understanding.

"It's the dope," I said. "It does that to some men, makes them melancholy."

His head rolled back until it smacked the side of the wall he was leaning against.

"Jesus!" he said again, a look of pain sliding behind his eyes. "Why you doing this?"

"I'll explain once I get you dry again."

"Well, that'll be a friggin' relief," he grumbled, then looked up at the red sky, the swirling flakes coming down. "Is that snow?"

"Come on," I said, shoving him along through the alley.

"Huh . . . ?"

"Just go."

I pushed him ahead of me until we reached Alex's and went in the back way. It was dark and we stumbled around while I looked for a lamp.

"You gonna light a lamp," he said, "or, are we just gonna stand around here in the dark like two old maids trying to save the fuel oil?"

"To tell the truth, Ed, I'm not sure I like you sober."

"Good!" he said. "You think I give a damn what you think?"

I checked the street from the front windows, saw no one outside, pulled the curtains, and struck a match to the wick in one of the lamps and slid the chimney down over it. The light danced around inside like it was alive and trying to free itself.

I spent the next fifteen minutes making a pot of mean black coffee. "Drink that," I ordered.

He looked at it, sniffed it, screwed his face up.

"Drink it!" I said.

He wasn't happy with the turn of events, but I kept reminding him of how much two thousand dollars was and what it looked like all together at one time—as if I really knew. He licked his lips when I talked about the money, and drank the coffee and gritted his teeth and drank some more of it.

The time dragged by, the opium clinging to his brain like ivy on a fence. Several times I checked the windows, and once or twice I saw men out on the street, but nearer to the main section of town. They carried torches; I could hear them shouting, their voices rising against the night.

But it didn't last long, and after a while they disappeared inside one of the saloons. I guess they weren't much for hunting down killers when it was cold the way it was and there was still more whiskey to be drunk. So much for Charley Coffey's vigilantes. At least for the night.

"Okay," Ed mumbled, after he had nearly finished the contents of the big pot of coffee. "Explain it to me once more, about the money, how I get to keep it all. My brain's starting to unfreeze from where you pushed it down in that goddamn horse trough! Tell me again about the money. And don't ever do that shit again, huh?"

"I've gone through that part already," I said. "You want me to tell you again?"

"Yeah, goddamn it, I want to hear about it one more time."

So I explained it to him, again; at least, as much as I thought necessary to explain. I told him the part about Charley and Davies and Leo Loop wanting me put in a plain pine box and have me carried up to the boneyard on Mount Moriah, where Bill Hickok and a lot of other disappointed dreamers were sleeping the long sleep.

He listened and kept interrupting me about the money. Having a conversation with Ed Siringo was like trying to fast dance with a one-legged woman.

"I don't care nothin' about that shit," Ed said impatiently, "them wantin' to kill you. Just tell me how it is I can get that two thousand dollars."

"I'm coming to that," I told him.

He nodded and shook his head irritably.

"All I want from you, Ed, is to back my play with that Navy of yours. I'm going after them full-bore. I need an extra gun. You back me up, you'll get the two thousand. That simple enough for you?"

"Yeah, that's what I like, simple," he said.

"The other thing," I said.

"What's 'at?"

"You decide to switch horses in the middle of the stream, take up with the other side, it's you I'll kill first. We clear on that?"

He looked plainly disappointed I had brought it up, his allegiance.

"What I look like, McCannon, some damn bush-whacker?"

"Those are the rules," I said. "Remember them."

"Rules . . ." he muttered.

29

"When and how do you want to do this thing, McCannon?" Ed Siringo moaned.

I'd been staring out into the night watching the snow falling from a sky that glowed red over the shadowy outlines of the town.

I turned to Siringo, holding his head in his hands, leaning forward, his wet hair hanging in loose strands. His muddy boots had soiled the carpet.

He looked up at me with reddened eyes when I didn't answer right away.

"Well?" he said.

"Not tonight," I said.

He looked relieved, dropped his head back into his hands.

"Maybe I'll catch me a little sleep, then," he muttered. "'At's what I need, a little sleep." I watched him stretch out on the divan he'd been sitting on.

I walked into the bedroom where Flora's trunk was. I lifted the lid, took out the diary, and put it in the pocket of the curly coat. I wasn't exactly sure what I was going to do with the book, but it was all I had to try and tie Johnny to Flora's murder.

But proving that Johnny killed Flora, didn't prove he killed the others, and it didn't prove Leo Loop was behind it, or anything else, and that was the real problem. Johnny had already paid for whatever sins he might have committed. It wasn't him I really wanted.

I walked back to the window. Ed Siringo was snoring, his right arm flung across his eyes.

I checked the street again; it was still quiet, almost evil quiet. I pulled my Ingersol and looked at the time; it was nearly two in the morning. *What now?*

I went over what few facts I already knew about the killings. Then went over what I believed. I knew with all certainty that Leo was behind the murders, even though I had no proof. The reason was obvious, Alex was hurting his business by running a first-class escort service and not the usual rough trade of a frontier town, the sort of trade Leo was good at running.

But the question still persisted: why, if Leo wanted Alex to fold her tent, didn't he just go after her directly? Why kill three of her young women instead?

Then there was Doc Holliday. How did he figure into the killings? The way I saw it, Doc could have prevented the murders, or he could have been in on them. He had the opportunity for doing either.

Doc was like a moving shadow against the night, a man you could easily forget about until the next time you ran into him—or until it was too late. But the question was, why he would kill the women, what did he have to gain from it?

Again I considered the possibilities: Doc could have done the killings for money. It takes a special kind of man to be a paid assassin, and I had little doubt that Doc possessed such abilities. Then, there was the possibility that he owed a debt to Leo—a gambling debt, perhaps—and Leo was willing to wipe the slate clean if Doc committed the murders. Doc was a notorious gambler, but the problem was, I'd never heard that he was a poor gambler. So it made the odds that Doc might have killed the women to erase a debt seem long.

The only other connection between Doc and the killings was Alex. Alex had told me that first night we talked that Doc had an interest in her. And he had more or less admitted the same thing that night he came to my room. Maybe Alex had rejected Doc's advances and it had made him angry and he killed the girls to hurt her. But that sure in the hell seemed a long way around the barn.

I stood there trying to piece the puzzle together. My reflection looked ghostly in the glass panes, and I wondered if I hadn't stepped into it, like Bill Hickok had done. According to Jane's version of the story, Bill had crossed someone in town and paid the ultimate price—a long, eternal sleep. I wondered if I wouldn't wind up finding myself sleeping next to him.

All the odds were stacked against me ever leaving Deadwood alive. And what did I have to fight with? The diary of a dead prostitute and a dope-addicted gunfighter. Somehow, it didn't seem nearly enough.

Absently, my hands rested in my pockets, the fingers of my right hand touching the grips of the self-cocker. My other hand felt the diary. Doc troubled me the most. And if any of them was going to kill me, Doc would be the one. At least that much I was sure of.

As far as the others, I wasn't all that concerned. I figured I could kill Charley six days out of seven if it came to a face-to-face showdown. Watching him beat his horse over that ridge at the ambush told me something about his nerve. The posse of drunken miners would scatter like quail once I either dropped Charley or a couple of them.

But Doc was another matter. Feeling Flora's diary in my pocket gave me an idea, perhaps a way to draw Doc out.

I had to know the truth about his involvement in the murders. And if the killing was going to begin, it might as well begin between Doc and me.

It was time I found out who had killed the fallen angels.

30

I went out the back door, leaving Ed Siringo stretched out on Alex's divan. The snow was nearly knee-deep and crunched under my boots as I sloughed through it.

I kept to the back streets and off the main drag as much as possible. With the snow, the night was nearly as light as day and the shadows were few. And the sky was still glowing red as old blood.

I slipped past the Number Ten and the Black Hills Brewery. The hour was late and the town was winding down from its nightly celebration. Miners were drifting back to their tents and lean-to's and boardinghouses and flophouses, wherever they could lay their heads down for another night's rest before going back into the hills again.

I crossed the street just before the Lucky Strike, and turned down an alley. I worked my way along a back street until I came to the narrow, raw lumber house Doc rented for himself and Kate.

There was a light showing behind the frosted glass and tatted curtain of the single window in the front of the house.

I knocked on the door and waited, my hand resting on the butt of the pistol in my pocket.

The knob turned, the door opened a crack.

"I've come to see Doc," I told Kate.

She was wearing a checked blanket robe, her right hand clutching the throat of it. She stared at me with unflinching eyes.

"Doc's in bed," she said. "Who're you?"

"I need to see him," I said, ignoring her question.

She shook her head.

"He ain't feeling well. Come back tomorrow, you want to see him."

She tried to close the door, but I put my hand on it.

"Ask him to see me," I said.

"Do I know you, mister? Have we met somewhere? I don't recall ever seeing you and Doc together."

"No, Kate, you and I haven't met, but Doc knows me."

She blinked, her face ruddy under the soft light.

"It's still snowing," she said, looking past me, leaning a little way out to get a better look. That's when I could smell the liquor on her breath. It was a warm, sour smell.

"It's also cold," I said. "Can I come in while you ask Doc?"

"No," she said. "Doc don't like strangers in the house."

"Then I'll wait. You go ask him to see me."

"I don't know . . ." she said. "Doc don't like being disturbed once he's gone to bed." She was trying her best to protect him, her manchild.

"This is important, Kate," I said. "Otherwise, I wouldn't be coming around this time of night."

Still she hesitated.

"It could mean Doc's life," I said. And in an odd way, it could—except that if it came to that, I would be the one trying to *take* his life, not trying to save it. But it did the trick, my saying how it had to do with Doc's safety.

"Who should I say?" she asked.

"Tell him McCannon. Tell him I've got a book I want to discuss with him. A book with names in it."

"Book?"

"Yeah."

"Just a minute," she said. "I'll go see if he's still awake."

I held the door ajar just so she couldn't close it and lock it. I wondered how Doc would take the news, my coming for a visit.

I heard Doc cough hard for several minutes. I heard Kate talking to him, saying something I couldn't make out because they were in another room, probably with that door closed. Then there was a silence, followed by the sounds of shuffling steps coming to the door. My hand closed on the Remington. Maybe Doc was coming better prepared than he'd been the last time we'd met.

Kate opened the door.

"Come in, mister; Doc's getting something on," she said.

I stepped into the room. It was a small, spare room without benefit of luxury or any sign of permanence: no pictures on the wall, no glass figurines on shelves, none of the things you would expect to see in a house that's been lived in for a time. It was the house of a temporary man.

In the center of the room stood a table and two chairs, both plain and simply made. On the table a magazine lay open, and next to it a bottle and a half-filled glass of whiskey. An oil lamp gave the room its light. The ceiling was plaster, cracked in places. The dingy wallpaper was peeled loose where it met the wainscoting. It was not a room you would want to spend much time in. Doc's hat hung on the back of one of the chairs.

"You want to stand or sit?" Kate asked.

"I'll stand."

She kept the robe clutched tight around her throat; some of her nightdress showed below the hem of the robe.

She went over and closed the magazine that was lying open on the table.

"It's the latest issue of *Harper's Bazaar*," she said. "It's got all the latest fashions and the best stories. I can't sleep sometimes at nights. It's why I read, so's I can get sleepy.

"Always thought maybe someday I'd write a story about me and Doc, about our life together and send it in to them. I bet it would make good reading," she said, in an attempt to be cheerful.

"Doc says I'm just foolish. I don't know, maybe I am."

I heard something rattle behind a closed door, then watched as it opened and Doc appeared wearing a long nightshirt, his thin legs exposed below the hem, his feet encased in a pair of carpet slippers.

His hair was tousled from where he'd been lying in bed. His eyes darted from me to Kate then back to me.

"Go on to bed, woman," he said to her.

"But Doc—" she started to protest.

He gave her a look of impatience.

"This is private, Kate. Between men," he added.

He hadn't put a hand on her, but she looked as if he had.

She went to the table, started to reach for the bottle and the partially filled glass.

"Leave it, Kate. Don't you think you've had enough . . . reading for one night?"

Something tugged at the corners of her mouth, some old wound, a hidden hurt or embarrassment.

"Not enough, Doc. Not yet. I'm still not real sleepy."

"Leave it," he said, only this time without the same demand in his voice.

Her hand came away and she slowly turned and retreated to the bedroom Doc had just emerged from. She picked up the magazine and carried it with her as though it was her only comfort.

He waited until she closed the door, waited until he heard the bedsprings squeak. Then he crossed the room, shuffling his feet so that the slippers whispered on the bare wood floors. He moved to the table, picked up the glass, and drank its contents.

"What is it you want, sir?" he said, pouring himself another glass from the bottle. He did not bother to turn his attention to me until he had completed the task. Wearing the nightshirt made him look small and old; his spine was curved and bony through the material.

"Kate said you told her you had a book with names in it. What does that have to do with me, and at this hour of night?"

"Flora Cash, Doc. You remember Flora Cash?"

He raised the glass to his mouth, the heavy well-trimmed moustaches parting, his eyes not inclined to meet my own as he drank. Then, when he finished, he lowered the glass and said, "What about her?"

The eyes had finally come to rest on me and they showed no sign they recognized anything I was talking about.

"She left a diary, Doc. She talked about things, about Deadwood, its dirty secrets. She wrote down names in her diary."

It was a long shot, getting Doc to believe that Flora had written his name in her diary and that she had some dirty little secret on him. I was playing a weak hand against a man, who by profession, was a gambler.

"I am surprised she could write," Doc said. "She didn't strike me as the type who knew how."

"She did, Doc. She had a good hand, and she put down everything Johnny Slaughter whispered to her on those warm, tender nights when he wasn't with his wife or his chippy."

Doc pulled one of the chairs out and sat on it, the hand holding the glass as steady as a surgeon holds his scalpel.

"Why trouble me with all this nonsense, sir?" he asked, his voice weary but his gaze unflinching.

I was holding a handful of low cards and the stakes were big. But it was too late to fold.

"She mentions you in her diary, Doc," I said, pulling the book from my pocket and holding it up for him to see.

He cocked his head slightly as though trying to gauge whether I was telling the truth about what was written in the diary.

"Really?" he said, almost in a whisper, his voice weak. "What did Miss Cash have to say?"

Doc was calling my bluff. I could either raise the ante or toss in my hand.

"She talks about you and Johnny Slaughter and Leo Loop and Edwin Davies," I said.

Doc snorted.

"What about us?"

"I've got enough here to show it was Johnny that killed her," I said, avoiding a direct answer to Doc's question.

"Well, it's a little late for that," Doc said, reaching for the bottle again, pouring himself another round of the nerve tonic.

"John Slaughter has met the fate of his namesake— you'll pardon the weak attempt at wit—it's either an early or late hour for me, depending on how one looks at it."

"Maybe Johnny can't be hanged for the killings," I said, "but the others involved sure the hell can be."

He set the glass on the table gently, with great care and deliberation.

"You mean the names you supposedly have in that book?" he said.

"Yeah, those names," I said.

"And I am reported to be one of those names?"

"She mentions you, Doc, there's no getting around that."

"She says that I was involved in killing those poor, sad women?"

"Tell me, Doc, were you?"

"What do you think, sir?" he said, not wavering his gaze

an eyelash. "Do I seem to you the sort that would murder women?"

The forefinger of his left hand reached up and calmly smoothed the heavy moustache, swiped away the whiskey dew.

"You have a habit of answering my questions with those of your own, Doc. Why not just give me a straight answer?"

Kate called his name from the back room: "Doc!"

He half turned in his chair. I was distracted by the sudden plea of her voice. And when Doc turned back round again, I saw it there in his hand, a small double Derringer aimed at my chest.

His ace card.

"You accuse me of something so heinous as the murder of prostitutes," he said, not raising his voice in spite of the anger that flared behind the eyes. "You come into my house, unwelcome, uninvited, disturb my privacy, and make accusations against me. What am I to do about that? What would you do, sir, given the same set of circumstances?"

Doc had proved himself a prophet: he had said when we last met, that the next time the odds would be different. He was right. No way could I get to the self-cocker before he fired off both loads of the Derringer; and at this short range, maybe eight feet, I knew that even the bulk of the curly coat wasn't going to save me this time.

"Give me the courtesy of telling me the truth before you pull those triggers, Doc. Let's just say that if I'm going to die, I'd like to think I learned the truth first."

"Truth," he said, spitting it out like a seed.

"The truth is whatever most people want it to be. Lie becomes truth, truth becomes lie. Enough people hear a lie told often enough, they think it is the truth. The real truth becomes buried beneath the lies. That, sir, is what truth is."

"You mean like what they say about you, Doc?"

He nodded his head.

"Yes, what they have said about me is an example of lie becoming truth, and truth being lost because the truth is not nearly as exciting as the lies. The truth is often too boring to repeat."

"Did you kill them, Doc? Did you have a hand in it?"

"Would you rather know the truth, or would you rather live?" he asked.

It was a good question.

He coughed suddenly. I thought about going for the self-cocker in that fraction of a second—I probably could have, but I didn't.

He stifled the cough, swallowed hard against it as it bloated his cheeks, the hand with the Derringer wavering slightly.

Then he quickly tossed down the last of what was left in his whiskey glass to drown the sickness that erupted from his lungs. He lowered the Derringer.

"No," he said, softly. "I didn't have anything to do with the death of those tragic women—it's not my style."

I believed him.

"You were supposed to be watching them, though," I said, taking my chances that he had decided not to kill me there in his living room.

"I took the job as bodyguard for one reason, and one reason only," he said. "Alex."

This time his hands shook as he medicated himself with the liquor. The cough wracked him again; he gripped the edge of the table, fought it until it abated, then took a small linen handkerchief from his pocket and wiped his mouth. The red stain showed through as he balled it up in his fist.

He drew breath before speaking again.

"Like you, like every man who's ever met her, I was smitten by her the first time I saw her." The first sign of anything other than fierce intensity shone in his eyes.

"She came to me, asked me if I would be a bodyguard for her and her girls. I didn't do it because I needed the money or had nothing better to do. I did it because she flattered me. She's very, very good at that, flattering a man." He seemed to be remembering it as though it had just happened.

"Hell, what did I know about being a bodyguard? What did I *want* to know about it? Figure it out, man. Wouldn't you have done the same if she'd asked you? Look what you are doing for her as it is. You are risking your life much more than I ever did. And for what? Only one answer," he said. "You were as taken by her as I was, as any man is."

"You're overstating it, Doc."

"Am I? Tell me, sir, would you risk your life this much for a lesser woman, one without an ounce of charm or guile?"

"You're not going to believe me, Doc, but I'm doing this for a friend, not for Alex."

He snorted his disbelief.

"Tell yourself what you will, sir. We all like to tell ourselves whatever lie that works. We choose to believe that we are too noble to risk our lives for something as simple and base as a beautiful woman. You see, truth becomes lies, and lies become the truth."

I wondered.

"Tell me how it was that I saw you and Johnny Slaughter and Tommy O'Dule talking privately outside the Number Ten the other night, if you and Johnny weren't involved in something."

"It was nothing, really," Doc said, his shoulders slumping visibly beneath the nightshirt. "Johnny heard I had paid you a visit. And Tommy had also told him that you had been asking a lot of questions about the killings. They stopped me outside the Number Ten, and Johnny asked me what I knew about you—what my business with you was all about. I told them to either go to hell or buy me a drink—either way they wanted it. They chose to buy me a drink. I am not inclined to discuss my business with men such as Johnny Slaughter, not even on the best of days." A small, persistent cough nagged him and he coughed into the handkerchief again.

Then, raising his gaze once more, he continued.

"My visit with you was strictly of a personal nature. Even our enmity toward each other is strictly of a personal nature. Johnny wanted to know what it was about. I told him it was none of his concern. That was the end of it."

"One more thing I need to know, Doc. Did you take that shot at me outside on the street that night?"

He stared into his whiskey glass for a long moment, then said with almost mild amusement, "I thought I'd already clarified that point with you, sir. Had I wanted to kill you, I would have. Now, if you don't mind, I'd like to go back to bed. Kate and I are leaving first thing in the morning for Prescott, Arizona. I hear the climate is much better there, in more ways than one. I have lost my appetite for this town. It will come to nothing in the end. There is no promise here."

He stood, but not quite straight, and concluded, "If you don't mind dropping the latch on the door on your way out . . .," then went into the bedroom and closed the door behind him. I could hear Kate say his name.

Stepping back out into the cold, clear night that lay in ghostly whiteness, I was relieved to know that Doc wasn't part of the murders.

There were still plenty of folks in Deadwood that wanted to see me dead, but Doc wasn't one of them. And just knowing that was its own kind of relief.

I was feeling better about the odds as I headed back to Alex's house. But in Deadwood, nothing good lasts for long.

31

The sound came out of the darkness, a long, punished wail of a sound. Something I heard and recognized.

I found her lying in a snowbank behind the Black Hills Brewery. She was struggling to regain her feet, but she was as drunk as I'd ever seen her. A trickle of blood leaked from her nose and she smelled the way no woman should smell, worse than any muleskinner.

"Goddamn it!" she swore, struggling to climb out of the snowbank. "Jeezus and Mary!" She rose to one knee, tumbled backwards before I could reach her.

I took hold of her, lifted her to her feet. She fought me for a little bit, trying to free herself.

"Ya ain't molestin' me!" she shrieked. "I ain't no goddam crib tramp ya think ya can just haul off in the weeds and have at it with! Turn me loose, ya sons a bitches!"

I locked my arms around her until she became still. It was like holding onto a mustang you know is going to try and kick you to death the minute you let go.

"Jane, it's Mac," I said, as reassuringly as I knew how.

Drunken wildcats weren't my specialty, but with Jane, I was getting used to it.

For a few long minutes, she stayed stark still in my arms, just waiting for me to turn her loose so she could kick me, bite me, or generally lay me out.

"You understand, Jane—it's me, Mac?"

I felt her give a little.

"Mac?"

"Yeah, you remember Mac, don't you?"

"Mac?" She twisted her head around to get a look at me. I wished she hadn't; her breath was something to behold.

"Mac!" she said, the light of recognition invading her eyes.

"I'm going to turn you loose now, Jane. Don't do anything stupid, like try to bite me, okay?"

"Oh, no, Mac, why'd I bite ya?"

I let her go; she nearly fell over. I grabbed her again and held her steady.

"Oh, Lordy," she gurgled. "I must be a sight fer ya, huh?"

"You're drunk again, Jane."

"Oh, hell, don't I know it, Mac!"

"If you had fallen asleep in that snowbank, they'd have laid you out in the morning, up there on Mount Moriah with Bill," I said.

"Oh, Jeezus, Mac! What I wouldn't give to be buried alongside my Bill! It's what I want, what I pray fer ever night—to be with my Billy."

"Well, you keep drinking that paint thinner, you'll probably get your wish." I asked myself as soon as I said it why I was lecturing to Jane Canary on the evils of drink. Who was I to stop a body from going down the road they chose to go? Except I'd been there and I knew there were demons waiting for you if you went. And if they were the same demons I'd known, I didn't want anyone else to have to know them. And to tell the truth, I'd sort of taken a liking to her in a way I couldn't explain, even to myself.

"No! It's only right I join him!" she declared. "Now that Bill's gone, there ain't no reason for me to live! What've I got to live fer, Mac? Tell me that."

"How about that daughter you mentioned, Jane? Isn't she worth living for?"

Her eyes teared over. The thought had stung her.

"She knew how awful terrible I am," she bawled, "she wouldn't want a thing to do with me!"

"Maybe you should let her be the judge of that," I suggested.

"Oh, Mac, you say the damndest things to make me feel bad!"

"I wasn't trying to make you feel bad, Jane. I just don't think you ought to end it in some damn snowbank!"

Her eyes grew large, tears spilling out of them onto her smudged cheeks.

"Ya don't, Mac?"

"No," I said. "No one should have to end up like that— not even the worst of us. And you're not in that crowd."

Strangely, it seemed to sober her more than if I'd poured a pot of coffee down her, or plunged her head into a horse trough.

"Ya know it ain't too late for me, Mac. I could start over. I could clean myself up and be a lady again—like the lady I was when me and Bill were an item. I could even go back east, see my baby girl. Did I tell you her name was Janey?"

"I believe you did."

She smiled sweetly; I hadn't know it was possible, but in that moment, I felt some of her great loneliness.

"I'm a damn mess, ain't I?" she said.

"I reckon you are. Why don't you let me help you home so you don't freeze to death out here?"

She nodded.

She had a cot behind a lumberyard, a shack no bigger than the length of her bed and not much wider. But it had a small stove and I made a fire and laid her on the bunk and pulled a blanket over her.

"Ya think it's too late, Mac," she said, "me gettin straightened out?"

"No, Jane, I don't," I told her. "You're looking at living proof."

"Not ya, Mac. Hell, anybody but ya, I'd believe."

"I don't have a reason to lie to you, Jane."

She smiled that sweet smile again, her lids drooping.

"Ever body calls me Jane," she said. "But my real name's Martha. Don't nobody call me that, though. Just Jane, Calamity Jane, ya know. Sometimes, I'd like it someone calls me Martha."

"Martha," I said.

She closed her eyes, the smile still on her lips.

"It's nice to hear, Mac, a man saying me real name like that."

I waited until she'd fallen asleep, made sure there was enough wood shoved into the stove to last the rest of the night, then closed the door to that little shed she called her home. In a way, she wasn't all that different from Rose or May, or even beautiful Alex, in that she was a woman who just wanted to be loved and cared about. In that way, she was no different from any of us.

I hoped, as I shuffled through the drifts of snow back to Alex's house, that Martha *would* awaken with the same thought she'd gone to sleep with: a fresh start on life. But I'd been around long enough to know that just wanting something wasn't always enough and that sometimes the demons are stronger than you are. I hoped for her sake that wasn't the case.

32

I entered the house through the back door, the same way I had gone out earlier. It was quiet, dark, except for the ghostly light reflecting off the snow that had begun to pile up in huge drifts outside.

I was tired and cold from my trek to Doc's house and from the day's events. I went to Alex's room and stretched out across the bed without bothering to take my clothes off. In four or five hours, it would be daylight again. Everything would start over, and I would confront the men who wanted to kill me. And they would confront me. I figured if I was to stand a chance, I'd have to make the first move.

I lay there thinking how I was going to prove that Leo Loop was behind the killings. I didn't know of anyway, except to get him to confess. But getting a confession from him wasn't going to be as easy as waving Flora's diary in his face. It would have to be something more formidable, like waving the self-cocker in his face. A man like Leo would understand such directness.

My thoughts turned to May; I wondered if she and Tess had made it far enough south on the stage to have missed the storm. Another day of heavy snow and the gulch would be impassable; no one would get in or out. It was turning into that kind of week.

I wondered how Alex and Rose and Cherry Bee were doing up in the old man's mountain cabin whether they'd have enough supplies to last them through the storm. It didn't seem like anything came easy in Deadwood, least of all survival.

Somewhere in the night, my thoughts turned into dreams as exhaustion closed in on me, only this time the dreams were different. I was in a mountain meadow playing with a child, tossing him into the air and catching him and listening to his laughter, and it filled me with a great joy, a joy born of bone and flesh.

The child's hair was golden, like the sun, and his eyes were bright blue and full of mischief and cleverness. He called me "Daddy" and threw his arms around my neck and put his face to mine. Sitting on a blanket was a woman, a woman whose face I could not clearly see. She was wearing a white summer dress and a hat made of straw that shaded her eyes and a red ribbon was tied about her waist.

I knew that I loved the woman, and that the little boy was our boy, and that the world was a perfect place.

Then the child began to call my name, only his voice had changed, had become deeper, like a man's voice, and he didn't call me Daddy, he called me McCannon. And I couldn't understand why he would call me by my last name like that.

McCannon. McCannon.

I opened my eyes.

"McCannon, wake the hell up."

When my sight adjusted, I could see where the child's voice had been coming from.

"Don't even think about it," Ed Siringo said. He had the barrel of the Whitney revolver pressed against my forehead.

"What's going on, Ed?"

"Been thinking," he said.

"About what?"

"About money, what else?"

"I thought we already discussed that. Why the pistol?"

"Just don't get froggy and try jumping around," he warned.

"Two thousand isn't enough for you, Ed, is that it?"

"It might be if I knew for sure you had it. But I got to asking myself, how do I know you got two thousand, other'n your word you got it?"

"My word's always been good enough, Ed."

"No, see, as much as you explained it to me, I still never did see no hard cash in your hand, or noplace else, for that matter. Now, was you to show me, say, even half the money, why, I'd put this old dog leg away and apologize for disturbing your rest."

"And if I don't show you the money," I asked, "what then?"

"Well, now, that's a good question. You see, one way or the other, I intend on leaving Deadwood with more than empty pockets. The plain truth is, I've never been a man to much care who was writing the check, if you know what I mean. So it don't make a rat's butt worth of difference to me whether it's you 'at pays me or someone else. Who do you suppose that someone else might be in this case?"

"You're thinking of giving me over to Leo and Charley, that it? You think maybe Leo would pay you good money for me?"

"I have to admit, it did cross my mind," Ed said, with a twisted grin.

"You remember what I said about the rules, Ed?"

His grin increased until his teeth showed through the crack in his beard.

"Yeah, that was the other thing," he said, "them damn rules you kept telling me about. I ain't a man that likes living by no rules, McCannon." It wasn't exactly a laugh, the sound Ed made, more like a long grunt.

"I meant what I said, Siringo."

He pressed the barrel a little harder into my forehead.

"Jaysus, McCannon. You forgetting I still owe you for pushing my head in that horse trough? That friggin' ice-water liked to have stopped my heart!"

"Next time, I'll keep it there, Ed, till it does."

He thumbed back the hammer of the Navy; I heard the sound it made, the double click, metal against metal. It was the second time in a couple of nights I had heard that sound, and I didn't like it either time. And this time I didn't expect Hector Torrez to come through the door, blazing away with his carbine.

"You pull that trigger, Ed, you'll get no money from either side," I said. "Or did you forget to think about that in all the other thinking you were doing?"

I could almost hear his brains moving around trying to understand it.

He eased the hammer down.

"See, what I'm going to do is tie you up and leave you here while I go over and have a chat with that Loop fellow. I'm going to ask him how much he'd pay for you. That is, unless you can show me your end of the money now."

"You either take my word for it, or do what you will," I told him. "Just remember what the rules were, Ed, what we agreed to."

He shoved a little harder with the cold steel.

"Jaysus! Shut up about them goddamn rules, will ya?"

"Tell you what I'm willing to do here, Ed. You slide that Whitney back in your pocket, tell me you're just having an off day and you didn't mean anything by sticking your piece in my face, and maybe I'll see it as just that, you having an off day."

"You think I look that dumb?"

"This is a bad game you're playing, Ed."

"Get up!" he ordered. "Do it slow, or I might just pop you!"

I got up slow, like he wanted. Ed was nervous, operating

on the edge. I figured it was the ill effects of the opium still worming through his mind.

"In there," he said, stepping around behind me and placing the muzzle of the Whitney against the back of my skull. "It won't take much, me pulling this trigger you decide to try anything funny. Remember that. About a second is all it'll take to pop you."

Ed directed me into the kitchen, had me sit on a chair, and light the lamp in the center of the table. There were several silk scarves lying next to the lamp.

"See, while you was gone and I was doing my thinking about all that money you promised but never showed me, I figured out how I was going to do this. I went into the ladies' rooms and found them silk scarves. You ever been tied up with silk scarves, McCannon? I hear it's getting to be all the rage in the Denver whorehouses."

When he finished tying my hands behind my back and my legs to the chair rungs, he straightened and admired his handiwork.

"There, you're all set for the ball," he said. "That ought to keep you until I get back from my negotiations."

"What if Leo decides to put a bullet in your brain instead of money in your pocket?" I said.

Some of the grin fell away.

"Why would he do that? It's you he wants. Most men are willing to pay for what they want."

"You think Leo's the sort of man that would hand over two thousand dollars easily," I said, "you don't know Leo."

"He might with a little convincing," Siringo said, spinning the cylinder of his Navy.

"And if he doesn't?" I said.

"Well, if he don't, he don't. Then I guess I'll find that sweet woman you're so fond of, the one who owns this fancy house, and get her to pay for you. How's that sound, like a plan, or what?"

He slid the pistol into his waistband.

"I'll go over there soon's it gets daylight," he said, sitting down opposite the table from me. "No sense waking Leo up and having him in a bad mood. I'll catch him at breakfast. A man don't mind talking when he's having his breakfast."

"All that money," I said.

"What about it?"

"It's going to buy you misery."

He grunted again.

"You think so?"

"You'll see."

"I've got to give it to you, McCannon, even trussed up like a hog waiting for the butcher, you've got *cojones*. Tell me how it was, shooting ol' King Fisher like you done. Did it feel good to kill that sonofabitch, or what? I bet when he felt that bullet going through his vitals he just about shit his pants!"

"You know what I think it felt like," I said.

"What's at?"

"About the same way it's going to feel when I put a round through you, Ed. Only maybe a little better."

"Well, how do you think you're going to manage, all tied up like a hog the way you are?" He grunted that strange way of laughing, half the sound coming through his nose.

We didn't talk for a while after that, waiting for the sky to break dawn. A couple of times, Ed rose and walked to the window and looked out, rubbing the frost off the panes with the heel of his hand.

"Snowing like a sonofabitch," he said every time he looked out. "Never seen so much goddamn snow. Soon's I get my hands on that money, I'm heading south, far as I can get south. Maybe Mexico, someplace like that."

Then, he would sit back down across from me and smoke himself a cigarette and blow the smoke in my direction. And sometimes he would take out the Whitney and rotate its cylinder between his thumb and forefinger enjoying the clicking sounds it made.

"Killed lots of men with this piece," he bragged at one point. "Killed Little Ray Barger over near Fargo on the Red River with it. You remember Little Ray?"

When I didn't answer, he continued as though I'd asked him to tell me about it.

"Little Ray was standing on the back porch, brushing his teeth. He was wanted for cattle rustling, stealing off the big bosses up that way. They put out a five-hundred-dollar reward on him." Ed aimed his pistol at some imaginary figure, squinted his eye, sighting down the barrel.

"They say Little Ray had the best teeth of any outlaw that was ever killed in the territory; I imagine it was because he brushed 'em so regular, wouldn't you think?"

He lowered the Whitney and looked at me, the side of his mouth turned up in a half grin.

"Anyway, Little Ray wasn't the only man I ever shot with this. There's been others, and there'll be more, I reckon. Maybe even you, McCannon," he said, showing me the piece again by aiming it at me.

Then there was more silence, more trips to look out the window at the falling snow, searching the sky for the first sign of daybreak.

"What time you figure a man like Leo gets up in the morning?" Ed asked. I didn't know and I didn't care. I let him draw his own conclusions.

"It's interesting how time can go so damn slow when you got nothing to do, ain't it? But when you're having fun, like if you're with a good-looking woman or winning at cards, time goes by just like that," he said, snapping his fingers.

"I don't suppose you ever thought about things like time, have you, McCannon?"

When I didn't answer, he said, "Well, did you ever think about things like why time does what it does?"

"No." He had the mind of a lunatic.

"Opium," he said. "Makes me think about things, like the way times passes. It's a whole different world, that opium world is. Damn if it ain't. Could use me a smoke of it now. I ain't forgot you pulled me out of that Chinaman's last night and put my head in the water and messed with me. That's why it feels good, me going over to see Leo, sell you off like some butcher hog to the highest bidder. Leo don't buy you, I reckon maybe that pretty lady will.''

"What if they don't, Ed, what then?"

"Oh, hell, let's worry about that when the time comes, all right?"

He paced over to the window again, looked out. The sky was growing lighter. Maybe an hour more before it was morning. He paced and he sat and drummed his fingers on the edge of the table and he talked about some of the men he had killed with his Navy revolver.

Finally, the morning came.

"You got a watch?" Ed asked.

"In my pocket," I said.

He retrieved it, snapped open the face, and said, "It's almost eight o'clock. I reckon it's time to go see Mr. Leo. You think he likes bacon with his eggs for breakfast?" he snorted.

He jammed the Navy in his waistband, buttoned his coat, and pulled his hat down to the tops of his ears before walking to the door.

"Now, don't go anywhere," he said. "You're like my new bank account; I wouldn't want to see you get lost." Then he closed the door behind him, and I sat there wondering if I could have stepped in it any deeper.

33

I wondered if maybe Ed had done some rope work in his time, because the knots he'd tied in the scarves were damn good ones and I couldn't work my way loose.

I felt like the biggest damn fool in the territory to have trusted a man like Ed Siringo, then to have gotten caught with my guard down by him. Of all the glorious ways I figured on dying, being tied to a chair and having a fat man like Leo Loop walk in and stick the barrel of his pocket pistol in my mouth and pull the trigger wasn't one of them.

But that was the way it was going to end for me unless I could find a way out of the mess I'd fallen into.

I worked my wrists against the scarves until my flesh burned from trying. It was no use. I finally gave up the effort.

Funny, what a man thinks of when he knows he's about to die. I was thinking about how good a smoke would taste, and a glass of good mash whiskey, and the company of a woman—Mary Lee, or even May Smith. I would have liked to take the opportunity to say some things to them I never got around to saying when I had the chance. Then it dawned on me, Alex wasn't the first woman to come to mind as someone I would have liked to spend my last few minutes on earth with. I guess it told me something I probably needed to know about myself, about her.

But in truth, none of it would matter in a few more minutes, anyhow.

It felt like a long time had passed since Ed walked out into the cold snowy morning and bid me *adiós*. But he had left my Ingersol lying face-up on the table, and when I checked the time, not more than a minute or two had passed.

Suddenly the front door banged open, letting a blast of cold snowy air. Something else entered the room besides the weather: Ed Siringo and two Mexican *vaqueros*. The *vaqueros* wore big sombreros and heavy serapes and they were escorting Ed at the end of their pistols.

One kicked the door closed behind him, and the other forced Ed to get down on his knees.

"Jaysus!" Ed was shrieking. "Jaysus!"

"You be quiet, eh, meester?" the Mexican holding his pistol to Ed's skull ordered. "You be quiet or I'll have to shoot you. What do you theenk about that?"

Then the other Mexican came and stood in front of me, his pistol pointed at my face.

"You know who I am, Meester Quint McCannon?"

"Yeah, I can guess," I told him. "I never thought you'd ride this far north, though. You people must hold a real strong grudge."

"I am Pedro Vega, Pancho Vega's cosin," the Mexican said. "You remember who Pancho Vega was, don't you? You remember you shoot heem?"

"That's a hard thing to forget."

"We almost keeled you in the alley the other night, but then one of you friends come by and shot Luis. You a very lucky man, *Señor;* Luis was not so lucky."

"It's a long way to ride just to take a bullet," I said.

"So you see, Meester McCannon, now you responsible for the deaths of two of our cosins—Pancho, *and* Luis," Pedro said, shaking his head as if he was greatly saddened.

"Me and Juan discussed thees for a long time, what we going to do with you. You know, like a vote. Oh, we going to keel you, sure. Juan, he'd like to keel you right now. But then I tell heem what I theenk, and he agrees with me. You want to know what I theenk, *Señor* McCannon?"

I really didn't want to know, so I didn't ask.

"What? You got nothing to say? It don't matter. I told Juan, I theenk we should take you back across the *Río Grande* and keel you there, in our village, where everyone can see. You know, like a beeg celebration. Maybe put ropes around you and drag you behind our *caballos*. What you theenk of that?"

"What the hell are they talking about, McCannon?" Ed cried. "I mean Jaysus Christ, does everybody in the friggin' territories want to see you dead?"

"Shut up, meester!" Juan ordered, as he shoved the barrel of his pistol hard against Siringo's bony skull.

"Hey, that hurts, goddamn it!"

"Ees going to hurt more, you don't shut up," Pedro warned him.

"You should have kept to your end of the bargain, Ed," I said. "Now it's too late. You won't collect a damn cent. These two *vaqueros* are the cousins of Pancho Vega, a Mexican bandit I shot and killed down in Del Rio. Pancho was highly thought of by his people, as you can see. Not many Mexicans would ride this far north to avenge a death— they don't like the winters any better than you do."

Pancho Vega pulled a sticker from under his serape and cut the silk scarves loose.

"What do we do with heem?" Juan asked, keeping his pistol pressed to the back of Ed's skull.

"Hee's your friend?" Pedro asked me.

I looked at Ed.

"No, he's not my friend," I said.

"Tha's too bad," Pedro pronounced. "Now we won't take no pleasure in keeling heem."

"Kill me? What the hell you going to kill me for? I didn't do anything! Fact is, I tied him up, made him easy for you to grab hold of him. Don't that count for nothing?"

"Face it, Ed, you've come down to bargaining with Mexicans, and you know how you always hated Mexicans."

Ed's mouth dropped open by several inches as the one behind him thumbed back the hammer of his piece.

"I never said I hated Mesicans!" he squalled.

Juan pulled the trigger, only the pistol didn't fire; the hammer fell on a dud. Ed screamed, lashed out, and struck the Mexican just below the belt, causing the *vaquero* to cry out in agony. The sudden act caused Pedro to take his attention from me for just as long as it was needed, maybe two seconds, and I pulled my self-cocker and shot him. The round caved him in and he fell face forward with a groan.

Ed Siringo was scrambling to his feet, trying to make the back door when Juan pulled the trigger a second time, and this time the round went off, catching Siringo in the middle of his spine and crashing him against the doorjamb.

Maybe if Juan hadn't been so damn upset with Ed for hitting him where a man least likes it, he might have thought things out and tried to shoot me first. It was a fatal mistake on his part. When I shot him he toppled over and did not move.

And for a few long seconds, there was a silence in the room that was greater than any other silence.

Both of the Mexicans lay dead or dying. And Ed was lying on his side near the door, a moan escaping his lips as his hand still sought to reach up for the doorknob, trying to escape the house.

I stepped over the body of Juan, looked down into his youthful brown face. He was too damn young to die. But I guess he hadn't thought of that way back when he crossed the *Rio* with Pedro and the other cousin, Luis. They were young hotbloods who'd made a pact to avenge the death of Pancho Vega. It was a matter of honor to them, and now they were all dead. Pancho was still killing from his grave. Maybe now, this would be the end of it, maybe no more cousins would ride across the border when these three didn't return. Maybe we could all put it to rest, the death of Pancho Vega.

I knelt beside Ed, looked into his troubled eyes.

"That Mesican got me good, dint he?"

I looked at the spreading stain of blood on back of his coat; it was a lot of blood.

"Can't goddam believe I ended up this way," he groaned.

"How did you think it would end, Ed?"

"Wha . . ." His eyes searched mine, trying to understand the question.

"I was just curious," I said.

"I can't move my legs . . . Jaysus Christ!'

"You want a drink?" I asked.

"My hands are cold . . ."

I went to the kitchen and searched the cupboards until I found the decanter of cognac. I grabbed a couple of drinking glasses and returned to where Ed was lying.

"I'll help you sit up," I said, reaching under his arms and pulling him up so his back rested against the jamb. "I don't feel nothing," he said. "When you pulled on me, I didn't feel nothing. Maybe it ain't so bad, after all." I wasn't the one to say.

I poured us each a glass of the cognac.

"Try this," I said. He drank it and said, "What is this?" I told him.

He blew out air through his cheeks.

"You were right," he said.

"About what?"

"About how that money was going to bring me misery."

"It usually does," I said.

"Well, least you was wrong about them damn rules," he said.

"How so?"

"You said, if I broke the rules, it'd be *you* that killed me. Didn't prove out that way, did it?"

"No, Ed, it did not."

His hand reached up and took hold of the front of my coat; his knuckles turned white gripping it. Sweat sheened his face; the eyes were beginning to lose their light.

"Jaysus, but I'm afraid of what's on the other side, McCannon . . ."

"Maybe it's not so bad," I said.

"I always thought I'd live a long time," he muttered. "Most of the men in my family lived a long time. But then . . . they dint do the same kinda work as me." He coughed; the blood was spreading out on the floor below him.

His hand, the one holding on to the front of my coat, shook hard.

"Jaysus! I'm afraid I'm going . . ." he gasped. "I'm so goddamn afraid . . . of dying!"

"We all are, when it comes down to it, Ed. You're no different in that way. I've got a feeling it's really a lot easier than it seems."

He stared at me in a strange way.

"You mean maybe it's like . . . going . . . to sleep . . . somethin' like that?"

"Maybe like that," I said.

"Oh, no!" he cried suddenly then took a deep breath and let it out. "Oh, hell no!" His eyes moved upwards until they showed white and his mouth opened and closed and his hand yanked at my coat. "No! No!" Then his lips moved like he was saying something to someone, only no words came out. He had a look in his eyes like they were seeing something only he could see. That went on for maybe a minute, then his face relaxed and his hand fell away from the front of my coat. I eased him back down again.

He no longer had to worry about leaving Deadwood with empty pockets. He no longer had to worry about how cold the winters would get. Just like King Fisher and Johnny Slaughter and Bill Hickok and the three *vaqueros*, Ed Siringo would be spending eternity in the shadows of the Black Hills.

The door opened slowly and I brought the self-cocker around.

"You can put that away," Hector Torrez said, looking around the room. "It looks like you've been busy."

34

Hector Torrez stepped around the bodies and helped himself to the cognac, then rolled a cigarette and claimed a chair to sit in.

"I lost count," he said.

"Of what?"

"The number of men you've killed since the trip up."

"What are you doing here, Hector? I thought you were looking for Leotis January."

"I found him."

I wasn't sure I was all that much interested in the news considering my own circumstances.

I wanted to make a cigarette, but my tobacco pouch was empty.

"You got any makings?" I asked Hector.

He pulled his from his coat pocket and handed them to me.

"Say, this is damn interesting liquor, what is it?"

"Cognac," I said.

He seemed to appreciate the information. The cigarette tasted good and improved my mood enough to ask him about the rest of his investigation into the disappearance of his brother.

"Okay, Hector, what did you find out from Leotis January?"

"I found out he'd dead, buried down near Lead."

"That's it?"

He looked suddenly old.

"Didn't find Bob," he said, and scratched behind his ear, tipping his battered hat forward on his head.

"That woman, Alice Fournier, the one I went to see over to that boardinghouse your lady told me about. She told me where I could find Leotis. She said she knew Bob because he and Leotis were partners; she said she didn't know Bob too well. She said Leotis left for Lead after some trouble they had here. I asked her what kind of trouble and she said he and Bob had found a small strike up north of here, but it was supposedly on some other man's claim and there had been a dispute. That's what she called it, a dispute."

"She say who the other man was?" I asked.

"That's the interesting part," he said, staring at the amber liquid in his glass. It was that Englishman, Davies." Torrez spoke around the cigarette hanging from his mouth, the smoke curling up into his eyes, and it caused him to squint.

"Well, now, that *is* a piece of interesting news," I said, more than a little interested. "I think I know where they may have found their claim."

Hector took the cigarette out of his mouth and flicked the ashes in the palm of his hand and then rubbed it against his pants leg, a habit some men had to avoid flicking their ashes on a woman's floor.

"What do you intend to do now?" I asked, but with only partial interest because of my own problems. My last hole card was lying dead, a victim of his own greed and the Vega family.

"I think that one gal over at that cathouse knows something more than what she's saying," Hector said in a flat voice, as though talking more to himself than to me. "I think I need to go and question her again."

"The one you've been keeping tabs on?" I said.

He nodded.

"What makes you think she'll tell you any more than what she already has?" I asked, wondering if Torrez didn't have more interest in the woman than just asking her questions.

"I got a feeling?" he muttered around the shuck.

"I thought you weren't much for gut reactions," I said.

He looked at me, his right hand wrapped around the same glass of cognac Ed Siringo had taken his last drink from.

"I've been doing this a long time, McCannon. Some things you just know."

"Because you're a professional lawman, that it?"

He stared hard.

"I didn't mean anything by what I said the other day," he said, "about that detective business. It's just my way."

"To hell with it," I said. "I'm too old to get my feelings hurt."

"How'd you wind up with Ed Siringo and these Mexican boys?" he asked, surveying the destruction.

"It's a long story," I said.

"You know, a Mexican by nature does not like the cold weather, and these are the first two I've seen this far north," Hector said. "Now, why would they come this far north?"

"Like I said, Hector, it's a long story and one I don't have time to sit around and tell you about."

He drank the last of his cognac. "I think I could get used to this," he said, setting the glass down on the table. "It's got sort of a pleasant feel about it."

"Look," I said, "why don't we help each other here?"

"What makes you think I need help?"

"Maybe you don't, Deputy, but I do."

His gaze shifted to the winter scene outside the window.

"You mean with Charley Coffey and his bunch?"

"Yeah, that's why Siringo was here, to back me. Only he decided to change the rules after I'd laid them out for him."

"So you killed him because of it?"

"Not exactly, but it worked out that way."

"I could end up like that, McCannon," he said, pointing with his chin toward the dead gunfighter. "Or either one of them two."

"If you do, it won't be by my hand."

"I'm not so sure about that," he snorted.

"Maybe I can work the girl for you, get her to tell me what she might not tell you," I said.

"What makes you think so?" he asked.

"She sees you as trouble," I said.

"I'm listening," he said, "but not real hard."

"I don't know what went on between the two of you, but something did, something that scared her enough she's not going to tell you anything. Maybe she already knows you're the law, or maybe she thinks you're the one that killed those other women."

"How in the hell would you know how she sees me?" he asked.

"The other day, when I ran into you out in front of the bagnio, you remember?"

His nod was hesitant.

"I saw her looking down from the window up on the second floor. Dark, pretty, that her?"

"You saw her looking out a window, so what?" he said, his irritation evident by the way his eyes grew darker, more fixed.

"She looked like she was afraid you might come back," I said."

"You're reading a lot into it, McCannon. "Maybe she was afraid I wouldn't come back. You ever think of that?"

"I think maybe you went there to question her," I said. "I think you tried. But I think she got to you in a way you hadn't counted on. I think you paid her and she took you up to her room and somewhere along the way, she became afraid of you."

His entire body stiffened like he had been struck a blow, his jaw muscles knotted and his hands clenched so hard the glass shattered in it.

"You think I . . ." He started to say something, then the words retreated into his throat. He had a lot of anger he was trying to keep in check. It took a couple of seconds for him to say what he wanted to say.

"I didn't hurt her, if that's what you're thinking," he said. "It wasn't like what you think. If she's afraid of me, it's not because I hurt her or laid a hand to her." He grudgingly measured out his words like they were the last words he was ever going to speak. Droplets of blood fell from his cut hand.

"I'm not judging you," I said. "But what would it hurt for me to try talking to her this time?"

"What is it you want, exactly, McCannon?"

"I need you to back me up when I take on Charley and his bunch," I said.

"I'm not a *pistolero*," he said, "or did you forget that?"

"I've seen your work, Torrez, it'll do."

"I'm a federal lawman," he said, as a last effort to relieve his conscience.

"Then take off the badge and put it away for now, if it will make you feel any better."

"It won't."

"Do we have a deal?"

"I don't make deals, McCannon. You want to go ask that chippy what she knows, see if she'll talk to you, that's fine with me. I ain't asking you to."

"And if I run into Charley and his bunch on the way?"

"Then they better be armed and ready for a fight," he said.

"That's all I needed to know. Let's go."

He stood up slowly, looked around the room once more.

"At the rate you're going, McCannon, Deadwood's going to end up a ghost town."

"That might not be the worst thing that could happen to it, Hector."

"Probably not," he said, and stepped past the dead men and out into the storm.

35

"Lucky for you," Hector said, as we trudged through the deep drifts on our way to the bagnio called The Miners' Retreat.

"How am I lucky?" I asked, glad to have the protection of the big curly coat. It was difficult to see more than ten feet in front of us, the way the wind was blowing snow.

"Lucky this storm came along when it did," Hector added. "It's kept Charley and his crowd at bay, holed up over there in the Lucky Strike. I don't know what they'll do once they run out of whiskey and lies to tell each other. Die of boredom, I guess."

It was true, the storm had been a fortunate turn of events in my favor. About time, I thought.

We walked with our heads bowed to the wind; the snow was drifted waist-deep in some places. And for the second time since I had arrived, Deadwood appeared peaceful.

Hector didn't bother to knock on the front door of the cathouse, he simply went inside. I kicked as much snow off my boots as was possible before following him in.

We found ourselves standing in a parlor. A mahogany

settee with crushed red velvet upholstery stood against one wall. Against the facing wall there was a horsehair divan with a black fringe border wide enough for two people to sit on. There were glass lamps and blue drapes and a coatrack.

"It's where the women come to get selected," Torrez stated matter-of-factly, as we stood in the room.

"You seem to know a lot about it," I said.

He tossed me a hard look.

A little bell above the door had tinkled our arrival and a short, plump woman entered the room from behind a curtained archway.

"Well, you boys must have a powerful itch, to hoof out on a day like this," she said.

She had rouged cheeks and a mole near the side of her mouth. Her platinum hair was done in sausage curls and she wore a bone corset and pantaloons and long purple stockings. "I'm Agnes, but they call me Big Annie." Then she stared at Hector and said, "Ain't I seen you here before?"

"We come to see Josephine," Torrez said without fanfare.

"Little Jo," the woman said. "Sorry, gents, she's laid up with the monthlies. I got other gals, though. And with it being a real slow day on account of this weather, why, you can take your pick. Let's see, there's Hettie, and Doreen, and Slo Foot Sue, except Sue's got a bad tooth that's been troubling her and ain't in the best of moods, if you know what I mean. Getting rode by a man when your wisdom tooth is aching ain't exactly something a girl looks forward to."

"We came to see Jo," Hector repeated.

"Mister, I told you, Jo is out of commission for a few days," the woman half scolded. But Hector was a single-minded man who didn't have much patience.

"We just want to talk to her, is all," I interjected.

She looked at me.

"Talk to her?"

"Yeah."

"You trudged through them snowdrifts just to talk to a whore? You ain't even wanting to ride one?"

"You mind telling me which room she's in?" I asked.

"It'll cost you," the woman said, "talk will."

"How much?"

"Say, two dollars."

I was broke; I had given May the last of my money.

"Pay her, Hector," I said.

Instead, he showed her his badge.

"You see this?" he said, stepping close to the madam. "I'm a federal lawman, and this is considered official business."

"Mister, I don't care if you're the king of Siam and you're here to hunt turkeys; it'll still cost you two dollars, you want to talk to Jo."

"Pay her, Hector. Let's get this over with," I said.

"I could arrest you and take you to Cheyenne," he told the woman. "How would you like to ride all the way to Cheyenne chained to the floor of a stagecoach?"

She held out her hand.

"You want to arrest me, go ahead. That, or pay the two dollars."

He looked at me.

"It's why we came," I said, "to talk to her."

He reached inside his shirt pocket and found the money and handed her two dollars.

"You both want to talk to her?" the woman asked.

"No, just me," I said. Hector was still a little put out by the demand of payment just to talk to a woman.

"She's third door down on your right, top of the stairs," the woman said. "I'd knock first."

"I'll wait here, if you don't mind," Hector said placing his flat stare on the woman.

"No, hon, I don't mind at all. Fact is, you change your mind, I'll be right back there the other side of that curtain," she said, offering a wink that Hector ignored. "Big Annie ain't too old nor too tired to go to the races."

Hector ignored the comment.

"I'll go up and talk to her and see what I can find out about Bob," I said, ascending the stairs.

"Yeah, I'll just sit here and cool my heels," Hector said, pulling his tobacco out to make himself a cigarette.

I knocked on the door and a soft voice on the other side asked who it was. I told her I wanted to talk to her. She said she wasn't feeling well and that Agnes must have made a mistake, sending me up. "I ain't up to taking care of customers," she said.

"I'm not a customer," I told her.

She opened the door a crack and peered through it.

"Then who are you?"

"Just someone that wants to ask you a few questions about a friend of mine," I said.

She was attractive with dark alert eyes, and dark skin. Young. I guessed her to be Indian, maybe a little Mexican blood mixed in.

"Agnes said it was all right that we talked," I said.

She looked uncertain but then opened the door wider and allowed me into the room.

It was a small, spare room with a bed, a vanity, and an oval mirror framed in walnut. The mirror was cracked. There was the scent of crushed flowers in the air.

She shuffled over and sat on the edge of the bed, and when she did, the iron springs creaked. She was wearing a long cotton shift and her hair was black and straight and long. She had small brown feet showing below the hem of the shift.

"What is it you want to ask me?" she said. I noticed the traces of blunted speech common to Indians when they spoke the white man's language. I figured maybe she was Sioux or Cheyenne. She looked a little hungry, thin, like lots of working girls I'd seen. Most of the time, it was the whiskey and hard life they led that kept them thin and hungry. For some, it was the opium they smoked in the Chinese dens that kept them emaciated. Then when the whiskey and dope no longer worked, they turned to poison, and that always worked. She was young and pretty, but I could already see the slow death in her eyes.

"I want to ask you about a man, an old friend of mine."

"Who?" She avoided my gaze, choosing instead to stare down at her bare feet.

"His name is Bob Torrez," I said. She looked up suddenly. I saw the light of recognition knot the edges of her mouth.

"No, mister, I don't know any Bob."

"I think you do," I said.

She went back to staring at her feet, like a child that had just been scolded. "I'm not feeling too good," she whispered, holding herself with those thin arms. "It's that time, you know."

"Look," I said, standing by the door, not wanting to pose a threat to her, "I just want to know what happened to Bob Torrez, that's all. I'm not looking to hurt anybody or cause you any trouble."

She still didn't look up. Her black coarse hair fell straight down over her face.

"I don't know this Bob," she repeated.

"You sent his things home to his family," I said. "You took the trouble to do that much. I figure you must have cared about him to do that."

She swallowed back emotion that was trying to lose itself from someplace deep within her.

"So what if maybe I did?"

"It was a right thing to do," I said. "It was a kindness on your part."

She rocked back and forth holding herself.

"The problem is," I said, "no one knows exactly what happened to him, because you didn't include a note. His mother is grieving for her youngest boy and she doesn't even know what became of him."

She bit her lower lip, trying hard to keep from saying more.

I went over and stood in front of her and waited until she looked up.

"Josephine," I said, "you did a good thing, sending his belongings home to his mother; it just wasn't everything that needed to be done. You can understand that, can't you? You've gone this far. Why not just tell me the rest and put it behind you?"

"You don't understand," she said.

"What?"

"If they know I told you, I could end up like them other girls—the ones that got killed."

"No one has to know but me and you," I reassured her. "You loved Bob, didn't you?"

Her chin trembled and she blinked several times trying to hold back the tears.

"He said he was going to marry me," she murmured. "He said soon's he could clear up his problems with his gold claim, we were going to get married and go away . . ."

"How'd he die, Jo?" I said, placing my hand on her shoulder.

"Them men . . . he had the trouble with . . . over his gold claim," she stammered. "They . . . killed him!" She rocked back and forth, fighting the emotion of loss and fear.

"I thought he was going to . . . take me away from here. I thought it was my chance to be something more than somebody's damn whore. Bob said he loved me. He said he didn't want me with other men no more . . ."

"How did they kill him, Josephine?"

Her trembling hands came up to her face, the fingers trying desperately to wipe back the tears; I guessed she could not have been more than sixteen years old.

"That man . . . that Johnny Slaughter," she said, forcing the words out. "He came here one night and he said that he was arresting Bob for trespassing. And him and Bob

got into an argument, but that lawman hit Bob with his
pistol and knocked him down. I tried to get him off Bob,
but he hit me, too. Then Bob tried to stop him from hitting me and Bob's face was bleeding from where that
lawman hit him. But Bob wasn't no match for that John
Slaughter . . ."

"So Johnny arrested Bob. Then what?"

She sniffed, her hand brushing under her nose.

"Then I don't see Bob no more, except the next day
when I heard that someone had found him in an alley
with his head broken in. By the time I could get down to
see him, they already got him over at that man who fixes
up dead people before they bury them . . ." Her words
broke under the sobs again. I walked over to the water
basin and poured some water over a small hand towel and
wrung it out and wiped her face with it. She held my hands
as I tried to ease her pain.

"Take your time, Josephine."

She really looked at me for the first time, and all the
hurt trapped within those dark obsidian eyes penetrated
my soul.

"That man—the one who took care of Bob—cleaned
him up and put a clean shirt on him," she said, trembling.
He combed Bob's hair wrong. Bob never combed his hair
like that man had it. I couldn't hardly believe it was even
him when I saw him there in that box. He didn't even
look real to me. I touched his hands and his face, and they
didn't feel real to me, either. They were cold and hard,
and it gave me a bad feeling, touching him like that, and
I had to run away from there."

"Where did they bury him, Jo?" I asked, as gently as I
knew how.

"Up on that hill, with them other dead people," she
said. "I didn't go up there until later. One, two weeks,
maybe. The grass was already beginning to grow again. I
didn't even know if it was the right place."

"I'm sorry this happened to you," I said.

She shook her head as though still not able to accept it.

"I thought we was going to leave this place," she said, "Bob and me. I don't know what I'm going to do now. Bob, he didn't mind I was doing this. Most men mind."

"Yeah," I said.

"I guess they don't want someone to live or get something decent from life, they just kill them, that's all . . ." she said.

"Do you have people somewhere you could go live with?" I asked.

Her cheeks were stained with her sorrow and bitterness.

"No, I don't have no one," she said. "My people are all gone from around here." She didn't elaborate where her people had gone, whether she meant they had died or simply left, or the circumstances of how she had come to prostitute herself in a Deadwood whorehouse at such a young age.

"I know it sounds a little late," I said, "but is there anything I can do?"

"No," she said. "There's nothing nobody can do. Just don't tell them men who killed Bob what I said, okay? I don't want no more trouble than what I got. This ain't no kind of life mister, but it's all the life I got."

"I won't tell them."

She nodded her head.

I turned to go, but there was one last thing I wanted to ask her before I left.

"Is Josephine your real name?"

She shook her head, a small light of something remembered came into her eyes.

"No," she said. "It's a name Big Annie gave me 'cause it sounded more like a white girl's name. Big Annie said some of the men wouldn't pay as much for an Indian as they would a white girl. She made me change it to, Josephine; she said it was a name that'd remind men of their sweethearts."

"What was it before?" I asked.

"Blue Water Dancing," she said.

"It's a nice name," I said.

"My grandmother gave it to me."

"Maybe someday you will meet another man like Bob," I said.

"Maybe."

"And maybe he will call you by your real name."

She offered a weak smile.

"I almost forgot my name" she said, shyly. "Nobody ever calls me that anymore."

"It's too pretty to forget," I said.

She shrugged.

"Living like this, it don't give a girl much hope of having pretty things. Maybe someday, I'll save a little money and go see my people. They went off to Canada. I'd like to see my grandmother again."

"Blue Water Dancing," I said.

She looked at me, her eyes full of curiosity now.

"You shouldn't forget," I said.

36

Hector Torrez was checking the heel on his right boot when I came down the stairs from Josephine's room. The heel was run-down, so were the soles of his boots. He looked up.

"Well, did you do any good up there?" he asked, lowering his foot to the floor.

It struck me that if Torrez had paid for that child's services, he wasn't quite the man I'd thought him to be.

"Tell me something, Hector?"

His eyes narrowed.

"You want to know did I buy her," he said.

"Yeah."

His nostrils flared.

"No, I didn't buy her. I bought her some whiskey and we talked and she tried to get me to go upstairs with her and I did. But I didn't pay her for what you're thinking," he snorted. I didn't know whether to believe him or not. A man like him, not accustomed to women, maybe he had paid her and just didn't want to admit to it.

"I can see where a man might be tempted," I said.

"Given the right circumstances, I can understand a man paying her."

He stood up, settled his battered sombrero on his head.

"That what you think?" he said, "that I went to bed with a child like that?"

I knew then he hadn't.

"No, I just thought if you had, it might have complicated things a little."

"You're a damn suspicious man," he said, his jaw working into a knot.

"She told me some things about Bob," I said. "But maybe we'd better take it outside." I wasn't sure who might be listening on the other side of the curtain where Big Annie had appeared from earlier.

We stepped back out into the storm that hadn't slowed at all; the winds whipped gusts of snow down the streets and plastered it to the sides of the buildings and support posts and piled it deep in front of doorways.

"Where to?" Torrez asked.

"Someplace private," I said.

Hector scrunched his hat down a little more on his head to keep the wind from blowing it away and I did the same.

"Someplace private's going to be a little hard for you, isn't it?" he asked, as we trudged down the street. "What with half the town wanting to arrest you."

"I know a place that might work," I said.

He didn't ask, he just walked alongside me until we reached the old man's stables.

"In here."

"You want to hold court in a barn?"

"Why not?"

It was at least out of the weather.

Toole was out cold, lying on a bed of straw, a bottle lying near his outstretched hand.

"Who's that?" Torrez asked. I told him. "You reckon he'd mind we shared his bottle?" Torrez said, bending and picking up the liquor bottle. He held it up to check how much was remaining.

"Two, three good swallows yet," he said, holding the bottle out to me.

"No, thanks," I declined. Torrez didn't bother to make a second offer but instead finished it off in one long pull, his Adam's apple bobbing up and down.

"So, what'd she tell you?" he asked, when he had finished off the old man's liquor and tossed the bottle aside.

"She told me what happened to Bob," I said, careful to watch the reaction in his eyes. I think he already knew it, that Bob was dead, but hearing it said caused his eyes to narrow and his shoulders to slump.

"She say who it was killed him?"

"She didn't know for certain," I said.

"Then you wasted your time."

I repeated to him what she had told me about Johnny Slaughter arresting Bob and how the next day he was found in an alley with his skull caved in. I told him the part, too, about her having gone to see him at the undertaker's, and that it was her who had sent his belongings home.

"Well, it was damn civil of her, don't you think?" he said sarcastically.

"Hold on, Torrez. Bob was going to marry her, she loved him."

He snorted his disgust.

"I don't want to hear that shit," he said. "You seen what she was. My brother wasn't going to marry a damn who—!"

I came up real close to him and put my hand on his chest.

"Don't!" I said. *"Don't say it!"*

He jerked back, surprised that I had challenged him.

"What the hell's got into you?" he grunted.

"She's maybe all of sixteen years old and she fell in love with your brother, who had promised to marry her and take her out of the life she's living. She had the common decency to send his belongings home; she didn't have to take the trouble. So don't say what you were going to say about her, not in front of me, Hector! Not in front of me!"

It was a long moment of waiting.

Finally, he turned away and walked to the front of the barn, where the doors allowed a crack of dull light in from the outside. A long finger of snow lay along the hard-packed dirt floor.

"She say where Bob was put?" he asked with his back to me.

"Up on Mount Moriah," I said, "at the little cemetery."

His hands opened and closed several times.

"She said Bob had some troubles with his claim," I said. "The same thing you heard—he'd had some sort of dispute."

"You think it had something to do with the Englishman?" he said.

"I can't say for certain, but if what I've heard is true, that he claims to own a good part of that country north of here and has several mining claims already up there, then it might be a place a man would want to look for gold. And maybe Bob and his partner did just that."

"How could the Englishman own land that belongs to the Sioux?" Hector asked.

"That's a good question, deputy. But who's to stop him, who's to throw him off the land? Think about it."

"Those two you killed the other day, his men," Torrez said, "maybe they were the ones, maybe they had a hand in killing Bob."

"It's real possible, Hector."

"Only one goddamn way to find out," he said.

"Yeah, I was thinking the same thing."

"You want to go take care of Charley Coffey and his bunch first?" Hector asked, still with his back to me. He looked dark and menacing, standing there in the unlit building with the single blade of winter light knifing through the crack in the doors.

"Well, as much as we both want to head up there to Davies's place," I said, "we wouldn't get far in this storm."

"No, we wouldn't get a mile," he agreed.

"Then let's walk down the street and see if we can find Charley," I said.

"Yeah, let's."

37

We pushed our way through the snowdrifts and the bone-chilling winds on a direct line to the Lucky Strike. There was something fearsome in it, the way we were going about taking on Charley and his bunch and whoever else decided to get in the way. It was a feeling I hadn't had in a long time.

I don't know exactly how to explain it, the coldness that takes over your thinking, the little extra your heart starts to beat when you know that you're walking into a fight. Your mind fixes on just that one event, the fight you know is up ahead waiting for you, and everything else is forgotten. All you think about is doing what you know you have to do, and nothing else is of consequence.

That's the way I was feeling, and if I had to guess, I'd guess that was the way Hector Torrez was feeling, too.

We didn't talk or discuss it beyond the decision we'd made before we left the old man's stable. Hector had thumbed a fresh cartridge in his carbine and checked the loads in the Peacemaker Colt he had taken off the stage robber. I changed loads in both my pistols, then placed them in the pockets of the curly coat so I could reach them easily.

The wind bit our faces and snapped at our clothes and tried to take our hats. But none of that seemed to matter, because as cold as your mind tends to become in a fighting situation, your blood feels like it's running hot in your veins.

We reached the Lucky Strike, exchanged glances, and went in prepared to do what we had come for.

There were a few of the town's citizens, mostly miners, sitting around, but overall, the place was quiet. Those sitting around looked up when Hector and me stepped into the room. The small talk came to an end; someone coughed.

"I'm looking for Charley Coffey," I said.

No one said anything for a moment. Then Harve, the barman, stepped out of the shadows from behind the bar. The swelling around his eyes from the fight he and Red had, had given him the look of an Oriental.

"Coffey's gone," he said.

"Where?"

Harve placed the palms of his hands atop the bar, looked from me to Torrez then back to me.

"Where?" I asked again.

He shrugged.

Hector crossed the room and took hold of Harve's shirt-front and nearly pulled him over the top of the bar.

"He asked you a question, mister!" Torrez growled.

"I don't . . . know," Harve stammered.

"Goddamn you don't!" Hector said. "And you better be faster with an answer than I am with this Peacemaker." Hector showed him just enough of the big pistol to get his attention.

I kept an eye on the others in the room, in case there were any who thought they had a reason to get involved; no one moved.

Hector put his face up close to that of Harve's, and

Harve tried to close his eyes, but was having difficulty because of the swelling.

"I bet it'd hurt like hell I was to punch you in that face of yours," Hector threatened.

"Please don't do . . . that," Harve begged.

I noticed Red, Harve's partner, standing there behind the bar, his hands hanging at his sides. He didn't seem to be in a fighting mood, watching the way Hector was handling Harve.

Torrez looked like he was going to do it, hit Harve in his tender face, when I stopped him by asking Harve, "Then where's Leo?"

Harve shifted his swollen eyes toward the back, where Leo's office was.

"Keep him and these others out here while I pay Leo a visit," I told Torrez. "I'll get Leo to tell me what Harve says he doesn't know. I come back without an answer, you can go ahead and bust him in the face."

Harve grunted, but Hector held him in a bulldog grip, pulled halfway over the bar top, his toes barely touching the floor.

I didn't bother to knock on Leo's door before I went in. He had a chippy kneeling before him, his head back, his eyes closed against the pleasure she was giving him.

"Leave off with that," I ordered her. They both jumped.

"What the hell . . . !" Leo started to protest, but I showed him the self-cocker.

"Go on, lady, find something else to do," I told her. She looked grateful and slid out of the room, closing the door behind her.

Leo sat there sputtering and trying to button up his front. "Leave it be," I said. His hands came away.

"Time for the truth, Leo."

He looked at me, his piggish eyes full of anger and fear. "Truth of what?" he squealed, his face flushed.

"Everything, Leo. Start with the reasons you had those

girls murdered, then go on to the part about where Charley Coffey is hiding."

"You don't know . . . what you're . . . saying!" he stammered. I thumbed back the hammer on the Remington.

"Christ, Leo, it would be so damn easy to kill you, I have to fight the urge to keep from doing it!"

The piggish eyes shifted to the pistol in my hand.

"Only thing is," I said, "I want to do it slow, maybe shoot you in the legs first. What do you think that would be like, getting shot in the legs, Leo?"

He lost most of his color when I said the part about shooting him in the legs; the flesh around his neck and jowls were ashen, gray as the winter sky; his face was a sheen of sweat, and the thin strands of his oily hair couldn't hide the glisten of his scalp.

"You . . . can't do . . . this, McCannon! It'd be murder!"

"You think I give a damn what anyone in this town would call it, Leo? Do you want to know who's backing my play out there in your bar right now? A deputy U.S. marshal. Do I look like a man that's worried about being charged with murder?"

"You can't do this . . ."

I put the front blade of the self-cocker just under the sag of neck that spilled down from his chin.

"Go ahead, Leo, tell me again how I can't do this."

He swallowed hard enough that the flab of neck pushed against the barrel of my pistol.

"It wasn't just me . . ." he muttered.

"Go on."

"It was . . . Johnny who did it . . . he's the one that killed them."

"But you ordered it done," I said.

He was trying to hold the bile down, choking on it, tasting it. He swallowed two or three times, and every time he did, the barrel of my pistol moved under the bob of his Adam's apple.

"Okay . . . all right!" he cried, throwing up his hands.

"You had Johnny kill those women because you didn't want the competition from Alex's operation, is that it, Leo?" His eyes rolled until they showed white.

"Wasn't there enough lonely miners to go around?" I said, "You had to get all the trade, cut everyone else out?"

He snuffled, a thin line of mucous leaking from his right nostril.

"She didn't . . . go along with the . . . operations," he said. "She wouldn't pay up . . . it was the principle of the . . . thing."

"Principle!" I was having a hard time holding my anger in. It *would* have been easy to pull the trigger and just walk away.

"You had those women killed for something as little as that?"

He nodded again, unable to speak because the bile was right there in his throat, and if he tried to saying anything, it was all going to erupt out of him.

"I don't get it, Leo. Why go after the women? Why not just kill Alex instead? If you wanted her out of business, why not just take her out?"

He was shaking now, shaking and sweating and leaking through his nose.

"He wouldn't let me . . ." he managed to mumble.

"Who wouldn't let you?"

"Davies!" he blurted. "He wouldn't let me have Johnny . . . do her."

So there it was, like the unspoken truth finally said.

"Tell me exactly how he fits into this, Leo," I said, shoving the front sight of the pistol a little harder into the doughy flesh. Leo was clamping his jaws shut, trying to keep from losing his breakfast all over his gaiters.

"We had a deal . . . I run things around here . . . he controls most of the big mining claims. He said between the two of us . . . we could control it all."

"He was already a rich man, Leo," I said. "Why bother?"

Leo swallowed again, like he couldn't get enough air.

"It ain't . . . about money with him. It's the . . . power."

"So you supplied the guns and he supplied what, Leo, the brains?"

"Yeah . . . something . . . like that." Leo was sweating more than a man should on such a cold day.

"Until Edwin came along with his schemes and money, you were just nickel-and-dime-ing it, that the way it was, Leo?"

He nodded his head.

"Nickel-and-dime-ing it . . . that's right."

"I still don't get murdering the women," I said. "Why didn't Davies just let you kill Alex and be done with it? Why go to all that trouble to try to scare her off?" Leo was having a hard time coming up with enough words.

"Let me guess," I said, losing patience with him. "Edwin was in love with her, that's why he wouldn't let you kill her."

"Not just . . . that," Leo groaned.

"What else?"

"She's his sis . . . sister, you know . . . they're related for Chrissake! Jeezus . . . can you quit poking me in the neck with that?"

I held the barrel against his soft flesh while the revelation sank in. It was a hell of a fact Alex had forgotten to mention in our conversations both in and out of bed. The whole thought of it was doing a slow dance in my head.

"I should kill you for lying, Leo," I said, hoping he would confess it as a lie. But his eyes bugged out and his mouth opened and closed like a fish out of water.

"Honest to Christ . . . McCannon, it's the truth!"

I wanted to close my eyes and pull the trigger and feel him slide away from my gun.

"I'm going out there to Davies's place, Leo. And when I've finished my business, I'm coming back here. You be ready to ride the stage with me back to Cheyenne to stand trial for the murders of those girls. You try running, I'll hunt you down and kill you myself," I warned him. "One way or the other, you're going to pay the check for this."

I let down the hammer and took the pistol away from his neck; a red mark showed against the doughy flesh where I had pressed it with the barrel.

"Remember, Leo, what I said about trying to run," I repeated the warning as I turned toward the door. He was busy bent over a spittoon.

I stepped back out into the bar, where Hector was still holding Harve by his shirt.

"What's up?" Torrez asked.

"You can turn him loose now," I said. Harve staggered backward from the way Hector released him.

We headed for the door when a sharp explosion sounded from behind the door to Leo's office.

Hector started to go back that way, but I stopped him.

"What the hell's going on, McCannon?"

"I think Leo just paid his bill," I said.

"For what?"

"His sins."

Hector walked over to the front doors, looked out.

"What's the next move, McCannon?"

"Soon as this weather lets up, we pay a visit to Edwin John-Davies," I said.

"Well, this must be your lucky day, then," Torrez said. "It just stopped snowing."

38

We trudged our way down to the livery. The old man was repairing a harness with the help of a rusty awl and a bottle of busthead whiskey. He looked up when he saw us walking through the shaft of gray light that filtered through doors. Hay dust danced in the light.

"We need a couple of horses," I said. He looked at Hector, then at me.

"You going up to see Alex?" His eyes were rimmed red and his hands shook as he tried to work an awl through the leather strapping of the harness.

"Not today, Toole."

"Who's at you got with you?" he said, switching his gaze from Hector to me.

Before I could answer, Hector told him who he was.

Toole grunted the words. "Deputy U.S. Marshal" like they were bitter seeds in his mouth.

"How about getting our horses?" I suggested.

He coughed, laid the harness aside, and stood.

"You want that same buckskin?"

I nodded.

Ten minutes later, he had both horses saddled.

"Eight dollars fer the pair, you don't mind," he said, holding the reins in one hand, extending his other.

"Hector?" I said.

Torrez looked unhappy at the request for more money but dug down deep into his pockets.

"I'll want a receipt," he told Toole.

"Receipt?" the old man responded. "What the hell I look like, a bank?"

"I don't care how you do it," Hector stated flatly, "but make me a receipt."

Toole grumbled, searched through an old wooden box he had in the corner, and found a pencil. He rummaged some more, then looked up. "I don't have a damn piece of paper to write on. What the hell am I supposed to write you a receipt on?"

I took the diary out of my pocket, found a blank page and tore it out.

"Write it on this," I said.

"Two horses, eight dollars . . ." Toole mumbled, as he made the marks on the paper. When he finished, he handed it to Hector. "There's your damn receipt." Hector folded it and carefully placed it in his pocket.

"The government is real particular about deputies keeping good books," he said. "A lawman that don't keep his books is just a man waiting to go to the poorhouse."

"Well, we wouldn't want that, now, would we?" Toole said, taking a pull at his bottle, clearly put out for the extra effort he had to make to rent us the horses.

"Be glad, old man, that I didn't just confiscate these horses from you," Hector said.

Toole spat.

"That'd be the day."

"Let's go, Hector," I said, walking the buckskin toward the doors. I didn't need any more problems.

"He's a feisty son of a bitch," Hector said, when we were nearly to the edge of town.

"He's an old man with old memories," I said. "He probably got locked up a few times when he was a cowboy and never got over the experience."

Hector didn't reply, but instead, looped his reins over the horn of his saddle and made himself a smoke. "You want one?" he asked holding out his makings when he had finished.

"No, I'd just as soon keep my fingers warm inside my pockets," I said.

We took the north road that wound up through the hills, hills that were now surrendered to the snow; the boughs of the trees bore white blankets. The land looked clean and untouched. The heavy snow had given the Black Hills an endless beauty, vast and lonely, as if a man riding into it would be swallowed by it and never found again.

The horses chuffed steam through their black, wet nostrils and ice formed on my moustaches. It was damn cold, but somehow, I wasn't all that bothered by the weather.

Maybe the reason I wasn't troubled by the coldness was because I was still thinking about what Leo Loop had told me about Alex and Edwin John-Davies. I couldn't stop wondering why the lie about him and her. What was she hiding, and why hadn't she trusted me? It was disturbing in a way that seemed to ache down in my bones and force me to fight the anger of being deceived.

The truth, what was it? Maybe Doc had been right in his assessment of Alex Dupage: She was a woman so alluring that she could get any man to do just about anything for her. Doc had nearly laughed at my reasoning when it came to her. He was right: *truth becomes lies, lies become the truth.*

It left a sourness in my gut.

"You look like you swallowed a nail," Hector said. It was hard to tell which was cigarette smoke, and which was vapor coming out of his mouth when he spoke.

"It sort of feels that way, too," I said.

"Tell me," he said, "we heading into a big fight up there at John-Davies's place?"

"It could be," I said. "It just depends on how much Charley Coffey wants to prove he's a real gunfighter, and how many others he convinced to throw in with him. Leo said he had five, six men with him. Then, there's John-Davies to consider. I'd say of any of them, he's is the one I'd worry about."

Hector nodded, smoking his shuck like I was telling him about the newest sport of baseball back east.

"Another thing you may want to keep in mind, Hector," I added. "Davies carries a sporting rifle. I've seen similar when Cody took the Grand Duke of Russia out to hunt buffalo. The damn thing could shoot a thousand yards accurately. My guess would be, John-Davies sees it as sport, killing a man. It's another reason I figured he left England and came west. Out here, you can still shoot men for sport. You might want to keep that in mind when we get up there."

Torrez grunted, flicked the shuck aside, and watched it sizzle in the snow.

"Yeah, well, I've been shot at by some pretty fair men in my time," he said. "I reckon some toad from wherever the hell he's from don't worry me too much."

Hector found a small flask inside his jacket pocket and brought it out.

"To hold off the chill," he said, tipping it to his mouth. Then he handed it to me and I took a small pull, just enough to feel the warmth course through my blood.

The heavy snow made traveling a slow process; the horses broke through chest-deep drifts in places, and in other places, Hector and me dismounted and gave them a blow.

"Listen, Hector," I said as we neared John-Davies's place. "I'm sorry about Bob."

"Me, too," he said.

"Maybe we'll get all of our questions answered once we have John-Davies in hand, Hector." He nodded but didn't say anything. A man that didn't say much when there was much to be said worried me. I didn't want Davies to die the quick, easy death that Hector probably had in mind for him. I wanted to see the son of a bitch taken to the nearest circuit court and stand trial, then face a hangman. That seemed like a lot more payback than a fast bullet to the brain.

We rode the last mile in silence, Hector with his thoughts, me with mine.

"There," he said, checking the reins on the steeldust he was riding.

I looked up and saw a strand of smoke rising in the distance against the white horizon.

"That must be his place there."

"Let's ride in slow until we get a better lay of the place," I said.

Hector turned his flat gaze on me.

"You think I've never done this sort of thing before, McCannon?"

"You want to spread out," I said, "or go in like we are?"

He seemed satisfied that I deferred to him on the matter.

"Ride maybe fifty yards apart," he said.

I angled the buckskin off at a right angle to him until I reached the distance he'd suggested. I saw him shift the carbine from where he'd been carrying it in front of him.

We got to within five hundred yards of the house when the first shots rang out from a stand of ponderosa pines off to our left. The first rounds blew up snow in front of our horses and caused them to buck and kick.

"Up there!" I shouted at Hector, who jerked his mount's head around to face the trees. He charged without even bothering to wait. I kicked the flanks of the buckskin and chased after him, levering rounds and firing the Creedmore rifle as rapidly as I could. It is damn hard to hit anything from a running horse, but then like the old Texas Ranger'd once told me, "What the hell do you have to lose?"

We were maybe twenty yards from the trees when Hector's horse took a round in the chest that buckled its forelegs and sent Hector sailing through the air. I pulled up hard on the reins, sliding the buckskin to a stop, and leaped from the saddle just as Hector hit a snowbank.

I fired into the trees from a kneeling position while Hector scrambled to recover his carbine. His horse kicked its legs and tried to get up, spraying a fountain of red blood across the white snow.

Then Hector took a hit that spun him around, but he quickly got back up and was firing the carbine and I saw one man pitch forward from the treeline, then I heard one scream from the direction I'd been firing the Creedmore, and right after, I saw three dark shapes darting away like frightened deer.

The sudden silence lay all around us, with not even an echo of a gunshot. It was like the earth itself was holding its breath.

Hector was fumbling with the breech of his carbine. I made sure there were no more shooters waiting in the trees before crossing the patch of snow that was now stained with the blood of Hector's steeldust, and some of his own.

"You hit bad?" I asked.

He looked down at the sleeve of his left arm.

"Busted my arm," he said. "I can't close my hand and load this damn Spencer."

"Leave it," I said. "Use the Peacemaker."

"Yeah. I hate to leave it, though. It's been a good gun."

"Christ, Hector, it only shoots one round at a time," I said, not understanding why any man would want an old single-shot like that in the first place.

"Maybe so," he said. "But it gives me plenty of time to think what I'm aiming at before I pull the trigger. Not like what I seen you doing with that Creedmore, shooting the bark of those trees. Did you even hit anybody?"

"You're a pisser, Torrez," I said. "You think you're up to more fight with that arm?"

He pulled back the sleeve and looked at it, then packed some snow around it. It was just a small purple pucker, but I could see where the bone had been broken underneath the skin, the way it bumped up at an odd angle.

I pulled my bandanna off and tied it around his forearm in an attempt to keep the bone from shifting around too much. He didn't say much when I did that, just looked off and tensed his jaw.

"I think we got one or two of them," I said, finishing my patchwork. He looked at it. "The rest scattered up through those trees. I don't think they'll come back."

"Who's that leave, then?" Hector asked.

"Just John-Davies and Charley Coffey and whoever else might be up at the house, as far as I know."

"Their first line of defense," Hector said, walking toward the trees until we found the man he'd shot lying face down. He turned him over. The face was smallish, the eyes set close together, like a ferret's. There was black under his fingernails. Then we walked through the trees until we found the other one, the one I'd hit with the Creedmore. I found a bottle of whiskey in his coat and twenty dollars—probably more money than he had ever made mucking for gold. Well, he didn't have to muck gold anymore.

"Miners!" Hector concluded. "Charley threw up these half-wits as a first line of defense, hoping they'd get lucky and kill us before we ever reached the house."

"Well, now they know," I said.

"What's that?"

"That they should have stayed miners."

"I guess the free drinks and a little cash money blinded their judgment," he said. "It don't take much to buy a man these days."

"It never has," I said.

"You mind helping me make a smoke before we go up to the house?" Hector said.

We each had a cigarette. There was no point in hurrying now. It wouldn't help John-Davies's and Charley Coffey's nerves any to have to sit up there waiting, wondering if their ambush had succeeded.

Hector glanced over at the downed steeldust; the horse had quit kicking.

"I reckon that old man back at the livery's going to be mad as hell because I got his horse shot," Hector said.

"Maybe you can give him a government voucher for the animal," I said.

Hector snorted. "Yeah, right."

"How do you want to do this the rest of the way, Hector?" I asked, remembering the last time I tried to give orders.

"Hell," he said, "what's wrong with just going up there and knocking on the door?"

"I don't think that's a good idea," I said.

"You don't, huh?"

"You feel free to go ahead, though, if that's what you want to do," I said.

"That sporting rifle," Hector said, "how far you say that toad could hit a man with it?"

"I'd say four, five hundred yards easy. And if he's real good, maybe a thousand."

Hector twisted his head in the direction of the house.

"What would you say from here to the house?" he said.

"Maybe five hundred yards, maybe six."

"That'd mean he could kill us without us getting even a step closer than we are right now."

"If he was that good," I reminded him.

"Well, one of us has to circle around and go in the back way, then."

"You want to be the one?" I said.

"It don't matter to me."

"No, I'll go, Hector, you're liable to bleed to death going that far out of your way. Then where would I be?"

"I'm always pulling your shank out of the fire, McCannon," Hector said, with a shake of his head. "But just the same, it's probably a good idea you go this time."

"See you up to the house, Hector."

"Yeah. Up to the house," he said, as I broke for the trees.

39

I cut through the stand of ponderosa pines moving at a right angle in order to make an approach to the rear of the house. I saw tracks in the snow of the fleeing men who had tried to ambush us. They were going away from the house, probably toward a remuda of horses they'd kept stashed.

Sun broke through the shifting clouds and splayed down through the tall, dark pines. Overhead I could see patches of blue sky. Where the sun hit it, the snow sparkled. A large snowshoe hare broke from the cover of a rock and darted away.

It took ten, maybe fifteen minutes for me to cut through the woods and come out the other side, where I could get a clear view of the house.

It was a long, low building with a shake roof and a stone chimney. There were several outbuildings and a couple of corrals holding some blooded brood mares whose dark bodies stood in direct contrast to the snow. Their ears pricked up when they caught wind of me and they moved around in the corral, coming to stand at the rails nearest my position. I waited until they settled down before moving toward the house.

I let several more minutes pass in case anyone in the house had caught sight of the horses stirring in the corral. Finally the mares lost interest and went back to feeding on the bundles of hay that were scattered on the ground.

There was a privy thirty yards distance from the house; I figured to make that my first stop when I left the woods. From the privy, I could make a dash to a small lean-to, and from there to the back wall of the house. Anyone watching from inside would have a clear shot at me through the window. And if they were even half good—well, I didn't want to think about it.

I rested the Creedmore against the trunk of a pine. There was no use carrying it, not if the fighting was going to be up close.

I watched the rear windows of the house for another half minute, and when I didn't see any movement, I broke for the privy. It seemed like it took me forever, crossing that patch of snowy ground. It was like one of those war dreams I'd sometimes have; the ones where I'd be in the middle of a battle and couldn't move, like I was caught in quicksand. I ran and ran and finally dove behind the outhouse. No one took a shot at me. I took a couple of deep breaths and rubbed snow out of the workings of my self-cocker.

The only thing between me and the house now was the lean-to. I could see a bellows and an anvil and a rack of tools hanging from hooks, the snow was ledged up around the opening.

If I could make the lean-to without taking a bullet, I could reach the back of the house.

I was carrying the self-cocker in my right hand. I reached in my pocket and took out the Colt Thunderer with the short barrel and held it in my left hand. I wanted all the hardware I could get in making that next run. A gunman in the window would have to be blind not to be able to drop me if he saw me coming.

I took a deep breath and broke for the lean-to. Suddenly, the glass shattered out of one of the windows and a pistol shot rang out. A bullet whined off the anvil just as I dropped in behind the thin plank wall of the lean-to.

I heard Charley Coffey's voice yelling to whoever was inside the house that he thought he got me. I was thinking, Anybody but you, Charley, could have made a killing shot from that distance.

The problem was, I was trapped behind that plank wall. It was still a good ten, fifteen feet to the back wall of the house, and even Charley wasn't likely to miss a second shot.

I could hear Charley yelling for John-Davies to come have a look, but there was no reply. Charley was saying how maybe I was already dead and that maybe Edwin ought to come have a look for himself.

Then, I heard the roar of the sporting rifle as it echoed out into the frozen silence and I knew then why John-Davies hadn't come to the back of the house: he was watching the front, waiting for Hector to come from that direction.

I heard Charley shout, "What the hell—" his voice trailing away from the rear of the house. That's when I charged to the back wall and slammed hard against it, just below the window Charley had busted out when he'd tried to kill me.

A spiritualist might have claimed it was my destiny to be shot at through windows.

"Your man," I heard Edwin shout from inside. "Did you get him?"

Charley said he was pretty sure he had gotten me.

"What'd you shoot at out there, Mr. John-Davies?" I heard Charley ask.

"The ultimate game," Edwin said, his manner cool,

assured. "There, can you see him lying in the snow, just about where we had those miners set up in the woods?"

Charley said, "Uh-huh, I think so."

"I waited until for just the right moment, Charles—that's quite important, waiting for just the right moment."

Edwin was right about that. I didn't wait any longer; I crashed through the back door just as Charley was returning to check his own handiwork. He had a dumb, startled look on his face when he saw me.

He was carrying his pistol down by his leg, not expecting the company. He was way too late.

The force of my slug carried him halfway across the room and slammed him against the wall. He still had the dumb, startled look on his face when he slid to the floor, his legs out in front of him.

"Charles!" I heard Edwin call. "What's going on back there?"

I stepped into the main room just as Edwin was turning away from the open window. Smoke was still curling from the blued barrel of his sporting rifle. He turned his eyes down to the expensive gun in his hands.

"Don't!" I said.

Some of his cool manner fell away and his teeth clenched.

"Lay it there on the floor and kick it away," I ordered.

"It's a two-thousand-dollar custom-made weapon, sir," he protested. As if I gave a damn.

"I don't care if Queen Victoria gave it to you in payment for stud services, lay it down and kick it away."

He did, a pained look on his face as his gaze followed it across the floor.

"Move away from the window," I said.

Soon as he stepped aside, I went over and glanced out the shattered maw of glass. Lying there in the snow, at a distance of a hundred and fifty yards, was Hector Torrez, facedown. I couldn't see any movement.

"It's over, John-Davies. Get your coat."

"Whatever are you talking about?" he said dryly.

I walked over and slapped him hard across the face with the back of my hand. He staggered back, then I slapped him again and he fell to one knee.

"It's not a debate," I said. "Get your coat!"

He was bleeding from the lips and from the nostrils and his smoothly shaven flesh was scarlet where I'd hit him. He struggled to stand, still wobbly from the blows.

His hand reached up to his mouth and came away smeared with his blood.

"You killed them?" he said. "All the men I'd posted in the woods?"

"Just the ones that needed it," I said. "The others got smart and ran."

He walked in a slow, pained manner to the coat rack and took down a greatcoat and put it on.

"What now?" he said.

"Out that way." I nodded toward the front door.

We walked the hundred and fifty yards to where Hector was lying. "Stand off a little," I told John-Davies. I waited until he walked off about twenty feet before I rolled Hector unto his back. He groaned when I did. The bullet had punched a fist-sized hole through him.

He looked up at me, coughed.

"Reach me my . . . flask . . . would . . . you?"

I reached inside his coat, pulled out the metal flask, smeared and sticky with his blood, unscrewed the cap, and handed it to him.

He looked in John-Davies's direction. "That the son of a bitch that . . . shot me?"

"Yeah, that's the son of a bitch," I said. John-Davies flinched, but I don't think it was from the cold or from having been slapped by me a couple of times.

"Ask him, will you?" Hector said, then coughed.

I turned my attention to Davies.

"He wants to hear you say it."

"What is that, may I ask?" he said forever the goddamn English gentleman in his above-it-all manner.

"He wants you to say that you had a hand in his brother's killing."

John-Davies shrugged. "I don't even know this man," he said.

"His name is Hector Torrez and his brother was Bob Torrez and the other man's name was Leotis January. You had Bob killed because of a gold claim up around here somewhere."

Hector was sipping the whiskey and coughing up blood and most of what life he had left was staining the snow beneath him. His eyes were a little glazed and he was slipping fast.

"Sorry," Davies said. "I don't know the man of whom you're speaking." The damn sad truth was, I believed John-Davies probably had not know Bob Torrez. At least not by his name. But the rest of it was true—that either he or Charley Coffey had killed Bob and scared Leotis January off. I was willing to bet the bank on that.

"What'd . . . he say?" Hector sputtered.

I looked at John-Davies hard.

"Go on, tell the deputy here that you had his brother killed over a claim," I said. Only it wasn't a request as much as it was a flat-out threat on my part.

"Maybe there was a man," Edwin said. "I believe I remember Charley saying something about it."

"There you go, Hector. We got your man: Bob's killer. You can rest now."

His eyes widened as though he'd suddenly thought of something, or seen something. He stiffened.

"Killed us . . . both," he muttered. "Goddamn toad like . . . that."

Then Hector Torrez died much as he had lived, without fanfare. He simply closed his eyes.

John-Davies was standing there shivering, looking on.

I stood up from the body of the lawman.

"I need to know something," I said.

"Well, I guess you are in the position to ask whatever questions you wish," Davies said in that way of his. It made me want to slap him again.

"You and Alex Dupage," I said. The question had been burning me up ever since Leo had told me. "She's your sister?"

He nodded.

"Funny she would lie to me about it," I said.

His right eyebrow arched.

"Are you so certain that is what she did—lie to you Mr. McCannon? Or was it more that she left out certain parts of her story when she was convincing you to do her bidding?" He sounded like a jealous suitor.

"I'm not buying it, John-Davies."

He smiled as much as a man with busted lips could smile.

"Well, I suppose a man of your low sensibilities would be blinded by a woman that was far beyond your station. I mean, look at you, a frontiersman!"

I didn't say anything to him. I just crossed the space between us and knocked him down, only this time I didn't slap him. I hit him and I felt his jaw snap.

Maybe I called him a sick son of a bitch; I don't know for certain. But I dragged him to his feet, put him on a horse, and prayed he would do something to make me kill him before we got back to Deadwood.

Go on, Edwin, I kept thinking the whole ride back. Make this easy for all of us. *Run.*

40

The old man was standing out in front of the livery like he was waiting for some great event to take place. He was just standing there chewing his cud and spitting brown rings in the snow. His eyes fixed on me and John-Davies and the body of Hector Torrez when we pulled up. He wiped a hand across his wet mouth and said, "You not only leave dead men out on the streets, now you're bringing 'em into town."

Toole looked at Edwin's busted lips and nose and saw how the blood had dried on the front of the expensive white shirt. Then he paid closer attention to Torrez. "That the lawman?"

"It is."

The old man took notice of the stud. "Nice horse." Edwin offered him a sour look.

"You want to do me a favor?" I asked the old puncher.

"What's 'at?" he said.

"Take Mr. John-Davies over and lock him up in that little log dungeon Johnny kept out back of his office."

"You want me to lock up this rich man?" Toole asked,

showing enough of a grin that some of his remaining teeth stuck out like old corn kernels.

"Yeah, that's what I'd like you to do."

"What about him?" Toole asked, pointing toward Hector Torrez.

"I'll take care of him myself," I said.

"You leave anybody alive back up in them hills, McCannon?"

"A few," I said.

"I wisht I'd been there," Toole said. "Damned if I don't."

"How about it?" I asked. "You want to take John-Davies over to the jail and lock him up?"

"Did somebody elect me to office?" he said, scratching a face that hadn't seen a razor in a long time.

"You want, I'll vote for you," I said.

He shrugged.

"Might not hurt if I had some authority," he said.

"Maybe if you were to take Johnny's job, become the new constable, how would that be?"

"Shit, I reckon that'd be all right," he said, his eyes glittering with the prospect.

"Okay," I said. I searched through Hector Torrez's pockets until I found his badge.

"I'm appointing you new town constable."

Toole rolled his eyes.

"Just like that?" he said. "I don't have to apply or nothing?"

"Look around. You see anybody else rushing to take the job?"

"At's about right," he said, swiping the badge alongside his pant leg to polish it. "Anybody that'd have the nerve or was crazy enough for the job is either dead, or has left town. The last of 'em left just this morning—Doc Holliday. Seen him and Kate boarding the stage."

"Raise your right hand," I said, and when he did, I said, "You're hired."

He jerked his head, took the badge, and pinned it to his frayed coat.

"Shit, how's it look?" he asked, when he got it pinned on just right.

"Looks like they better get the women and children off the streets," I said.

His grin touched both ears.

"Come along, Mr. John-Davies," Toole said, taking the reins of the man's horse.

"Oh, another thing I forgot to mention," I called after him. He stopped, turned around and said, "What's 'at?"

"As an officer of the court, you have the right to confiscate that horse as evidence. And if they hang Edwin here, you can make a claim to the horse and keep him." Toole squinted.

"You're tugging my peaches," he said.

"Look at it this way, Toole. Being the only damn law there is around here, who's going to stop you from setting the rules?"

"At's true." He nodded. "You're a pisser, McCannon. I'll give you that."

I found the undertaker, a man named Clovemyer, and gave him instructions for Hector's burial. I asked him to buy Hector a new suit and a shirt. "A man ought to look his best," Clovemyer agreed.

"You want paid mourners?" he asked.

"No, I don't think Hector cared much for strangers. But get him a headstone with his name marked on it." Clovemyer said that if the ground was frozen, he wouldn't be able to bury Hector until the spring.

"I might have to keep him in the icehouse till the ground thaws," he stated. "Winter's a bad time to die."

"I didn't know there was a good time," I said.

"Huh?"

I turned to leave as Clovemyer began stripping the body.

"What about his personal effects, his money belt and rifle and pistol?" Clovemyer pointed at the belt tied around

Hector's waist. I asked how much money was in the belt. Clovemyer opened it and counted out the money. "Nearly four-hundred and eighty dollars," he said. "Should I take my fee out of this?"

"No. A man pays all his life for the living he does, he shouldn't have to pay for the dying. You take that money over to the Miners' Retreat—you know the place?" He nodded.

"You give the money to a girl name Josephine, tell her it's from Hector Torrez, Bob's brother. She'll know. Tell her Hector wanted her to go see her people up in Canada. Tell her that's what the money's for. That and whatever else she needs."

"And his weapons?"

"Sell them if you like, he won't be needing them."

I rode up into the hills following the directions Alex had given me to the old man's cabin. It looked peaceful the way it was nestled in a narrow valley; a curl of black smoke rose from the stone chimney and the long shadows of the pines stretched across the sparkling snow.

Cherry Bee opened the door and offered me a warm greeting, saying how she was happy to see me as she let me into the cabin. Rose rushed to greet me like she was my daughter. "I was worried about you," she said. "I'm glad you came back."

Alex sat in a highbacked rocker by the fireplace. She had not moved, but her gaze met mine.

"Quint," she said as she stood, smoothing her skirts, then the loose strands of hair around her face. She seemed slightly flushed.

"We need to talk, Alex."

She blinked like she already knew what I'd come for.

She looked at the other two women. The room was small, not a place to hold a private conversation.

"I'll get my cloak," she said. "We'll go for a walk."

She was wearing a checked shirt and breeches and boots

that laced up. She put on a gray woolen capote that draped over her shoulders.

The clouds had lifted and were replaced by a dome of blue sky and a warming sun that seeped through our clothes. The weather had turned surprisingly mild, and it was a welcome relief. Maybe the worst of it really was over, I told myself.

We'd walked a short distance from the cabin. I was trying to figure out the best way to ask her about the truth and the lies.

"Tell me," she said, breaking the great silence that surrounded us in that place. "Is it finished?"

"All but one thing," I said.

She didn't say anything for a time and we walked in among some pines; the air was thick with their scent.

"Edwin told you about us," she said.

"Yes."

"Then you know my secrets."

"I know it's damn confusing," I said. "And I sure as hell don't appreciate being lied to."

She turned and put her hand on my wrist.

"Don't," she said. "Don't accuse me of things you don't fully understand."

"Then explain it," I said, trying hard not to let my anger get between us.

She sighed and removed her hand.

"My mother was once an actress," she said. "In New York. She was quite beautiful, but not very talented. Her beauty earned her parts in plays that she might not otherwise have gotten. She was smart enough to know it wouldn't always be that way.

"One evening, a man came to see a play she was acting in. He immediately became smitten with her and began to pursue her. He was very wealthy, very charming, and very attentive to her, sending her rooms full of flowers after each performance.

"Mother found it impossible to resist him, and in short

order he asked her to marry him and return to with him to his home in England. She agreed because she'd fallen in love with him, and because she'd become pregnant with me.''

The sun collected in her hair as she talked and we wove in and out of the light that splintered down through the pines. She really was a beautiful woman.

"His name was Arthur and he had a small son waiting for him to return. The boy's mother had died giving birth to the boy. I was born shortly after Mother and Arthur arrived in England. So you see, the timing was good.'' She had tried to make light of it, but the effort was painful.

Alex moved among the trees, touching them as she talked, lost in a world of memory she had not visited in a long time, judging by the sound of her voice as she recalled the past.

"For several years I lived a very charmed life as the daughter of a rich man. We lived in a large house on a bluff that overlooked the Thames. And in the summer we could see the young college men racing their boats through the green water. It was such a happy time for me.''

Her voice broke slightly as she stopped long enough to turn and look at me.

"But as I grew into a young woman, my half-brother, Edwin, began to prevail upon me for my affections. At first I thought very little of it; it started out as a game we played whenever no one was around. Edwin said he was my handsome knight and I was his fair maiden. He would sometimes pretend to rescue me and then kiss me. And the more we played the game, the more serious he became. After a time, I thought of myself as being in love with him.''

Her hands trembled as she averted her gaze.

"As it turned out, on one occasion when everyone was gone from the house, I allowed myself to be taken in by him. It was a house with such large rooms. I remember at one point hearing the hall clock sounding as if it were the heartbeat of an old man beating in the great silence . . ." Her voice trailed off and a gust of wind swept over a ridge lifting a tail of snow high in the air.

I wasn't sure I wanted to hear any more. But Alex seemed compelled to tell me everything, as though she had to say the secrets she bore or they would suddenly kill her.

"He came into my room. I was watching the boats on the river. He came up behind me and touched me through the fabric of my dress . . ." She raised her chin, her eyes once again staring into mine.

"I won't say that I didn't like it, I did. I was fourteen, he was nearly twenty. I lived in a land of castles and tales of brave knights who slew dragons for the honor of maidens." She shook her head, biting down into her lower lip. "I had grown to believe that Edwin really was my brave knight."

"You don't have to tell me any more," I said.

"No. You asked; I will tell you."

I found my makings and rolled a cigarette. My hands felt heavy and I'd seemed to have run out of words to say to her that would make a difference in her pain.

"As soon as it was over," she said, "I knew what a terrible mistake it had been. The next time Edwin approached me, I tried to deny him. But by then he had already made up his mind that he was no longer going to be my knight. It happened several more times after that; each time I tried to fight him. I begged mother to take me away, back to America, to New York, the place she'd told me so many wonderful stories about. I saw it as a way out of my situation. At first she refused. But then I told her what had happened. She went to Arthur and he sided with his son. He looked straight at me and said that I was tramping around with the local boys, that Edwin was too well bred to have done such a thing. Then he accused Mother of having lied to him about her pregnancy; he said that I was not his child to begin with . . ."

I wondered as she told me these things, if I hadn't made

a mistake in not finishing off John-Davies when I'd had the opportunity.

"It broke my mother's heart to have Arthur turn on us, and she immediately left him and returned with me to New York. It ended up costing her her life. She contracted tuberculosis from someone on the ship on the voyage over. She died within the year. I was then fifteen years old, alone in a city where orphans slept on the streets and ate other people's garbage to survive. I decided I would never eat garbage or depend on a man for my survival. Look what it had cost my mother. Shortly after, I saw an ad in the papers advertising for young women to go west with a local touring group of actors. At least, that was what the manager in charge called us at first. Later, in the cow towns of Kansas, he called us something else. The fact is, we were called lots of things other than what we were."

She gave me a weak smile, the pain still there, buried deep, trying to rise to the surface.

"The names men have for their whores," she said with a toss of her head. "Chippies, Cyprians, doxies, bawds, brides of the multitudes."

"And fallen angels," I said.

Her gaze revealed something tender.

"Yes, and fallen angels, lest we forget. Clever names to hide the truth. Do you think it is easer, Quint, that men call us those names in order to justify their own lust?"

"Maybe so, Alex," I said, remembering again what Doc had said about truth.

"How was he able to find you here?" I said.

"Purely by accident, as far as I know. I had arrived in Deadwood only a few weeks before Edwin. I couldn't believe it when I ran into him. He wanted to start up with me again. I told him I would die first." Alex hesitated, the emotion of it cutting off her words.

"But still you saw him again," I said. "That's the part I don't understand."

She took a deep breath.

"I have a daughter," she said. "She is back east, attending a Boston finishing school. She is Edwin's daughter, a result of his raping me. I did everything within my power to keep her protected, to keep her from finding out the truth of her birthright."

Her hair shone rich and red under the blades of sunlight piercing through the tops of the trees.

"Edwin somehow learned of her. He threatened that if I did not see him again, he would go to her and tell her the truth about me. *His* version of the truth, whatever that was.

"Why would a man do that to his own daughter?" I asked.

"Because he enjoys his own madness."

"So you gave into him?"

"What choice did I have? Even if I had left Deadwood, he could still find me, or find our daughter and tell her whatever lies he wanted to." Alex paused. "Her name is Angelique."

"Like in angel."

"Yes, like in angel."

"So to hide the truth from me, you made it sound like he was just someone in your life when the subject came up between us that night," I said.

"Yes, and I would do it over again if it was to protect my daughter. I would tell whatever lies I had to, do whatever it took, to protect her."

"And you never suspected that Edwin might be behind the killings?"

"No. I knew he was after me, that he wanted me, to control me, to keep me for his own private sickness. But I never suspected he had anything to do with the murders. Did he confess them to you?"

"No, Leo did."

"You have them both?" she said.

"Leo's dead. I'm taking Edwin back to Cheyenne to stand trial. If the law doesn't hang him, I will."

"Then that's the end of it," she said.

"Yes, I guess so."

"What about us? Have you thought about us, Quint?"

"I have, Alex. I've thought a lot about us."

"And what did you conclude?"

"I guess I still have some things from my own past I need to deal with," I said. "Some memories I need to put to rest before I can move on."

"I see," she said. "But there could still be a chance for us later, when you've dealt with those things?"

"Yeah. Maybe if I get things cleared up, I'll find you and we'll take it from there."

"I'd like to believe that, Quint."

"I'm catching the morning stage to Cheyenne," I said. "Maybe you could lend me the money for a pair of tickets."

She nodded. "It's the least I could do."

"Another thing, Hector was killed in the shootout we had with Edwin and Charley Coffey. I told the undertaker I'd come by before I left town and take care of the bill."

"I'll see to it," she said.

"You think you'll stay here in Deadwood now?" I asked.

"No. I think I will go to Boston and see Angelique and maybe find something there—teaching, perhaps. I've always thought it would be a worthwhile vocation, teaching."

"The pay's not so good," I said.

"Oh, I've a little saved," she said, a slight smile curving her mouth. "Which brings me to the matter of the reward money; you've earned it."

"Just the stage tickets," I said, "and Hector's funeral expenses. The rest you can send to Ben directly."

"Can I ask a kiss of you one last time before you go?"

"I'd be damn disappointed if you didn't," I said.

It was warm and gentle, the way she kissed me. But it was a sad kiss as well, and it would stay with me for the entire ride back to Cheyenne and for a long time after that.

Before I left, I asked Rose what her plans were. She said Alex had asked her and Cherry Bee to go to Boston with her.

"You ever been to Boston?" I asked.

"No, Mr. McCannon, I haven't," she said. "Do you think I should go?"

"I think you'd like it," I said. "And I think Alex would be a good influence on you, teach you what you will need to know."

"I think she could, too," Rose said. "Me and Cherry Bee have become the best of friends, and Alex is near like a mother to me."

I kissed her on the top of the head and she said, "That ain't hardly a kiss at all." So I kissed her lightly on the lips, and said, "That's all the kiss you'll get from me," and she smiled and hugged me.

We rode back to town together and they left me off at my hotel.

The desk clerk was waiting for me.

"All the shooting going on," he said, "I nearly rented out your room, thinking maybe you'd fallen victim to the violence."

"Why didn't you?"

His mouth broke open until his purple gums showed above his stained teeth.

"Hell, so many of my tenants have dropped like flies lately, I'm having trouble filling the vacancies as it is."

"Well, you'll have one more come the morning, I'm catching the stage out."

"Aw, hell," he said.

41

My last night in Deadwood I decided to spend in a tub of hot, clean water. I found a bathhouse three doors down from the hotel and had the man fill me a bath.

I sank down in the tub, remembering how damn good it felt and how damn long it seemed since I'd last had the pleasure of hot water and a bottle of mash whiskey and the peace of being alone.

In the morning, I would be taking Davies back to Cheyenne. I'd told Toole to have him at the stage depot early and in chains. I didn't mind everyone seeing what a rich man looked like in chains. He was a damn murderer and all his money wasn't going to change that.

It felt good, the bath and whiskey and the rest of it, and knowing I'd survived and broken the case.

"Here's to you, Pancho Vega, wherever your damn soul is hanging out these days!" I said, lifting a glass to an old friend and an old enemy who in spite of everything I missed just a little. Pancho had kept a little spice in things when he was alive. Men like Pancho Vega were disappearing fast, and the frontier was going to be a lot less interesting without them.

"And to your cousins, who honored you by following you to the grave," I added, taking another pull of the bottle. "Brave damn men, and honorable ones . . ."

"Jesus Mac, ya've gone to talkin' to yarself!"

I didn't want to believe it, but there she stood.

"Calamity," I said. "How'd you find me here?"

"Aw, hell, hon, I'd be able to find ya in the middle of the Atlantic Ocean!"

For once she wasn't drunk or indecent. She had on clean clothes, and I couldn't swear to it, but it looked like she'd taken some care in washing and fixing her hair as well.

"If you came for a loan, Jane, you caught me at the wrong time."

She slid a chair over, turned it around, and sat down on it.

"Didn't come fer no loan, Mac."

"A drink?"

She looked at the bottle.

"Well, maybe just a little one," she said, holding her thumb and forefinger apart a couple of inches.

"Help yourself."

She took a swallow, then set the bottle back down again.

"You've changed," I said.

She smiled.

"Time to get on with my life, Mac. I've mourned Bill long enough. Let the dead rest in peace, that's what I say!"

"Sounds like a good plan," I said.

"Going to Denver," she said. "I met me a drummer and he wants to take me to Denver and asked me to be his loving wife."

"You agreed to that?"

"Not yet I ain't. I'll have to see how it washes out, me and him, first. Give it a few weeks, ya know."

"You look happy," I said. "Maybe it's the right thing, going to Denver with your drummer friend."

"Ya know the best thing about him, Mac?"

"No."

"He calls me Martha. Says it's a lot prettier than Jane. Ya know how I liked to be called Martha."

"It suits you."

"Damned if it don't," she said.

She sat there with a pleased look on her face and didn't say any more until I said my water was getting cold.

"Well, ya better get out of there before ya catch pneumonia, then," she said.

"What, with you in the room?"

She grinned sheepishly.

"Don't hurt to try, does it?" she said.

"Good luck with your drummer, Martha."

"See ya around, Mac." She stood and walked in that stiff way she had, closing the door behind her.

I hoped the drummer and Denver would be kind to her.

I'd lied to her about the water growing cold; I just wanted a little more time to myself and a chance to finish the bottle. I thought of the long ride back to Cheyenne and meeting Ben, and what I was going to tell him when I got back. I thought of Alex, what we had shared with each other, and what she had shared with me in our last conversation.

I owed Ben our friendship, but I owed Alex her private pain. I thought about it for a long time, until the water did grow cold and the bottle rang on empty.

Then I knew what I was going to tell Ben: I was going to tell him why Charley Weed had been wearing a dress the day I'd brought him back to Cheyenne in the rain.